C.J. CHERRYH

CYTEEN

"At once a psychological novel, a murder mystery, and an examination of power on the grand scale, encompassing light-years and outsize lifetimes [that] only hint at the richness of CYTEEN. Cherryh goes deep into political and scientific conflicts . . . examines the differing natures of born-men and azi, deals with the subtle shadings of love, desire, kinship. . . . The whole ambitious enterprise succeeds brilliantly."

—*Locus*

"A future as detailed as that of Herbert's *Dune*, with dozens of complex characters . . . all the paranoid tension of a spy thriller . . . and the plot sheds new light on several of Cherryh's important earlier novels. *Cyteen* could easily make Cherryh into SF's next household name. Strongly recommended."

—*Newsday*

"Complex and thoughtful. Churning with political intrigue and heavyweight powerbrokering, thick with knotty conspiracies and plot."

—*Kirkus Reviews*

"Tackles a variety of ethical, social, and political issues. . . . Cherryh's world building is ambitious and her main characterizations are well individualized . . . ultimately fascinating in concept and [its] very detail."

—*Booklist*

"Unmistakable weight and ambition . . . readers will find [   ] enjoy [   ] ng and pleasant surprise from

—*Publishers Weekly*

Also by C.J. Cherryh

*Cyteen: The Rebirth**
*Cyteen: The Vindication**

Published by
POPULAR LIBRARY   *forthcoming

C.J. CHERRYH
CYTEEN.

THE BETRAYAL

POPULAR LIBRARY

An Imprint of Warner Books, Inc.

A Warner Communications Company

POPULAR LIBRARY EDITION

Popular Library®, the fanciful P design, and Questar® are
registered trademarks of Warner Books, Inc.

This work is volume one in a trilogy first published in hardcover in
one volume entitled CYTEEN.

Book design by H. Roberts
Cover illustration by Don Maitz

Popular Library books are published by
Warner Books, Inc.
666 Fifth Avenue
New York, N.Y. 10103

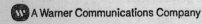 A Warner Communications Company

Printed in the United States of America

Originally published in hardcover by Warner Books.
First Printed in Paperback: February, 1989

10 9 8 7 6 5 4 3

CYTEEN:
THE BETRAYAL

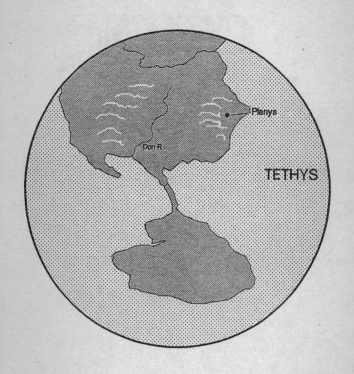

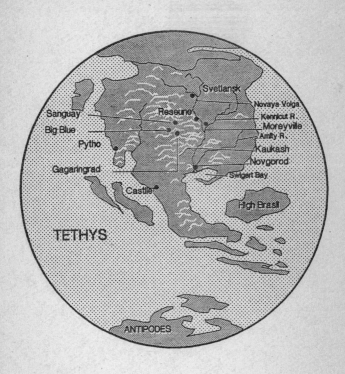

Svetlansk

Novaya Volga
Kennicut R.
Sanguay
Reseune
Moreyville
Big Blue
Amity R.
Pytho
Kaukash
Novgorod
Gagaringrad
Swigert Bay
Castile

High Brasil

TETHYS

ANTIPODES

Verbal Text from:
THE HUMANE REVOLUTION
"The Company Wars": #1

**Reseune Educational Publications: 4668-1368-1
approved for 80+**

Imagine all the variety of the human species confined to a single world, a world sown with the petrified bones of human ancestors, a planet dotted with the ruins of ten thousand years of forgotten human civilizations—a planet on which at the time human beings first flew in space, humans still hunted a surplus of animals, gathered wild plants, farmed with ancient methods, spun natural yarns by hand and cooked over wood fires.

Earth owed allegiance to a multitude of chairmen, councillors, kings, ministers and presidents; to parliaments and congresses and committees, to republics, democracies, oligarchies, theocracies, monarchies, hegemonies and political parties which had evolved in profusion for thousands of years.

This was the world which first sent out the starprobes.

Sol Station existed, a much more primitive Sol Station, but altogether self-sustaining; and favored with a system of tax remission in return for scientific benefit, it launched a number of ambitious projects, including the first large-engine starprobe, and ultimately the first crewed pusher-ship cluster toward the near stars.

The first of the pusher-modules was of course the venerable

Gaia, *which was to deliver the Alpha station-component at the star known at that time as Barnard's, and leave thirty volunteer scientists and technicians in what in those days meant inconceivable isolation. They would build their station out of the star's expected system-clutter of rock and ice, perform scientific research and maintain long-distance communication with Earth.*

The first concept had been disposable pushers, hardly more than robotic starprobes; but human passengers mandated an abort-and-return capacity which, considering all the possibilities for disaster, was negotiated finally to mean a full-return capacity. That led to the notion of a crewed pusher-module to stay at Barnard's should the star prove impossibly deficient in raw materials necessary for self-sufficiency of the Alpha module, in which event Gaia *might remain for a number of years, then strip the station to the essential core and return the mission to Earth. If the star proved a viable home for the station,* Gaia *would remain only a year or so until the Alpha Station module was fully functioning and stable in its orbit. Then it would return to Sol with its tiny complement of crew and surrender the* Gaia *module to a second mission, which would, after refitting, go out again with such supplies as trace minerals and materials which the infant station might not have available. Equally important with the supplies, those early pioneers theorized, was the human link, the reassurance of face-to-face contact with other human beings across what in those days was an inconceivably lonely expanse of space.*

Earth, with years' advance warning via the constant data-flow from Gaia *and Alpha Station that the mission was abundantly successful and that* Gaia *was returning, trained a replacement crew and dutifully prepared the return mission.*

But the crew of Gaia, *subject to relativistic effects, running into an information stream indicating greater and greater changes in the Earth they had left, had become more at home in the ship than in the mainstream of a Terran culture gone very alien to them. Their sojourn on Sol Station was intensely unhappy, and they re-occupied* Gaia *by a surprise move which immensely disconcerted station authorities, but which finally won them their ship and relegated the replacement crew to waiting on the next pusher-craft.*

Other crews of further missions reached the same decision, regarding themselves as permanent voyagers. They considered their small ships as home, had children aboard, and as star stations and attendant pushers multiplied, asked of Earth and the stations only fuel, provisions, and the improvement of their ships with larger compartments, more advanced propulsion— whatever had become available since their last docking.

Star-stations at half a dozen stars linked themselves by the regular passage of such ships. But in the isolation of those days in which messages traveled at mere light-speed and ships traveled slower still, every station was at least four or five years time-lagged from every other human habitation, be it ship or station, and learned to exist in these strangely fluxing time-referents which were impossibly alien to the general population of Earth.

The discovery of intelligent life on the planet at Pell's Star, the star Earth once called Tau Ceti, was more than ten years old by the time the word of it reached Earth. The dealing of human beings with the Downers was more than two decades advanced by the time Earth's elaborate instructions could arrive at Pell; and it was much longer before Terran scientists could reach Pell, up the long route that led them station by station into a human culture almost as foreign to them as were the Downers.

As it is difficult from our viewpoint to imagine Earth of that time, it was virtually impossible for Earth to comprehend the reasoning of spacers who refused to leave their ships and who, in their turn, found the (to them) teeming corridors of Sol Station chaotic and terrifying. It was virtually impossible even for Sol Station to understand the life of their contemporaries in the deep Beyond—contemporaries whose culture was built on history and experiences and legendry that had much more to do with the hardships of life in remote stations and famous ships, than with events in a green and chaotic world they saw only in pictures.

Earth, beset with overpopulation and political crises largely attributable to its ancient rivalries, had nevertheless flourished while it was the focus of human development. The unexpected rush of stationers to new construction at Pell, following the prospect of abundant biostuffs, a native population primitive and friendly, and exploitable free-orbiting resources, became a panic flood. Stations between Earth and Pell shut down, disrupting the trade of the Great Circle, and creating economic chaos on Earth and Sol Station.

Earth reacted by attempting to regulate—across a ten-year time lag: Terran politicians could not readily conceive of the economic strength the remaining stations might achieve, given the unification of population that rush to Pell had created. The concentration of population and the discovery of vast resources combined with the psychological impetus to exploration . . . meant that Earth's now twenty-year-old instructions arrived in a situation in such rapid flux even a month's lag would have been significant.

Earth found itself increasingly isolate, subject to internal pressures from a faltering trade system, and in a desperate and ill-advised action imposed a punitive tariff which led to smuggling and an active black market; which in turn led to a sudden fall-off of trade. Earth's response was the declaration of most-favored-status for certain ships; which led in turn to armed hostilities between ships from Earth and ships which had not been built by Earth and which did not hold any allegiance to its convolute and wildly varying politics.

Further, Earth, convinced that emigration of scientists and engineers from Sol System was feeding the spacer cultures with the best and brightest and robbing Earth of its best talent, slammed down an emigration ban not only on travel from Earth and Sol Station, but on further moves of citizens in certain professions from station to station.

Gaia made her last trip to Earth in 2125, and left, vowing never to return.

A general wave of rebellion and mutiny swept through the stars; stations were mothballed and deserted; probes and missions sought further stars not only with economic motive now—but because there were more and more people anxious to move outward, seeking political freedom before restrictions came down.

Viking Station and Mariner sprang into existence as stationers found even Pell too vulnerable to Earth's influence and as Pell's now established economy afforded less opportunity for highly profitable initial-phase investment.

By 2201 a group of dissident scientists and engineers sponsored by financial interests on Mariner founded a station at Cyteen, about a world vastly different from Pell. The brilliant *work of one of those scientists combined with the economic power of Cyteen's new industries sent the first faster-than-light probe out from Cyteen in 2234, an event which altered the time-scale of spaceflight and forever changed the nature of trade and politics.*

Cyteen's early years were characterized not only by a burst of growth and invention unparalleled in human history, but, ironically, by the resurrection of long disused technologies out of ship archives: combustion engines, gravity-dependent processing, all to save soft-landing the enormous mass-requirements of a full-scale terrestrial development. In addition, there were new on-planet technologies specific to Cyteen, to create pockets of breathable atmosphere in the otherwise deadly environment—all this effort because Cyteen represented a major biological opportunity for the human species. It had no intelligent indigenes. It did have a varied and entirely alien ecosystem—virtually two ecosystems, in fact, because of the extreme isolation of its two continents, differing significantly from each other but vastly different from Earth and Pell.

It was a biologist's paradise. And it offered, by its absence of intelligent life, the first new cradle of terrestrial human civilization since Earth itself.

It was not politics alone which led to the Company Wars. It was the sudden acceleration of trade and population mobility, it was the stubborn application of outmoded policies by Terran agencies out of touch with the governed, and finally it was the loyalty of a handful of specially favored Terran merchanter captains attempting to maintain a fading trade empire for a motherworld which had become only peripheral to human space.

It was a doomed effort. Cyteen, no longer alone in the Beyond, but motherworld itself to Esperance, Pan-paris, and Fargone Stations, declared its independence from the Earth Company in 2300, an action which, reported now with the speed of the Faster-Than-Lights, prompted Earth to build and dispatch armed FTLs to bring the dissident stations back into line.

Merchanters quickly fled the routes nearer Pell, thus reducing the availability of supplies, while Earth itself, even with FTL technology, was by no means able to supply the mass re-

quirement of its fleet over such distances. Over a span of years the Earth Company fleet degenerated to acts of piracy and coercion which completely alienated the merchanters, always the Earth Company's mistake.

The formation of the merchanters' Alliance at Pell established the second mercantile power in the Beyond and put an end to Earth's attempt to dictate to its scattered colonies.

Surely one of the more ironical outcomes of the War, the Treaty of Pell and the resulting economic linkages of three human societies, drawing on three vastly different ecosystems, now exist as the driving forces in a new economic structure which transcends all politics and systems.

Trade and common interests have proven, in the end, more powerful in human affairs than all the warships ever launched.

CHAPTER

1

It was from the air that the rawness of the land showed most: vast tracts where humanity had as yet made no difference, deserts unclaimed, stark as moons, scrag and woolwood thickets unexplored except by orbiting radar. Ariane Emory gazed down at it from the window. She kept to the passenger compartment now. Her eyesight, she had had to admit it, was no longer sharp enough, her reflexes no longer fast enough for the jet. She could go up front, bump the pilot out of the chair and take the controls: it was her plane, her pilot, and a wide sky. Sometimes she did. But it was not the same.

Only the land was, still most of the land was. And when she looked out the window, it might have been a century ago, when humankind had been established on Cyteen less than a hundred years, when Union was unthought of, the War only a rumbling discontent, and the land looked exactly like this everywhere.

Two hundred years ago the first colonists had come to this unlikely star, made the beginnings of the Station, and come down to the world.

Forty-odd years later the sublight ships were coming in, few and forlorn, to try to convert their structure and their operations to faster-than-light; and time sped up, time hurtled at translight speeds, change came so fast that sublight ships met ships they took for alien—but they were not: it was worse news for them. They were human. And the game was all changed.

The starships went out like seeds from a pod. The genetics labs upriver at Reseune bred humanity as fast as it could turn them out from the womb-tanks, and every generation bred others and worked in labs breeding more and more, till there were people enough, her uncle had said, to fill the empty places, colonize the world, build more star-stations: Esperance. Fargone. Every place with its own labs and its own means to breed and grow.

Earth had tried to call her ships back. It was all too late. Earth had tried to tax and rule its colonies with a hard hand. That was very much too late.

Ariane Emory remembered the Secession, the day that Cyteen declared itself and its own colonies independent; the day the Union began and they were all suddenly rebels against the distant motherworld. She had been seventeen when the word came down from Station: *We are at war.*

Reseune bred soldiers, then, grim and single-minded and intelligent, oh, yes: bred and refined and honed, knowing by touch and reflex what they had never seen in their lives, knowing above all what their purpose was. Living weapons, thinking and calculating down one track. She had helped design those patterns.

Forty-five years after the Secession the war was still going on, sometimes clandestine, sometimes so remote in space it seemed a fact of history—except at Reseune. Other facilities could breed the soldiers and the workers once Reseune had set the patterns, but only Reseune had the research facilities, and it had fought the war in its own dark ways, under Ariane Emory's directorate.

Fifty-four years of her life . . . had seen the Company Wars over, humanity divided, borders drawn. The Earth Company Fleet had held Pell's Star, but the merchanters of the newly formed Alliance had taken Pell and declared it their base. Sol had tried to ignore its humiliating defeat and go off in another direction; the remnant of the old Company Fleet had turned to piracy and still raided merchanters, no different than they had ever done, while Alliance and Union alike hunted them. It was only hiatus. The war was cold again. It went on at conference tables where negotiators tried to draw lines biology did not, and make borders in boundless, three-dimensional space—to keep a peace that had never, in all Ariane Emory's life, existed.

All of that might not have been yet. It might have been a hundred years ago, except that the plane was sleek and fine, not the patch-together that had run cargo between Novgorod and Reseune: in those days everyone had sat on bales of plastics and containers of seed and whatever else was making the trip.

Then she had begged to sit by the dusty windows and her mother had said to put her sunscreen on, even so.

Now she sat in a leather seat with a drink at her elbow, in a jet snugly warm inside, immaculately maintained, with a handful of aides talking business and going over their notes, a noise just barely enough to get past the engines.

No traveling nowadays without a clutter of aides and bodyguards. Catlin and Florian were back there, quiet as they were trained to be, watching her back, even here, at 10,000 meters and among Reseune staff whose briefcases were full of classified material.

Much, much different from the old days.

Maman, can I sit by the window?

She was anomalous, child of two parents, Olga Emory and James Carnath. They had founded the labs at Reseune, had begun the process that had shaped Union itself. They had sent out the colonists, the soldiers. Their own genes had gone into hundreds of them. Her quasi-relatives were scattered across lightyears. But so were everyone's, these days. In her lifetime even that basic human thinking had changed: biological parentage was a trivial connection. Family mattered, the larger, the more extended . . . the safer and more prosperous.

Reseune was her inheritance. Hence this jet, *not* a commercial airliner. No hired plane, either, and no military jet. A woman in her position could call on all these things; and still preferred mechanics who were part of the Household, a pilot whose psych-patterns she was sure of, bodyguards who were the best of Reseune's designs.

The thought of a city, the subways, life among the clerks

and techs and cooks and laborers who jostled one another and hurried about their schedules to earn credit . . . was as frightening to her as airless space. She directed the course of worlds and colonies. The thought of trying to buy a meal in a restaurant, of fighting crowds to board a subway, of simply being on a topside street where traffic roared and people were in motion on all sides—filled her with an irrational panic.

She did not know how to live outside Reseune. She knew how to arrange a plane, check out the flight plans, order her luggage, her aides, her security, every little detail—and found a public airport an ordeal. A serious flaw, granted. But everyone was due a phobia or two and these things were far from the center of her worries. It was not likely that Ariane Emory would ever face a Novgorod subway or a station's open dock.

It was a long, long while before she saw the river and the first plantation. A thin ribbon of road, finally the domes and towers of Novgorod, a sudden, remarkably sudden metropolis. Under the jet's wings the plantations widened, the towers of electronic screens and precipitators shadowed the fields and traffic crawled along the roads at ground-bound pace.

Barges chained down the Volga toward the sea, barges and pushers lined the river dockage past the plantations. There was still a lot of the raw and industrial about Novgorod, for all the glitter of the new. This side of it had not changed in a hundred years, except to grow bigger, the barges and the traffic becoming ordinary instead of a rare and wonderful sight.

Look, maman, there's a truck.

The blue of woolwood thicket blurred by under the wing. Pavement and the end-stripes of the runway flashed past.

The tires touched smoothly and the jet came rolling to a stop, for a left turn toward the terminal.

A little panic touched Ariane Emory at this stage, despite the knowledge that she would never get to the crowded hallways. There were cars waiting. Her own crew would handle the baggage, secure the jet, do all these things. It was only the edge of the city; and the car windows would permit vision out, but none in.

All those strangers. All that motion, random and chaotic. In the distance she loved it. It was her own creation. She knew its mass motions, if not its individual ones. At a distance, in the aggregate, she trusted it.

At close range it made her hands sweat.

Cars pulling up and a flurry of hurrying guards in the security entrance of the Hall of State said that it was no mere senatorial arrival. Mikhail Corain, on the balcony outside the Council Chamber, flanked by his own bodyguards and aides, paused and looked down on the echoing stone lower floor, with its fountain, its brass railings on the grand stairway, its multiple star-emblem in gold on the gray stone wall.

Imperial splendor for imperial ambitions. And the chief architect for those ambitions made her entrance. The Councillor from Reseune, in company with the Secretary of Science. Ariane Carnath-Emory with her entourage, late, dependably late, because the Councillor was damned confident of her majority, and only deigned to visit the Hall because the Councillor had to vote in person.

Mikhail Corain glared and felt that speeding of his heart that his doctors had told him to avoid. Calm down, they were wont to say. Some things are beyond your control.

Meaning, one supposed, the Councillor from Reseune.

Cyteen, by far the most populous of the entities in the Union, had consistently managed to capture *two* seats in the executive, in the Council of Nine. It was logical that one of them was the Bureau of Citizens, which meant labor and farming and small business. It was not logical that the electors in the sciences, far and wide across the lightyears Union reached, with a dozen eminently qualified potential candidates, persisted in returning Ariane Emory to the halls of government.

More than that. To a position which she had held for fifty years, *fifty damned years*, during which she had bribed and browbeaten interests on Cyteen and every station in Union and (rumored but never proved) in Alliance and Sol as well. You wanted something done? You asked someone who could get the Councillor of Science to arrange it. What were you willing to pay? What would you take in trade?

And the damned Science electorate, made up of supposed intellects, kept voting her in, no matter what the scandals that attached to her, no matter that she virtually owned Reseune labs, which was legally equal to a *planet* in Union's government, which did things within its walls that countless investigations had tried (and failed, on technicalities) to prove.

Money was not the answer. Corain had money. It was Ariane Emory herself. It was the fact that most of the population of Cyteen, most of the population of Union itself, had come in one way or another from Reseune; and those who did not, used tapes . . . that Reseune devised.

Which that woman . . . devised.

To doubt the integrity of the tapes was paranoid. Oh, there were a few who refused to use them; and studied higher math and business without them, and never took a pill and never lay down to dream what the masses clear across Union dreamed, knowledge pouring into their heads, as much as they could absorb, there in a few sessions. Drama—experienced as well as seen . . . at carefully chosen intensity. Skills—acquired at a bone and nerve level. You used the tapes because your competition would, because you had to excel to get along in the world, because it was the only way to know things fast enough, high enough, wide enough, and the world changed and changed and changed, in any human lifespan.

The Bureau of Information vetted those tapes. Experts reviewed them. There was no way any subliminals could get past them. Mikhail Corain was not one of the lunatic fringe who suspected government com-tapping, Alliance poisoning of cargoes, or mind-enslaving subliminals in the entertainment tapes. That sort of purist could refuse rejuv, die old at seventy-five, and live off public works jobs because they were self-taught know-nothings.

But damn it, *damn* it, that woman kept getting elected. And he could not understand it.

There she was, getting a little stoop to the shoulders, allowing a little streak of gray to show in the black hair, when anyone who could count knew she was older than Union, on rejuv and silver-haired under the dye. Aides swarmed round her. Cameras focused on her as if there was no other center to the universe. Damn bony bitch.

You wanted a human being designed like a prize pig, you asked Reseune. You wanted soldiers, you wanted workers, you wanted strong backs and weak minds or a perfect, guaranteed genius, you asked Reseune.

And senators and Councillors alike came to bow and scrape and mouth politenesses—Good God, someone had brought her flowers.

Mikhail Corain turned away in disgust, plowed himself a way through his aides.

Twenty years he had been sitting as head of the minority party in the Nine, twenty years of swimming against the tide, gaining a little now and again, losing all the big ones, the way they had lost the latest. Stanislaw Vogel of the Trade electorate had died, and with the Alliance violating the treaty as fast as they could arm their merchant ships, the Centrists ought to have been able to carry that seat. But no. The Trade electorate elected Ludmilla deFranco, Vogel's niece. Moderate, hell, deFranco was only steering a careful course. She was no less an Expansionist than her uncle. *Something* had changed hands. Someone had been bought, someone had tilted Andrus Company toward deFranco, and the Centrists had lost their chance to install a fifth member in the Nine and gain the majority of the executive for the first time in history.

It was a crushing disappointment.

And there, there in the hall downstairs, in the middle of the sycophants and all the bright young legislators, was the one who had pulled the strings money could not pull.

Political favor, then. The unprovable, untraceable commodity.

On that, the fate of the Union hinged.

He entertained the most terrible fantasy, not for the first time, that somehow, on the steps outside, some lunatic might run up with a gun or a knife and solve their problem at one stroke. He felt a profound disturbance at that thought. But it would reshape the Union. It would give humankind a chance, before it was everlastingly too late.

One life—weighed very little in those scales.

He drew deep breaths. He walked into the Council chambers and made polite conversation with the few who came to commiserate with the losers. He gritted his teeth and walked over to pay his polite congratulations to Bogdanovitch, who, holding the seat of the Bureau of State, chaired the Council.

Bogdanovitch kept his face absolutely bland, his kindly, white-browed eyes the image of everyone's grandfather, full of gentility and civility. Not a trace of triumph. If he had been that good when he negotiated the Alliance settlement, Union would own the codes to Pell. Bogdanovitch was always better at petty politics. And he was another one who lasted. His electorate was all professional, the consuls, the appointees, immigration, the station administrators—a minuscule number of people to elect an office which had started out far less important than it had turned out to be. God, how had the framers of the Constitution let themselves play creative games with the political system? The 'new model,' they had called it; 'a government shaped by an informed electorate.' And they had thrown ten thousand years of human experience out the hatch, a damned bunch of social theorists, including, *including* Olga Emory and James Carnath, back in the days when Cyteen had five seats of the Nine and most of the Council of Worlds.

"Tough one, Mikhail," Bogdanovitch said, shaking his hand and patting it.

"Well, will of the electorate," Corain said. "Can't quarrel with that." He smiled with absolute control. "We did get the highest percentage yet."

Someday, you old pirate, someday I'll have the majority. And you'll live to see it.

"Will of the electors," Bogdanovitch said, still smiling, and Corain smiled till his teeth ached, then turned from Bogdanovitch to Jenner Harogo, another of that breed, holding the powerful Internal Affairs seat, and Catherine Lao, who held the Bureau of Information, which vetted all the tapes. Of course.

Emory came sailing in and they left him in mid-sentence to go and join her claque. Corain exchanged a pained look with Industry, Nguyen Tien of Viking; and Finance, Mahmud Chavez of Voyager Station, Centrists both. Their fourth seat, Adm. Leonid Gorodin, was over in a grim confluence of his own uniformed aides. Defense was, ironically, the least reliable—the most prone to reassess his position and shift into the Expansionist camp if he conceived near-term reasons. That was Gorodin, Centrist only because he wanted the new Excelsior-class military transports kept in near space where he could use them, not, as he put it, 'out on our backside while Alliance pulls another damn embargo. You want your electorates hammering at your doors for supplies, you want another hot war, citizens, let's just send those carriers out to the far Beyond and leave us depending on Alliance merchanters. . . .'

Not saying, of course, that the Treaty of Pell, which had agreed that the merchanters' Alliance would haul cargo and build no warships; and that Union, which had built a good many of those haulers, would maintain its fleet, but build no ships to compete with the merchanters . . . was a diplomatic buy-off, a ransom to get supply flowing again. Bogdanovitch had brought that home and even Emory had voted against it.

The stations had passed it. The full General Council had to vote on it, and it got through by a hair's breadth. Union was tired of war, that was all, tired of disrupted trade, scarce supplies.

Now Emory wanted to launch another wave of exploration and colonization out into the deep Beyond.

Everyone *knew* there was trouble out there to find. What Sol had run into on the other side of space proved that well enough. It had brought Sol running back to the Alliance, begging for trade, begging for markets. Sol had neighbors, and its reckless poking about was likely to bring trouble in the Alliance's back door and right to Union space. Gorodin hammered on that point constantly. *And* demanded a larger share of the budget for Defense.

Gorodin's position was weakest. He was vulnerable to a vote of confidence. They could lose him, if he failed to get the ships the Fleet wanted, in the zones that mattered.

And the news from the Trade electorate was a blow, a severe one. The Centrists had thought they had won this one. They had truly thought they had a chance of stopping Emory, and all they could do now was force a point of order, persuade the Council that no vote ought to be taken on the Hope project, since it involved ship appropriations and a major budget priority decision, until deFranco could get in from Esperance and assume her seat.

Or . . . they could break the quorum and send it to a vote in the Council of Worlds. Emory's cabal would flinch at that. The representatives were far more independent, especially Cyteen's large bloc, who were mostly Centrist. Let them get their teeth into a bill of this complexity not already hammered out by the Nine, and they would be at it for months, sending up changes the Nine would veto, and round and round again.

Let Gorodin have another try at persuading the Expansionists to delay the vote. Gorodin was the one on the fence, the one with the medals, the war hero. Throw him at them, see if he could swing them. If not, the Centrists would walk, all four of them. It had political cost, profound cost, to break the quorum and close the meeting.

But time was what they needed, time to get to key lobbyists, time to see if they could pull a few strings and see if deFranco, when she arrived, could be persuaded to be the moderate she proclaimed herself—or at least tilt to the Centrist side on a bill that critical to her constituency. She might, *might*, vote to table.

Councillors drifted toward their seats. Emory's group came up last. Predictably.

Bogdanovitch rapped with the antique gavel.

"Council is in session," Bogdanovitch said, and proceeded to the election results and the official confirmation of Ludmilla deFranco as Councillor for the Bureau of Trade.

Moved and seconded, Catherine Lao and Jenner Harogo. Emory sat expressionless. She never made routine motions. The bored look on her face, the slow revolutions of the stylus in her long-nailed fingers, proclaimed a studied patience with the forms.

No discussion. A polite, pro forma round of ayes, officially recorded.

"Next item of business," Bogdanovitch said, "acceptance of Denzill Lal voting proxy for sera deFranco until her arrival."

Same routine. Another bored round of ayes, a little banter between Harogo and Lao, small laughter. From Gorodin, Chavez, Tien, no reaction. Emory noticed that: Corain saw her laugh shortly and take in that silence with a sidelong glance. The stylus stopped its revolutions. Emory's glance was wary now, sharp as she glanced Corain's way and gave a slow, slight smile, the kind that might mitigate an accidental meeting of eyes.

But the eyes were not smiling at all. *What* will you do? they wondered. What are you up to, Corain?

There were not that many guesses, and a mind of Emory's caliber would take a very little time to come up with them. The stare lingered, comprehended, threatened like a blade in fence. He hated her. He hated everything she stood for. But, God, dealing with her was like an experience in telepathy: he stared flatly, returning the threat, quirked a brow that said: You can push me to the brink. I'll carry you over it. Yes, I will do it. Fracture the Council. Paralyze the government.

The half-lidding of her eyes, the fondness of her smile said: Good strike, Corain. Are you sure you want this war? You may not be ready for this.

The fondness of his said: Yes. This is the line, Emory. You want crisis, right when two of your precious projects are coming up, and you can have it.

She blinked, slid a glance to the table and back again, the smile tight, the eyes hooded. War, then. A widening of the smile. Or negotiation. *Watch my moves, Corain: you'd make a serious mistake to make this an open breach.*

I'll win, Corain. You can stall me off. You can force elections first, damn you. And that will waste more time than waiting on deFranco.

"The matter of the Hope Station appropriations," Bogdanovitch said. "First scheduled speaker, sera Lao. . . ."

A signal passed between Emory and Lao. Corain could not see Lao's face, only the back of her blonde head, the trademark crown of braids. Doubtless Lao's expression was perplexed. Emory signaled an aide, spoke into his ear, and that aide's face tightened, mouth gone to a thin line, eyes mirroring dismay.

The aide went to one of Lao's aides, and Lao's aide went and whispered in her ear. The move of Lao's shoulders, the deep intake of breath, was readable as her now profiled, frowning face.

"Ser President," Catherine Lao said, "I move we postpone debate on the Hope Station bill until sera deFranco can take her seat in person. Trade is too profoundly affected by this measure. With all respect to the distinguished gentleman from Fargone, this is a matter that ought to wait."

"Seconded," Corain said sharply.

A murmur of dismay ran among the aides, heads leaning together, even Councillors'. Bogdanovitch's mouth was open. It took him a moment to react and tap the gavel for decorum.

"It has been moved and seconded that debate on the Hope Station bill be postponed until sera deFranco takes her seat in person. Is there discussion?"

It was perfunctory, Emory complimenting the proxy, the gentleman from Fargone, agreeing with Lao.

Corain made the request for the floor solemnly to concur with Lao. He might have made some light banter. Sometimes they did, Expansionists with Centrists, with irony under it, when matters were settled.

This one was not. Emory, damn it, had stolen his fire and his issue, given him what he demanded, and looked straight at him when he had uttered the tedious little courtesy to Denzill Lal, and taken his seat.

Watch me closely, that look said. That will cost.

The vote went round, unanimous, Denzill Lal voting proxy in the vote that took the Hope appropriations bill out of his hands.

"That concludes the agenda," Bogdanovitch said. "We had allotted three days for debate. The next bill on the calendar is yours, sera Emory, number 2405, also budget appropriations, for the Bureau of Science. Do you wish to re-schedule?"

"Ser President, I'm ready to proceed, but I certainly wouldn't want to rush a measure through without giving my colleagues adequate time to prepare debate. I *would* like to move it up to tomorrow, if my distinguished colleagues have no objection."

A polite murmuring. No objections. Corain murmured the same.

"Sera Emory, would you like to put that in the form of a motion?"

Seconded and passed.

Motion to adjourn.

Seconded and passed.

The room erupted into more than usual disorder. Corain sat still, felt the weight of a hand on his shoulder and looked up at Mahmud Chavez's face. Chavez looked relieved and worried at the same time.

What happened? that look said. But aloud: "That was a surprise."

"My office," Corain said. "Thirty minutes."

Lunch was a matter of tea and sandwiches couriered in by aides. The meeting had grown beyond the office and filled the conference room. In a fit of paranoia, the military aides had gone over the room for bugs and searched other aides and the scientists for recorders, while Adm. Gorodin sat glumly silent through everything, arms folded. Gorodin had been willing to go along with the walkout. Now things had slid sideways, and the admiral was glowering, anxious, silent, as it developed they had cornered Emory on the Hope corridor budget and might have an ultimatum on their hands.

"It's information we're after," Corain said, and took a glass of mineral water from an aide. In front of him, in front of all of them and most of the aides, eight hundred pages of exposition and figures that constituted the Science budget, in hard-copy, with certain items underlined: there were Centrists *inside* the Science Bureau, and there were strong rumors of sleepers in the bill. There always were. And every year no few of them involved Reseune. "The damn place doesn't *ask* for budget itself, the only thing we've got on it is the gross tax returns, and why in hell does Reseune want to get Special Person status for a twenty-year-old chemist on Fargone? Who in hell is Benjamin P. Rubin?"

Chavez sorted papers on his table, took one that an aide slid under his hand and gnawed at his lip, following the aide's finger down the paper. "A student," Chavez said. "No special data."

"Is there any way it's part of the Hope project? By any stretch of the imagination?"

"It's at Fargone. It's on the route."

"We could ask Emory," Chavez said sourly.

"We damn well may have to, on the floor, and take whatever documentation she comes up with."

There were dour looks all around. "We're beyond jokes," Gorodin said.

Lu, the Secretary of Defense, cleared his throat. "There is a contact we might trust, at least a chain of contacts. Our recent candidate for Science—"

"He's a xenologist," Tien objected.

"And a personal friend of Dr. Jordan Warrick, of Reseune. Dr. Warrick is here. He came in as part of Councillor Emory's advance staff. He's asked, through Byrd, for a meeting with, mmnn, certain members of Science."

When Lu spoke with that much specificity, he was often saying more than he could officially say in so many words. Corain looked straight at him, and Gorodin was paying full attention. The admiral had come in from military operations, would go back to military operations and leave the administrative details of the Bureau of Defense to the Secretary and his staff: it was axiomatic—Councillors might be the experts in their respective fields, but the Secretaries ran the apparatus and the department heads knew who was sleeping with whom.

"Byrd among them?"

"Very likely," Lu said primly, and shut his mouth.

Mark that one down, Corain thought.

"Is that an old friendship?" Tien asked in a low voice.

"About twenty years."

"How safe is that for Warrick?" Gorodin asked. "What are we jeopardizing?"

"Very little," Lu said. "Certainly not Warrick's friendship with Emory. Warrick himself has his own offices, rarely enters hers, and vice versa. In fact there's considerable hostility there. He's demanded autonomy inside Reseune. He has it. There *are* no Centrists in Reseune. But Warrick is—not an Emory partisan. He's here, in fact, to consult with the Bureau on a transfer."

"He's one of the Specials," Corain said, for those not from Cyteen, and not, perhaps, entirely aware who Warrick was. A certified genius. A national treasure, by law. "Forty-odd years old, no friend of Emory's. He's had a dozen chances to leave and found his own facilities, and she keeps blocking it in the Bureau, cut him off at every turn." He had made a personal study of Reseune *and* Emory. It was only reasonable. But some pieces of information were not as available as others, and Lu's tracing of connections was one of them. "Byrd can contact him?"

"Schedules have gone amok," Lu said softly, in his scholarly way. "Of course things have to be rearranged all along the agenda. I'm sure something can be done. Do you want me to mark that down?"

"Absolutely. Let's break this up. Get the staffs to working."

"That leaves us meeting in the morning," Tien said.

"My staff will be here," Corain said, "very late tonight. If anything comes up that we have to—" He shrugged. "If anything comes up, of the nature—you understand, something of a need to know nature—" *Walk-out* was not a word they used openly, and not all the staff present knew that that was in the offing, particularly the clerks. "My staff will contact you directly."

And quietly, catching Gorodin and Lu as the rest of them drifted out to offices and staff meetings in their own Bureaus and departments:

"Can you get Warrick?"

"Lu?" Gorodin said, and Lu, with a lift of clerkly shoulders:

"I should think."

He was an ordinary enough man who showed up in the Hall of State conference room, wearing a brown casual suit, carrying a briefcase that looked as if it had been sent through baggage once too often. Corain would not have picked him out of any crowd: a brown-haired, handsome, athletic sort, not looking quite his forty-six years. But bodyguards would have attended this man until military police took him under their own wing, and very likely servants had all but dressed him and staffers attended him on ordinary business. By no means would Jordan Warrick have come by commercial carrier or a baggage department gotten its hands on that briefcase.

Emory was a Special. There were three at Reseune, the highest number at any single installation. One was this man, who devised and debugged psych tape structures, so they said, in his head. Computers ordinarily did that kind of work. When an important enough tape program had to be built or debugged, they gave it to Jordan Warrick's staff, and when a problem was more than any or all of them could handle it went to Warrick himself. That was as much as Corain understood. The man was a certified genius and a Ward of the State. Like Emory. Like the other dozen Special Persons.

And presumably if Emory wanted to accord that status to a twenty-year-old chemist on Fargone, and, the rumor said, open an office there to attach him to Reseune staff, *and* seemed to imply she attached a priority to that project that made it worth something in the scales right along with her cherished colonial push, there was a damned good reason for it.

"Ser Lu," Warrick said, shaking Lu's offered hand. "Adm. Gorodin. A pleasure." And a worried look but an overall friendly one as he looked toward Corain and offered his hand. "Councillor. I hadn't expected you."

Corain's heart did a little skip-and-race. Danger, it said. Warrick, he reminded himself, was not one of those bright types who operated in some foggy realm of abstract logic completely detached from humanity: he was a psychsurgeon, manipulation was his work, and he was quite in his element stripping people down to their motives. All this lay behind that sober pleasantness and those younger-than-forty eyes.

"You may have guessed," Lu said, "that this is more than I told you it would be."

A little alarm registered on Warrick's face. "Oh?" he said.

"Councillor Corain very much wanted to speak with you—without public attention. This is political, Dr. Warrick. It's quite important. Certainly if you would rather get on to your other meeting, for which you will otherwise be perhaps ten minutes late—we will understand that you don't want to involve yourself with our questions, and I hope you'll accept my personal apologies in that case. It's my profession, you understand, a disposition to intrigue."

Warrick drew a breath, distanced himself the few paces to the conference table, and set his briefcase down on it. "Is this something to do with Council? Do you mind explaining what, before I make any decision?"

"It's about the bill coming up. The Science appropriations bill."

Warrick's head lifted just the little bit that said: Ah. A small smile touched his face. He folded his arms and leaned back against the table, in every evidence a relaxed man. "What about the bill?"

"What's in it," Corain asked, "—really?"

The secret smile widened and hardened. "You mean what's it covering? Or something else?"

"Is—what it's covering—in any way connected to the Hope project?"

"No. Nothing in that budget to do with it. Nothing I'm aware of. Well, SETI-scan. But that's fairly general."

"What about the Special appointment? Is Reseune interested?"

"You might say. You want to know about Fargone in general?"

"I'm interested in whatever you have to say, Dr. Warrick."

"I can spare the ten minutes. I can tell you in less than that what's going on. I can tell you in one word. Psychogenesis. Mind-cloning, in the popular press."

It was not the answer Corain had expected. It was certainly not what the military expected. Gorodin snorted.

"What's it covering?"

"Not a cover," Warrick said. "Not the process in the popular press. Not exact duplicates, but duplicate capabilities. Not real significant for, say, a child trying to recover a lost parent. But in the case of, say, a Special, where the ability is what you want to hang on to— You're familiar with the attempt to recover Bok.''

Estelle Bok. The woman whose work led to faster-than-light. ''They tried,'' Corain said. ''It didn't work.''

''Her clone was bright. But she wasn't Bok. She was a better musician than she was a physicist, and desperately unhappy, thanks to all the notoriety. She wouldn't take her rejuv for days on end, till the effects caught up with her and she'd have to. Wore herself down that way, finally died at ninety-two. Wouldn't even leave her room during the last few years of her life.

''What we didn't have then was the machinery we have now; and the records. Dr. Emory's work in the war, you know, the studies with learning and body chemistry—

''The human body has internal regulating systems, the whole complex that regulates sex and growth and defense against infection. In a replication, the genetic code isn't the whole game. Experience impacts the chemical system the genetic code set up. This is all available in the scientific journals. I could give you the actual references—''

''You're doing quite well,'' Corain said. ''Please.''

''Say that we know things now that we didn't when we cloned Bok. If the program does what Dr. Emory hopes, we can recover the ability in the same field. It involves genetics, endocrinology, a large array of tests, physiological and psychological; and the records have to be there. I don't know all of it. It's Dr. Emory's project, it's secret, and it's in a different wing. But I do know that it's serious and it's not extremely far off the present state of the art. A little speculative, perhaps; but you have to understand, in our science, there's a particularly difficult constraint: the scientist himself has to live long enough to draw his conclusions; and Dr. Emory is not young. Every azi experimentation takes at least fifteen years. The Rubin project is going to take at least twenty. You see the difficulty. She has to take some small risks.''

''Health problems?'' Corain said quietly, recollecting the subtle change in skin tone, the loss of weight. Rejuv lasted an unpredictable number of years. Once it started to lose its effect—problems started. And aging set in with a vengeance.

Warrick's eyes left his. He was not going to answer that question frankly, Corain reckoned before he said anything. He had pressed too closely.

"Mortality is an increasing concern," Warrick said, "for anyone her age, in our field. It's what I said: the *time* the projects take."

"What's your estimate of this project?" Gorodin asked.

"It's very, very important to her: all her theories, understand, all her personal work, her work on endocrine systems and genetics, on psych-structures—lead toward this."

"She's a Special. She can requisition damn near anything she needs—"

"Except the Special status that would protect her subject from what happened to Bok. I agree with her on the matter of *not* using someone inside Reseune. The clone will be at Reseune, but not Rubin. Rubin is young. That's a prerequisite. He's brilliant, he was born on a station, and every move he's ever made down to buying a drink out of a machine is there in station records. He was also born with an immune deficiency, and there are extensive medical records that go back to his infancy. That's the most important part. Ari can do it without the Council's approval; but she can't keep Fargone's local government from doing something that might compromise her results."

"Is Rubin supposed to be aware of this?"

"He'll be aware he's a blind control on an experiment at Reseune. More significantly, his clone won't know Rubin exists until he's the same age Rubin is now."

"Do you think it's a valid project?" Corain asked.

Warrick was silent a moment. "I think whether or not one equals the other, the scientific benefits are there."

"You have reservations," Lu said.

"I see minimal harm to Rubin. He's a scientist. He's capable of understanding what blind control means. I would oppose any meeting of the two, at any future date. I'll go on record on that. But I wouldn't oppose the program."

"It's not yours."

"I have no personal work involved in it."

"Your son," Corain said, "does work closely with Dr. Emory."

"My son is a student," Warrick said, expressionless, "in

tape design. Whether or not he'll be involved is up to Dr. Emory. It would be a rare opportunity. Possibly he might apply for the Fargone office, if it goes through. I'd like to see that."

Why? Corain wondered, and wished he dared ask it. But there were limits with a hitherto friendly informant, and there were persistent rumors about Emory that no one proved.

"Student," Lu said, "at Reseune, means rather more than student at the university."

"Considerably, yes," Warrick said. All liveliness had left his face. It was guarded now, extremely careful of expressions and reactions.

"How do *you* feel about the Hope project?" Corain asked.

"Is that a political question?"

"It's a political question."

"Say that I avoid politics, except as a study." Warrick looked down and up again, directly at Corain. "Reseune no longer depends on the azi trade. We could live quite well off our research, whether colonies go out or not, —there'll be a need for what *we* do, never mind the fate of the other labs— who couldn't undercut us. We have too great a head start on other fields. We wouldn't be as rich, of course. But we'd do quite well. It's not economics that troubles me. Someday we should talk."

Corain blinked. That was not what he expected, a feeler from a Reseune scientist. He put his hands in his coat pockets and looked at the others. "Can Dr. Warrick miss that meeting—without it leaking?"

"No difficulty," Lu said; and added: "If Dr. Warrick wants to miss it."

Warrick drew a long breath, then set the briefcase on the floor and pulled a chair back at the conference table. "I'm willing," he said, and sank into the chair.

Corain sat down. Gorodin and Lu took the chairs at the end. Warrick's face held no expression still. "I know these gentlemen," he said with a slide of the eyes toward the military. "I know your reputation, Councillor Corain. I know you're an honest man. What I'm going to tell you could cost me— considerably. I hope you'll use this—only for what it contains, and I hope you won't lay it to personal dislike. Dr. Emory and I have had our differences. You understand—working at

Reseune, you have to make a lot of critical decisions. Our material is human. Sometimes the ethics of a situation are—without precedent. All we operate on is our best estimation, and sometimes those estimates don't agree.

"Dr. Emory and I have had—more than the average number of confrontations. I've written papers opposing her. We have a conflicting view of—certain aspects of her operations. So if she finds out I've been talking to you, she'll believe I've tried to do her damage. But I hope to God you give her this program at Fargone. It doesn't cost the government anything but that Special—"

"It creates a dangerous precedent, to create a Special just to satisfy a research project. Just to keep a subject in your reach."

"I want myself and my son transferred out of Reseune."

Corain stopped breathing a moment. "You're a Special, the same as she is."

"I'm not political. I don't have her pull. She'll claim I'm essential, under the very terms that make me a Special—I'm bound to stay where the government needs me. And so far it arranges to need me at Reseune. Right now my son is working in her program for two reasons: first because it's his field and she's the best; second, because he's my son and Ari wants a hold on me, and in the politics inside Reseune, there's nothing I can do about that. I can try again to get myself out of there, and if *I'm* out from under her direction, I can request my son over to the other project on a personal hardship transfer. That's one reason I'm anxious to see this Fargone facility built. It would be the best thing for the state. It would be the best thing for Reseune. God knows it would be the best thing for Reseune."

"Perhaps some things would come out. Is that what you're saying?"

"I'm not making any charges. I don't want to go public with any of this. I'm saying that Ari has too damn much power, inside Reseune and out. There's no question of her scientific contributions. As a scientist I have no quarrel with her. I only know the politics inside the house and politics outside it is the only way I see to get free of a situation that's become increasingly—explosive."

One had to be careful, very careful. Corain had not spent

twenty years in government to take everything at face value. Or to frighten a cooperating witness. So he asked softly: "What do you want, Dr. Warrick?"

"I'd like to see that project go through. Then I'm going to transfer. She's going to try to prevent that. I'd like support—in my appeal." Warrick cleared his throat. His fingers were locked, white-edged. "The pressure at Reseune is considerable. A move would be—everything I want. I'll tell you, . . . I'm *not* in agreement with this colonization effort. I agree with Berger and Shlegey, there *is* harm dispersing humankind to that degree, that fast. We've just finished one social calamity; we're *not* what left Earth, we're not what left Glory Station, we're not going to be what our founders anticipated; and if we make this further push there's going to be a critical difference between us and our descendants—there's no miracle, no Estelle Bok, no great invention going to close up this gap. That's my view. I can't express that from Reseune."

"Dr. Warrick, are you telling me your communications are limited there?"

"I'm telling you there are reasons I can't express that view there. If you leak this conversation to the press I'll have to take Reseune's official position."

"Are you telling me, Dr. Warrick, that that transfer is what you're holding out for?"

"The transfer, Councillor. Myself. And my son. Then I would have no fear of expressing my opinions. Do you understand me? Most of us in the field that could speak with authority against the Hope project—are in Reseune. Without voices inside Science, without papers published—you understand that ideas don't gain currency. Xenology is strongly divided. The most compelling arguments are in our field. You do *not* have a majority in the nine electorates, Councillor. It's Science itself you have to crack, Ari Emory's own electorate. *This*, this psychogenesis project is very dear to her heart—so much her own, in fact, that she doesn't let her aides handle it. It's the time factor again. On the one hand, there's so very little in a lifetime. On the other—a process that involves a human life has so many hiatuses, so many periods when nothing but time will produce the results."

"Meaning we'll still have her to deal with."

"As long as she lives, definitely, you'll have her in Council to deal with. That's why the Fargone project is an advantage to both of us. I'd like to take a public position, on your side. An opposition from inside Reseune, as it were, particularly from another Special—would have considerable credibility in Science. But I can't do it now, as things are.''

"The important question," Gorodin said, "aside from that: *is* the Rubin project likely to work? Is it real?''

"It's very likely that it will, Admiral. Certainly it's a much more valid effort than the Bok project was. You may know, we don't routinely create from the Specials' genesets. Even our genetic material is protected by statute. On a practical level, it's the old 'fine line' business—genius and insanity, you know. It's not total nonsense. When we create azi, the Alpha classes take far more testing and correction. Statistically speaking, of course. What went wrong with the Bok clone was what could have gone wrong with Bok, give or take her particular experiences, and influences we don't have record of. Our chances of recovering a currently living Special are much better. Better records, you understand. Bok came here as a colonist, her records went with her ship, and it was one of the de-built ones: too much was lost and too much just wasn't recorded. I'm not sure we ever will get Bok's talent back, but it certainly won't be in the present project. On the other hand—recovering, say, Kleigmann . . . who's, what?— pushing a century and a half . . . would be a real benefit.''

"Or Emory herself," Corain said under his breath. "God. Is *that* her push? Immortality?''

"Only so far as any human might want progeny like himself. It's not immortality, certainly no sense of identity. We're talking about mental similarity, two individuals more like each other than identical twins tend to be, and without a dominant twin. Essentially the recovery of an ability latent in the interface between geneset and what we call tape in an azi.''

"Done by tape?''

Warrick shook his head. *"Can't* be done with tape. Not by present understanding.''

Corain thought it through again. And again.

"Meaning," Gorodin said, "that with our lead in genetics and reconstructive psych, we might replicate living Specials as well as dead ones.''

"That is a possibility," Warrick said quietly, "if certain

laws were changed. Practically—I'd speak against that. I understand why they're starting with one. But the potential for psychological trouble is very strong, even if the safeguards keep the two from meeting. Even dead ones— If I were such a subject—I'd worry about my son, and that individual—who would not, in any meaningful sense, be his brother; or his father. Do you see, it's very complicated when you're dealing with human lives? The Nine took a strong interest in the Bok case. Too strong. In this much I agree with Dr. Emory: only the Bureau of Science, in specific, only Reseune ought to have any contact with the two subjects. That's what she wants on Fargone. We're not talking about an office or a lab. We're talking about an enclave, a community Rubin will not leave except as I leave Reseune: rarely and with escorts for his protection.''

"My God," Gorodin said, "Fargone will veto it."

"A separate orbiting facility. That's what she's had to promise Harogo. A compartmentalized area. Reseune will pay the construction."

"You know, then, what deals she's made."

"I happen to know that one. There may be others. That's a fat contract for certain construction companies at Fargone."

It rang true. All the way down. Corain gnawed his lip.

"Let me ask you a difficult question," Corain said. "If there were other information—"

"I would give it."

"If there were other information yet to come—"

"You're asking me to be an informant."

"A man of conscience. You know my principles. I know yours. It seems there's a great deal in common. Does Reseune own your conscience?"

"Even the admiral hasn't been able to requisition me. I'm a ward of the state. My residencies have to be approved by the Union government. That's the price of being a Special. The admiral will tell you: Reseune will call me essential. That's an automatic five votes of the Nine. That means I stay in Reseune. I'll tell you what I'm going to do, Councillor. I'm going to slip Adm. Gorodin a request for transfer, *just* as soon as that Special status is voted for Rubin, *before* the appropriations vote for the Hope Station project. Officially—that's when it will happen.''

"God! You think you're worth a deal like that?"

"Councillor, —you can't win the Hope Station vote. DeFranco is in Ari's pocket. Or her bankbook, via Hayes Industries. The arrangement is—deFranco's going to try to abstain, which at least is going to show a little backbone for her constituency. Forget you heard that from me. But if you *don't* throw the vote into a tie and send the business into the General Council, it's inevitable. You buy me *and my son* out of Reseune, Councillor—and I'll start talking. I'll be worth far more—outside her direct surveillance, in the Reseune facility on Fargone. She might get Hope Station. But she can be stopped, Councillor. If you want a voice inside Science, I can be that."

It was a moment before Corain felt in command of his breathing. He looked at Lu, at Gorodin, suddenly trying to remember how Lu had maneuvered him into this meeting, suspecting these two dark eminences among the Nine, who played behind a screen of secrecies.

"You should go into politics," he said to Warrick then, and suddenly remembered to his disturbance who he was talking to: that this was a Reseune psychmaster, and that this mind was one of those twelve Union considered too precious to lose.

"Psych is my field," Warrick said, with a disturbing directness to his gaze, which no longer seemed ordinary, or harmless, or average. "I only want to practice it without harassment. I'm fully aware of politics, Councillor. I assure you it never leaves us, at Reseune. Nor we, it. Help me and I'll help you. It's that simple."

"It's not simple," Corain objected, but to Warrick it was. Whoever had drawn him into this meeting—be it Lu, be it Gorodin—be it Warrick—

He was not sure, suddenly, that it was not Emory. A man could grow insane, dealing with the potential in the Specials, especially those Specials who dealt with perception itself.

One had to trust someone sometime. Or nothing got done.

iii

"The first bill on the agenda is number 2405, for the Bureau of Science. Ariane Emory sole sponsor, regarding the regular appropriations for the Bureau of Science, under the provisions of Union Statute 2595, section 2. . . .''

Emory looked Corain's way. Well? that half-lidded stare said. Will you defy me, over something so routine?

Corain smiled. And let the bitch worry.

The gavel hammered down, again early: "We are in recess," Bogdanovitch said. The murmuring in the Council chamber was subdued.

Ariane Emory drew a whole breath, finally. The first stage was passed. Rubin had his status, barring a veto from the Council of Worlds, and there would be none. Corain might orchestrate a double-cross, but he would save it for something important. Something *Corain* considered important. The Hope Station project could serve as a decoy until then. DeFranco might want to abstain. But she would not, when the heat came on.

Aides surged doorward, accompanying their Councillors. The press was, thank God, held downstairs, away from the chamber as long as there was no adjournment. A two-hour lunch and consideration of the dispensation of the rest of the Science permissions afterward, a tedious long list of permissions which, in the way of a good many things in a government which had started small and cozy and grown into an administrative monster within a single lifespan, the executive Nine were supposed to clear, but which in fact had devolved to the Secretarial level and which had become routine approval.

Still, she would not breathe easy until that clearance was given—until the obfuscated facts of permission to use a geneset from a living Special went through in the list of Reseune projects that required routine permissions.

There had been, each year, an attempt to cancel the whole Science permissions grant from the floor of General Council. Every year the Abolitionists or some other lunatic group got up a proposal to outlaw azi and to outlaw human experimentation. Every year the Council of Worlds sensibly voted it down. But there was that lunatic element, which the Centrists could in some attempt to exert leverage against the Hope project—use against the Science bill. If the fringes and the Centrists *did* combine on an issue in that body, it came dangerously close to a plurality against the Expansionist party.

She was worried. She had worried ever since her informers

told her that the Centrists were talking walk-out. Corain's sudden willingness to deal bothered her.

And if it would not have raised the issue of an unseemly haste, she would gladly have urged the chair to put the Science bill up before noon. As it was, obstacles were falling too fast, things were going too well, everything was sliding on oil. What had looked to be a lengthy session would end in a record three days, sending the Nine back to their civilian lives for at least another six months.

It had been intended as a means to speed up government, that the Nine would meet and pass all measures that impacted their various spheres of interest, then leave the staff of the Bureaus and the elected representatives of the Council of Worlds and the various senates and councils to handle the routine and the ordinary administrative detail.

In fact, the Nine, being top professionals, were very efficient. They met briefly, did their job, and went away again to be what they were—but some of them exerted an enormous control over the Bureaus they oversaw, wielding power that the framers of the constitution had not entirely foreseen, no more than they had foreseen Reseune's work in the war, or the fact that population would become what it was, or the defection of Pell from both Sol and Union, and the developments that had entrained. The Bureau of State had been conceived as carefully controlled by professionals in diplomatic service; but distances pushed it into greater and greater dependency on the Defense Bureau's accurate reporting of situations it was not there to see.

The Bureau of Science, considering the discovery of alien life at more than Pell's Star, had to take on diplomatic functions and train potential contact specialists.

The Bureau of Citizens had become a disproportionately large electorate, and it had elected an able and dangerous man, a man who had still the sense to know when he was trapped.

Possibly Corain did not know that deFranco was solidly hers. That would explain his willingness to risk his political life on a walk-out. Surely he did not think he had any hope of swinging the Pan-paris trade loop, which Lao dominated. He could do nothing but cost the government money, with which other interests would not be patient. It was certainly not likely that he would create any objection on the Science bill.

Surely.

"Dr. Emory." Despite her aides and her bodyguards a touch reached her arm, and Catlin was there too, instantly, her body tense and her expression baffled, because the one who had touched her was no one's aide, it was Adm. Gorodin himself who had just brushed by Catlin's defense. "A word with you."

"I'm on a tight schedule." She had no desire to talk to this man, who, already with an enormous share of the budget at his disposal, with sybaritic waste in his own department, argued with her about the diversion of ten ships to the Hope project; *and* sided with Corain. She had other contacts inside Defense, and used them: a good section of Intelligence and most of Special Services was on her side, and a new election inside the military might unseat both Gorodin and Lu: let Corain consider *that* if he wanted a fight.

"I'll walk with you," Gorodin said, refusing to be shaken, his aides mingling with hers.

"One moment," Catlin said, "ser." Florian had moved in. They were not armed. The military were. But it did not prevent them: they were azi, and they answered to her, not to logic.

"It's all right," Ariane said, lifting a hand in a signal that confirmed what she said.

"An inside source tells me," Gorodin began, "you've got the votes on the Hope project."

Damn. Her heart raced. But aloud, with a stolid calm: "Well, then, your source might be right. But I don't take it for granted."

"Corain's upset. He's going to lose face with this."

What in hell is he up to?

"You know we can stall this off," Gorodin said.

"Likely you can. It won't win you anything. If you're right."

"We have a source on deFranco's staff, Dr. Emory. We are right. We also have a source inside Andrus Company; and inside Hayes Industries. Damn good stock buy. Are they finally going to get that deep-space construction?"

My God.

Gorodin lifted a brow. "You know, Hayes has defense contracts."

"I don't know what you're getting to, but I don't like to talk

finance anywhere near the word *vote*. And if you've got a recorder about your person, I take strong exception to it.''

"As I would to yours, sera. But we're not talking finance.
As it happens, I set my people to talking to people in Hayes
when we heard that. And we know very well that the Reseune
extension is connected to the Rubin bill, *and* when my staff
spent last night investigating the Reseune Charter, a very help-
ful young aide came up with a sleeper in the articles that gives
Reseune the unique right to declare any subsidiary facilities
part of its Administrative Territory. That means what you're
going to build at Fargone *won't* be under Fargone control. It's
going to be under yours. An independent part of Union. And
Rubin has something to do with it.''

*This is more than he could come up with on his own. Damn,
but it is. Someone's spilled something and he keeps naming
Hayes and Andrus. That's who I'm supposed to blame.*

"This is all very elaborate," she muttered. They had
reached the intersection of the balcony and the hall to the
Council offices, where she wanted to go. She stopped and
faced the admiral. "Go on."

"We find this of military interest. A Reseune facility at
Fargone poses security risks.''

For a moment everything stopped. It was not from the direction she had expected. It was not sane. It *was*, if one was
worried about merchanter contacts.

"We're not talking about labs, admiral.''

"What *are* we talking about?''

"Rubin's going to be working there. Mostly it'll be his
lab.''

"You have enormous faith in this young man.''

Trap. My God, where is it? "He's a very valuable young
man.''

"I'd like to discuss the security aspects of this. Before the
vote this afternoon. Can we talk?''

"Dammit, I've got a luncheon appointment.''

"Dr. Emory, I honestly don't want to send this to committee. I'm trying to be cooperative. But I feel this is going
through much too fast. I have other concerns that I *don't* think
you want me to mention here.''

Someone's talked. He's gotten to someone.

But aloud, to Florian: "Tell Yanni I'm caught in a crisis.

Tell him to sit in for me. I'll get there when I can.'' She looked at the admiral, calmer, reckoning that it sounded like bargaining, not a torpedo from the flank. ''Your place or mine?''

''Thank you,'' Ariane said, taking the coffee from Florian, who knew how she liked it. It was her office, her conference room, and her bodyguards present, the military aides staying outside, the admiral's own offer.

Conciliation, perhaps.

The admiral took his coffee black. Most did, who got a taste of it on special occasions. It was rare and real, imported all the way from Sol, Earth's southern hemisphere. It was one of Ariane's cultivated vices. And she took hers white. Real milk. A second extravagance.

''AG is still working on this,'' she said. ''Someday.'' Cyteen had been a silicate-polluted hell when they started agriculture in the low-lying valleys, where domes and the precipitators could create mini-climate.

Another small flash: so much brown, so much blue-green on the hills. The lines spun above the valley like a webfly's work. The big mirrors caught light from space and flung power down from the hills. And the weathermakers in orbit raked the land with storms, terrible storms— *We're safe, Ari*, maman would say. *It's only noise. It's weather, that's all*—

Leonid Gorodin sipped his coffee with a tranquil look. And smiled. And said: ''The rumor inside the Bureau is that this Rubin project is yours. Personally. There's nothing you do that doesn't change the balance between us and Alliance, us and Sol. I've talked to Lu. We have a lot of anxiety about this.''

''We manage our own security. We've always managed it.''

''Tell me this, Dr. Emory. Is the project you're undertaking . . . going to have any strategic significance?''

Trap. ''Admiral, I suspect the development of a new toilet seat has strategic significance with some of your advisers.''

Gorodin chuckled politely, and waited.

''That's fine,'' she said calmly. ''We'll appreciate a vote of support from your Bureau. You want us to move the facility, we'll move it, even to Cyteen Station. We're very accommodating. We just don't want to lose Rubin.''

''That important?''

''That important.''

''I'll make a proposition to you, Dr. Emory. You've got an

agenda. You want it passed. You want these things to go through, you want them to go through with a clean bill from Finance, you certainly don't want any long delays. You want to get back to Reseune. I want to get back to my command. I've got business out there, and between you and me, I'm allergic as hell to something around here and I hate the socializing.''

"I'm also anxious to get home," she said. It was a dance. It would get where it was going in Gorodin's own time.

"You level with me," Gorodin said, "about the Fargone project."

"Say it's genetics. It's experimental."

"Are you going to have advanced labs out there?"

"No. Medical wing. Analysis. Administrative work. None of the classified equipment."

"Meaning you're following-up, not creating."

"In practical terms, yes. No birth-lab."

Gorodin looked at the empty cup, and at the two azi, and held his out.

"Florian," Ariane said, and the azi, with a quiet nod, took the pot from the sideboard and filled it. Gorodin followed Florian's moves with his eyes, thoughts proceeding.

"You can rely on their discretion," Ariane said. "It's quite all right. They're not sensitive to discussion. Reseune's best work. Aren't you, Florian?"

"Yes, sera," Florian said, preparing her second cup. He offered it.

"Beauty and brains," Ariane said, and smiled with the mouth, not the eyes. "Alliance *won't* develop birth-labs. They have no worlds to fill."

"Yet. We have to think about that. —Who's going to manage that facility at Fargone?"

"Yanni Schwartz."

Gorodin frowned, and sipped slowly at the incongruously tiny cup.

Ah, Ariane thought. *Now, now, we get closer to it.*

"I'll tell you, Dr. Emory. A lot of my people rely on the psych hospital at Viking. For reasons which are only politics—I'd like to have a facility a lot closer to that Hope Station route you're promoting. I'd like to have a place to send some of my worse cases—where Cyteen *won't* take them through the station facility."

"Any particular reason for that?"

"We're talking about special operations. People whose IDs change. People whose faces—you understand—I don't want seen. These are people who live anxious lives. They feel exposed at the big stations. They'd feel a hell of a lot better if there were a way to get to a Reseune facility—not on Cyteen."

Ariane frowned, not bothering to hide her perplexity. It sounded halfway sane.

"What I want," Gorodin said, "is access. A facility where my people feel—safe. Where I know they are. I want to throw some of the covert budget in there. Some of my staff."

"No military."

"We're talking about unanimous support for that facility. I can deliver that."

"No military. Reseune staff. And it better be a damn large contribution. You'll force a redesign. I'm not having my project compromised by your people strolling through Reseune boundaries. There'll be a total separation between any military hospital and our offices."

"We can go with that. But we want a liaison between our side and yours that we have confidence in. Someone we've worked with."

The thought hit like ice water. It was hard not to react, to keep the fingers relaxed on the fragile handle of the cup. "Who did you have in mind?"

"Dr. Warrick. He designed the training tapes. We want him, Dr. Emory."

"Does he want you?" Calmly. Very calmly.

"We can ask him."

"I think I know your source, admiral. I'm damned sure I know your source. What else did he tell you?"

"I think you're jumping to conclusions."

"No, I'm not. I was afraid of something like this. You want him, do you? You want a man in charge of your highest security operations, who quite readily betrayed my interests."

"I've told you my sources."

"Of course you have. You're quite willing to have some Hayes employee's head on the block, some poor sod of an engineer, no doubt, that they'll find a way to blame if I come down on them. You want Jordan Warrick. Did he tell you why?"

"He didn't tell me anything."

"Admiral, you're a damn good poker player, but remember how I make my living. Remember how he makes his. What's he done? Offered to go public with his opinions? Is that how you'll guarantee me Corain?"

"Dr. Emory, you know I can deliver what I promise."

"Of course you can. And Jordan Warrick promises you my head on a platter. He promises you he can swing votes in Science. I'll tell you what I'll do. You can have him. I'll transfer him and his whole damned staff. If you want to put him over a top-secret facility, go right ahead. If he wants to make speeches and write papers against my policies, fine." She set the cup down. "Do we have a deal, admiral? We can get out of this damned city days early, if that's the case. You support me in a request to let us leave sealed ballots on the Hope bill, and if you can guarantee they'll be unanimous, none of us will have to show up here to call a question. Deal?"

"I think we can go with that."

She smiled. "Excellent. If you want Warrick's wing at Fargone, that'll have to be written up. I'll trust your staff for that. Mine's busy. But it'll wait on the establishment of a secure facility. And I do trust you know how to lay your hands on Warrick to get his signature on the request."

Gorodin swallowed his coffee in some haste and set his cup down. "Thank you, Dr. Emory. I'm sure this will work to everyone's good." He rose and offered his hand.

Ariane rose and reciprocated a strong handshake. And smiled at him all the way to the door.

The azi Catlin closed it then, her face as blank as any soldier at attention.

Florian picked up the cups, trying not to look at her either.

They knew when to be afraid.

Verbal Text from:
PATTERNS OF GROWTH
A Tapestudy in Genetics: #1
"A Reseune Calendar: 2396"

Reseune Educational Publications: 8970-8768-1
approved for 80+

BATCH AL-5766: FOUR UNITS:

The technician begins a routine procedure at Reseune, the transfer of genetic material already replicated. Ten units of AL-5766 remain unused in the genebank, standard operating procedure for commercial and experimental materials.

AL-5766 is female, Alpha class. Alpha, the highest intelligence in the A-Z non-citizen classifications, ranges upward from 150 on the Rezner scale, to a current known high of 215. AL-5766 is 190, which verges on genius. Alphas are generated only rarely except for specific executive assignments, experimental studies or colonial operations in which there is minimum population density and considerable latitude for independent judgment. Alphas without early socialization are prone to personality disorders: the best successes in non-social Alphas have been achieved with positive feedback in early training and an accelerated early tapestudy consisting of world awareness, reading, and mathematics skills, with minimal intervention except for reward. The most reliably successful Alphas are those given to human parentage from the

*moment of birth: in such cases the behavioral and social statis-
tics follow the same profile as citizen-born individuals of equal
Rezner values. It should always be remembered that an azi
geneset's traits and to some extent, classification, are determined by the tape designed specifically for that geneset; and
that the primary failing with Alphas seems to be in tape design.*

*AL-5766 has shown developmental patterns in human par-
entage situations which are within acceptable ranges, but
which indicate a propensity toward aggression. Within azi
communities the AL-5766 statistics are wholly unacceptable,
involving violent behaviors, moodiness, and abnormal and irrational anxieties. AL-5766 disorders once manifested find no
amelioration through tape, and only rarely find relief through
interventive counseling, although some salvage has been ef-
fected on two occasions by transfer to military situations where
hardship and physical challenge is extreme.*

*Neither case, however, has utilized the high potential of the
AL-5766s in mathematics, and not even experimental use has
been made of the AL-5766 geneset since 2353. Now, however,
Reseune believes it has a tape-fix for the problem, of interest
since AL-5767 proved out as Beta-class, lacking the traits
which made 5766 both brilliant and troublesome.*

*There are four sets in this group because a tape-design team
has come up with two fixes, subtly different. Two each will provide adequate comparisons for a first run. There is no need of
a control using the original tape: AL-5766s have forty-six
years of data behind them, and no one needs to prove that the
old tapes were faulty.*

*The eggs lack a code of their own until they receive the full
diploid set of AL-5766. This is standard, for azi and citizen
replications.*

*The womb into which each egg goes is bioplasmed and con-
tractile, the whole environment closely duplicating a specific
natural pregnancy which has served Reseune for forty-nine
years: it replicates all the movements, the sounds, the chemical
states, and the interactive cycles of a living womb.*

BATCH EU-4651: TEN UNITS:

*The AL-5766 units are a day along, four motes of life with
identical genetic codes busily dividing and growing in the dark*

of the wombs. The EU-4651s, male, have an identical start; and there are the usual ten units left in the genebank.

EU-4651 is an old type, Eta-class, between 90 and 95 on the Rezner scale and outstandingly stable, one of the most successful Etas in industrial and military fields, and not restricted to Cyteen, but patented in all its sets and derivative sets. Ordinarily Reseune would have simply sold the requisite eggs in whatever number the purchasing lab requested, but this is a new application for the EU-4651s, most of whom are in military service. An EU-4651 has shown an uncommon and late-developing aptitude under an emergency situation which might mean reclassification and upgrading of the type if a tape program could take advantage of it either in existing individuals or in future EU-4651s.

BATCH RYX-20: TWENTY UNITS:

This set is Rho-class, Rezner 45 and below. Rho is the last of the azi classes which Reseune deliberately engineers on a commercial basis. Rho-class azi perform very well with positive feedback and minimal intervention, having little inclination to deviate from program. Their ability to rebound from mishandling and so-called bad tape make them valuable initial test subjects in any new tape structure, which, along with general labor, will be the usefulness of these twenty azi in Reseune. Because they are prone to physical strain during their lives they are, like classes N through Ps, generally not given rejuv, which of course does little to alleviate skeletal damage; but they are given a value structure which provides great satisfaction in continuance of the genotype.

BATCH CIT-*-**-**-**-****: ONE UNIT:

CIT--**-**-**-**** goes directly from processing to cryogenics, flown via company jet to a courier service in Novgorod, to make the scheduled shuttle lift on the weekend, weather permitting.*

Reseune maintains a special service to the general public, whereby it receives certain tax exemptions and utilizes equipment during its slack hours.

CIT--**-**-**-**** is from a tissue sample of a seven-*

year-old child from ***, who suffered a fatal fall. The release form has advised the mother there will be no identity transference: the replicate by law must have special counseling, but at the will of the parent, the clone may bear the name and must bear the citizen number of the deceased, being a posthumous replicate of the child, beloved daughter of Susan X. (Actual name and numbers withheld.) The embryo will develop in ***'s lab, indebted only with the minimal freight charge so tiny a canister requires on a scheduled military transport. In due course she will be delivered from the womb-tank into her genetic mother's arms.

BATCH CIT-*-**-**-****PR: ONE UNIT:

Cloning individuals who want a personal twin instead of a genetically mixed offspring has become a lucrative business for the ordinary lab, since the cost runs upward of 500,000 credits; but Reseune, as a research and development laboratory, has no interest in this practice, sometimes called vanity cloning, except for the rare genotype Reseune finds of commercial or experimental interest. This is such a case, a fetus near term. In fact, Reseune has absorbed all cost on this replication, whose designation is CIT-*-**-***-****PR: the parent-subject is uniquely talented, willing to trade genetic uniqueness for one replicate, and willing to sign a release opening all informational records of applicable interest to Reseune: Reseune will store that data for future development of the geneset, but will not release the geneset for commercial use until fifty years after the decease of parent and replicate.

Reseune puts ten genesets in storage as A**-1.

BATCH AGCULT-789X: ONE UNIT:

A day along, in a womb-tank in a large building somewhat downhill from the last facility, is AGCULT-789X. AGCULT-789X, experimental as the X-designation indicates, closely resembles the RYX-20s or the EU-4651s, except that the genetic codes of the RYX-20s and the EU-4651s indicate two feet while that of AGCULT-789X indicates four, and the RYX-20's and the EU-4651's codes indicate smooth skin, while AGCULT-

789X's indicates a sleek bay hide and a superlative ability to run.

AGCULT-789X is exceedingly rare material, Terran in origin, another attempt at a species with which Cyteen has had limited success. The AGCULT programs, involving not only animal species, but also botanical studies, have had far more success with the algae and with the lower end of a food-chain which may one day support the descendants of Terran species. In a much-heralded gesture toward peace, Earth has provided Cyteen with genesets and data on the whole range of Terran species, with particular emphasis on the endangered or extinct, along with human genesets which may contain genetic information missing from Union and Alliance genepools.

Reciprocally, Union has released representative genesets of Union populations to Terran genetic archives, in an exchange program designed to provide a valuable comparison between the two populations, and to provide a reference in event of global catastrophe or unforeseen lapse in contact.

Of the two worlds presently supporting human colonies, one, Downbelow, is, of course, a protectorate, and there is no question of changing the environment to any extent that would wipe out the indigenes. Humanity remains a visitor to Downbelow.

Cyteen, far less hospitable, harboring no species more advanced than the various platytheres and ankyloderms, was far more suitable for radical terraforming, and Cyteen's ability to store genetic material against irrevocable climatic and atmospheric change at least raises hopes of selective recoveries in specific protected habitats should changes exceed their intended limits.

Terraforming, while wreaking havoc on many native species, has provided a unique opportunity to study interface zones and compare adaptive changes in Terrene and indigenous species, advancing our understanding of catastrophic changes which have impacted Terrene species over geologic time, and of the degree of change facing the human species in its radical changes of habitat.

Understanding that genetic changes are inevitable but not always desirable, Earth has begun to look on Cyteen as a repository for genetic information on species threatened with extinction. Some of the more ambitious projects involve *large-mammal habitat, from the bottom of the food-chain up. Ironically, the experience in terraforming Cyteen, destructive as it has been of Cyteen's indigenous life, is making possible the recovery of certain threatened ecosystems on Earth, and the establishment of more fragile systems on Mars, fourth planet of Sol system.*

Certain of the proposed future exchanges are quite ambitious.

Earth is particularly anxious for the success of cetaceans and higher primates on Cyteen. It has proposed a joint study program as soon as the cetacean project is viable, for the study of cetacean development and the comparison of whalesong on Cyteen and on Earth.

Cyteen finds such projects of interest too, for the future. But the present emphasis in terraforming and recovery is far more concerned with the immediate problems in large-scale atmospheric changes, and the problems of interface zones, high salinity, and trace minerals in Swigert Bay, at the delta of the heavily-colonized Novaya Volga, which offers the most favorable conditions for large-scale marine aquaculture . . .

CHAPTER
2

Reseune from the air was a patch of green in the deep valley of the Novaya Volga, a protected, low-lying strip stretching yearly longer on the riverside, white buildings at the last, and the AG pens, the barracks, the sprawling complex of Reseune proper spread out under the left-side window that was always hers. Ariane Emory latched up her papers, quite on schedule as the gear came down and Florian appeared beside her seat to take temporary custody of her personal kit.

She kept the briefcase.

Always.

The jet touched down, concrete coming up under the delta wings; it braked, taxiing to a gentle stop at Reseune terminal as ground crews swung into action, personnel transport, baggage crews, cleaning crews, mechanics, a crisp and easy operation from decontamination to docking that matched anything Novgorod could muster.

They were all azi, all staff born to Reseune. Their training went far beyond what Novgorod counted sufficient. But that was true of most Reseune personnel.

They were known faces, known types, and everything about them was in the databanks.

For the first time in days Ariane Emory felt herself secure.

The Security hand-off had gone smoothly enough, control passing to Reseune offices the moment the word reached Giraud Nye's office that *RESEUNE ONE* had left the ground at Novgorod—with no more than an hour's advance warning. Ari's movements were usually sudden and unscheduled, and she did not always give advance notice even to him, who was head of Reseune Security—but this was a record suddenness.

"Advise the staff," he had told Abban, his own bodyguard, who did that, quickly, seeing to the transfer of logs and reports. *He* called his brother Denys, in Administration, and Denys advised Wing One as soon as the plane was on final approach.

The last was routine, the standard procedure on Ariane's returns, whenever *RESEUNE ONE* came screaming in and Ariane Emory settled into the place that was hers, in her wing, in her residency.

The word had come on yesterday's news that the Hope project had been tabled, and the stock market had reacted with a shock that might well run the length and width of space, although analysts called it a procedural delay. The good news was a tiny piece following, with biographical clip provided from Science Bureau files, that an obscure chemist on Fargone had been afforded Special status: *that* bill, at least, had gone through. And the Council had wrapped up in a marathon session that had extended on into the small hours: more ripples in the interstellar stock market, which loathed uncertainties more than it disliked sudden reverses of policy. The news bureaus of every polity in Union had held a joint broadcast of commentary and analysis, preempting scheduled morning broadcasts, senior legislative reporters doing their best to offer interpretations, frustrated in the refusal of even opposition Councillors to grant interviews.

The leader of the Abolitionist faction in the Centrist coalition had granted one: Ianni Merino, his white hair standing out in its usual disorder, his face redder and his rhetoric more extreme than ever, had called for a general vote of confidence of the entire Council and threatened secession from the Centrist party. He did not have the votes to do the one: he might well do the other, and Giraud Nye had sat listening to that, knowing more than the commentators and still wondering along with the news bureaus just what kind of deal had been struck and why Mikhail Corain had been willing to go along with it.

A triumph for Reseune?

A political disaster? Something lost?

It was not Ariane's habit to consult back during the sessions in Novgorod except in dire emergency, certainly not by phone, not even on Bureau lines; but there were staff couriers and planes always available.

That she had not sent—meant a situation under control, despite that precipitate adjournment—one hoped.

The social schedule had been thrown into utter confusion, the Councillors had canceled meetings right and left, and the Councillors from Russell's and Pan-paris had sped back to Cyteen Station to make passage on a ship bound for Russell's Star, departure imminent. Their Secretaries had been left to sit proxy, one presumed, with definite instructions about their votes.

It was more than protocol that brought Giraud Nye and his brother Denys to meet the small bus as it pulled up in the circle drive at the front of Reseune.

The bus door opened. The first one down was, predictably, the azi Catlin, in the black uniform of Reseune security, her face pale and set in a forecast of trouble: she stepped down and reached back to steady Ari as Ari made the single step—Ari in pale blue, carrying her briefcase herself as usual, and with no visible indication of triumph or catastrophe until she looked straight at Giraud and Denys with an expression that foretold real trouble.

"Your office," she said to Denys. Behind her, exiting onto the concrete with the rest of the staff, Giraud saw Jordan Warrick, who was not supposed to be with that flight, who had flown out five days ago on *RESEUNE ONE* and was supposed to come back at the end of the week, on a RESEUNEAIR special flight.

There was trouble. Warrick arriving in Ari's company was as great a shock as Centrists and Expansionists suddenly bedding down together. Warrick's staff was not with him, only his azi chief-of-Household, Paul, who followed along with a so-ber, anxious look, carrying a flight-kit.

Abban might collect gossip from the staff, the ones who were Family, and free to talk. Giraud gave Abban the order and fell in with Ari and Denys, silent Florian heading off to the left hall the moment they cleared the doors, Catlin walking along behind with Denys' azi Seely.

Not a word until they were inside Denys' inmost office, and Denys turned on the unit that provided sound-screening in the room. Then:

"We've got a problem," Ari said, opening the briefcase very carefully, very precisely on the expensive imported ve-neer of Denys' desk.

"Hope's in trouble?" Denys asked, accepting the fiche she handed him. "Or is it Jordan?"

"Gorodin is promising us unanimous approval for Hope—if Jordan gets a liaison post at a Fargone military psych facility *we're* going to have hidden in our budget."

"God," Giraud said, and sat down.

"You tell me how you buy Mikhail Corain's vote, and why Jordan Warrick's transfer has to be part of Gorodin's bar-gain."

Giraud had no doubts. It was certain that Ari had none.

"He's become a problem," Ari said.

"We can't touch him," Giraud said. Panic welled up in him. Sometimes Ari forgot she *had* limits, or that prudence did.

"He's counting on that, isn't he?" So, so quietly. Ari set-tled into the remaining chair. "It still has to be voted. It doesn't need to be voted until the facility exists. And we just got the appropriation."

Giraud was sweating. He resisted the impulse to mop his face. The sound-screening tended to make his teeth ache, but at the moment the discomfort was mostly in his gut.

"Well, it's not that bad," Denys said, and tilted his chair back, folding his hands on his ample stomach. "We can map this out. Jordie's being a fool. We can merge his wing right back into Administration, absorb his staff and his records, that for a start."

"He's not a fool," Ari said. "I want to know if we're miss-ing files."

"You think he's left something in Novgorod?"

"What's ever stopped him?"

"Dammit," Giraud said, "Ari, I warned you. I warned you."

Ari tilted her head, regarding him sidelong. "I'll tell you one thing: even if he goes, son Justin won't."

"We've got five more years of budget to fight through! What in hell are we going to do when Jordie's out there in front of the cameras?"

"Don't worry about it."

"What do you mean, don't worry about it?"

"He's here, isn't he? Left his aides, his staff, everyone but Paul in Novgorod. I didn't confront him about the leak. I just sent Florian to advise him he was wanted. He's well aware what he's done and that I know he's done it."

"If you touch him— Listen to me. He won't have done this without advance preparation. God knows what kind of harm he can do us. Or what kind of information he's smuggled out of here. My God, I didn't see this coming."

"Jordan and his little feuds. His requests for transfer. His bickering on staff. Oh, we're still friendly. We have our little policy debates. We had one on the way home. And smiled at each other over drinks. Why not? There's always the chance I *believed* Gorodin."

"He knows damn well you didn't!"

"And he knows that I know that he knows, round and round. So we smile at each other. I'll tell you something: I'm not worried. He's sure I won't move until I know what he's got. He's manipulating the situation. Our Education Special thinks he's the best there is. He's gambling everything on things going the way he predicts. He'll make me a counter-offer soon. And I'll make mine. And that's how we'll pass the months. He's sure he can match me move for move. We'll see. I'm going to my apartments. I'm sure Florian's run his checks by now. I'm going to have a shower, put my feet up a while, and read the logs. *And* have a decent meal. *Formal* dinner tonight. It's a session-end, isn't it? Catlin can approve the menu."

"I'll tell the staff," Denys said. The thought of food turned Giraud's stomach.

"It's not a total disadvantage," she said. "Have you seen

the news? The Centrist coalition is showing seams this morning. Corain's made Ianni Merino very, very upset. An old hand like Corain—this is moving much too fast for him. Corain had his people ready to walk, now he shifts stance on them—the Abolitionists will suspect a sell-out . . . won't they? Let the Abolitionists peel off and start talking about dismantling the labs again. It's bound to make the moderates a little anxious.''

"That's where Jordan can do us the most damage! If he goes to the press—''

"Oh, you don't think the Abolitionists are going to credit a voice out of Reseune.''

"If he's saying the right things they damn well will.''

"Then we have to do something about his credibility, don't we? *Think* about it, Gerry. Corain's going to end up acquiescing—no, *voting for*—the establishment of a Reseune lab right on the Hope colony route. The Abolitionists haven't gotten saner, just quieter; and we have our own sleepers in their rank and file. Keep Corain quite busy putting out fires on his own decks. Gorodin may find the whole noise a bit more than he wants: there are always deals we can offer him: he always stands with his feet either side of the line. Lu is the problem, that double-crossing bastard. But we can persuade him. This facility is exactly the kind of thing that may do it. I want you to look into these things, I don't need to tell you how discreetly. Use your military contacts. The Science Bureau is dispatching a ship to notify Rubin of his status. They're also going to take measures to establish him a protective residency in Fargone Blue Zone: the team is on its way Sunday, when *Atlantis* pushes off for Fargone.''

"Harogo's going to be aboard?'' Denys asked.

"Absolutely. There's not going to be a hitch. He'll get our staff right through customs, and *Atlantis* is running light.''

"Military can beat her.''

"A worry. But Harogo's a much higher card, on his own station, and he's bringing home the second biggest construction project Fargone's ever lusted after. *First* being the Hope corridor, of course. There won't be a hitch. If the Centrists try anything with Rubin, Harogo can fry them, no question. We'd love that kind of ammunition. Did you see the clip? Rubin's a wide-eyed innocent. Pure science and total vulnerability. I thought that came across rather well."

"They can throw that back at us too," Giraud said.

"We can rely on Harogo, I think. At certain times, you have to let a thing go."

"Even Warrick?"

"If they want him by then."

ii

Ari smiled gently across the table, across the salad with vinaigrette, product of their own gardens, and dusted it liberally with a spoonful of Keis, synthetic cheese, a salted yeast, actually: spacer's affectation. Her mother had used it. Ari still liked the tang of it, and imported it downworld at some little trouble.

Most of the Family abhorred it.

It was the formal dining hall: one long table for the Family, and a large U-shaped table around the outside for the azi who were closer than relatives, and somewhat more numerous, about two to one.

Herself at the head: that had been the case since the day uncle Geoffrey died. To her right, Giraud Nye, to her left his brother Denys; then Yanni Schwartz rightside, left again, his sister Beth; and across from her, Beth's son by Giraud Nye, young Suli Schwartz, long-nosed and thin-faced, and looking preoccupied as usual: sixteen and bored; left next, and right and right again, Petros Ivanov and his two sisters Irene and Katrin, then Katrin's current passion the dark-skinned Morey Carneth-Nye; old Jane Strassen looking like a dowager empress in black and an ostentatious lot of silver; daughter Julia Strassen in green, a truly amazing decolletage; dear cousin Patrick Carnath-Emory, who was *far* more Carnath than Emory, and absolutely butter-fingered—he was already mopping his lap; Patrick's daughter Fideal Carnath, olive-skinned and lovely, and her thirty-two-year-old son Jules who they had thought was Giraud's until they ran the genetics and found it was, of all people, Petros'. Then Robert Carnath-Nye and his daughter young Julia Carnath; *and* of course, endmost, Jordan and Justin Warrick, who looked exactly like father and son, unless you had known Jordan thirty years ago and knew that they were twins.

Vanity, vanity.

Jordan had had his passages. (Who had not?) But when it came to bestowing his heredity he had not trusted nature. Or women. It was the temptation to godhood, perhaps. Or the belief that he, being a Special, was bound to produce another.

A replicate citizen was not azi. There were considerable legal differences between young Justin, say, and elegant, red-haired Grant, at the second rank of tables, so, so close in all respects . . . born in the same lab, an insignificant day apart. But Justin, dark-haired, square-jawed, and, at a handsome, broad-shouldered seventeen, so very much Jordan's younger image . . . was CIT 976-88-2355 *PR*, that all-important Citizen prefix and that expensive Parental Replicate suffix— replicate except for the little accidents like the break in Jordan's nose, the little scar on Justin's chin, and oh, indeed, the personality, *and* the ability. When Justin was a mote in a womb-tank, the Bok project had already failed—but (Ari was amused) Jordan had entertained notions that his tapes and his genes could overcome all odds.

The lad was bright. But he was not Jordan. Thank God.

Grant's number, on the other hand, was ALX-972, experimental: a design of her own, aesthetic in the extreme, and with an excellent antecedent—another Special geneset, but, for certain legal reasons, she had corrected a genetic fault, incidentally expressing a few aesthetic recessives, to an extent that the legitimate descendants of a certain slightly myopic, brown-haired, unathletic biologist with a heart defect . . . would find astounding.

Neither was Grant a biologist. An excellent student in tape-design, an Alpha capable of working on the structures which had made him what he was—structures wherein lay the legal difference, *not* in the substitution of certain sequences in the geneset, *not* in the wombs which gestated them.

One infant had gone to a father's arms, to lie in a crib in the House, to hear—nothing, at times; or to deal with the fact that Jordan Warrick might be busy at some given time, and a meal might be late, or a noise startle him—

The other had gone to a crib where human heartbeat gave way at intervals to a soothing voice, where activity was monitored, crying measured, reactions clocked and timed—then extensive tape and training for three years until Ari had asked Jordan to take the boy in, nothing unusual: they fostered-out the suspected Alphas, as a rule, and in those days her relations with Jordan had been stormy but professional. A member of the House with a son the same age was a natural thought, and an Alpha companion was a high-status prize for a household, even at Reseune.

I have every confidence in Justin, she had said that day to Jordan. It's such a natural pairing. I'm perfectly willing to let that happen, on a personal basis, you understand, as long as I can continue my tapes and my tests with Grant.

Meaning that the azi as he grew might pass into Justin's care, become his companion—which implied her faith that young Justin would be in that small percentage licensed to work with Alphas—that Justin's own scores would be Alpha-equivalent.

Not entirely to her astonishment it had worked out very well. The correction was a routine one, minor, not likely to affect the azi's intelligence, . . . although, within certain parameters, that had not been a primary concern in creating the set.

So, so convenient to have a link to troublesome Jordan in those years, not informational, since there was hardly anything a ten-, a thirteen-year-old azi knew in the House that *she* did not.

But one never knew—when it might be of use.

She finished the salad, chatted with Giraud while the serving staff took away the plates and brought in the next course: a fine ham. Terrestrial pigs thrived at Reseune, on the residue of the gardens, in sufficient numbers to provide seed stock for several other farms. Pigs and goats, humankind's oldest and hardiest foodstock, with sense enough not to poison themselves on a stray sprig of native shrubbery.

Horses and cattle had the damnedest self-destructive bent.

"Do you know," she said, over the dessert, a simple ice, tangy and pleasant. "We are going to have to make some far-reaching adjustments in staff."

Amazing how many ears were pricked at table, and how quiet a room could get, when she was only speaking to Denys.

"I really don't anticipate any difficulty with the Hope bill."

They were all listening now, not pretending to do otherwise. She smiled at her family, put down the spoon and picked up the little cup of strong coffee. "You know how to read that. No difficulty. Forget the news reports. Everything is proceeding tolerably well on schedule, and we have a very exciting prospect in front of us . . . certainly a very exciting prospect, a military psych facility at Fargone—in addition. Which is going to make a real difference in operations here. You can congratulate Jordan for laying the groundwork—really, just everything that may put the Hope route in our laps; *and* the new labs; everything. *That's* what's going on. Jordan should have a lot of the credit for that."

Jordan's face was absolutely devoid of expression. "Let's drop the pretense. We're *home*, we're not in front of the cameras."

Ari flashed a smile. "Jordan, I don't bear you the least ill will. I'm sorry if that offends you, but you've done Reseune—and me—a great favor. I truly don't begrudge you the rewards of it."

"The hell!"

Ari laughed gently and took another sip of coffee. "Jordie, dear, *I* know you'd like to have upstaged me with this; but as it happens, Gorodin came to *me*, and I'm going to give you everything you asked for, on a platter. You'll *get* that long-awaited transfer, you and anyone in your wing who wants to go to Fargone, just as soon as the official request for military liaison comes down the tubes."

"What *is* this?" Yanni Schwartz asked.

"I don't say it'll be a bad thing," Ari said quite honestly, still smiling. "I'm not pulling surprises on you, Yanni—Jordan pulled this one on me. I think everyone should think about it, those who'll prefer to go out to the frontier, those who'd rather stay with the comforts of Reseune—God *knows*, some of us would miss ham and fresh fruit. But the opportunities out there are worth thinking about." Another sip of coffee, slow and thoughtful, watching Jordan's eyes like a fencer. "The Educational wing here will continue, of course. There are some of you we can't transfer, you understand that. We'll have to restructure here, rather well replicate the whole wing—" A little wider smile. It was a joke. Suli Schwartz woke up, a quick look around to see if people were supposed to laugh. "Jordie, you'll have to lay out some recommendations."

"Of course," Jordan said. "But I'm sure you'll use your own list."

She laughed, to keep it polite. "You know damn well I will. But I really will respect your choices wherever I can—after all, I'll assume anyone on your list *wants* to transfer, and I'll assume you want them. Yanni, you can deal with Jordie on that."

There was a growing wariness behind the attentive faces. Young Suli finally seemed to have understood what was going on, perhaps to have figured out for the first time in his life what it was to sit in this room on Family Occasions, and not with the juniors down the hall. No one moved, not the Family, not the azi at the tables round about.

A sonorous clearing of the throat from Denys. "Well," he said, "well, Ari, after all—" Another clearing of the throat. "I don't suppose we could have some of those little cookies we had last night, hmmn?" Wistfully.

"Yes, ser," a server said, close by the door, and slipped out, while Denys ladled sugar into his coffee.

"Hum. The essential thing is Reseune, isn't it? Ari, Jordie, Yanni, really, we all have the same thing at heart, which is the freedom to do our work. We all hate these administrative messes, we all do, it's such a damned waste of our time and there's so much more important on our desks than a lot of little regional authorities bickering away in Novgorod. I'm sure it's important whether station administrators can or can't hold stock in their own stations, but it's just not the kind of thing that *we* ought to have to sit through—I mean, the whole idea of the Bureaus was never meant to take valuable people completely away from work. Council's certainly no great inconvenience to Corain, or Chavez, or, God knows, Bogdanovitch, but it's not really productive to have Gorodin on a short string, and Science, my God, Science is an absolute tragedy—I mean, really, Ari, it's a dreadful waste of your time and energy—"

"I don't know why," Jordan said from his end of the table, with a wry lift of his wineglass, a rivalry old as their existence in Reseune, dinner witticisms, "since Ari just considers the whole damned universe her province."

Ari laughed, pro forma. Everyone was relieved. Everyone

laughed, because to do other than that was an Incident, and no one wanted it, not even Jordan.

"Well, you'll have your chance, won't you?" she said. "The whole Hope route right off Fargone, and you'll be working with old friends, so it's not like you'll be out there alone. If I were younger, Jordie, damned if I wouldn't jump at it; but Denys is right. The politics is done, the whole course is laid, and I'm sure I'm anxious to get on about my work, you're anxious to get yours underway. I hate like hell to drop another administrative job in your lap, but I really want your expertise. You've got to set us up another Educational wing here, really, really an opportunity for you to hand us on a legacy, Jordie, I'm very serious—"

"I left that in cryogenics," Jordan said. Another small round of anxious laughter. "Do you want another sample?"

Ari chuckled and took a sip of her coffee. "What? Jordie, I thought you went the other way. But we do have a second source."

Justin blushed. People turned to see if he had. There was another laugh, much too thin.

"I'm sure Jordie will cooperate," Denys said, intervening before the knives came out: it was the ancient rule in this room—nothing unpleasant. One retaliated with wit here, nothing else, and not too far.

"I'm sure," Ari said. And seriously: "We do have restructuring to do. I'm going to be doing some of my Council work by proxy, figuring it's going to be a little tamer now we have the major projects mapped out. There really shouldn't be any difficulty. I suppose I can fly down if they need me, but Denys is very right: I'm a hundred twenty years old—"

"You've got a few more," Denys said.

"Oh, yes, but I see the wall—true." The room was quiet again. "The Rubin project will take a great deal of my time. I'm not getting morbid. But you know and I know that there's not an infinite amount of time for getting this thing moving. I'll leave most of the Fargone set-up to you, Yanni. I'll be asking data from this department and that. I'll be wanting to oversee the process myself—just a desire to have hands-on again. Maybe a little vanity." She chuckled softly. "I'm going to be writing on my book, doing a little side research—preparation. Retirement, I suppose."

"The hell," Jordan said.

She smiled, covered her cup with her hand when the server wanted to pour more coffee. "No, dear, I've caffeine enough to see me to my rooms. Which is where I ought to go, figuring that the floor is still going up and down—we had a bitch of a lot of turbulence over the Kaukash, didn't we? And I don't think I really slept in Novgorod. Catlin?"

A chair moved, and Catlin was there, and Florian with her. Catlin drew her chair back for her.

"Good night, all," she said; and to Florian, quietly, as chairs went back and people began leaving: "Tell Grant I'm reclaiming him."

"Sera?"

"I need him," she said. "Tell him I've filed a new assignment for him. Jordan never did have legal custody of him. He surely realizes that."

iii

"A moment," the azi Florian said, when Justin and Grant started out the door after Jordan and Paul, in the general mill of family and azi headed their separate ways.

"Later," Justin said. His heart began to pound, the way it did anytime he came near Ari or her bodyguards on anything but coldest business, and he took Grant by the arm and tried to get him out the door as Florian blocked Grant's path.

"I'm very sorry," Florian said, looking as if he were. "Sera has said she wants Grant. He's assigned to her now."

For a moment Justin did not realize what he had heard. Grant stood very still in his grip.

"He can retrieve his belongings," Florian said.

"Tell her *no*." They were blocking the Schwartzes from exit. Justin moved confusedly into the hall, drawing Grant with him, but Florian stayed with them. "Tell her—tell her, dammit, if she wants my cooperation in anything, he stays with me!"

"I'm terribly sorry, ser," Florian said—always soft-spoken, soft-eyed. "She said that it was already done. Please understand. He should get his things. Catlin and I will watch out for him the best we can."

"She's not going to do this," Justin told Grant, as Florian slipped back into the dining hall, where Ari delayed. He was cold through and through. His supper sat uneasy at his stomach. "Wait here." His father was waiting with Paul a little down the hall, and Justin crossed the distance in a half-dozen strides, face composed, showing no more, he hoped, than an understandable annoyance; and please, God, not as pale as he was afraid it was. "Something's come up with a project," he told Jordan. "I have to go see about it."

Jordan nodded, had questions, perhaps, but the explanation seemed to cover it; and Justin walked back again to the doorway where Grant stood. He put a hand on Grant's shoulder in passing, and went inside where Ari lingered talking to Giraud Nye.

He waited the few seconds until Ari deliberately passed her eye across him, a silent summons; she seemed to say something dismissing Giraud, because Giraud looked back too, then left.

Ari waited.

"What's this about Grant?" Justin asked when he was face to face with her.

"I need him," Ari said, "that's all. He's a Special geneset, he's relevant to what I'm working on, and I need him now, that's all. Nothing personal."

"It is." He lost control of his voice, seventeen and facing a woman as terrible as his father. He wanted to hit her. And that was not an option. Ari, in Reseune, could do anything. To anyone. He had learned that. "What do you want? What do you really want out of me?"

"I told you, it's not personal. Nothing like it. Grant can get his things, he can have a few days to calm down— You'll see him. It's not like you're not working in that wing."

"You're going to run tape on him!"

"That's what he's for, isn't it? He's an experimental. Tests are what he pays for his keep—"

"He pays for his keep as a designer, dammit, he's not one of your damn test-subjects, he's—" *My brother*, he almost said.

"I'm sorry if you've lost your objectivity in this. And I'd suggest you calm yourself down right now. You don't have your license to handle an Alpha yet, and you're not likely to get it if you can't control your emotions better than this. If you've given him promises you can't keep, you've mishandled him, you understand me? *You've* hurt him. God knows what else you've done, and I can see right now you and I are due for a long, long talk—about what an Alpha is, and what you've done with him, and whether or not you're going to get that license. It takes more than brains, my lad, it takes the ability to think past what you want, and what you believe, and it's about time you learned it.''

"All right, all right, I'll do what you want. He will. Just leave him with me!"

"Calm down, hear? Calm down. I'm not leaving him with anyone in that state. Also—'' She tapped him on the chest. "You're dealing with *me*, dear, and you know I'm good at getting my own way: you know you always lose points when you show that much to your opposition, especially to a professional. You get those eyes dry, you put yourself in order, and you take Grant home and see he comes with everything he needs. Most of all you calm him down and don't frighten him any further. Where are your sensibilities?"

"Damn you! What do you *want?*"

"I've got what I want. Just go do what I tell you. You work for me. And you'll show up polite and respectful in the morning. Hear me? Now go take care of your business."

"I—"

Ari turned and walked out the door that led to the service area and a lift upstairs; Catlin and Florian barred his way, azi, and without choice.

"Florian," she called from some distance, impatient, and Florian left Catlin alone to hold the doorway—the worse, because Catlin had no compunction such as Florian had, Catlin would strike him, and strike hard, at the next step beyond her warning.

"Go the other way, young ser," Catlin said. "Otherwise you'll be under arrest."

He turned abruptly and walked back to the other door, where Grant stood, very pale and very quiet, witness to all of it.

"Come on," Justin said, and grabbed him by the arm. Ordinarily there would be a slight, human resistance, a tension in the muscles. There was none. Grant simply came, walked with him when he let him go, and offered not a word till they were down the hall and in the lift that took them up to third level residencies.

"Why is she doing this?"

"I don't know. I don't know. Don't panic. It's going to be all right."

Grant looked at him, a fragile hope that hit him in the gut, as the lift stopped.

Down the hall again, to the apartment that was theirs, in a residential quiet-zone, only a handful of passersby at this hour. Justin took his keycard from its clip on his pocket and inserted it with difficulty in the slot. His hand was shaking. Grant had to see it.

"No entries since last use of this key," the monitor's bland voice said, and the lights came on, since that was what he had programmed his Minder to do for his entry at this hour, all the way through the beige and blue living room, to his bedroom.

"Grant's here," he mumbled at it, and more lights came on, Grant's bedroom, visible through the archway leftward.

"I'll get my things," Grant said; and, the first sign of fracture, a wobble in his voice when he asked: "Shouldn't we call Jordan?"

"God." Justin embraced him. Grant held on to him, trembling in long, spasmodic shivers; and Justin clenched his own arms tight, trying to think, trying to reason past his own situation and the law inside Reseune which said that he could not protect the azi who had been a brother to him since he could remember.

Grant knew everything, knew everything that he knew. Grant and he had no difference, none, except that damning X on Grant's number, that made him Reseune property as long as he lived.

She could interrogate him about Jordan, about everything he knew or suspected, test systems on him, put him under tape with one structure and another, put sections of his memory under block, do any damned thing she wanted, and there was no way he could stop it.

It was revenge against his father. It was a hold on him, who, the same way Grant had just been transferred, had been Aptituded into Ari's wing. Let her, he had said to his father. Let her take me into her staff. Don't contest it. It's all right. You can't afford a falling-out with her right now, and maybe it's a good place for me to be.

Because he had had a notion then that his father, harried with plans (again) for getting a transfer, could lose too much.

You tell me, Jordan had said with the greatest severity, *you tell me* immediately *if she makes trouble for you.*

There had been trouble. There had been more than trouble, from his second day in that wing—an interview with Ari in her office, Ari too close and touching him in a way that started out only friendly and got much too personal, while she suggested quietly that there was more reason than his test scores that she had requisitioned him into her wing, and that he and Grant both could . . . accommodate her, that others of her aides did, and that was the way things were expected to be on her staff. Or, she had hinted, there were ways to make life difficult.

He had been disgusted, and scared; and worst of all, he had seen Ari's intention, the trap laid—slow provocations, himself the leverage she meant to wield against Jordan, a campaign to provoke him to an incident she could use. So he had gone along with it when she put her hands on him, and stammered his way through reports while she sat on the arm of his chair and rested her hand on his shoulder. She had asked him to her office after hours, had asked him questions, pretending to fill out personnel reports, and he mumbled answers, things he did not dwell on, things he did not want even to remember, because he had never even had a chance to do the things she asked him about, and never wanted in his life to do some of the things she talked about; and suspected that without tape, without drugs, without anything but his own naivete and her skill, she was in the process of twisting his whole life. He could fight back—by losing his capacity to be shocked, by answering her flippantly, playing the game—

—but it was her game.

"I'll think of something," he said to Grant. "There's a way out of this. It'll be all right." And he let Grant go off to his rooms to pack, while he stood alone in the living room in the grip of a chill that went to his bones. He wanted to phone Jordan, ask advice, whether there was anything legal they *could* do.

But it was all too likely Jordan would go straight to Ari to negotiate Grant free of her. Then Ari might play other cards, like tapes of those office sessions—

—O God, then Jordan *would* go straight to the Science Bureau, and launch a fight that would break all the careful agreements and lose him everything.

Query the House computers on the law—but there was nothing he dared use: every log-on was recorded. Everything left traces. There was no way that Reseune would not win a head-on challenge. He did not know the extent of Ari's political power, but it was enough that it could open new exploration routes, subvert companies on distant star-stations and affect trade directly with old Earth itself; and that was just the visible part of it.

Beyond the archway, he heard the sounds of the closet door, saw Grant piling his clothes onto the bed.

He knew suddenly where Grant *was* going—the way they had dreamed of when they were boys, sitting on the banks of the Novaya Volga, sending boats made of old cans floating down to Novgorod, for city folk to marvel at. And later, on a certain evening when they had talked about Jordan's transfer, about the chance of them being held until Jordan could get them out.

It was that worst-case now, he thought, not the way they had planned, but it was the only chance they had.

He walked into Grant's room, laid a finger on his lips for silence, because there *was* Security monitoring: Jordan had told him it went on. He took Grant's arm, led him quickly and quietly out into the living room, toward the door, took his coat from the closet—no choice about that: it was close to freezing outside, people came and went from wing to wing in the open, it was ordinary enough. He handed Grant his, and led him out into the hall.

Where to? Grant's worried look said plainly. *Justin, are you doing something stupid?*

Justin took his arm and hauled Grant along, down the hall, back to the lift.

He pushed T, for the tunnel-level. The car shot downward. God, let there be no stops on main—

"Justin—"

He shoved Grant against the wall of the lift, held him there, never mind that Grant was a head taller. "Quiet," he said. "That's an order. Not a word. Nothing. *Hear?*"

He did not speak to Grant that way. Ever. He was shaking. Grant clamped his jaw and nodded, terrified, as the lift door opened on the dingy concrete of the storm-tunnels. He dragged Grant out, backed him against the wall again. Calmer this time.

"Now you listen to me. We're going down to the Town—"

"I—"

"Listen to me. I want you to go null. Deep-state, all the way. Right now. Do it. And stay that way. That's an order, Grant. If you never in your life did exactly what I said, —do it now. Now! Hear me?"

Grant took a gulp of air, composed himself then, expressionless in two desperate breaths.

No panic now. Steady. "Good," Justin said. "Put the coat on and come on."

Up another lift, to the Administration wing, the oldest; back to the antiquated Ad wing kitchens, where the night shift staff did dinner clean-up and breakfast prep for the catering service. It was the escape route every kid in the House had used at one time or another, through the kitchens, back where the ovens were, where the air-conditioning never was enough, where staff from generation to generation had propped the fire-door with trash-bins to get a breeze. The kitchen workers had no inclination to report young walk-throughs, not unless someone asked, and Administration never stopped the practice—that routed juvenile CIT truants and pranksters past witnesses who would, if asked, readily say yes, Justin Warrick and his azi had gone out that door—

—but not until they were missed.

Shhh, he mimed to the kitchen azi, who gave them bewildered and anxious looks—the late hour, and the fact they were older than the usual fugitives who came this way.

Past the trash-bin, down the steps into the chill dark.

Grant overtook him by the pump shed that was the first cover on the hill before it sloped rapidly to the road.

"We're going down the hill," Justin said then. "Taking the boat."

"What about Jordan?" Grant objected.

"He's all right. Come on."

He broke away and Grant ran after him, pelted downslope to intercept the road. Then they strolled at a more ordinary pace down through the floodlit intersections of the warehouses, the repair shops, the streets of the lower Town. The few guards awake at this hour were on the perimeters, to mind the compound fences and the weather reports, not two boys from the House bound down toward the airport road. The bakery and the mills ran full-scale at night, but they were far off across the town, distant gleam of lights as they left the last of the barracks.

"Is Jordan getting hold of Merild?" Grant asked.

"Trust me. I know what I'm doing."

"Justin, —"

"Shut *up*, Grant. Hear me?"

They reached the edge of the port. The field lights were out right now, but the beacon still blipped its steady strobe into the dark of a mostly vacant world. Far off, the freight warehouses and the big RESEUNEAIR hangar showed clear, brightly lit, night-work and maintenance going on with one of the commercial planes.

"Justin, —*does he know?*"

"He'll handle it. Come on." Justin set out at a run again, leaving Grant no breath for questions, down the road that passed the end of the runway to the barge-dock and down across the concrete bridgeway to the low-lying warehouses at the edge of the river.

No one locked the doors down here at the small boathouse. No one needed to. He pushed at the door of the shabby prefab, winced at the creak of the hinge. Inside, an iron grid whispered hollowly under their feet. Water splashed and slapped at the pilings and buffers, starlight reflecting wetly around the outlines of the boats moored there. The whole place smelled of river-water and oil and the air was burning cold.

"Justin," Grant said. "For God's sake—"

"Everything's all right. You go exactly the way we planned—"

"*I* go—"

"I'm not leaving. You are."

"You're out of your mind! Justin!"

Justin clambered aboard the nearest boat, opened up the

pressurized cabin door and left Grant nothing to do but follow him aboard with his objections.

"Justin, if you stay now, they can arrest you!"

"And if I take you out of here there's no way in hell I'll ever get certified to be near you, you know that. So I'm not down here tonight. I don't know a thing about this. I just go back up there, say I never left my room, how am I to know where you went? Maybe a platythere ate you and got indigestion." He flipped the on-switch, checked the gauges, one toggle-switch and another. "There you go, everything's full, batteries all charged. Wonderful how the staff keeps things up, isn't it?"

"Justin." Grant's voice was shaking. He had his hands in his pockets. The air was bitter chill near the water. "Listen to *me* now, let's have some sense here. I'm azi. I was listening to tape in the cradle, for God's sake. If she runs something on me I can handle it, I can rip the structures apart and tell you if there were any bugs in it—"

"The hell you can."

"I can survive her tests, and there's no way she can axe my Contract, there's no axe-code. I know for a fact there's not—I *know* my sets, Justin. Let's just forget this and go up the hill and we'll figure out another way. If it gets bad, we always have this for an option."

"Shut up and listen to me. Remember how we mapped this out: first lights you see on your right are still Reseune: that's the number ten precip station, up on the bluffs. The lights on your left two klicks on will be Moreyville. If you run completely dark you can pass there before Ari gets wind of this, and it's a clear night. Remember, stay to the center of the channel, that's the only way to miss the bars, and for God's sake, be careful of snags. Current comes from the left when you get to the Kennicutt. You turn into it, and the first lights you see after that, two, maybe three hours on, that's Krugers. You tell them who you are and you give them this—" He turned on a dim chart-light and scribbled a number down on the pad clipped to the dash. Under the number he wrote: MERILD. "Tell them call Merild, no matter the hour. You can tell Merild when he gets there—tell him Ari's blackmailing Jordan through me, dammit, that's all he has to know. Tell him I can't come until my father's free, but I had to get you out of there, you're one more hostage than Jordan can cope with. Understand?''

"Yes," Grant said in a faint voice, azi-like: *yes.*

"The Krugers won't betray you. Tell them I said sink the boat if they have to. It's Emory's. Merild will handle everything else.''

"Ari will call the police."

"That's fine. Let her. *Don't* try to go past the Kennicutt. If you have to, the next place on down the Volga is Avery, overnight, maybe more, and she *could* intercept you. Besides, you'd get caught up in Cyteen-law and police down there, and you know what that could be. Krugers is it. It has to be." He looked back at Grant's face in the faint glow of the chart-light, and it struck him suddenly that he might not see him again. "Be careful. For God's sake, be careful."

"Justin." Grant embraced him hard. "You be careful. Please."

"I'll push you out of here. Go on. Dog the seals down."

"The other boat—" Grant said.

"I'll take care of it. Go!" Justin turned and ducked out of the door, hopped up on the deck and onto the echoing grating. He cast off the ties then, threw them aboard, shoved the big boat back with his foot and with his hands till it drifted clear, scraping the buffers.

It swung round sideways, inert and dark, then caught the current off the boathouse and drifted, following the sweep of the main channel, turning again.

He opened up the second boat and threw up the cover on the engine.

The starter was electronic. He pulled the solid state board, dropped the cover down, closed the hatch behind him, and dropped the board into the water before he made the jump between the boat and the metal grid of the dock.

In the same moment he heard the distant, muffled cough of Grant's engine.

Solid then, chugging away.

He cleared the boathouse, latched the door and ran. It was dangerous to be down here on the river-edge, in the dark, dangerous anywhere less patrolled, where something native could have gotten in, weed in the ditch, stuff carried in the air—God

knew. He tried not to think about it. He ran, took up on the
road again, walking as he caught a stitch in his side.

He expected commotion. He expected someone on night
shift at the airport to have seen the boat, or heard its engine
start. But the work at the hangars was noisy. Maybe someone
had had a power wrench going. Maybe they thought it was
some passing boat from Moreyville or up-Volga, with a balky
engine. And they had the bright lights to blind them.

So far their luck was a hundred percent.

Till he got to the House and found the kitchen door locked.

He sat down a while on the steps, teeth chattering, trying to
think it through, and gave it a while, time for a boat to get well
on its way. But if he sat there the night, then it was unarguable
that it was conspiracy.

If he gave them evidence of that—

It would land on Jordan.

So there was nothing to do finally but use his key and trip the
silent warnings he knew would be in place by now.

Security showed up to meet him in the halls by the kitchens.
"Ser," the azi in charge said, "where are you coming from?"

"I felt like a walk," he said. "That's all. I drank too much.
I wanted some cold air."

The azi called that in to the Security office; Justin waited,
expecting the man's expression to change then, when the order
came back. But the azi only nodded. "Good evening, ser."

He walked away, weak-kneed, rode the lift up and walked
all the lonely way to the apartment.

The lights came on inside. *"No entries since the last use of
this key,"* the dulcet voice of the Minder said.

He went into Grant's room. He picked things up and hung
them back in the closet and put them in drawers. He found
small, strange things among Grant's belongings, a tinsel sou-
venir Jordan had brought back from holiday in Novgorod, a
cheap curio spacer patch of the freighter *Kittyhawk* that he had
brought back from Novgorod airport, for Grant, who had not
been allowed to go. A photo of the pair of them, aged four,
Grant pale-skinned, skinny, and shockingly red-haired, himself in that damned silly hat he had thought was grown-up,
digging in the garden with the azi. Another photo of them, at a
mutually gawky ten, standing on the fence of the livestock

pens, barefoot, toes curled identically pigeon-toed over the rail, arms under chins, both grinning like fools.

God. It was as if a limb had been cut off, and the shock had not quite gotten to the brain yet, but it had hit his gut, and it told him it was going to get worse.

Ari would call him now, he had no doubt.

He went back to the living room, sat down on the couch, hugged his arms about himself and stared at the patterns in the veneer of the table, anything but shut his eyes and see the boat and the river.

Or think of Ari.

Only Grant? Merild would ask, when he got that phone message. Merild would take alarm. Merild might well call Reseune and try to talk to Jordan; and he could not afford that: he tried to think what he would say, how he would cover it. Grant could tell Merild enough, maybe, to set Merild working on a rescue of some sort; but, oh, God, if something got to Jordan about Ari and him, either from Grant, from Merild, or from Ari—and Jordan blew up—

No. Jordan was too cagy to do something without thinking it out—

The time passed. The air of the apartment felt cold as the chill outside; he wanted to go in to his own bed, and pull the covers about him, but he asked the Minder for more heat and kept to the living room, fighting to stay awake, afraid he would sleep through a Minder call.

None came.

Small boats went out of one port and never got to another, that was all. It happened even to experienced pilots.

He thought about every step he had taken, every choice he had, over and over again. He thought about calling Jordan, telling him everything.

No, he told himself. No. He could handle it with Ari. Jordan needed help, and Jordan *not* knowing was the only way it worked.

------------------------------ **iv** ------------------------------

A plane flew over. Grant heard it even above the steady noise of his own engines, and his hands sweated on the wheel as he ran down the clear middle of the river, his meager speed boosted by the current. He had no lights on, not even the small chart-light on the panel, for fear of being spotted. He did not dare increase the speed of the engines now, for fear of widening the white boil and curl of wake that might show to searchers.

The plane went over and lost itself in dark and distance.

But in a little time it circled back again: he saw it coming up the river behind him, a searchlight playing over the black waters.

He put the throttle up full, and felt the easy rock of the boat become an increasing vibration of waves as the bow came up. To hell with the wake, then, and with the floating snags that had sunk many a boat in the Novaya Volga.

If they had sent boats out from Moreyville, or from the other end of Reseune, and if someone on those boats had a gun, shots could go through the cabin, breach the seals fatally even if they missed him, or go through the hull and maybe hit the fuel tanks—but they had rather put a hole in the boat and slow it with waterlogged compartments. They would not, he was sure, want him dead if they had a choice.

He did not intend to harm Justin, that was his first determination: not to be used against Justin, nor against Jordan. And beyond that, even an azi had a right to be selfish.

The plane roared directly over him, throwing the decks into bright light, blinding glare through the cabin windows. The beam passed on a moment, leaving him half blind in the sudden dark. He saw it light the trees on the far side of the river, pale gray of native foliage against the night.

Suddenly the bow fell off to starboard and that floodlit view of the bank turned up off the bow, not the beam. In a moment's fright he thought the propeller might have fouled, and then he knew it was current he had run into—the Kennicutt's effluence into the Volga.

He put the helm over, still blind except for the fleeting glimpse the searchlight had shown him of the wooded ground on the far side. He could run aground. He dared not turn the lights on.

Then he saw the shadow of the banks, tall trees black against the night sky on either side of an open space of starlit water.

He drove for it; and the boat shuddered and jolted to impact along the keel, scrape of sand and a shock that threw him violently as the boat slewed out of control.

He caught himself against the dash then, saw a black wall in front of him and swerved with everything the boat had.

Something banged against the bow and scraped portside. Snag. Sandbar and snag. He heard it pass aft, saw the clear water ahead of him and hoped to God it was the Kennicutt he was in after that sort-out and not the Volga. He could not tell. It looked the same as the other, just black water, glancing with starlight.

He risked the chart-light for a second to sneak a look at the compass. Bearing northeast. The Volga could bend that much, but he thought it had to be the Kennicutt. The plane had not come back. It was even possible that the maneuver had confused it, and he was not, God knew, running with the Locator beacon on. Ari's power was enough to get Cyteen Station in on the hunt, and that plane's beacon could guide the geosynchronous surveillance satellites to a good fix, but so far as he knew there was no strike capacity on the Locators, and he could still, he hoped, outrun any intercept from Moreyville or further down the Volga.

First lights after that, Justin had said. Two, maybe three hours further on, up a river that *had* no further development on its banks. Krugers' Station was a mining outpost, largely automated, virtually all related to each other: what azi they brought in all got their CIT papers within the year, and a share of Kruger Mines on top of it—a dream of an assignment, the kind of place azi whispered among themselves did exist, if one were very, very good—

And if one's Contract was affordable.

Nothing like that existed for a seventeen-year-old azi with an X on his number, and all the political sense a boy could gain, living in Reseune and in the House, advised him that Justin had done something for his sake desperate beyond all reason—

Advised him that the Krugers might well have welcomed a Warrick with an azi he had a valid Contract for, but that there were good reasons they might not welcome that azi by himself.

God knew.

He was, the more he had time to think about it, a liability on all accounts, except for what he knew about Reseune, Ari, and

Warrick business, which people might insist he give up; and he had had no instructions on that. He was Alpha, but he was young and he was azi, and all that he had learned only told him that his responses were conditioned, his knowledge limited, his reasoning potentially flawed— (Never worry about your tapes, Jordan had told him gently. If you ever think you're in trouble, come to me and tell me what you think and what you feel and I'll find the answer for you: remember I've got your charts. Everything's all right—)

· He had been seven then. He had cried in Jordan's arms, which had embarrassed him, but Jordan had patted him on the back and hugged him the way he hugged Justin, called him his other son and assured him even born-men made mistakes and felt confused.

Which had made him feel better and worse, to know that born-men had evolved out of old Earth by trial and error, and that when Ari had decided he should exist, she had done something of the same thing. Trial and error. Which was all the X on his number meant to a seven-year-old.

He had not understood then that it meant Jordan could not deliver what he promised, or that his life was Reseune's and not Jordan's. He had clutched that 'my other son' to him like daylight and breath, a whole new horizon of being.

Then he had grown enough, when he and Justin were twelve and Justin discovered girls, to know that sex made things very different.

"Why?" he had asked Jordan; and Jordan had walked him into the kitchen, his arm about his shoulders while he explained that an Alpha was always mutating the instructions the tapes gave him, that he was very bright, and that his body was developing and that he really should go to the azi who specialized in that.

"What if I make somebody pregnant?" he had asked.

"You won't," Jordan had said, which he had not asked about then, but he knew later he should have. "You just can't mess around with anyone in the House. They aren't licensed."

He had been outraged. And thought there was a kind of irony in it. "You mean because I'm an Alpha? You mean whoever I go to bed with—"

"Has to be licensed. You don't get a license at your age.

Which lets out all the girls your age. And I don't want you sleeping with old aunt Mari, all right?''

That had been halfway funny. At the time. Mari Warrick was decrepit, on the end of her rejuv.

It had gotten less funny later. It was hard to stay cool while a Carnath girl put her hands where they did not belong and giggled in his ear; and to be supposed to say: "I'm sorry, sera, I can't."

While Justin, poor Justin, got girlish giggles and evasions, because *he* was Family; and Justin's azi was fair game—or would have been, if he had only been Beta.

"Lend him, can't you?" Julia Carnath had asked Justin outright, in Grant's presence, when Grant knew damned well that Justin was courting Julia for himself. Grant had wanted to sink through the floor. As it was, he had gone blank-faced and proper, and kept very quiet later when Justin sulked and said that Julia had turned him down.

"You're better-looking," Justin had complained. "Ari made you perfect, dammit. What chance have I got?"

"I'd rather be you," he had answered faintly, realizing for the first time that was the truth. And he had cried, for the second time in his life that he remembered, just cried for no reason that he could figure out, except that Justin had hit a nerve. Or a tape-structure.

Because he was made of both.

He had never been sure after that, until Jordan had let him see the structures of his own tapes when he was sixteen and starting into advanced design studies. He had figured out enough of his tape-structures on his own that Jordan had opened the book for him and let him see what he was made of; and so far he had not traced any lines that could lead to fear of sex.

But Alphas mutated their own conditioning, constantly. It was a constant balancing act, over an abyss of chaos. Nothing could dominate. Balance in everything.

Or the world became chaos.

Dysfunction.

An azi who had become his own counselor was begging for trouble. An azi was so terribly fragile. And so very likely to get into a situation he could not handle, in a larger game than anyone had bothered to tell him about.

Dammit, Justin!

He wiped his eyes with his left hand and steered with the right, trying to watch where he was going. He was, he told himself, acting the fool.

Like a born-man. Like I was like them.

I'm supposed to be smarter. I'm supposed to be a damn genius. Except the tapes don't work that way and I'm not what they wanted me to be.

Maybe I just don't use what I've got.

So why didn't I speak up louder? Why didn't I grab Justin and haul him off to his father if I had to hit him to do it?

Because I'm a damn azi, that's why. Because I go to jelly inside when someone acts like they know what they're doing and I stop using my head, that's why. Oh, damn, damn, damn! I should have stopped him, I should have dragged him aboard with me, I should have taken him to the Krugers and gotten him safe, and then he could have protected both of us; and Jordan would be free to do something. What was he thinking of?

Something I couldn't?

Dammit, that's the trouble with me, I haven't got any confidence, I'm always looking to be sure before I do anything, and I don't do a damn thing, I just take orders—

—because the damn tapes have got their claws into me. They never told me to hesitate, they just make me do it, because the tapes are sure, they're so damned fucking sure, and nothing in the real world ever is—

That's why we never make our own minds up. We've known something that has no doubt, and born-men never have. That's what's the matter with us—

The boat hit something that jolted the deck, and Grant threw the wheel over and corrected furiously, sweating.

Fool, indeed. He suddenly arrived at the meaning of it all and damned near holed his boat, which was the kind of thing that happened to born-men, Justin would say, just the same as anybody else; which was how things worked—a second cosmic truth, in sixty seconds. His mind was working straight or he was scared into hyperdrive, because he suddenly had a sense what it was to be a born-man, and to be a fool right on top of understanding everything: one had to swallow down the doubts and just go, how often had Jordan told him that. *The doubts aren't tape. They're life, son. The universe won't break* if you fuck up. It won't even break if you break your neck. Just your private universe will. You understand that?

I think so, he had said. But that had been a lie. Till now, that it jumped into clear focus. *I'm free*, he thought. *Out here, between here and the Krugers, I'm free, on my own, the first time in my life*. And then he thought: *I'm not sure I like it*.

Fool. Wake up. Pay attention. O my God, is that the plane coming back?

As a light showed suddenly behind him.

A boat. O God, O God, it's a boat back there.

He shoved the throttle wide. The boat lifted its bow and roared along the Kennicutt. He turned the lights on. They shone on black water, on water that swirled with currents, on banks closer than the Volga's, banks overgrown with the gangling shapes of weeping willies—trees that tended to break as they aged and rot worked on them, trees which shed huge gnarled knots of dead wood into the Volga, navigation hazards far worse than rocks, because they floated and moved continually.

The lights were less risk now, he figured, than running blind.

But there would be guns back there, maybe. Maybe a boat that could overpower the runabout. He would be surprised if Moreyville had had something that could outrun him; damned surprised, he thought, with a cold knot of fear at his gut, watching the light wink out around a turning of the river; and then reappear in his rearview mirror.

A boat out of the precip station, maybe; maybe that end of Reseune had boats. He had no idea.

He applied his attention forward after that brief glance; center of the channel, Justin had warned him. Justin at least had taken the boat back and forth to Moreyville and down to precip ten; and he had talked to people at Moreyville who had gone all the way to Novgorod on the river.

Justin had done the talking; and Grant had paid attention mostly to the Novgorod part, because that had been what he was curious about. He and Justin—talking together about taking a boat that far someday, just heading down the river.

He steered wildly around a snag floating with one branch high.

A whole damned *tree*, that one. He saw the root-mass following like a wall of tangled brush in the boat's spot; and swerved wider, desperately.

God, if one of those came floating sideways—if the bow caught it—

He kept going.

And the light stayed behind him until he saw the lights Justin had promised him shining on the right, out of the dark— Ambush, he thought in the second heartbeat after he had seen them, because everything had become a trap, everything was an enemy.

But they were too high, they were too many: lights that twinkled behind the screen of weeping willies and paperbarks, lights that were far too high for the river, lights blinking red atop the hills, warning aircraft of the obstacles of precip towers.

Then his knees began feeling weak and his arms began shaking. He missed the light from behind him when he looked to see; and he thought for the first time to put Justin's note in his pocket, and to take the paper that had been under it, in the case someone returned the boat to Reseune.

He throttled back, seeking some dockage, alarmed as the spotlight showed up a low rusty wall on the riverside, and another, after that—

Barges, he realized suddenly. Kruger's was a mining settlement. They were ore barges, not so big as the barges that came down from the north; but the whole place was a dock; and there was a place for a little boat to nose to, there was a ladder that went up from a lower dock to an upper one, which meant he was not in the wild anymore, and he could breach the seals: but he did not do that. He did not think he ought to use the radio, since Justin had not told him anything about it; and he was not sure how to work it in any case. He just blew the horn, repeatedly, until someone turned the dockside lights on, and people turned out to see what had come to them from the river.

V

"You have a phone call," the Minder said, and Justin started out of what had become sleep without his knowing it, lying as he had all night curled up on the living room couch; the sound

brought him up on his elbow and onto his arm and then, as the Minder cut in and answered it, to his feet— "I'm here," he said aloud, to the Minder, and heard it tell the caller:

"Justin is in. A moment, please."

He rubbed a face prickly with the faint stubble he could raise, eyes that refused to focus. "I'm here," he said, his heart beating so hard it hurt, and waited for bad news.

"Good morning," Ari said to him. *"Sorry to bother you at this hour, Justin, but where is Grant?"*

"I don't know," he said. *Time. What time?* He rubbed his eyes and tried to focus on the dim numbers of the clock on the wall console. *Five in the morning. He's got to be at Kruger's by now. He's got to.* "Why? Isn't he there?" He looked beyond the arch, where the lights were still on, where Grant's bed was unslept-in, proof that everything was true, Grant *had* run, everything he remembered had happened.

We can't *have gotten away with it.*

"Justin, I want to talk with you, first thing when you get in today."

"Yes?" His voice cracked. It was the hour. He was shivering.

"At 0800. When you get in. In the Wing One lab."

"Yes, sera."

The contact went dead. Justin rubbed his face and squeezed his eyes shut, jaw clamped. He felt as if he was going to be sick.

He thought of calling his father. Or going to him.

But Ari had given him plenty of latitude to do that; and maybe it was what he was supposed to do, or maybe it was Ari trying to make him think it was what he was supposed to do, so that he would shy away from it. Trying to out-think her was like trying to out-think his father.

And he was trying to do both.

He made himself a breakfast of dry toast and juice, all he could force onto his unwilling stomach. He showered and dressed and paced, delaying about little things, because there was so much time, there was so damned much time to wait.

It was deliberate. He knew that it was. She did everything for a reason.

Grant might be in the hands of the police.

He might be back at Reseune.

He might be dead.

Ari meant to drop something on him, get some reaction out of him, and get it on tape. He prepared himself for anything she could say, even the worst eventuality; he prepared himself, if he had to, to say: *I don't know. He left. I assumed he was going to you. How could I know? He's never done anything like this.*

At 0745 he left his apartment and took the lift down to the main hall; passed Wing One security, walked to his own office, unlocked the door, turned on the lights, everything as he usually did.

He walked down the corridor where Jane Strassen was already in her office, and nodded a good morning to her. He rounded the corner and took the stairs down to the lab-section at the extreme end of the building.

He used his keycard on the security lock of the white doors and entered a corridor of small offices, all closed. Beyond, the double doors gave onto the dingy Wing One lab, with its smell of alcohol and chill and damp that brought back his early student days in this place. The lights were on. The big cold-room at the left had its vault door standing wide, brighter light coming from that quarter.

He let the outer doors shut and heard voices. Florian walked out from the vault-door of the lab.

Not unusual for a student to be here, not unusual for techs to be in and out of here: Lab One was old, outmoded by Building B's facilities, but it was still sound. Researchers still used it, favoring it over the longer walk back and forth to the huge birthlabs over in B, preferring the old hands-on equipment to the modern, more automated facilities. Ari had been down here a lot lately. She kept a lot of her personal work in the old cold-lab, as convenient a storage for that kind of thing, he had figured, as there was in Wing One.

Rubin project, he thought. Earlier her presence down here had puzzled him, when Ari did not need to do these things herself, when she had excellent techs to do the detail work. It no longer puzzled him.

I'll be wanting to oversee the process myself—just a desire to have hands-on again. Maybe a little vanity. . . .

It was also private, the kind of situation with her that he had spent weeks trying to avoid.

"Sera is expecting you," Florian said.

"Thank you," he said, meticulously ordinary. "Do you know what about?"

"I would hope you do, ser," Florian answered him. Florian's dark eyes said nothing at all as he slid a glance toward the cold-lab door. "You can go in. —Sera, Justin Warrick is here."

"All right," Ari's voice floated out.

Justin walked over to the open door of the long lab where Ari sat on a work-stool, at a counter, working at one of the old-fashioned separators. "Damn," she complained without looking up. "I don't trust it. Got to get one out of B. I'm not going to put up with this." She looked up and the hasty lift of her hand startled him as his hand left the vault door. He realized he had moved the door then, and caught it and pushed the massive seal-door back, steadying it in frustration at his own young awkwardness, that rattled him when he most wanted composure.

"Damn thing," Ari muttered. "Jane's damn penny-pinching—you touch it, it swings on you. *That's* going to get fixed. —How are *you* this morning?"

"All right."

"Where's Grant?"

His heart was already beating hard. It picked up its beats and he forced it to slow down. "I don't know. I thought he was with you."

"Of course you did. —Grant stole a boat last night. Sabotaged the other one. Security tracked him to Kruger's. What do you know about it?"

"Nothing. Nothing at all."

"Of course not." She turned on the stool. "Your companion planned the whole thing."

"I imagine he did. Grant's very capable." It was going too easily. Ari was capable of much, much more; of spinning it out, instead of going straight to the point. He held himself back from too much relief, as if it were a precipice and the current were carrying him too quickly toward it. Florian was still outside. There were no witnesses to what she said—or what she ordered. There was a lock on the doors out there. And there might well be a recorder running. "I wish he *had* told me."

Ari made a clicking with her tongue. "You want to see the

security reports? You both went out last night. You came in alone.''

''I was looking for Grant. He said he was going to borrow a carry-bag from next door. He never came back.''

Ari's brows lifted. ''Oh, come, now.''

''Sorry. That's what I was doing.''

''I'm really disappointed in you. I'd expected more invention.''

''I've told you everything I know.''

''Listen to me, young friend. What you did is *theft*, you know that? You know what happens if Reseune files charges.''

''Yes,'' he said, as calmly, as full of implication as he could make it. ''I really think I do.''

''We're not Cyteen.''

''I know.''

''You're very smug. Why?''

''Because you're not going to file charges.''

''Do you want to bet on that?''

He was supposed to react. He smiled at her. He had himself that far under control, not knowing, not at all knowing whether or not Grant was in her hands. ''I'm betting on it,'' he said, and held his voice steady. ''You've got me. You haven't got Grant. As long as things go right with me and my father, Grant keeps his mouth shut and we're all just fine.''

''That's why you stayed behind.''

That had bothered her. The irrational act.

He smiled wider, a thin, carefully held triumph, alone, in her territory. ''One of us had to. To assure you we'll keep quiet otherwise.''

''Of course. Did Jordan plan this?''

He did react then. He knew that he had. It was an unexpected and offhanded praise.

''No,'' he said.

''You did.'' Ari gave a breath of a laugh; and he did not like that, even when all the movements of her body, her rocking back against the back of the lab-stool, her rueful smile, all said that she was surprised.

Ari played her own reactions the way his father did—with all her skill, all the way to the end of a thing.

So must he. He gave a matching, deprecatory shrug.

"It's really very good," Ari said. "But you have to put so much on Grant."

He's dead, he thought, bracing himself for the worst thing she could say. *She might lie about that.*

"I trust him," he said.

"There's one flaw in your set-up, you know."

"What would that be?"

"Jordan. He's really not going to like this."

"I'll talk to him." His muscles started to shake, the cold of the cryogenics conduits that ran overhead seeming to leach all the warmth from him. He felt all his control crumbling and made a profound effort to regroup. It was a tactic his father had taught him, this alternate application of tension and relief she was using, watching cues like the dilation of his eyes, the little tensions in his muscles, everything fallen into a rhythm like a fencer, up, down, up, down, and then something out of the rhythm the moment he had discovered the rules. He saw it coming. He smiled at her, having gotten command of himself with that thought. "He'll be amused."

He watched a slow grin spread over Ari's face, either his point or a deliberate dropping of the shield for a moment to make him think it was.

"You really have nerve," Ari said. "And you aren't at all cocky, are you? Damn, boy, the edges are ragged, you're not real confident you've got all the pieces in your hands, but I'll give it to you, that's a damned good maneuver. Harder than hell to do twice, though."

"I don't need to leave till my father does."

"Well, now, that *is* a problem, isn't it? Just how are we going to disengage this little tangle? Have you thought it all the way through? Tell me how it works when it comes time for Jordan to go off-world. I'm interested."

"Maybe you'll make me an offer."

Ari flashed a bright smile. "That's marvelous. You were so quiet. What did you do, try to throw those test scores?"

"You're supposed to be able to figure that out."

"Oh, cheek!" She outright laughed. "You *are* bright. You've taught me something. At my age, I value that. You're very fond of Grant, to give up your camouflage for him. *Very* fond of him." She leaned against the counter, one elbow on it, looking soberly up at him. "Let me tell you something, dear.

Jordan loves you—very much. Very, very much. It shows in the way you behave. And I must say, he's done a marvelous job with Grant. Children need that kind of upbringing. But there's a dreadful cost to that. We're mortal. We lose people. And we really hurt when they hurt, don't we? —Families are a hell of a liability. What are you going to tell Jordan?''

"I don't know. As much as I have to.''

"You mean, as much as will let him know he's won?''

Break and reposition. He only smiled at her, refusing a debate with a master.

"Well," she said, "you've done Jordan proud in this one. I don't say it's wise. The plan was very smart; the reasons are very, very stupid, but then, —devotion makes us fools, doesn't it? What do you suppose Jordan would do if I charged you with this?''

"Go public. Go to the Bureau. And you *don't* want that.''

"Well, but there's a lot else we can do, isn't there? Because his son really *is* guilty of theft, of vandalism, of getting into files that don't concern him—And there's so much of that that doesn't have to happen. Jordan can make charges, I can make charges; you know if this breaks, that appointment he wants won't make it, no matter what interests are behind it. They'll desert him in a flash. But you know all that. It's what makes everything work, isn't it—unless I really wanted to take measures to recover Grant and prosecute those friends of yours. That's what you've missed, you know. That I can do just exactly what you did, break the law; and if someone brings out your part in this, and if your father has to listen to your personal reasons, our little private sessions, hmmn? —it's really going to upset him.''

"It won't do you any good if I go to court, either. You can't afford it. You've got the votes in Council right now. You want to watch things fall apart, you lay a hand on Grant—and I talk. You watch it happen.''

"You damned little sneak," she said slowly. "You think you understand it that well.''

"Well enough to know my friends won't use a card before they have to.''

"What have you got on the Krugers, that they'd risk this kind of trouble for you? Or do you think the other side won't use you? Have you taken that into account?''

"I didn't have much choice, did I? But things ought to be safe as long as the deal for Jordan's transfer is going to hold up and you keep your hands off Grant. If they put *me* under probe they'll hear plenty—about the project. I don't think you want outsiders questioning anyone in Reseune right now."

"Damned dangerous, young man." Ari leaned forward and jabbed a finger in his direction. "*Did* Jordan map this out?"

"No."

"Advise you?"

"No."

"That amazes me. It's going to amaze other people too. If this goes to court, the Bureau isn't going to believe he didn't put you up to this. And *that's* going to weigh against him when it comes to a vote, isn't it? So we'll keep it quiet. You can tell Jordan as much as you want to tell him; and we'll call it stalemate. I won't touch Grant; I won't have the Krugers arrested. Not even assassinated. And yes, I can. I could arrange an accident for you. Or Jordan. Farm machinery—is so dangerous."

He was shocked. And frightened. He had never expected her to be so blunt.

"I want you to think about something," she said. "What you tell your father will either keep things under control—or blow everything. I'm perfectly willing to see Jordan get that Fargone post. And I'll tell you exactly what deal I'll strike to unwind this pretty mess you've built for us. Jordan can leave Reseune for Fargone just as soon as there's an office there for him to work in. And when he ships out from Cyteen Station, you'll still be here. You'll arrange for Grant to follow him as soon as the Hope corridor is open and the Rubin project is well underway. You can take the ship after his. And all of that should keep your father—and you—quiet long enough to serve everything I need. The military won't let Jordan be too noisy— They hate media attention to their projects. —Or, *or*, we can just blow all of this wide right now and let us fight it out in court. I wonder who'd win, if we just decided to pull Rubin back to Cyteen and give up the Fargone facility entirely."

I've fallen into a trap, he thought. *But how could I have avoided it? What did I do wrong?*

"Do you agree?" she asked.

"Yes. So long as you keep your end of it. And I get *my* transfer back to my father's wing."

"Oh, no, that's *not* part of it. You stay here. What's more, you and I are going to have an ongoing understanding. You know—your father's a very proud man. You know what it would do to him, to have to choose whether to go to the Bureau and lose everything over what you've done, or keep his mouth shut and *know* what you're involved in to keep that assignment for him. Because that's what you've done. You've handed me all the personal and legal missiles I need—if I have to use them. I've got a way to keep your father quiet, an easy way, as it happens, that doesn't involve him getting hurt. And all you've got to do is keep quiet, do your work, and wait it out. You've got exactly the position you bargained for—hostage for his release; and his good behavior. So what I want you to do, young man, is go put in an honest day's work, give me the BRX reports by the time your shift's over, and let me see a good job. You do what you like: call your father, tell him Grant's gone missing, tell him as much as you like. I certainly can't stop you. And you come to my Residency, oh, about 2100, and you tell me what you've done. Or I'll assume it's gone the other way."

He was still thinking when she finished, still running through all of it, and what she meant; but he knew that. He tried to find all the traps in it. The one he was in, he had no trouble seeing. It was the invitation he had dreaded. It was where everything had been going.

"You can go," she said.

He walked out past Florian in the outer lab, out into the hall, out through the security doors and upstairs into the ordinary hallways of Wing One operations. Someone passed him on the way to his office and said good morning to him; he realized it half the hall further on, and did not even know who it had been.

He did not know how he was going to face Jordan. By phone, he thought. He would break the news by phone and meet his father for lunch. And get through it somehow. Jordan would expect him to be distraught.

Ari was right. If Jordan got involved in it, everything that was settled became unsettled, and for all that he could figure, Jordan had no hand to play.

At best, he thought—go along with it till he could get control of himself enough to think whether telling Jordan the whole story was the thing to do.

Whatever the time cost.

─────────────── vi ───────────────

"What we did . . ." Justin turned the stem of his wineglass, a focus to look at, anything but Jordan's face. "What we did was what we always planned to do, if one of us got cornered. Her taking Grant—was to pressure me. I know—I know you told me I should come to you. But she sprang that on us, and there wasn't time to do anything but file a protest with the Bureau. That'd have been too late for Grant. God knows what she might have put him through before we could get any kind of injunction, if we could get one at all—" He shrugged. "And we couldn't win it, in the long run, the law's on her side and it would foul everything up just after everything was settled on the Fargone deal, so I just—just took the only chance I thought would work. My best judgment. That's all I can say."

It was a private lunch, in the kitchen in Jordan's apartment. Paul did the serving, simple sandwiches, and neither of them did more than pick at the food.

"Damn," Jordan said. He had said very little up to that point, had let Justin get it out in order. "Damn, you should have told me what was going on. I *told* you—"

"I couldn't get to you. It'd make everything I did look like it was your doing. I didn't want to lay a trail."

"Did you? Did you lay one?"

"Pretty plain where I'm concerned, I'm afraid. But that's part of the deal. That's why I stayed here. Ari's got something on me. She's got me to use against you, the way she planned to use Grant against me. Now she doesn't need him, does she?"

"You're damn right she doesn't need him! My God, son—"

"It's not that bad." He kept his voice ever so steady. "I called her bluff. I stayed around. She said— She said that this is the way it's going to work: you get your transfer as soon as the facility is built, earnest of her good faith. Then I get Grant to go out there to you, earnest of mine. That way—"

"That way you're left here where she can do anything she damn well pleases!"

"That way," he reprised, calmly, carefully, "she knows that she can hold on to me and keep you quiet until her projects are too far advanced to stop. And the military won't let you go public. That's what she's after. She's got it. But there's a limit to what she can do—and this way all of us get out. Eventually."

Jordan said nothing, for a long, long while, then lifted his wineglass and took a drink and set it down.

And still said nothing, for minutes upon minutes.

"I should never, never have kept Grant," Jordan said finally, "when things blew up with Ari. I knew it would happen. Damn, I knew it would, all those years ago. Don't ever, *ever* take favors from your enemies."

"It was too late then, wasn't it?" Justin said. The bluntness shocked his nerves, brought him close to tears, an anger without focus. "God, what could we do?"

"Are you sure he's all right?"

"I haven't dared try to find out. I think Ari would have told me if she knew anything different. I set everything up. If the number I gave him doesn't answer, Krugers will keep him safe till it does."

"Merild's number?"

Justin nodded.

"God." Jordan raked his hair back and looked at him in despair. "Son, Merild's no match for the police."

"You always said—if anything happened— And you always said he was a friend of the Krugers. And Ari's not going to call the police. Or try anything herself. She said that. I've got all the ends of this. I really think I have."

"Then you're a damn sight more confident than you ought to be," Jordan snapped. "Grant's somewhere we're not sure, Krugers could have the police on their doorstep—Merild may or may not be available, for God's sake, he practices all over the continent."

"Well, I couldn't damn well phone ahead, could I?"

Jordan's face was red. He took another drink of wine, and the level in the glass measurably diminished.

"Merild's a lawyer. He's got ethics to worry about."

"He's also got friends. Hasn't he? A lot of friends."

"He's not going to like this."

"It's the same as me coming to him, isn't it?" He was suddenly on the defensive, fighting on the retreat. "Grant's no different. Merild knows that, doesn't he? Where's ethics, if it turns Grant over to the police?"

"You'd have been a hell of a lot easier to answer for. If you'd had the sense to go *with* him, for God's sake—"

"He's not ours! He belongs to the labs! My being with him couldn't make it legal."

"You're also a minor under the law and there're extenuating circumstances—you'd have been *out* of here—"

"And they'd bring it to court and God knows what they could find for charges. Isn't that so?"

Jordan let go a long breath and looked up from under his brows.

He wanted, he desperately wanted Jordan to say no, that's wrong, there is something— Then everything became possible.

But: "yes," Jordan said in a low voice, dashing his hopes.

"So it's fixed," Justin said. "Isn't it? And you don't have to do anything unless the deal comes unfixed. I can tell you if I'm getting trouble from Ari. Can't I?"

"Like this time?" Jordan returned.

"Better than this time. I promise you. I promise. All right?"

Jordan picked at his sandwich, sidestepping the question. It was not all right. Justin knew that. But it was what there was.

"You're not going to end up staying here when I transfer," Jordan said. "I'll work something out."

"Just don't give anything away."

"I'm not giving a damned thing away. Ari's not through. You'd better understand that. She doesn't keep her agreements longer than she has to. Grant's proof of that. She's damned well capable of cutting throats, hear me, son, and you'd better take that into account the next time you want to bluff. She doesn't think any more of you or me or anyone than the subjects in her labs, than the poor nine-year-old azi down there in the yards that she decides to mindwipe and ship off to some damn sweathouse because he's just not going to work out; because she needs the space, for God's sake! Or the problem cases she won't solve, she won't even run them past my staff—she's not going to use that geneset again anyway and she damned well put three healthy azi down last month, just declared them hazards, because she didn't want to take the time with them, the experiment they were in is over, and that's all she needed. I can't prove it because I didn't get the data, but I know it happened. That's who you're playing games with. She doesn't give a damn for any life, God help her lab subjects, and she's gotten beyond what public opinion might make of it—that's what she's gotten to, she's so smart they can't figure out her notes, she's answerable only to Union law, and she's got that in her pocket—she just doesn't give a damn, and we're all under her microscope—'' Jordan shoved his plate away and stared at it a moment before he looked up. "Son, *don't* trust there's anything she won't do. There isn't.''

He listened. He listened very hard. And heard Ari saying that accidents at Reseune were easy.

_____ vii _____

His watch showed 2030 when he exited the shower and picked it up to put it on . . . in an apartment entirely too quiet and depressingly empty.

He was halfway glad not to spend the night here, with the silence and Grant's empty room, glad the way biting one's lip did something to make a smashed finger hurt less, that was about the way of it. Losing Grant hurt worse than anything else could, and Ari's harassment, he reckoned, even became a kind of anodyne to the other, sharper misery she had put him to.

Damned bitch, he thought, and his eyes stung, which was a humiliation he refused to give way to on her account. It was Grant had him unhinged, it was the whole damned mess Grant was in that had his hands shaking so badly he had trouble with the aerosol cap and popped it a ricocheting course around the mirrored sink alcove. It infuriated him. Everything conspired to irritate him out of all reason, and he set the bottle down with measured control and shaved the scant amount he had to.

Like preparing a corpse for the funeral, he thought. Everyone in Reseune had a say in his future, everyone had a mortgage on him, even his father, who had not asked his son whether he wanted to grow up with a PR on his name and know every line he was to get before he was forty, not, thank God, a bad sort of face, but not an original, either, —a face carrying all sorts of significances with his father's friends—

and enemies; and Ari cornering him that first time in the lab storage room—

He had not known what to do, then; he had wished a thousand times since he had grabbed hold of her and given her what she was evidently not expecting out of a seventeen-year-old kid with a woman more than twice old enough to be his grandmother. But being seventeen, and shocked and not having thought through what his choices were before this, he had frozen and stammered something idiotic about having to go, he had a meeting he had to make, had she got the report he had turned in on a project whose number he could not even remember—

His face burned whenever he thought about it. He had gotten out that door so fast he had forgotten his clipboard and the reports and had to rewrite them rather than go back after them. He headed toward this appointment of Ari's, this damnable, no-way-out-of-it meeting, with a carefully nurtured feeling that he might, maybe, get something of his self-respect back if he played it right now.

She was old, but she was not quite beyond her rejuv. She looked—maybe late forties; and he had seen holos of her at twelve and sixteen, a face not yet settled into the hard handsomeness it had now. As women six times his age went, she was still worth looking at, what she had was the same as Julia Carnath's in the dark, he told himself with a carefully held cynicism—and better than Julia, at least Ari was up front with what she was after. Everybody in Reseune slept with everybody else reasonable at some time or another, it was not totally out of line that Ari Emory wanted to renew her youth with a replicate of a man who would have been three times too young for her when *he* was seventeen. The situation might have deserved a real laugh, if things were not so grim, and he were not the seventeen-year-old in question.

It was not sure he could do a damned thing, but, he told himself, she might at least be an experience: his was limited to Julia, who had ended up asking him for Grant—which had hurt so badly he had never gone back to her. Which was about the sum of his love affairs, and he had almost decided Jordan was right in his misogyny. Ari was a snake, she was everything reprehensible, but the key to the whole thing, he thought, was his own attitude. If he used it, if he handled it as if it were what

Jordan called one of his damnfool stunts, then Ari had no weapon to use. That was the best way to take care of the problem, and that was what he had made up his mind to do—be a man, go along with the whole mess, learn from it (God *knew* a woman Ari's age had something to teach him . . . in several senses)—let Ari do what she wanted, play her little games, and either lose interest or not.

He reckoned he could take a page from Ari's notebook— that a seventeen-year-old wasn't going to be besotted with a woman her age—but a woman her age might have a real emotional need for a handsome, good-humored CIT bedmate. Let her get hooked.

Let *her* have the problem, and him have the solution.

Age and vanity might be the way to deal with her, the weakness no one else could find, because no one else was the seventeen-year-old boy she wanted.

viii

His watch showed 2105 when he walked up to the door and rang the bell of Ari's apartment—the five because he meant to make Ari wonder if he was going to show or if instead he and Jordan were going to come up with something; and no more than five because he was afraid if Ari thought that, then Ari might initiate some action even she might not be able to stop.

It was Catlin who opened the door, on an apartment he had never seen—mostly buff travertine and white furniture, very expensive, the sort of appointments Ari could afford and the rest of them only saw in places like the Hall of State, on newscasts: and blond, braid-crowned Catlin immaculate in her black uniform, very formal—but then, Catlin always was. "Good evening," Catlin said to him, one of the few times he had ever had a pleasant word from her.

"Good evening," he said, as Catlin let the door close. There was a drift of music, barely intruding on the ears . . . electronic flute, cold as the stone halls through which it moved. He felt a shiver in his bones. He had eaten nothing but that handful of salted chips at lunch and a piece of dry toast at suppertime, thinking that if there were anything in his stomach he would throw up. Now he felt weak in the knees and light-headed and regretted that mistake.

"Sera doesn't entertain in this end of the apartments," Catlin said, leading him through to another hall. "It's only for appearances. Mind your step, ser, these rugs are treacherous on the stone. I keep telling sera. —Have you heard from Grant at all?"

"No." His stomach tightened at the sudden, mildly delivered flank attack. "I don't expect to."

"I'm glad he's safe," Catlin said confidentially, as she might have said how nice the weather was, that same silky voice, so he had no idea whether Catlin was ever glad of anything or ever cared for anyone. She was cold and beautiful as the music, as the hall she led him through; and her opposite number met them at the end of the hall, in a large sunken den, paneled in glazed woolwood, all gray-blue and fabric-like under a sheen of plastic, carpeted in long white shag furnished with gray-green chairs and a large beige couch. Florian came from the hall beyond, likewise in uniform, dark and slight to Catlin's athletic fairness. He laid a companionable hand on Justin's shoulder. "Tell sera her guest is here," he said to Catlin. "Would you like a drink, ser?"

"Yes," he said. "Vodka and *pechi*, if you've got it." *Pechi* was an import, extravagant enough; and he was still in shock from the richness Ari managed inside Reseune. He looked around him at Downer statuary in the far corner beyond the bar, wide-eyed ritual images; at steel-sculpture and at a few paintings about the woolwood walls, God, he had seen in tapes as classics from the sublight ships. Stuck in this place, where only Ari and her guests saw them.

It was a monument to self-indulgence.

And he thought of the nine-year-old azi his father had mentioned.

Florian brought him the drink. "Do sit down," Florian said, but he walked the raised gallery about the rim of the room looking at the paintings, one after the other, sipping at a drink he had only had once in his life, and trying to calm his nerves.

He heard a step behind him, turned as Ari walked up on him, Ari in a geometric-print robe lapped at the waist, that glittered with the lights, decidedly no fit attire to meet business company. He stared at her, his heart hammering away in him in the panicked realization that Ari was very real, that he was in a situation he did not know the limits of, and there was no way out from here.

"Enjoying my collection?" She indicated the painting he had been looking at. "That's my uncle's. Quite an artist."

"He was good." He was off his stride for a moment. Least of all did he expect Ari to start off with reminiscences.

"He was good at a lot of things. You never knew him? Of course not. He died in '45."

"Before I was born."

"Damn, it's hard to keep up with things." She slipped her arm into his and guided him toward the next painting. "That one's a real prize. Fausberg. A naive artist, but a first view of Alpha Cent. Where no human goes now. I love that piece."

"That's something." He stared at it with a strange feeling of time and antiquity, realizing it was real, from the hand of someone who had been there, to a star humankind had lost.

"There was a time no one knew what that was worth," she said. "I did. There were a lot of primitive artists on the first ships. Sublight space gave them a lot of time to create. Fausberg worked in chart-pens and acrylics, and damn, they had to invent whole new preservation techniques up on station—*I* insisted. My uncle bought the lot, I wanted them preserved, and that's why the *Argo* paintings got saved at all. Most of them are in the museum at Novgorod. Now Sol Station wants one of the Fausberg *61 Cygni*'s really, really bad. And we may agree—for something of equal value. I have a certain Corot in mind."

"Who's Corot?"

"God, child. Trees. Green trees. Have you seen the Terran tapes?"

"A lot of them." He forgot his anxiety for a moment, recollecting a profusion of landscapes stranger than native Cyteen.

"Well, Corot painted landscapes. Among other things. I should lend you some of my tapes. I should put them on tonight— Catlin, have you got that *Origins of Human Art* series?"

"I'm sure we do, sera. I'll key it up."

"Among others. —That, young friend, is one of our own. Shevchenki. We have him on file. He died, poor fellow, of lifesupport failure, when they were setting up Pytho, up on the coast. But he really did remarkable work.''

Red cliffs and the blue of woolwood. That was too familiar to interest him. *He* could do that, he thought privately. But he was too polite to say it. He sketched. He even painted, or had, when he was fresh from the inspiration of the explorer-painters. Ground-bound, he imagined stars and alien worlds. And had never in his life expected to get clear of Reseune.

Until it looked like Jordan might.

Florian came up and offered Ari a drink, a bright golden concoction in a cut-crystal glass. ''Orange and vodka,'' she said. ''Have you ever tasted orange?''

''Synthetic,'' he said. Everyone had.

''No, real. Here. Have a sip.''

He took a little from the offered glass. It was strange, a complicated, sour-sweet-bitter taste under the alcohol. A taste of old Earth, if she was serious, and no one who had these paintings on her walls could be otherwise.

''It's nice,'' he said.

''Nice. It's marvelous. AG is going to make a try with the trees. We think we have a site for them—no messing about with genetics: we think the Zones can accommodate them just the way they are. It's a bright orange fruit. Just like the name. Full of good things. Go on. Take it. Florian, do me another, will you?'' She locked her arm tighter, steered him toward the steps and down, toward the couch. ''What did you tell Jordan?''

''Just that Grant was out of the way and everything was all right.'' He sat down, took a large swallow of the drink, then set it down on the brass counter behind the couch, having gotten control of his nerves as much as he figured was likely in this place, in present company. ''I didn't tell him anything else. I figure it's my business.''

''Is it?'' Ari settled close to him, at which his stomach tightened and felt utterly queasy. She laid her hand on his leg and leaned against him, and all he could think of was the azi Jordan had talked about, the ones she had put down for no reason at all, the poor damned azi not even knowing they were dying— just some order to report for a medical. ''Sit a little closer, dear. That's all right. It's just pleasant, isn't it? You really shouldn't tense up like that, all nervous.'' She slipped her arm about his ribs and rubbed his back. "There, relax. That feels good, doesn't it? Turn around and let me do something for those shoulders."

It was like when she had trapped him in the lab. He tried to think what to answer to something that outrageous and failed, completely. He picked up the drink and took a heavy swallow and another and did not do what she asked. Neither did her hand stop its slow movement.

"You're so tight. Look, it's a simple little bargain. And you don't have to be here. All you have to do is walk out the door."

"Sure. Why don't we just go into the bedroom, dammit?" His hands were close to shaking. The chill of the ice went right through his fingers to the bone. He finished the drink without looking at her.

I could kill her, he thought, not angrily. Just as a solution to the insoluble. *Before Florian and Catlin could stop me. I could just break her neck. What could they do then?*

Psychprobe me and find out everything she did? That'd fix her.

It might be the way. It might be the way to get out of this.

"Florian, he's out of orange juice. Get him another. —Come on, sweet. Relax. You really can't do anything like that, you know better and I know better. You want to try it yourself? Is that the problem?"

"I want the drink," he muttered. Everything seemed unreal, nightmarish. In a moment she was going to start talking to him the way she had in the interviews, and that was all part of it, a sordid, dirty business he did not know how to get through, but he wanted to be very drunk, very, very drunk, so that possibly he would get sick, turn out incapable, and she would just give up on this.

"You said you never had experimented around," Ari said. "Just the tapes. Is that the truth?"

He did not answer. He only twisted round on the couch to see how long it was going to take Florian to get him the drink, to have any distraction that might turn this in some other direction.

"Do you think you're normal?" Ari asked. He did not answer that either. He watched Florian's back as Florian poured and mixed the drink. He felt Ari's hands on his back, felt the cushion give as she shifted against him, as her hand came around his side.

Florian handed him the drink, and he leaned there with his elbow on the back of the couch sipping the orange drink and feeling the slow, light movement of Ari's hands on his back.

"Let me tell you something," Ari said softly, behind him. "You remember what I told you about family relationships? That they're a liability? I'm going to do you a real favor. Ask me what that is."

"What?" he asked because he had to.

Her arms came around him, and he took a drink, trying to ignore the nausea she made in his gut.

"You think tenderness ought to have something to do with this," Ari said. "Wrong. Tenderness hasn't got a thing to do with it. Sex is what you do for yourself, for your own reasons, sweet, just because it feels good. That's all. Now sometimes you get real close to somebody and you want to do it back and forth, that's fine, and maybe you trust them, but you shouldn't. You really shouldn't. The first thing you have to learn is that you can get it anywhere. The second thing—it ties you to people who aren't family and it mucks up your judgment unless you remember the first rule. That's how I'm going to do you a favor, sweet. You're not going to confuse what we're doing here. Does that feel good?"

It was hard to breathe. It was hard to think. His heart was hammering and her hands did quiet, disturbing things that made his skin all too sensitive, the edge of pleasure—or intense discomfort. He was no longer sure which. He drank a large gulp of the orange and vodka and tried to put his mind anywhere else, anywhere at all, in a kind of fog in which he was less and less in control of himself.

"How are you doing, dear?"

Not well, he thought, and thought that he was drunk. But at the edge of his senses he felt a dislocation, a difficulty in spatial relationships—like the feeling that Ari was a thousand miles away, her voice coming from behind him and not straight back, but aside in a strange and asymmetrical way—

It was a cataphoric. Tapestudy drug. Panic raced through his brain, chaotic, stimuli coming in on him too fast, while the body seemed to lag in an atmosphere gone to syrup. Not a high dosage. He could see. He could still feel Ari tug his shirt up, run her hands over his bare skin, even while his sense of balance deserted him and he felt his head spinning, the whole room going around. He lost the glass and felt the chill of ice and liquid spreading against his hip and under his buttocks.

"Oh, dear. Florian. Get that."

He was sinking. He was still aware. He tried to move, but confusion set in, a roaring muddle of sound and sensation. He tried to doubt. That was the hardest thing. He was quite aware that Florian had rescued the glass and that his head was back in Ari's lap, in the hollow of her crossed legs, that he was gazing up into Ari's face upside down and that she was unfastening his shirt.

She was not the only one unfastening his clothing. He heard a murmur of voices, but none of them involved him. "Justin," a voice said, and Ari turned his head between her hands. "You can blink when you need to," she whispered, the way the tapes would. "Are you comfortable?"

He did not know. He was terrified and ashamed, and in a long nightmare he felt touches go over him, felt himself lifted up and dragged off whatever he was lying on and down onto the floor.

It was Catlin and Florian who hovered over him. It was Catlin and Florian who touched him and moved him and did things to him that he was aware of in a kind of vague nowhere way, which were wrong, wrong and terrible.

Stop this, he thought. *Stop this. I don't agree with this.*

I don't want this.

But there was pleasure. There was an explosion in his senses, somewhere infinite, somewhere dark.

Help me.

I don't want this.

He was half conscious when Ari said to him: "You're awake, aren't you? Do you understand now? There's nothing more than this. That's as good as it gets. There's nothing more than this, no matter who it's with. Just biological reactions. That's the first and the second rule. . . ."

"Watch the screen."

Tape was running. It was erotic. It blurred into what was happening to him. It felt good and he did not want it to, but he was not responsible for it, he was not responsible for anything and it was not his fault. . . .

"I think he's coming out of it. . . ."

"Just give him a little more. He'll do fine."

"There's nothing can do to you what tape can do. Can it, boy? No matter who it is. Biological reactions. Whatever does it for you. . . ."

"Don't move. . . ."

"Pain and pleasure, sweet, are so thin a line. You can cross it a dozen times a minute, and the pain becomes the pleasure. I can show you. You'll remember what I can do for you, sweet, and nothing will ever be like it. You'll think about that, you'll think about it for the rest of your life . . . and nothing will ever be the same. . . ."

He opened his eyes and found a shadow over him, himself naked, in a bed he did not know, a hand patting his shoulder, moving to brush hair from his brow. "Well, well, awake," Ari said. It was her weight that pushed down the edge of the mattress, Ari sitting there dressed and he—

His heart jumped and started hammering.

"I'm off to the office, sweet. You can sleep in, if you like. Florian will serve you breakfast."

"I'm going home," he said, and dragged the sheet over him.

"Whatever you like." Ariane got up, releasing the mattress, and walked across to take a look in the wall mirror, demonstrative unconcern that crawled over his nerves and unsettled his stomach. "Come in when you like. —Talk to Jordan if you like."

"What am I supposed to do?"

"Whatever you like."

"Am I supposed to *stay* here?" Panic sharpened his voice. He knew the danger in Ari hearing it, acting on it, working on it. It was a threat she had just made. He thought that it was. Her tone was blank, void of cues. Her voice tweaked at nerves and made him forget for a handful of seconds that he had a counter-threat in Grant, upriver. "It won't work."

"Won't it?" Ari gave her hair a pat. She was elegant, in a beige suit. She turned and smiled at him. "Come in when you like. You can go home tonight. Maybe we'll do it again, who knows? Maybe you can tell your father and get him to pass it off, hmmn? Tell him whatever you like. Of course I had a recorder on. There's plenty of evidence if he wants to go to the Bureau.''

He felt cold through and through. He tried not to show it. He glared at her, jaw set, as she smiled and walked out the door. And for a long while he lay there cold as ice, sick to his stomach, darts of headache going from the top of his skull through to the nape of his neck. His skin felt hypersensitized, sore in places. There were bruises on his arm, the marks of fingers.

—Florian—

A flash came back to him, sensation and image from out of the dark, and he plunged his face into his hands and tried to shove it out. Tape-flash. Deep-tape. More and more of them would come back. He did not know *what* could come back. And they would, bits of memory floating up to the surface and showing a moment, a drift of words and feeling and vision, before they rolled over and sank again into the dark, nothing complete—just more and more of them. He could not stop it.

He threw the sheets back and got out of bed, unfocusing his eyes where it came to his own body. He staggered into the bathroom, turned on the shower and bathed, soaped himself again and again and again, scrubbed without looking at himself, trying not to feel anything, remember anything, wonder anything. He scrubbed his face and hair and even the inside of his mouth with the perfumed soap, because he did not know if there was anything else to use; and spat and spat and gagged from the sharp, soapy taste, but it did not make him clean. It was a scent he remembered as hers. Now *he* smelled like it, and tasted it in the back of his throat.

And when he had chafed himself dry in the shower-cabinet blower and he had come out into the cold air of the bathroom, Florian walked in with a folded stack of his clothes.

"There's coffee, ser, if you like."

Bland as if nothing had happened. As if none of it were real. "Where's a shaver?" he asked.

"The counter, ser." Florian motioned toward the mirrored end of the bath. "Toothbrush, comb, lotion. Is there anything you need?"

"No." He kept his voice even. He thought of going home. He thought of killing himself. Of knives in the kitchen. Of pills in the bathroom cabinet. But the investigation afterward would open everything up to politics, and politics would swallow his father up. In the same moment he thought of subliminals that might have been buried in his mind last night, urges to suicide, God knew what. Any irrational thought was suspect. He could not trust them. A series of tape-flashes ripped past him, sensations, erotic visions, landscapes and ancient artworks. . . .

Then real things, set in the future. Images of Jordan's outrage. Himself, dead, on the floor of his kitchen. He rebuilt the image and tried to make it something exotic: himself, just walking out beyond the precip towers, a body to be found like a scrap of white rag by air-search a few hours later . . . "Sorry, ser, looks like we've found him—"

But that was not a valid test of any suspected subliminal Ari might have put into his tape. When a mind drank in tapestudy, it incorporated it. Tape images faded and resident memory wove itself into the implant-structure and grew and grew in its own way. There was no reliable way to detect an embedded command; but it could not make him act when he was conscious, unless it accurately triggered some predisposition. Only when drugs had the threshold flat, then he would take in stimuli without censoring, answer what he was asked, do whatever he was told—

Anything he was asked, anything he was told, if it slipped past the subconscious barriers of his value-sets and his natural blocks. A psychsurgeon could, given time, get answers that revealed the sets and their configurations, then just insert an argument or two that confounded the internal logic: rearrange the set after that, create a new microstructure and link it where the surgeon chose—

All those questions, those questions in the damned psychtests Ari had given him, calling them routine for Wing One aides . . . questions about his work, his beliefs, his sexual experiences . . . that he, being a fool, had thought were simply Ari's way of tormenting him . . .

He dressed without looking at the mirrors. He shaved and brushed his teeth and combed his hair. There was nothing wrong with his face, no mark on it, nothing to betray what had happened. It was the same ordinary face. Jordan's face.

She must have gotten a real satisfaction out of that.

He smiled at himself, testing whether he could control himself. He could. He had that back, as long as he was not facing Ari herself. Her azi he could handle.

Correction. *Florian* he could handle. He thanked God it was Florian she had left with him and not Catlin, and then a wild flutter of mental panic wanted to know why he reacted that way, why the thought of dealing with Catlin-the-icicle sent a disorganizing quiver through his nerves. Fear of women?

Are you afraid of women, sweet? You know your father is.

He combed his hair. He wanted to throw up. He smiled instead, a re-testing of his control, and carefully wiped the tension of the headache from the small muscles around his eyes, relaxed the tension from his shoulders. He walked out and gave that smile to Florian.

He'll report to her. I can't think with my head splitting. Damn, just let him tell her I was all right, that's all I have to do, keep my face on straight and get out of here.

The sitting room, the white rug, the paintings on the walls, brought back a flash of memory, of pain and erotic sensation.

But everything had happened to him. It was a kind of armor. There was nothing left to be afraid of. He took the cup from Florian and sipped at it, stopping the tremor of his hand, a shiver which hit of a sudden as internal chill and a cold draft from the air-conditioning coincided. "Cold," he said. "I think it's the hangover."

"I'm really sorry," Florian said, and met his eyes with an azi's calm, anxious honesty: at least it seemed to be and probably it was very real. There was not a shred of morality involved, of course, except an azi's, which was to avoid rows with citizens who might find ways to retaliate. Florian had real cause to worry in his case.

—Florian, last night: *I don't want to hurt you. Relax. Relax—*

The face had nothing to do with the mind. The face kept smiling. "Thanks."

Far, far easier to torment Florian. If it was Ari, he would fall apart. He had, last night. Seeing Florian afraid . . .

. . . pain and pleasure. Interfaces . . .

He smiled and sipped his coffee and enjoyed what he was doing with a bitter, ugly pleasure even while he was scared of what he was doing, meddling with one of Ari's azi; and twice scared of the fact that he enjoyed it. It was, he told himself, only a human impulse, revenge for his humiliation. He would have thought the same thing, done the same thing, the day before.

Only he would not have known *why* he enjoyed it, or even *that* he enjoyed it. He would not have thought of a dozen ways to make Florian sweat, or considered with pleasure the fact that, if he could maneuver Florian into some situation, say, down at the AG pens, far away from the House, on terms that did not involve protecting Ari, he could pay Florian in kind—Florian being azi, and vulnerable in a dozen ways he could think of . . . without Ari around.

Florian undoubtedly knew it. And because Florian was Ari's, Ari probably fed off Florian's discomfiture in leaving Florian alone with him. It fitted with everything else.

"I feel sorry for you," Justin said, and put his hand on Florian's shoulder, squeezed hard. On the edge of pain. "You don't have a real comfortable spot here, do you? You *like* her?"

—The first thing you have to learn is that you can get it anywhere. The second thing—it ties you to people who aren't family and it mucks up your judgment unless you remember the first rule. That's how I'm going to do you a favor, sweet. You're not going to confuse what we're doing here. . . .

Florian only stared at him, not moving. Even though the grip on his shoulder undoubtedly hurt, and even though Florian could break it with a shrug. And maybe his arm, into the bargain. That stoic patience was, Justin thought, what one could expect, in this place, of Ari's azi.

"What does Ari really want me to do?" Justin asked. "Have you got it figured out? Am I supposed to stay here? Am I supposed to go home?"

As if he and Florian were the same thing. Co-conspirators, azi both. He loathed the thought. But Florian was, in a way, his ally, a page he could read and a subject he could handle; and he still could not read the truth in Ari's eyes, not even when she was answering his questions in all sobriety.

"She expects you to go home, ser."

"Do I get other invitations?"

"I think so," Florian said in a quiet, quiet voice.

"Tonight?"

"I don't know," Florian said. And added: "Sera will probably sleep tonight."

As if it were all a long-familiar sequence of events.

A queasiness went through his stomach. They were all caught in this.

Attitude, Jordan would say. Everything is attitude. You can do anything if you're in control of it. You have to know what your profit is in doing it, that's all.

Life was not enough, to trade a soul for. But power . . . power to stop it happening, power to pay it back, that was worth the trade. His father's safety was. The hope someday of being in a position to do something about Ariane Emory—that was.

"I'm going to go home," he said to Florian, "take something for my headache, get my messages, and go on to the office. I don't suppose my father's called my apartment."

"I wouldn't know, ser."

"I thought you kept up with things like that," he said, soft and sharp as a paper-cut. He set down the coffee cup, remembering where the outside door was, and headed off through the halls, with Florian trailing him like an anxious shadow . . . Ari's guard, too polite to show it, and much too worried to let him walk that course through Ari's apartments unwatched.

For half a heartbeat he thought ahead to the safety of his own rooms upstairs and expected Grant would be there to confide in, the two of them would think things out—it was the habit of a lifetime, a stupid kind of reflex, that suddenly wrenched at a stomach ravaged by too little food, too much drink, too many drugs, too much shock. He went light-headed and grayed out, kept walking all the same, remembering the way from here, that it was a straight course down a hall decorated with fragile tables and more fragile pottery.

A triple archway, then, of square travertine pillars. And the reception room, the one Catlin had said was for show. He remembered the warning about the rugs and the floor, negotiated the travertine steps and crossed the room, up the slight rise to the door.

He reached to the door-lock to let himself out, except Florian interposed his hand and pushed the latch himself. "Be careful, ser," Florian said. And meant more, he was sure, than the walk home.

He remembered the nine-year-old. And the azi Ariane had killed. Remembered the vulnerability any azi had, even Grant.

And saw Florian's—who had never had a chance since the day he was created and who was, excepting his dark side, gentle and honest as a saint, because he was made that way and tapes kept him that way despite all else Ari made him be.

It was that enigma that dogged him out the door and down the hall, in a confusion of graying vision and weakness, all part of the nightmare that crowded on his senses—tape-flash and physical exhaustion.

Ari had shaped Florian—in both his aspects, with all his capacities—the dark and the light. She might not have made him in the first place, but she maintained him according to the original design . . . from her own youth.

To have a victim? he wondered. Was that all it was?

Test subject—for an ongoing project?

Interface, the answer came rolling up to the surface and dived down again, nightmarish as a drowned body. *Crossing of the line.*

Truth lies at the interface of extremes.

Opposites are mutually necessary.

Pleasure and pain, sweet.

Everything oscillates . . . or there's nothing. Everything can be in another state, or it can't change at all. Ships move on that principle. The stars burn. Species evolve.

He reached the lift. He got himself inside and leaned against the wall until the door opened. He walked into a reeling hall, kept his balance as far as his own apartment and managed the key.

"No entries since the last use of this key."

Can't depend on that, he thought, in gray-out, in a sudden weakness that made the couch seem very far away, and nothing safe. *Can't depend on anything. She can get into anything, even the security systems. Probably bugged the place while I was out. She'd do a thing like that. And you can't know if the Minder can catch the kind of things she can lay hands on. State of the art. Expensive stuff. Classified stuff. She could get it.*

Maybe Jordan can.

He reached the couch and sat down, lay back and shut his eyes.

What if I'm not alone?

Ari's voice, soft and hateful:

I planned your father's actions. Every one of them. Even if I couldn't predict the microstructures. Microstructures aren't that important.

Tape-designer's aphorism: macrostructure determines microstructure. The value-framework governs everything.

I even planned you, sweet. I planted the idea. Jordan has this terrible need for companionship. Am I lying? You owe your existence to me.

He imagined for a heartbeat that Grant would walk in from the other room, Grant would ask what was the matter, Grant would help him unweave the maze in which he found himself. Grant had experienced deep-tape. God knew.

But it was only a ghost. A habit hard to break.

And Grant, certainly, I planned. I made him, after all.

He had to go to the lab. He had to get out of the isolation in which the tape-structures could fester and spread before he could deal with them. He had to get about routine, occupy his mind, let his mind rest and sort things out slowly.

If the body could only have a little sleep.

"Messages, please," he murmured, remembering he had to know, *had* to know if he had calls from Jordan. Or elsewhere.

They were generally trivia. Advisories from the wing. From Administration. A note of reprimand about the illicit entry. He drifted in the middle of it, woke with a start and a clutch at the couch, the erotic flush fading into a lightning-flash clinical recollection that he was going to have to wear long sleeves and high collars and put some Fade on the bruises: he could put Jordan off with a claim that Ari had him on extra lab duty, logical, since Ari had no reason, in what he had told Jordan, to be pleased with him. He could *not* face Jordan at close quarters until he had better control of himself.

In the next heartbeat as the Minder's half-heard report clicked off, he realized that he had lost track of the playback, and that two days ago he had defaulted the Minder's message-function to play-and-erase.

ix

Grant could see the plane long before they reached the strip—not the sleek elegance of RESEUNEAIR by any stretch of the imagination, just a cargo plane with shielded windows. The car pulled up where people were waiting. "There," the driver said, virtually the only word he had spoken the entire trip, and indicated the people he was supposed to go to.

"Thank you," Grant murmured absently, and opened his own door and got out, taking his lunchbag with him, walking with pounding heart up to total strangers.

Not all strangers, thank God, Hensen Kruger himself was there to do the talking. "This is Grant. Grant, these people will take you from here." Kruger stuck out his hand and he was supposed to shake it, which he was not used to people doing: it made him feel awkward. Everything did. One of the men introduced himself as Winfield; introduced the woman in the group, the pilot, he supposed, in coveralls and without any kind of badge or company name, as Kenney; and there were two other men, Rentz and Jeffrey, last name or first or azi-name, he was not sure. "Let's get going," Kenney said. Everything about her was nervous: the shift of her glance, the stiffness of her movements as she wiped her hands on her grease-smeared coveralls. "Come on, let's move it, huh?"

The men exchanged looks that sent little twitches through Grant's taut nerves. He looked from one to the other, trying to figure whether he was the object of contention. Arguing with strangers was difficult for him: Justin always fended problems for him. He knew his place in the world, which was to handle what his employer wanted handled. And Justin had told him to object.

"We're going to Merild?" he asked, because he had not heard that name, and he was determined to hear it before he went anywhere.

"We're going to Merild," Winfield said. "Come on, up you go. —Hensen—"

"No problem. I'll contact you later. All right?"

Grant hesitated, looking at Kruger, understanding that things were passing he did not understand. But he knew, he thought, as much as they were going to tell him; and he went ahead to the steps of the jet.

It had no company markings, just a serial number. A7998. White plane, with paint missing here and there and the spatter of red mud on its underside. Dangerous, he thought. Don't they foam it down here? Where's Decon? He climbed up into the barren interior, past the cockpit, and uncertainly looked back at Jeffrey and Rentz, who followed him, a little ahead of Winfield.

The door whined up and Winfield locked it. There were jump-seats of a kind, along the wall. Jeffrey took him by the arm, pulled a seat down and helped him belt in. "Just stay there," Jeffrey said.

He did, heart thumping as the plane took its roll and glided into the sky. He was not used to flying. He twisted about and lifted a windowshade to look out. It was the only light. He saw the precip towers and the cliffs and the docks passing under them as they came about.

"Leave that down," Winfield said.

"Sorry," he said; and drew the shade down again. It annoyed him: he very much wanted the view. But they were not people to argue with, he sensed that in the tone. He opened the bag the Krugers had fixed for him, examined what he had for breakfast, and then thought it was rude to eat when no one else had anything. He folded it closed again until he saw one of them, Rentz, get up and go aft and come back with a few canned drinks. Rentz offered one to him, the first kind gesture he had had out of them.

"Thank you," he said, "they sent one."

He thought it would be all right to eat, then. He had been so exhausted last night he had only picked at supper, and the salt fish and bread and soft drink Krugers had sent were welcome, even if he had rather have had coffee.

The jet roared away and the men drank their soft drinks and took occasional looks out under the shades, mostly on the right side of the aircraft. Sometimes the pilot talked to them, a kind of sputter from the intercom. Grant finished his fish and bread and his drink and heard that they had reached seven thousand meters; then ten.

"Ser," someone had said that morning, opening the door to his room in Kruger's House, and Grant had waked in alarm, confused by his surroundings, the stranger who had to be speaking to him, calling *him* ser. He had hardly slept; and finally drowsed, to wake muddled and not sure what time it was or whether something had gone wrong.

They had taken his card last night, when the night watch had brought him up from the dock and the warehouses, into the

House itself, up the hill. Hensen Kruger himself had looked it over and gone somewhere with it, to test its validity, Grant had thought; and he had been terrified: that card was his identity. If anything happened to it, it would take tissue-typing to prove who he was after that, even if there *was* only one of him, which he had never, despite Jordan's assurances, been convinced was the case.

But the card had turned up with the stack of clothing and towels the man laid on the chair by the door. The man told him to shower, that a plane had landed and a car was coming for him.

Grant had hurried, then, rolled out of bed, still dazed and blurry-eyed, and staggered his way to the bathroom, rubbed his face with cold water and looked in the mirror, at eyes that wanted sleep and auburn hair standing up in spikes.

God. He wanted desperately to make a good impression, look sane and sensible and not, not what Reseune might well report to them—an Alpha gone schiz and possibly dangerous.

He could end up back in Reseune if they thought that. They would not even bother with the police; and Ari might have tried some such move. Justin would have answered to Ari by now—however he was going to do it Grant had no idea. He tried not to think about it, as he had tried to send the thoughts away all night long, lying there listening to the sounds of a strange House—doors opening and closing, heaters and pumps going on, cars coming and going in the dark.

He had showered in haste, dressed in the clothes they had laid out for him, a shirt that fit, trousers a bit too large or cut wrong or something—given his hair a careful combing and a second check in the mirror, then headed downstairs.

"Good morning," one of the household had said to him, a young man. "Breakfast on the table there. They're on their way. Just grab it and come on."

He was terrified for no specific cause, except he was being rushed, except that his life had been carefully ordered and he had always known who would hurt him and who would help him. Now, when Justin had told him he would be free and safe, he had no idea how to defend himself, except to do everything they told him. Azi-like. Yes, ser.

He dropped his head onto his chest while the plane droned

on, and shut his eyes finally, exhausted and having nothing to look at but the barren deck, closed windows, and the sullen men who flew with him: perhaps, he thought, if he simply said nothing to them the trip would be easier, and he would wake up in Novgorod, to meet Merild, who would take care of him.

He waked when he felt the plane change pitch and heard a difference in the engines. And panicked, because he knew it was supposed to be three hours to Novgorod, and he was sure it had not been. "Are we landing?" he asked. "Is something wrong?"

"Everything's fine," Winfield said; and: "Leave that alone!" when he reached for the shade, thinking it could surely make no difference. But evidently it did.

The plane wallowed its way down, touched pavement, braked and bumped and rolled its way, he reckoned, toward the Novgorod terminal. It stopped and everyone got up, while the door unsealed and the hydraulics began to let the ladder down; he got up, taking the wadded-up paper bag with him—he was determined not to give them a chance to complain of his manners—and waited as Winfield took his arm.

There were no large buildings outside. Just cliffs and a deserted-looking cluster of hangars; and the air smelled raw and dry. A bus was moving up to the foot of the ladder.

"Where are we?" he asked, on the edge of panic. "Is this Merild's place?"

"It's all right. Come on."

He froze a moment. He could refuse to go. He could fight. And then there was nothing he could do, because he had no idea where he was or how to fly a plane if he could take it over. The bus down there—he might use to escape; but he had no idea where in the world he was, and if he ran beyond the fuel capacity in raw outback, he was dead, that was all. Outback was all around them: he could see the land beyond the buildings.

He could hope to get to a phone, if they got the idea he was compliant enough to turn their backs on. He had memorized Merild's number. He thought of all that in the second between seeing where he was and feeling Winfield take his arm.

"Yes, ser," he said meekly, and walked down the steps where they wanted him to go—which still might be to Merild.

He still hoped that they were telling the truth. But he no longer believed it.

Winfield took him down to the waiting bus and opened the door to put him in, then got in after, with Jeffrey and Rentz. There were seven seats, one set by each window and across the back; Grant took the first and Winfield sat beside him as the other pair settled in behind them.

He scanned the windows and doors: elaborately airsealed. An outback vehicle.

He clasped his hands in his lap and sat quietly watching as the driver started up and the bus whipped away across the pavement, not for the buildings: for a line road, probably the one they used to get to the precip towers. In a little time they were traveling on dirt, and in a little time more they were climbing, up from the lowland and onto the heights beyond the safety the towers maintained.

Wild land.

Perhaps he was going to die, after they had stripped his mind down for what he knew. They might be Ari's; but it was a very strange way for Reseune to handle its problems, when they could easily bring him back to Reseune without Jordan or Justin knowing, just land like one of the regular transport flights and send him off in the bus to one of the outlying buildings where they could do whatever they liked till they were ready (if ever) to admit they had him.

They might, more likely, be Ari's enemies, in which case they might do almost anything, and in that case they might not want him to survive to testify.

Whatever had happened, Kruger was involved in it, beyond a doubt, and it could even be monetary . . . perhaps everything rumor had said about Kruger's humanitarian concerns was a lie. Reseune was full of lies. Perhaps it was something Ari herself maintained. Perhaps Kruger had just fooled everyone, perhaps he was engaged in a little side business, in forged Contracts whenever he got a likely prospect. Maybe he was being sold off to some mining site in the hinterlands, or, God, some place where they could try to retrain him. *Try.* Anyone who started meddling with his tape-structures on a certain level, he could handle. On others . . .

He was not so sure.

There were four of them, counting the driver, and such men might well have guns. The bus seals were life itself.

He clasped his hands together and tried desperately to think the thing through. A phone was the best hope. Maybe stealing the bus once they trusted him, once he knew where civilization was and whether the bus had the fuel to get there. It could take days to get a chance. Weeks.

"I think you know by now," Winfield said finally, "this isn't where you're supposed to be."

"Yes, ser."

"We're friends. You should believe that."

"Whose friends?"

Winfield put his hand on his arm. "Your friends."

"Yes, ser." *Agree to anything. Be perfectly compliant. Yes, ser. Whatever you want, ser.*

"Are you upset?"

Like a damned field supervisor, talking to some Mu-class worker. The man *thought* he knew what he was doing. That was good news and bad . . . depending what this fool thought he was qualified to do with tape and drugs. Winfield had mismanaged him thus far. He did not give way to instincts simply because he reckoned that they did not profit him in this situation, and because there was far more profit in keeping his head down . . . reckoning that his handlers were not stupid, but simply too ignorant to realize that the Alpha-rating on his card meant he could not have the kind of inhibitions born-men were used to in azi. They should have drugged him and transported him under restraint.

He was certainly not about to tell them so.

"Yes, ser," he said, with the breathless anxiousness of a Theta.

Winfield patted his arm. "It's all right. You're a free man. You will be."

He blinked. That took no acting. 'Free man' added a few more dimensions to the equation; and he did not like any of them.

"We're going up in the hills a ways. A safe place. You'll be perfectly all right. We'll give you a new card. We'll teach you how to get along in the city."

Teach you. Retraining. God, what am I into?

Is there any way this could be what Justin intended?

He was afraid, suddenly, in ways that none of the rest of this had touched . . . that he did *not* have it figured, that defying these people might foul up something Justin had arranged—

—or Jordan, finding out about it, intervening—

They *might* be what the only friends he had in the world had intended for him, they *might* be heading him for real freedom. But retraining, if that was what they had in mind, would reach into all his psychsets and disturb them. He did not have much in the world. He did not own anything, even his own person and the thoughts that ran in his brain. His loyalties were azi-loyalties, he knew that, and accepted that, and did not mind that he had had no choice in them: they were real, and they were all he was.

These people talked about freedom. And teaching. And maybe the Warricks wanted that to happen to him and he had to accept it, even if it took everything away from him and left him some cold *freedom* where home had been. Because the Warricks could not afford to have him near them anymore, because loving him was too dangerous for all of them. Life seemed overwhelmed with paradoxes.

God, now he did not know, he did not know who had him or what he was supposed to do.

Ask them to use the phone, get a message to Merild to ask whether this was all right?

But if they were not with Merild that would tip them off that he was not the compliant type they took him for. And if they were the other thing, if this was not the Warricks' doing, then they would see he had no chance at all.

So he watched the landscape pass the windows and endured Winfield's hand on his arm, with his heart beating so hard it hurt.

X

It was surreal, the way the day fell into its accustomed order, an inertia in the affairs of Reseune that refused to be shaken, no matter what had happened, no matter that his body was sore and the damnedest innocent things brought on tape-flashes that hour by hour assumed a more and more mundane and placid level of existence—of *course* that was what it felt like, of course people from the dawn of time had done sex with mixed partners, paid sex for safety, it was the world, that was all, and he was no kid to be devastated by it—it was more the hangover that had him fogged, and now he was on the other side of an experience he had rather not have had, he was still alive, Grant was downriver safe, Jordan was all right; and he had damned well better figure Ari Emory had more than that in mind—

Shake the kid up, play games with his mind, go on till he cracked.

You wanted Grant free, boy, you can substitute, can't you?

—leave the apartment, report to the office, smile at familiar people and hear the business go on about him that had gone on yesterday, that went on every day in Wing One—Jane Strassen cursing her aides and creating a furor because of some glitch-up in equipment repair; Yanni Schwartz trying to mollify her, a dull murmur of argument down the hall. Justin kept to his keyboard and immersed himself in a routine, in a problem in tape-structure Ari had sent him a week ago, complex enough to keep the mind busy hunting linkages.

He was careful. There were things the AI checker might not catch. There were higher-level designers between his efforts and an azi test-subject, and there were trap-programs designed to catch accidental linkages in a particular psychset but it was no generic teaching-tape: it was deep-tape, specifically one that a psychsurgeon might use to fit certain of the KU-89 subsets for limited managerial functions.

A mistake that got by the master-designers could be expensive—could cause grief for the KU-89s and the azi they might manage; could cause terminations, if it went truly awry—it was every designer's nightmare, installing a glitch that would run quietly amok in a living intellect for weeks and years, till it synthesized a crazier and crazier logic-set and surfaced on some completely illogical trigger.

There was a book making the rounds, a science fiction thriller called *Error Message*, that had Giraud Nye upset: a not too well disguised Reseune marketed an entertainment tape with a worm in it, and civilization came apart. There was a copy in library, on CIT-only check-out, with a long waiting list; and he and Grant had both read it—of course. Like most every House azi except Nye's, it was a good bet.

And he and Grant had tried designing a worm, just to see

where it would go. —"Hey," Grant had said, sitting on the floor at his feet, starting to draw logic-flows, "we've got an Alpha-set we can use, hell with the Rho-sets."

It had scared him. It had gone unfunny right there. "Don't even think about it," he had said, because if there was such a thing as a worm and they designed one that would work, *thinking* about it could be dangerous; and it was Grant's own set Grant meant. Grant had his own manual.

Grant had laughed, with that wicked, under the brows grin he had when he had tagged his CIT good.

"I don't think we ought to do this," Justin had said, and grabbed the notebook. "I don't think we ought to mess around with it."

"Hey, there isn't any such thing."

"I don't want to find out." It was hard to be the Authority for the moment, to pull CIT-rank on Grant and treat him like that. It hurt. It made him feel like hell. Suddenly and glumly sober, Grant had crumpled up his design-start, and the disappointment in Grant's eyes had gone right to his gut.

Till Grant had come into his room that night and waked him out of a sound sleep, saying he had thought of a worm, and it worked—whereupon Grant had laughed like a lunatic, pounced on him in the dark and scared hell out of him.

"Lights!" he had yelled at the Minder, and Grant had fallen on the floor laughing.

Which was the way Grant was, too damned resilient to let anything come between them. And damned well knowing what he deserved for his pretensions to godhood.

He sat motionless at the keyboard, staring at nothing, with a dull ache inside that was purely selfish. Grant was all right. Absolutely all right.

The intercom blipped. He summoned up the fortitude to deal with it and punched the console button. "Yes," he said, expecting Ari or Ari's office.

"Justin." It was his father's voice. "I want to talk to you. My office. Now."

He did not dare ask a question. "I'm coming," he said, shut down and went, immediately.

He was back an hour later, in the same chair, staring at a

lifeless screen for a long while before he finally summoned the self-control to key the project-restore.

The comp brought the program up and found his place. He was a thousand miles away, halfway numb, the way he had made himself when Jordan told him he had gotten a call through to Merild and Merild had given a puzzled negative to a coded query.

Merild had gotten no message. Merild had gotten nothing at all that he would have recognized as the subject of Jordan's inquiry. Total zero.

Maybe it was too soon. Maybe there was some reason Krugers had held Grant there and not called Merild yet. Maybe they were afraid of Reseune. Or the police.

Maybe Grant had never gotten there.

He had been in shock as Jordan had sat down on the arm of the office chair and put his arm about him and told him not to give up yet. But there was nothing they could do. Neither of them and no one they knew could start a search, and Jordan could not involve Merild by giving him the details over the House phone. He had called Krugers and flatly asked if a shipment got through. Krugers avowed it had gone out on schedule. Someone was lying.

"I thought we could trust Merild," was all he had been able to say.

"I don't know what's going on," Jordan had said. "I didn't want to tell you. But if Ari knows something about this she's going to spring it on you. I figured I'd better let you know."

He had not broken down at all—until he had gotten up, had said he had to get back to his office, and Jordan hugged him and held him. Then he had fallen apart. But it was only what a boy would do, who had just been told his brother might be dead.

Or in Ari's hands.

He had gotten his eyes dry, his face composed. He had walked back through the security checkpoint and into Ari's wing, back past the continuing upset in Jane Strassen's staff, people trying to get a shipment out on the plane that was going after supplies, because Jane was so damned tight she refused to move with anything but a full load.

He sat now staring at the problem in front of him, sick at his stomach and hating Ari, *hating* her, more than he had ever conceived of hating anyone, even while he did not know where Grant was, or whether he himself had killed him, sending him out in that boat.

And he could not tell Jordan the full extent of what was going on. He could not tell Jordan a damned thing, without triggering all the traps set for him.

He killed the power again, walked out and down the hall to Ari's office, ignoring the to-do in the hall. He walked in and faced Florian, who had the reception desk. "I've got to talk to her," he said. "Now."

Florian lifted a brow, looked doubtful, and then called through.

"How are we?" Ari asked him; and he was shaking so badly, standing in front of Ari's desk, that he could hardly talk.

"Where's Grant?"

Ari blinked. One fast, perhaps-honest reaction. "Where's Grant? —Sit down. Let's go through this in order."

He sat down in the leather chair at the corner of her desk and clenched his hands on its arms. "Grant's gone missing. Where is he?"

Ari took in a long slow breath. Either she had prepared her act or she was not troubling to mask at all. "He got as far as Krugers. A plane came in this morning and he might have left on it. Two barges left this morning and he could have been on those."

"Where is he, dammit? Where have you got him?"

"Boy, I do appreciate your distress, but get a grip on it. You won't get a thing out of me by shouting, and I'd really be surprised if the hysteria is an act. So let's talk about this quietly, shall we?"

"Please."

"Oh, dear boy, that's just awfully stupid. You know I'm not your friend."

"Where is he?"

"Calm down. I don't have him. Of course I've had him tracked. Where *ought* he to be?"

He said nothing. He sat there trying to get his composure back, seeing the pit in front of him.

"I can't help you at all if you won't give me anything to work on."

"You can damn well help me if you want to. You know damn well where he is!"

"Dear, you really can go to hell. Or you can answer my questions and I promise you I'll do everything I can to extricate him from whatever he's gotten into. I won't have Krugers arrested. I won't have your friend in Novgorod picked up. I don't suppose Jordan's phone call a while ago had anything to do with your leaving your office and coming in here. You two really aren't doing well this week."

He sat and stared at her a long, long moment. "What do you want?"

"The truth, as it happens. Let me tell you where I think he was supposed to go and you just confirm it. A nod of the head will do. From here to Krugers. From Krugers to a man named Merild, a friend of Corain's."

He clenched his hands the tighter on the chair. And nodded.

"All right. Possibly he was on his way on the barges. It was supposed to be air, though, wasn't it?"

"I don't know."

"Is that the truth?"

"It's the truth."

"Possibly he just hasn't left yet. But I don't like the rest of the pattern. Corain isn't the only political friend Kruger's got. Does the name de Forte mean anything to you?"

He shook his head, bewildered.

"Rocher?"

"Abolitionists?" His heart skipped a beat, hope and misery tangled up together. Rocher was a lunatic.

"You've got it, sweet. That plane this morning landed over at Big Blue, and a bus met it and headed off on the Bertille-Sanguey road. I've got people moving on it, but it takes a little organizing even for me to get people in there that can get Grant out without them cutting his throat— They *will*, boy. The Abolitionists aren't all in it for pure and holy reasons, and if they've played a hand that blows Kruger, you can damn well bet they aren't doing it for the sake of one azi, are you hearing me, boy?"

He heard. He thought he understood. But he had not done

well in this, Ari had said it; and he wanted it from her. "What do you think they're after?"

"Your father. And Councillor Corain. Grant's a Reseune azi. He's a Warrick azi, damn near as good as getting their hands on Paul; and de Forte's after Corain's head, boy, because Corain sold out to *me*, Corain made a deal on the Fargone project and on the Hope project, your father's the center of it, and damned if you didn't go and throw Grant right into Kruger's lap."

"You're after him to haul him back."

"I want him back. *I want him away from Rocher*, you damned little idiot, and if you want him alive, you'd better start telling me any secrets you've got left. You *didn't* know about the Rocher connection, did you, didn't know a thing about Kruger's radical friends—"

"I didn't. I don't. I—"

"Let me tell you what they'll do to him. They'll get him out someplace, fill him full of drugs and interrogate him. Maybe they'll bother to give him tape while they're at it. They'll try to find out what he knows about the Rubin project and the Hope project and anything else he knows. They'll *try* to subvert him, God knows. But that isn't necessarily what they're after. I'll tell you what I think has happened. I think Kruger's being blackmailed by this lot, I think they had a man in his organization, and I think when they knew what you'd dropped in his lap, Merild never got a word of it: Rocher did, and Rocher's picked him up. Probably they have him sedated. When he does come around, what's he going to think? That these are friends of yours? That everything that's happening to him is your doing?"

"For God's sake—"

"It *is*, you know. Calm down and think this through. We can't go breaking in shooting Rocher's people if we aren't damned sure he's with them. We're getting a Locator into position. We missed a shot at the Bertille airport; we're not sure we're going to get any fix on them at Big Blue. We'll try. In the meanwhile we aren't a hundred percent sure he's not still at Kruger's. Now, I can get a warrant for a search there. But I'm going to take another tack. I can damn well guess how they're blackmailing Kruger: I can bet a lot of his azi contracts are real suspect; and I can arrange an audit. I've got a plane on its way over there. In the meanwhile Giraud is going to fly over to Corain at Gagaringrad and talk to him. *You're* going to explain this to Jordan, and tell Jordan I'd really appreciate it if he'd get onto this and get Merild on Kruger's case.''

"We get him out," he said, "and he goes to Merild. Merild won't blow anything.''

"Sweet," Ari said, "you know me better than that. We get him out and he comes right back to Reseune. He'll have been in their hands better than forty-eight hours, best we can do, if it isn't longer than that. We'll have to have him in for a check, —won't we? They could have done him all sorts of nastiness. And you wouldn't want to leave him to nurse that kind of damage all on his own, now, would you?''

"You want this blown wide open—''

"Sweet, *you* don't want it blown wide open. *You* don't want your father involved. He's going to be well aware when we pull Grant back here. If we can get him back alive. He's going to be well aware we have Grant in hospital, —isn't he? And he's going to be worried. I'll trust you keep your bargain with me, sweet.''

He said nothing, finding no argument, no weapon left.

"That's supposing," she said, "that he's salvageable. It may take years of treatment—if I can straighten him out. Of course, we have to get him away alive. That's first.''

"You're threatening me.''

"Sweet, I can't predict what Rocher will do. Or where shots may go. I'm only warning you—''

"I told you I'd do what you want!''

"For your father's sake. Yes. I'm sure you will. And we'll talk about Grant after I've got him.'' She flipped the cover on the intercom and punched a button. "Jordan? Ari here.''

"What is it?'' Jordan's voice came back.

"I've got your son in my office. Seems we've both noticed a little problem. Would you mind calling your contact in Novgorod again and telling him he really needs to get Kruger to give me a call. . . .''

_____ **xi** _____

There was break-time, finally, in the dingy little precip station where they had pulled in—an underground garage and a concrete stairs and this place, that was mostly crumbling concrete. There were only three rooms to it, excluding the bath and the kitchen. It had no windows, because windows were a liability in a place like this, just a kind of a periscope rig that would give a 360° scan of the area; but Grant had no access to it. He sat and answered questions, most of the time truthfully, often enough not, which was the only defense he could muster. There was not a phone in the place. There was a radio. He had no idea in the world how to work it, except having seen Jordan use one on the boat years ago.

He was still not sure what they were. Or whose they were. He just mumbled answers to Winfield's questions and complained, complained about the lack of coffee, complained about the uncomfortable accommodations, complained about everything, figuring to push them as far as he could, make them mad if he could, and get them to react. He played a slow relaxation, a gathering confidence in his safety, flowered into the worst bitch House-azi he could script—he built off Abban, as it happened, Giraud Nye's insufferable staffer, who was a prime pain to the janitorial and the kitchen staff, not mentioning any azi he thought he outranked.

There was a tape-machine in the bedroom. He did not like the look of that. It was not an unexpected thing to find in an out-of-the-way place: entertainment would be high among priorities for a line-keeper stationed out here, wherever *here* was. But it was not a little entertainment rig; it was new equipment, it looked like it had monitor plugs, and he was nervous about it. He figured to push them to the point where any reasonable CIT would lose his temper and see what sort they were.

"Sit down," Rentz said when he got up to follow Winfield to the kitchen.

"I thought I could help, ser. I—"

He heard a car. The others heard it too, and all at once Rentz and Jeffrey were on their feet, Winfield coming back from the kitchen, Winfield very quick to take a look with the periscope.

"Looks like Krähler."

"Who's—" Grant asked.

"Just sit down." Rentz put a hand on Grant's shoulder and shoved him into the chair, held him there while the sound of the car grew louder. The garage door went up without anyone in the room doing anything.

"That's Krahler," Winfield said. The lessening of tension was palpable, all around the room.

The car drove in, the noise vibrating through the wall that divided them from the underground garage, the garage door went down, the Decon spray hissed for a moment, then, car doors opened and slammed, and someone came up the steps.

"Who's Krahler, ser?"

"A friend," Winfield said. "Jeffrey, take him on into the bedroom."

"Ser, *where* is Merild? Why hasn't he come? Is—"

Jeffrey hauled him out of the chair and headed him for the bedroom, pushing him at the bed. "Lie down," Jeffrey said, in a tone that encouraged no argument.

"Ser, I want to know where Merild is, I want to know—"

Rentz had followed him. It was the best set he was likely to have. He whirled and took out Jeffrey with his elbow, Rentz with his other hand, and rushed the other room, where Winfield had realized his danger—

Winfield pulled a gun from his pocket, and Grant dodged. But Winfield did not panic as he might. Winfield had a steady hand and an unmissable shot; and Grant froze where he was, against the doorframe, while the door from the garage opened and a trio of men came in, two of them fast and armed.

One of the men behind him was getting up. Grant stood very still, until someone grabbed him from behind. He could have broken the man's arm. He did not. He let the man pull him back, while Winfield followed up and kept the gun on him.

"This the way it's been going here?" one of the newcomers asked.

Winfield did not laugh. "Lie down," he said to Grant, and Grant backed up to the bed and sat down. *"Down!"*

He did what Winfield wanted. Jeffrey got cord from his pocket and tied his right wrist to the bedframe, while Rentz was moaning on the floor and the several armed men stood there with their guns aimed in Grant's direction.

The other wrist, then, at an uncomfortable stretch. Grant looked at the men who had come in, two of them large, strong men; and one older, slight, the only one without a gun. It was his look Grant distrusted. It was this man that the others deferred to.

Krahler, the others had called him. More names he did not know, names that had nothing to do with Merild.

They put away the guns. They helped Rentz up. Jeffrey stayed while all the others left, and Grant stared at the ceiling, trying not to think how unprotected his gut was at the moment.

Jeffrey just pulled the drawer open under the tape machine and took out a hypospray. He put it against Grant's arm and triggered it.

Grant winced at the kick and shut his eyes, because he would not remember to do that in a few moments and he did not trust them to remind him. He gathered up the defenses he had in his psychset and thought mostly of Justin, not wasting time with the physical attack that had gone wrong: the next level of this was a fight of a very different sort. He had no more doubts. The guns had proved it. What they were about to do proved it. And he was, azi that he was, a Reseune apprentice, in Ariane Emory's wing: Ariane Emory had created him, Ari and Jordan had done his psychsets, and damned if somebody he had never heard of could crack them.

He was slipping. He felt the dissociation start. He knew that the Man was back and they were starting the tape. He was going far, far under. Heavy dose. Deep-tape with a vengeance. He had expected that.

They asked his name. They asked other things. They told him they owned his Contract. He was able to remember otherwise.

He waked finally. They let him loose to drink and relieve himself; they insisted he eat, even if it nauseated him. They gave him a little respite.

After that they did it all again, and the time blurred. There might have been more such wakings. Misery made them all one thing. His arms and back ached when he came to. He answered questions. Mostly he did not know where he was, or remember clearly why he had deserved this.

Then he heard a thumping sound. He saw blood spatter across the walls of the room. He smelled something burning.

He thought that he had died then, and men came and wrapped him in a blanket, while the burning-smell grew worse and worse.

Up and down went crazy for a while. And tilted, and the air had a heartbeat.

"He's waking up," someone said. "Give him another one."

He saw a man in blue coveralls. Saw the Infinite Man emblem of Reseune staff.

Then he was not sure of anything he had surmised. Then he was not sure where the tape had started or what was real.

"*Get the damn hypo!*" someone yelled in his ear. "*Dammit, hold him down!*"

"*Justin!*" he screamed, because he believed now he had always been home, and there was the remote chance Justin might hear him, help him, get him out of this. "*Justin—!*"

The hypo hit. He fought, and bodies lay on him until the weight of the drug became too much for him, and the world reeled and turned under him.

He waked in a bed, in a white room, with restraints across him. He was naked under the sheets. There were biosensors on a band about his chest and around his right wrist. The left was bandaged. An alarm beeped. He was doing it. His pulse rate was, a silent scream he tried to slow and hush.

But the door opened. A technician came in. It was Dr. Ivanov.

"It's all right," Dr. Ivanov said, and came and sat down on the side of his bed. "They brought you in this afternoon. It's all right. They blew those bastards to bloody hell."

"Where was I?" he asked, calmly, very calmly. "Where am I now?"

"Hospital. It's all right."

The monitor beeped again, rapidly. He tried to calm his pulse. He was disoriented. He was no longer sure where he had been, or what was real. "Where's Justin, ser?"

"Waiting to see you're coming round. How are you doing? All right?"

"Yes, ser. Please. Can you take this damn stuff off?"

Ivanov smiled and patted his shoulder. "Look, lad, you know and I know you're sane as they come, but for your own good, we're just going to leave that on a while. How's the bladder?"

"I'm all right." It was one more indignity atop the rest. He felt his face go red. "Please. Can I talk to Justin?"

"Not a long talk, I'm afraid. They really don't want you talking to much of anybody till the police have a go at you— it's all right, just formalities. You just answer two questions, they'll make out their reports, that's all there is to it. Then you'll take a few tests. Be back up at the House in no time. Is that all right?"

"Yes, ser." The damned monitor beeped and stopped as he got control of his pulse-rate. "What about Justin? Please."

Ivanov patted his shoulder again and got up and went to the door and opened it.

It was Justin who came in. The monitor fluttered and steadied and went silent again; and Grant looked at him through a shimmering film. Jordan was there too. Both of them. And he was terribly ashamed.

"Are you all right?" Justin asked.

"I'm fine," he said, and lost control of the monitor again, and of his blinking, which spilled tears down his face. "I guess I'm in a lot of trouble."

"No," Justin said, and came and gripped his hand, hard, saying different things with his face. The monitor fluttered and quieted again. "It's all right. It was a damn fool stunt. But you're coming back to the House. Hear?"

"Yes."

Justin bent over and hugged him, restraints and all. And drew back. Jordan came and did the same, held him by the shoulders and said:

"Just answer their questions. All right?"

"Yes, ser," he said. "Can you make them let me go?"

"No," Jordan said. "It's for your safety. All right?" Jordan kissed him on the forehead. He had not done that since he was a small boy. "Get some sleep. Hear? Whatever tape you get, I'll vet. Personally."

"Yes, ser," he said.

And lay there and watched Jordan and Justin go out the door.

The monitor beeped in panic.

He was lost. He had hell to go through before he got out of this place. He had looked at Justin's face past Jordan's shoulder and seen hell enough right there.

Where was I? What really happened to me? Have I ever left this place?

A nurse came in, with a hypo, and there was no way to argue with it. He tried to quiet the monitor, tried to protest.

"Just a sedative," the nurse said, and shot it off against his
arm.

Or Jeffrey had. He went reeling backward and forward and
saw the blood spatter the white wall, heard people yelling.

_____ xii _____

"Good enough?" Ari asked Justin, in her office. Alone.

"When can he get out?"

"Oh," Ari said, "I don't know. I really don't know. Like I
don't know now about the bargain we worked out—which
seems rather moot, right now, doesn't it? What coin have you
left to trade in?"

"My silence."

"Sweet, you have a lot to lose if you break that silence. So
does Jordan. Isn't that why we're doing all this?"

He was trembling. He tried not to show it. "No, we're doing
this because you don't want your precious project blown. Because *you* don't want publicity right now. Because you've got a
lot to lose. Otherwise you wouldn't be this patient."

A slow smile spread on Ari's lips. "I like you, boy, I really
rather like you. Loyalty's the rarest thing in Reseune. And you
have so much of it. What if I gave you Grant, untouched,
unaltered? What's he worth to you?"

"It's possible," Justin said, in a measured, careful tone,
"you can misjudge how far you can push me."

"What's he worth?"

"You release him. You don't run tape on him."

"Sweet, he's a little confused. He's been through hell. He
needs rest and treatment."

"I'll see he gets it. Jordan will. I'm telling you; don't push
me too far. You don't know what I'd do."

"Oh, sweet, I know what you can do. A lot of it really ex-
quisite. And I don't have to deal with you about Grant at all. I
have some very different kind of tapes. Your father would die,
he would outright die."

"Maybe you underestimate him."

"Oh? Have you told him? —I thought not. You have to understand the situation, you see. It's not just his son. It's not 'some woman.' You're his twin. It's *me*, Ari Emory. Not mentioning the azi.'' She chuckled softly. ''It's a marvelously good try, it really is. I respect that. I respect it enough to give you a little latitude. Come here, boy. Come here.''

She held out her hand. He hesitated in confusion and finally held out his own within her reach. She took it gently, and his nerves jumped, his pulse fluttered and a flush came over his skin, confusing all his thinking.

He did not jerk away. He did not dare. He could not formulate a sarcasm. His mind was darting too fast in a dozen directions, like something small and panicked.

''You want a favor? You want Grant back? I'll tell you what, sweet: you just go on cooperating and we'll just make that our private little deal. If you and I get along till your father goes, if you keep your mouth shut, I'll make him a present to you.''

''You're using deep-tape.''

''On you? Nothing to really bend your mind. What do you think, that I can take a normal, healthy mind and redesign it? You've been reading too many of those books. The tapes I used with you—are recreational. They're what the Mu-class azi get, when they're really, really good. You think you can't stand them? You think they've corrupted you? Reseune will do worse than that, sweet, and I can teach you. I told you: I *like* you. Someday you'll be a power in Reseune—here, or Fargone, or wherever. You've got the ability. I'd really like to see you survive.''

''That's a lie.''

''Is it? It doesn't matter.'' She squeezed his fingers. ''I'll see you at my place. Same time. Hear?''

He drew his hand back.

''It's not like I don't give you a choice.'' She smiled at him. ''All you have to do is keep things quiet. That's not much, for as much as you're asking. You make my life tranquil, sweet, and stand between me and Jordan, and I won't have his friends arrested, and I won't do a mindwipe on Grant. I'll even stop giving you hell in the office. You know what the cost is, for all those transfers you want.''

''You sign Grant over to me.''

''Next week. In case something comes up. You're such a clever lad. You understand me. Make it 2200 this evening. I'm working late.''

Verbal Text from:
PATTERNS OF GROWTH
A Tapestudy in Genetics: #1

Reseune Educational Publications: 8970-8768-1
approved for 80+

ATTENTION OPERATOR
BATCH ML-8986: BATCH BY-9806: FINALFINALFINAL

The computers flash completion, appealing for human intervention. The chief technician alerts the appropriate personnel and begins the birth-process.

There are no surprises: the womb-tanks, gently moving and contracting, have all manner of sensors. The two ML-8986s, female, Mu-class, have reached the mandated 4.02 kilo birthweight. There are no visible abnormalities. The two BY-9806s, Gamma-class, are likewise in good health. The techs know their charges. The BY-9806s, highly active, are favorites, already tagged with names, but the names will not stay with them: the techs will have no prolonged contact with them.

The wombs enter labor-state, and after a space, send their contents sliding down into fluid-cushioned trays and the gloved hands of waiting techs. There are no crises. There is little stress. The Mu-class females are broad-faced, placid, with colorless hair; the two Betas are longer, thin-limbed, with shocks of dark hair, not so handsome as the Mu-classes. They make faces and the techs laugh.

The cords are tied, the afterbirth voided from the bottom of the tray, and clean warm water gives the infants their first baths. The techs weigh them as a formality, and enter the data on a record which began with conception, two hundred ninety-five days ago, and which will have increasingly fewer entries as the infants pass from a state of total moment-by-moment dependency into the first unmonitored moments of their lives.

Azi attendants receive them, wrap them in soft white blankets, to be tenderly handled, held and rocked in azi arms.

In intervals between diaper changes and feeding, they lie in cribs which, like the wombs, gently rock, to the sound of human heartbeat and distant voice, the same voice that spoke to them in the womb, soft and reassuring. Sometimes it sings to them. Sometimes it merely speaks.

Someday it will give them instruction. The voice is tape. As yet it is only subliminal, a focus of confidence. Even at this point it rewards good behavior. One day it will speak with disapproval, but at this stage there are no misbehaviors, only slight restlessness from the Betas. . . .

BATCH AGCULT-789X: EMERGENCYEMERGENCY

AGCULT-789X is in trouble. The experimental geneset is not a success, and after staff consultations, a tech withdraws lifesupport and voids AGCULT-789X for autopsy.

The azi techs swab out the womb, flush it repeatedly, and the chief tech begins the process that will coat it in bioplasm.

It will receive another tenant as soon as the coating is ready. The staff waits results of the autopsy before it attempts the fix.

In the meanwhile the womb receives the male egg AGCULT-894, same species. This is not the first failure. Engineering adaptations is a complex process, and failures are frequent. But AGCULT-894 is a different individual with a similar alteration: there is the chance it will work. If it fails it will still provide valuable comparisons.

Reshaping the land and altering the atmosphere is not enough to claim a world for human occupation. The millions of years of adaptation which interlocked Terran species into complex ecosystems are not an option on Cyteen.

Reseune operates in the place of time and natural selection. Like nature, it loses individuals, but its choices are more rapid and guided by intelligence. Some argue that there are consequences to this, a culling of the ornamental and nonfunctional elements which give Terran life its variety, with an emphasis on certain traits and diminution of others.

But Reseune has lost nothing. It plans deepspace arks, simple tin cans parked around certain stars, vessels without propulsion, inexpensive to produce, storage for genetic material in more than one location, shielded and protected against radiation. They contain actual genetic samples; and digital recording of genesets; and records to enable the reading of those genesets by any intelligence advanced enough to understand the contents of the arks.

A million years was sufficient for humankind to evolve from primitive antecedents to a spacefaring sapient. A million years from now humankind will, thanks to these arks, have genetic records of its own past and the past of every species to which Reseune has access, of our own heritage and the genetic heritages of every life-bearing world we touch, preserved against chance and time. . . .

The arks preserve such fragmentary codes as have been recovered from human specimens thousands of years old, from Terran genepools predating the development of genebanks in the 20th century, from the last pre-mixing genepools of the motherworld, and from remains both animal and human preserved through centuries of natural freezing and other circumstances which have preserved some internal cellular structure.

Imagine the difference such reference would make today, if such arks had preserved the genetic information of the geologic past. Earth, thus far unique in its evidences of cataclysmic extinctions of high lifeforms, might, with such libraries, recover the richness of all its evolutionary lines, and solve the persistent enigmas of its past. . . .

Reseune has never abandoned a genetic option. It has seen to the preservation of those options to a degree unprecedented in the history of the human species, and, working as it does with a view toward evolutionary change, has preserved all the possible divergences. . . .

CHAPTER 3

————————————— i —————————————

Time stopped being. There was just the tape-flow, mostly placid, occasionally disturbing. There were intervals of muzzy waking, but the trank continued—until now, that Grant drifted closer to the surface.

"Come on, you've got a visitor," someone said, and a damp cloth touched his face. The washing proceeded downward, gently, neck and chest, with an astringent smell. "Wake up."

He slitted his eyes. He stared at the ceiling while the washing proceeded, and hoped they would let him loose, but it was not much hope. He wished they would give him trank again, because the fear was back, and he had been comfortable while it lasted.

He grew chill with the air moving over damp skin. He wanted the sheet back again. But he did not ask. He had stopped trying to communicate with the people that handled him and they did not hurt him anymore. That was all he asked. He remembered to blink. He saw nothing. He tried not to feel the cold. He felt a twinge when the tech jostled the needle in his arm. His back ached, and it would be the most wonderful relief if they would change the position of the bed.

"There." The sheet settled over him again. A light slap popped against his face, but he felt no pain. "Come on. Eyes open."

"Yes," he murmured. And shut them again the moment the azi tech left him alone.

He heard another voice then, at the door, young and male. He lifted his head and looked and saw Justin there. He distrusted the vision at once, and jerked at the restraints.

But Justin came to him, sat down on the side of his bed and took his hand despite the restraint that gave him only a little movement. It was a warm grip. It felt very real.

"Grant?"

"Please don't do this."

"Grant, for God's sake— Grant, you're home. You understand me?"

It was very dangerous even to think about believing. It meant giving up. There was no secret sign his own mind could not manufacture. There was no illusion tape could not create. Justin was what they would use. Of course.

"Grant?"

Tape could even make him think he was awake. Or that the mattress gave, or that Justin held him by the shoulder. Only the keen pain in his back penetrated the illusion. It was not perfect.

Reality—had such little discordances.

"They won't let me take you back to the apartment yet. Ari won't. What are they doing? Are you all right? Grant?"

Questions. He could not figure how they fitted. There was usually a pattern. These had to do with credibility. That was the game.

"Grant, dammit!" Justin popped his hand against his cheek, gently. "Come on. Eyes open. Eyes open."

He resisted. That was how he knew he was doing better. He drew several breaths and his back and shoulders hurt like hell. He was in terrible danger . . . because he thought that the illusion was real. Or because he had lost the distinction.

"Come on, dammit."

He slitted his eyes cautiously. Saw Justin's face, Justin with a frightened look.

"You're home. In hospital. You understand? Ari blew them all to hell and got you out."

(Blood spattering the walls. The smell of smoke.)

It looked like hospital. It looked like Justin. There was no test that would confirm it, not even if they let him out to walk around. Only time would do that, time that went on longer than any tape-illusion.

"Come on, Grant. Tell me you're all right."

"I'm all right." He drew a breath that hurt his back and realized he could get things out of this illusion. "My back's killing me. My arms hurt. Can you move the bed?"

"I'll get them to take those off."

"I don't think they will. But I'd like the bed moved. There—" The surface under him flexed like a living thing and shifted upward, bringing his head up. The whole surface made a series of waves that flexed muscles and joints. "Oh, that's better."

Justin settled back on the edge, making a difference in the ripples. "Ari tracked you to Kruger's. Kruger was being blackmailed. He handed you over to the Abolitionists. I had to go to Ari. She got somebody—I don't know who—to go in after you. She said they'd been running tape."

He had had no structure for that time. No division between there and here. He examined the gift very carefully. "How long?"

"Two days."

Possible.

"You've been *here* two days," Justin said. "They let Jordan and me in right after they brought you in. Now they say I can visit."

It frightened him. It wanted to move in permanently, an illusion against which his defenses were very limited. He was losing. He sat there and cried, feeling the tears slip down his face.

"Grant."

"All right." He was nearly gone. "But if I tell you to leave, you leave."

"Grant, it's not tape. You're *here*, dammit." Justin squeezed his hand till the bones ground together. "Focus. Look at me. All right?"

He did. "If I tell you to leave—"

"I'll go. All right. Do you want me to?"

"Don't do that to me. For God's sake—"

"I'll get Ivanov. Damn them. Damn them."

Justin was on his way to his feet. Grant clenched his hand, holding on to him. Held on and held tight; and Justin sat down again and hugged him hard.

"Unnnh." It hurt. It felt real. Justin could pull him back. Justin knew what he was doing, knew what was the matter with him, knew why he was afraid. Was his ally. Or he was lost. "It's going to take a while."

"About a week to get you out of here. Ari says."

He remembered crises other than his own. He looked at Justin as Justin sat back. Remembered why he had gone down the river. "She give you trouble?"

"I'm all right."

Lie. More and more real. Tape was better than this. In a while Justin would go away and he would remember believing it and be afraid. But in the meanwhile it made him afraid for a different, more tangible reason. Jordan's transfer; Justin's sending him away—the fragments assumed a time-sense. *When* existed again. The real world had traps in it, traps involved Ari, Justin had tried to get him free, he was home and Justin was in trouble.

No. Careful.

Careful.

"What did she do when she found out I was gone?"

"I'll tell you later."

Dammit, he did not need worry to upset his stomach. It felt like home. Secrets, Ari, and trouble. And everything he loved. He took in a slow, long breath. "I'm holding on," he said, knowing Justin would understand. "I don't want any more tape. I don't want any more sedation. I need to stay awake. I want them to leave the lights on. All the time. I want to get this damn tube out of my arm."

"I haven't got any authority. You know that. But I'll tell Ivanov. I'll make it real strong with him. And I'll take the tube out. Here."

It stung. "That's going to drip all over the floor."

"Hell with it. There." He stopped the drip. "They're going to put a phone in here. And a vid."

His heart jumped. He remembered why a phone was important. But he was not there anymore. Or none of it had happened. Or there were possibilities he had missed.

"You know I'm not really well-hinged."

"Hell, I don't notice a difference."

He laughed, a little laugh, automatic, glad Justin was willing to joke with him; and realized that had come totally around a blind corner. Surprised him, when he had been expecting smooth, professional pity. It was not a funny laugh. Surprise-laugh.

Tape could hardly get Justin down pat enough to do something his mind had not expected, not when he was resisting it and not cooperating out of his subconscious.

He laughed again, just to test it, saw Justin look like he had glass in his gut, and hope at the same time.

"It's a worm," he told Justin. And grinned wide, wider as he saw an instant of real horror on Justin's face.

"You damn lunatic!"

He laughed outright. It hurt, but it felt good. He tried to draw his legs up. Wrong. "Oh, damn. You think they can get my legs free?"

"Soon as you know where you are."

He sighed and felt tension ebbing out of him. He melted back against the moving bed and looked at Justin with a placidity different than tape offered. It still hurt. Muscle tension. Sprain. God knew what he had done to himself, or what they had done to him. "I had you, huh?"

"If you put this on for an act—"

"I wish. I'm fogged. I think I'm going to have flashes off this. I think they'll go away. I'm really scared, if you don't come back. Dr. Ivanov's running this, isn't he?"

"He's taking care of you. You trust him, don't you?"

"Not when he takes Ari's orders. I'm scared. I'm really scared. I wish you could stay here."

"I'll stay here through supper. I'll come back for breakfast in the morning; every hour I can get free till they throw me out. I'm going to talk to Ivanov. Why don't you try to sleep while I'm here? I'll sit in the chair over there and you can rest."

His eyes were trying to close. He realized it suddenly and tried to fight it. "You won't leave. You have to wake me up."

"I'll let you sleep half an hour. It's nearly suppertime.

You're going to eat something. Hear? No more of this refusing food.''

''Mmnn.'' He let his eyes shut. He went away awhile, away from the discomfort. He felt Justin get up, heard him settle into the chair, checked after a moment to be sure Justin really was there and rested awhile more.

He felt clearer than he had been. He even felt safe, from moment to moment. He had known, if the world was halfway worth living in, that Justin or Jordan would get to him and pull him back to it. Somehow. When it came he had to believe it or he would never believe anything again, and never come back from the trip he had gone on.

ii

The reports came in and Giraud Nye gnawed his stylus and stared at the monitor with stomach-churning tension.

The news-services reported the kidnapping of a Reseune azi by radical elements, reported a joint police–Reseune Security raid on a remote precip station on the heights above Big Blue, with explicit and ugly interior scenes from the police cameras—the azi, spattered with the blood of his captors, being rescued and bundled aboard a police transport. It had taken something, for sharpshooters in outback gear to hike in, break into the garage via a side door, and make a flying attack up the stairs. One officer wounded. Three radical Abolitionists killed, in full view of the cameras. Good coverage and bodies accounted for, which left no way for Ianni Merino and the Abolition Centrists to raise a howl and convoke Council: publicly, Merino was distancing himself as far and as fast as he could from the incident. Rocher was deluging the Ministry of Information with demands for coverage for a press conference: he got nothing. Which meant that the police would be watching Rocher very carefully—the last time Rocher got blacked out, someone had unfurled a huge Full Abolition banner in the Novgorod subway and sabotaged the rails, snarling traffic in a jam the news-services could not easily ignore.

God knew it had not won Rocher the gratitude of commuters. But he had his sympathizers, and a little display of power meant recruits.

About time, he thought, to do something about Rocher and de Forte. Thus far they had been a convenient embarrassment to Corain and to Merino, discrediting the Centrists. Now Rocher had crossed the line and become a nuisance.

Convenient if the damage to Grant had been extreme. A before-and-after clip given to the news-services would show the Abolitionists up for the hounds they were. Honest citizens never saw a mindwipe in progress. Or botched. Convenient if they could take the azi down for extreme retraining—or take him down altogether. God knew he was Alpha, and a Warrick product, and God knew what Rocher's tapes had done: *he* had rather be safe; he had told Ari as much.

Absolutely not, Ari had said. What are you thinking of? In the first place, he's a lever. In the second, he's a witness against Rocher. Don't touch him.

Lever with whom, Giraud thought sourly. Ari was holding night-sessions with young Justin, and Ari was, between driving Jane Strassen to ulcers over the refitting of Lab One and the relocation of eight research students, so damned wrapped up in her obsession with the Rubin project that nobody got time with her *except* her azi and Justin Warrick.

Got herself a major triste. *Lost youth and all of that.*

Goes off and leaves me to mop up the mess in Novgorod. 'Don't touch Merild or Krugers. We don't want to drive the enemy underground. Cut a deal with Corain. That's not hard, is it?'

The hell.

The phone rang. It was Warrick. Senior. Demanding Grant's release to his custody.

"That's not my decision, Jordie."

"Dammit, it doesn't seem to be anybody's, does it? I want that boy out of there."

"Look, Jordie—"

"I don't care whose fault it isn't."

"Jordie, you're damn lucky no one's prosecuting that kid of yours. It's his damn fault this came down, don't yell at me—"

"Petros says you're the one has to authorize a release."

"That's a medical matter. I don't interfere in medical decisions. If you care about that boy, I'd suggest you let Petros do his job and stay—"

"He passed the mess to you, Gerry. So did Denys. We're

not talking about a damn records problem. We're talking about a scared kid, Gerry.''

"Another week—"

"The hell with another week. You can start by giving me a security clearance over there, and get Petros to return my calls.''

"Your son is over there right now. He's got absolute clearance, God knows why. He'll take care of him.''

There was silence on the other end.

"Look, Jordie, they say about another week. Two at most.''

"Justin's got clearance.''

"He's with him right now. It's all right. I'm telling you it's all right. They've stopped the sedation. Justin's got visiting privileges, I've got it right here on my sheet, all right?''

"I want him out.''

"That's real fine. Look, I'll *talk* to Petros. Is that all right? In the meantime your kid's with Grant, probably the best medicine he could get. Give me a few hours. I'll get you the med reports. Will that satisfy you?''

"I'll be back to you.''

"Fine, I'll be here.''

"Thanks,'' came the mutter from the other end.

"Sure,'' Giraud muttered; and when the contact broke: "Damn hot-head.'' He went back to the draft of the points he meant to make with Corain, interrupted himself to key a query to Ivanov's office, quick request for med records on Grant to Jordan Warrick's office. And added, on a second thought, because he did not know what might be *in* those records, or what Ari had ordered: SCP, *security considerations permitting*.

iii

The new separator was working. The rest of the equipment was scheduled for checkout. Ari made notes by hand, but mostly because she worked on a system and the Scriber got in her way: in some things only state of the art would do, but when it came to her notes, she still wrote them with a light-pen on the TranSlate, in a shorthand her Base in the House system continually dumped into her archives because it knew her handwriting: old-fashioned program, but it equally well served as a privacy barrier. The Base then went on to translate, transcribe and archive under her passwords and handprint, because she had given it the password at the top of the input.

Nothing today of a real security nature. Lab-work. Student-work. Any of the azi techs could be down here checking things, but she enjoyed this return to the old days. She had helped wear smooth the wooden seats in Lab One, hours and hours over the equipment, doing just this sort of thing, on equipment that made the rejected separator look like a technologist's dream.

That part of it she had no desire to recreate. But quite plainly, she wanted to say *I* in her write-up of this project. She wanted her stamp on it and her hand on the fine details right from the conception upward. *I was most careful, in the initiation of this project—*

I prepared the tank—

There were very few nowadays who *were* trained in all the steps. Everyone specialized. She belonged to the colonial period, to the beginnings of the science. Nowadays there were colleges turning out educated apes, so-named scientists who punched buttons and read tapes without understanding how the biology worked. She fought that push-the-button tendency, put an especially high priority on producing methodology tapes even while Reseune kept its essential secrets.

Some of those secrets would come out in her book. She had intended it that way. It would be a classic work of science—the entire evolution of Reseune's procedures, with the Rubin project hindmost in its proper perspective, as the test of theories developed over the decades of her research. *IN PRINCIPIO* was the title she had tentatively adopted. She was still searching for a better one.

The machine came up with the answer on a known sequence. The comp blinked red on an area of discrepancy.

Damn it to bloody hell. Was it contamination or was it a glitch-up in the machine? She made the note, mercilessly honest. And wondered whether to lose the time to replace the damn thing again and try with a completely different test sample, or whether to try to ferret out the cause and document it for the sake of the record. Doing the former, was a dirty solution. Being reduced to the latter and, God help her, failing to find solid evidence, which was a good bet in a mechanical glitch-up, made her look like a damn fool or forced her to have recourse to the techs more current with the equipment.

Dump the machine *and* consign it to the techs, run the suspect sample in a clean machine, and install a third machine for the project, *with* a new sample-run.

Every real-life project is bound to have its glitch-ups, or the researcher is lying . . .

The outer lab-door opened. There were distant voices. Florian and Catlin. And another one she knew. Damn.

"Jordan?" she yelled, loud enough to carry. "What's your problem?"

She heard the footsteps. She heard Florian's and Catlin's. She had confused the azi, and they trailed Jordan as far as the cold-lab door.

"I need to talk to you."

"Jordie, I've got a problem here. Can we do it in about an hour? My office?"

"Here is just fine. Now. In private."

She drew a long breath. Let it go again. *Grant*, she thought. *Or Merild and Corain.* "All right. Damn, we're going to have Jane and her clutch traipsing through the lab out there in about thirty minutes. —Florian, go over to B and tell them their damn machine won't work." She turned and ejected the sample. "I want another one. We'll go through every damn machine they've got if that's what it takes. I want the thing cleaner than it's providing. God, what kind of tolerances are they accepting these days? And you bring it over yourself. I don't trust those aides. Catlin, get up there and tell Jane she can take her damn students somewhere else. I'm shutting down this lab until I get this thing running." She drew a second long breath and used the waldo to send the offending sample back through cryogenics, then ejected the sample-chamber to a safe-cell and sent it the same route. When she turned around the azi were gone and Jordan was still standing there.

<hr>

iv

It was a hike from the hospital over to the House itself, a long round-about if the weather made it necessary to go through the halls and the tunnel, a good deal shorter to walk over under open sky. Justin opted for the open air, though the shadows of the cliffs had cut off the sun and he ought to have brought a coat. He got tape-flash. He got it almost everywhere. The sensations got to him most, and his stomach stayed upset— *"You eat the damn stuff,"* Grant had challenged him, since hospital staff had brought two dinners. "I'll match you."

He had gotten it down. He was not sure it was going to stay there. It had been worth everything to have Grant able to sit up and laugh—they had let him free to have his supper and Grant had sat cross-legged in bed and managed the dessert with some enthusiasm. Even if the nurses said they were going to have to put the restraints back on when he was alone for the night.

He would not have left for the night at all, and Ivanov would have let him stay; except he had an appointment with Ari, and he could not tell Grant that. Late work at the lab, he had said. But Grant had been a hundred percent better when he had left him than when he had come in, quickly exhausted, but with liveliness in his eyes, the ability to laugh—perhaps a little too much, perhaps a little too forced, but the way the eyes looked said that Grant was back again.

Just when he was leaving the mask had come down, and Grant had looked sober and miserable.

"Back in the morning," Justin had promised.

"Hey, you don't have to, it's a long walk over here."

"I want to, all right?"

And Grant had looked ineffably relieved.

That was the good in the day. It was worth everything he paid for it. He felt for the first time since that day in Ari's office, that there might be a way out of this.

If—if Ari had enough to keep her busy, if—

He thought of Grant and Ari, Grant already on the edge of his sanity—

Grant, who had the looks, the grace that every girl he had ever known had preferred to him—

He waded through tape-flash that diminished only to shameful memory, through a muddle of anguish and exhaustion. He was not going to be worth anything. He wanted to go somewhere and be sick—he could call Ari and plead that he was sick, truly he was, he was not lying, she could ask him the next time he—

O God. But then there was the agreement that let him get to

Grant. There was the agreement that promised Grant would be free. She could mindwipe Grant. She could do anything. She had threatened Jordan. Everything was on him, and he could not tell Grant, not in the state Grant was in.

He took in his breath and slogged on down the path that led around the corner toward the main door—a jet was coming in. He heard it. It was ordinary. RESEUNEAIR flew at need, as well as on a weekly schedule. He saw it touch down, walking along by the gravel bed and the adapted shrubbery that led to the front doors. The bus started up from in front of the doors and passed him on its way around the drive and down toward the main road. On its way to pick up someone on the jet, he reckoned, and wondered who in the House had been downriver in all this chaos.

He walked in through the automatic doors, using his keycard in the brass slot, clipped the keycard back to his shirt and headed immediately for the lift that would take him up to his apartment.

Phone Jordan first thing he got in and tell him Grant was better. He wished he had had time to call while he was in the hospital, but Grant had not wanted him out of his sight, and he had not wanted to upset him.

"Justin Warrick."

He turned and looked at the Security guards, putting their presence together with the plane and the bus and instantly thought that some visitor must be coming in.

"Come with us, please."

He indicated the lift buttons. "I'm just going up to my room. I'll be out of here."

"Come with us, please."

"Oh, damn, just use the com, ask your Supervisor— You don't touch me!" As one of them reached for him. But they took him by the arms and leaned him up against the wall. "My God," he said, unnerved and exasperated, as they proceeded to search him thoroughly. It was a mistake. They were azi. They got their instructions upside down and they went damned well too far.

They wrenched his arms back and he felt the chill of metal at his wrists.

"Hey!"

The cuffs clicked shut. They faced him about again and

walked him down the hall. He balked, and they jerked him into
motion, down the hall toward the Security office.

God. Ari had filed charges. On him, on Jordan, Kruger, everyone involved with Grant. That was what had happened.
Somewhere she had gotten the leverage she wanted, something
to silence them and bring everything down on them; and he had
done it, he, thinking he could deal with her.

He walked where they wanted him to go, down the hall and
into the office with the glass doors, where the Supervisor sat.
"In there," the Supervisor said with a wave of her hand toward the back of the office.

"What in hell's going on?" he demanded, trying bluff in the
absence of everything else. "Dammit, *call Ari Emory!*"

But they took him past steel doors, past the security lock,
put him in a bare, concrete room, and shut the door.

"Dammit, you have to read me the charges!"

There was no answer.

---

v

The body was quite, quite frozen, fallen right at the vault door,
mostly prone, twisted a little. Surfaces in the vault still were
frost-coated and painful to the touch. "Patch of ice," the investigator said, and recorded the scene with his camera, posthumous indignity. Ari would have resented that like hell,
Giraud thought, and stared at the corpse, still unable to think
that Ari was not going to move, that stiff limbs and glazed eyes
and half-open mouth were not going to suddenly find life. She
was wearing a sweater. Researchers would, who worked in the
antiquated cold-lab: nothing heavier. But no cold-suit would
have saved her.

"There wouldn't have been any damn patch of ice then,"
Petros muttered. "No way."

"She work with the door shut?" The investigator from
Moreyville, small-town and all the law there was for a thousand miles in all directions, laid his hand on the vault door. It
started swinging to at that mere touch. "Damn." He stopped it
with a shove, balanced it carefully and gingerly let go of it.

"There's an intercom," Petros said. "That door's swung to
on most of us, sooner or later, we all know about it. It's some-

thing in the way the building's settled. You get locked in, you just call Security, you call Strassen's office, and somebody comes down and gets you out, it's no big thing.''

"It was this time." The investigator—Stern, his name was—reached up and punched the button on the intercom. The casing broke like wax. "Cold. I'll want this piece," he said to his assistant, who was following him with a Scriber. "Does anyone hear?"

There was no sound out of the unit.

"Not working."

"Maybe it's the cold," Giraud said. "There wasn't any call."

"Pressure drop was the first you knew something was wrong."

"Pressure in the liquid nitrogen tank. The techs knew. I got a call a minute or so later."

"Wasn't there an on-site alarm?"

"It sounded," Giraud said, indicating the unit on the wall, "down here. No one works back here. The way the acoustics are, no one could figure out where it was coming from. We didn't know till we got the call from the techs that it was a nitrogen line. Then we knew it was the cold-lab. We came running down here and got the door open."

"Ummn. And the azi weren't here. Just Jordan Warrick. Who was back upstairs when the alarm went off. I want a report on that intercom unit."

"We can do that," Giraud said.

"Better if my office does."

"You're here for official reasons. For the record. This is not your jurisdiction, captain."

Stern looked at him—a heavy-set, dour man with the light of intelligence in his eyes. Intelligence enough to know Reseune swallowed its secrets.

And that, since Reseune had friends high in Internal Affairs, promotion or real trouble could follow a decision.

"I think," Stern said, "I'd better talk to Warrick." It was a cue to retire to private interviews. Giraud's first impulse was to follow him and cover what had to be covered. His second was a genuine panic, a sudden realization of the calamity that had overtaken Reseune, overtaken all their plans, the fact that the brain that had been so active, held so much secret—was no more than a lump of ice. The body was impossible, frozen as it was, to transport with any dignity. Even that simple necessity was a grotesque mess.

And Corain— This is going to hit the news-services before morning.

What in hell do we do? What do we do now?

Ari, dammit, what do we do?

Florian waited, sitting on a bench in the waiting room, in the west wing of the hospital. He leaned his elbows against his knees, head against his hands, and wept, because there was nothing left to do, the police had Jordan Warrick in custody, they would not let him near Ari, except that one terrible sight that had made him understand that it was true. She was dead. And the world was different than it had ever been. The orders came from Giraud Nye: report for tape.

He understood that. Report to the Supervisor, the rule had been from the time he was small; there was tape to heal distress, tape to heal doubts—tape to explain the world and the laws and the rules of it.

But in the morning Ari would still be dead and he did not know whether they could tell him anything to make him understand.

He would have killed Warrick. He still would, if he had that choice; but he had only the piece of paper, the tape order, that sent him here for an azi's comfort; and he had never been so alone or so helpless, every instruction voided, every obligation just—gone.

Someone came down the hall and came in, quietly. He looked up as Catlin came in, so much calmer than he—always calm, no matter what the crisis, and even now—

He got up and put his arms around her, held her the way they had slept together for so many years he had lost count, the good times and the terrible ones.

He rested his head against her shoulder. Felt her arms about him. It was something, in so much void. "I saw her," he said; but it was a memory he could not bear. "Cat, what do we do?"

"We're here. That's all we can do. There's no place else to be."

"I want the tape. It hurts so much, Cat. I want it to stop."

She took his face between her hands and looked in his eyes.

Hers were blue and pale, like no one else's he knew. There was always sober sense in Cat. For a moment she frightened him, that stare was so bleak, as if there was no hope at all.

"It'll stop," she said, and held him tight. "It'll stop, Florian. It'll go. Were you waiting for me? Let's go in. Let's go to sleep, all right? And it won't hurt anymore."

Steps came up to the door, but people went back and forth every few minutes, and Justin had shouted himself hoarse, had sat down against the cold concrete wall and tucked himself up in a knot until he heard the door unlocked.

Then he tried for his feet, staggered his way up against the wall and kept his balance as two security guards came in after him.

He did not fight them. He did not say a word until they brought him back to a room with a desk.

With Giraud Nye behind it.

"Giraud," he said hoarsely, and sank down into the available round-backed chair. "For God's sake—what's going on? What do they think they're doing?"

"You're an accused accessory to a crime," Giraud said. "That's what's going on. Reseune law. You can make a statement now, of your own will. You know you're subject to Administrative rules. You know you're subject to psychprobe. I'd truly advise you be forthcoming."

Time slowed. Thoughts went racing in every direction, sudden disbelief that this could be happening, surety that it was, that it was his fault, that his father was involved because of him— Psychprobe would turn up everything.

Everything. Jordan was going to find out. They would tell him.

He wished he were dead.

"Ari was blackmailing me," he said. It was hard to coordinate speech with the world going so slow and things inside him going so fast. It went on forever, just hanging there in silence. *Mention Jordan and why Grant had to leave? Can they find that? How far can I lie?* "She said Grant could go, if I did what she wanted."

"You didn't know about Kruger's link to Rocher."

"No!" That was easy. Words tumbled one onto the other. "Kruger was just supposed to get him away safe because Ari was threatening to hurt him if I—if I didn't—she—'' He was going to be sick. Tape-flash poured in on him, and he leaned back as much as his arms let him and tried to ease the knot in his stomach. "When Grant didn't get to the city I went to her myself. I asked for her help."

"What did she say?"

"She called me a fool. She told me about Rocher. I didn't know."

"All that. You didn't go to your father."

"I couldn't. He didn't know about it. He'd—"

"What would he do?"

"I don't know. I don't know what he'd have done. I did everything. He didn't have anything to do with it."

"With stealing Grant, you mean."

"With anything. With Kruger. Rocher. Anybody."

"And Ari was going to let this happen."

It did not sound reasonable. Trap, he thought. *She let it happen. Maybe she hoped he'd get through. Maybe—*

—maybe some other reason. She was mad about it. She was—

But you never know with Ari. She plays reactions like most people use a keyboard.

"I think we'll ask the rest of the questions under probe. Unless you have anything else you want to tell me."

"Who's going to do it?" There were technicians and there were technicians, and it made a difference who he was going to be spilling his guts to. "Giraud, if I go on record, Ari's not going to like it. Does she know where I am? Does she know—" *God, is this some politics between Ari and Giraud, has he snatched me up to get something on her?* "I want to talk to Ari. I'm supposed to meet with her. She's going to be asking where I am. If she doesn't hear from me she's going to start—" *—start after Jordan, maybe do something even she can't undo. They're going to tell him. Giraud will tell him. Maybe Administration wants something on Jordan, maybe this is some team action Ari and Giraud are running, her on me and Giraud on Jordan. O God, O God! what have I walked into?* "—Start asking where I am. Hear me?"

"I don't think so. And I'm going to be asking the questions myself. You want to walk down to the room or are you going to make trouble about it? It'll go worse if you fight it, in all

senses. You understand that. I just want to make sure you remember it.''

"I'll walk."

"Fine." Giraud got up, and Justin sat forward and got up on
shaking legs. He was halfway numb with cold, and the
thoughts that had tumbled one onto the other lost all variety,
became just a circle without escape.

He walked out the door Giraud opened for him, walked
ahead of Giraud and the waiting guards, down the hall to a
place he had heard about all his life, a room very like the
rooms over at the hospital, in that wing where azi came for
tape-adjustment, green walls, a plain couch. There was a
camera-rig in the corner.

"Shirt," Giraud said.

He knew what they wanted. He peeled it off and laid it on
the counter. He sat down on the couch and took the shot one of
the azi had ready for him, tried to help them attach the sensors,
because he always did his own, with tape; but his coordination
was shot. He let himself back in the hands that reached to help
him, felt them lift his legs up onto the couch. He felt them
working with the patches. He shut his eyes. He wanted to tell
Giraud to send the azi out, because what he had to say involved
Ari, and the azi who heard that—would be in for selective
wipe, there was no else about it.

Giraud asked him questions, gently, professionally. He was
aware of the first ones. But that slipped. He could have been in
the hands of one of the techs, but Giraud was the best interro-
gator he could have hoped for—quiet and not given to leaving
an emotional load behind him. Professional, that was all. And
if Giraud was checking the truth, Giraud was at least trying to
find out what it was.

Giraud told him so. And under the drug it was true.

Giraud would not be shocked at what Ari had done. He had
lived too long and seen too much. Giraud was truly sorry for
him, and believed everything he said. A young boy of his
qualifications, in Ari's vicinity—he had to understand this was
not the first time. That Ari would try to work leverage on his
father, of course. Who could doubt it? Jordan had surely
known.

No, he argued, with a flash of white ceiling and bright light:

he came that far to the surface. He remembered Giraud touching his shoulder.

You really took care not to have your father know. Of course. What do you suppose he would do if he found out?

Go to the Bureau.

Ah.

But he didn't know.

You can sleep now. You'll wake up rested. You can let go. You won't fall.

Something was still wrong. He tried to lay hold of it. But it slid sideways, out of his vision.

"I don't think there's much doubt," Giraud said, looking at Jordan from across his desk. At forty-six, Jordan was far too athletic, far too capable physically to take a chance with; and they were careful, for other reasons, not to put a bruise on him. The restraints they used were webbing: no psychprobe, to be sure: Jordan Warrick was a Special, a national treasure. Not even the Bureau of Internal Affairs could do anything that might damage him, in any sense.

A Special was charged with murdering another Special. It was a situation that had no precedent. But Jordan Warrick could murder a dozen infants in Novgorod Plaza at noonday, and they could neither ask him why nor remand him to probe nor give him as much as the adjustment a public vandal would get.

Jordan glared at him from the chair Security had tied him to. "You know damn well I didn't do it."

"What will you do? Ask for a probe to prove it? We can't do a thing to you. *You* know that. You knew it when you did it."

"I didn't do it. Dammit, you haven't even got an autopsy yet."

"Whatever she died of, the cold was enough. The pipe didn't just break, Jordan, you know it and you know why it broke. Save us all the trouble. What did you do? Score the pipe and fill the lab tank is my guess. Fill the lab tank to capacity, then stop the main valve and turn the backflow pump to max. That'd blow the line at its weakest point, wherever someone damaged it."

"So you know how to do it. You seem to know the plumbing a hell of a lot better than I do. I do my work with a computer, Gerry, a *keyboard*. I'm sure I never cared where the pipes run in Wing One lab. I don't understand the cryogenics systems and I never cared to learn. There's one other thing wrong with your theory. I haven't got access there."

"Justin does. His azi had."

"Oh, you're really reaching. Grant's in hospital, remember?"

"We've questioned your son. We're starting to question the azi. Yours and his."

Jordan's face settled into stony calm. "You won't turn up a damn thing, because there isn't anything to turn up. You're going to have charges up to your eyeballs, Giraud. You had better plan on it."

"No, I won't. Because I know your motive."

"*What* motive?"

Giraud punched a button on the office recorder, on a preloaded clip.

"He passed the mess to you, Gerry. So did Denys. We're not talking about a damn records problem. We're talking about a scared kid, Gerry."

"Another week—"

"The hell with another week. You can start by giving me a security clearance over there, and get Petros to return my calls."

"Your son is over there right now. He's got absolute clearance, God knows why. He'll take care of him." Pause. "Look, Jordie, they say about another week. Two at most."

"Justin's got clearance."

End tape.

"What in hell has that got to do with anything?"

"That's when you went down to see Ari. Isn't it? Straight down there, right after that conversation."

"Damn right. You couldn't get off your ass."

"No. 'Justin's got clearance,' you said. That surprised you. A, Justin hadn't told you something he should have told you. B, Ari never gave away her advantages. C, you know Ari's habits. Right then, you guessed something you'd picked up on all along, right when you got onto the deal your son cut for Grant."

"Sheer fantasy."

"Your son tried to blackmail Ari. It was really quite a

scheme. You thought he'd held Ari off. You let him run with it. But when Ari hauled Grant home, Ari had all the cards. Didn't she? *All* of them. Your son went to Ari for help, not to you. And your son got a favor out of her you couldn't get for all your threats. I wonder how.''

"You have a hell of an imagination. I never suspected it of you.''

"You confronted Ari, Ari either told you or you already knew—what your boy'd been doing for his tuition. And you killed her. You jammed a valve and turned a pump on, *no* great amount of time involved. Everyone in Wing One knew about that door. It was supposed to be an accident, but then you had to improvise.''

Jordan said nothing for a moment. Then: "It doesn't work.''

"Why not?''

"Let me tell you who else knew I was going down there. You knew. I left. Ari and I talked and I left. Check the Scriber.''

"She didn't run one. You know that damn TranSlate. There isn't any spoken record. And she didn't leave us any notes. She didn't have time. You knocked her out, fixed the pipe, slammed the door, raised the pressure. By the time the alarm went off, you were back upstairs.''

"I didn't do it. I don't say I'm shedding any tears. But I didn't do it. And Justin was over in hospital, you say so right on that tape you've got. You edit it and I'll make a liar out of you.''

"Now you're reaching. Because if you go to trial, Jordie, I've got other tapes that belong in evidence. I'm going to run one for you.''

"You don't have to.''

"Ah. Then you guess what they are. But I want you to watch, Jordie. I'll run them all if you like. And you can tell me what you think.''

"You don't have to.''

"Ari said—you'd had your own passage with her . . . some years ago.''

Jordan drew in a long breath. The mask was down. "You listen to me,'' he said on that breath. "You listen to me real well, slime, because you *think* you're handling this. If Ari's dead, and I'm gone, Reseune's got two wings in complete disorder. Reseune's got agreements it can't keep. Reseune's going to have real trouble meeting its contracts and all its political bedfellows are going to scramble for their pants. Fast. You're forgetting: if a Special dies, there's got to be an inquiry. And what they find out is going to be real interesting, *not* just for us lucky souls inside Reseune. When this hits the news-services, you're going to see department heads and corporation presidents running like bugs with the lights on. You're right. You can't question me. *I* can't testify by anything but my given word. You know what I'll tell them. I'll tell them you used tape on me. And they can't tell without a psychprobe. Which the law won't even let me volunteer for. You put me in front of a mike. You just go ahead and do that. That's the kind of coverage I've been waiting for. Best damn coverage I could get. Ari and her friend Lao could black me out. But you know the way it is—some stories are too big to silence. Murdering the head of Reseune is one of them. I'm damn sorry I didn't think of it."

"That's true. That's all very true."

"Right now you're thinking about killing me. *Do* it. You think *one* Special dead is hard to explain."

"But there's something so damned final about old news. A little scandal. A lot of silence after that."

"But *you* wouldn't be on Council. Damned sure you wouldn't. We can do murder in the streets but we can't cover it up. No political power. No dark spots for the bugs to snuggle in. Public contempt. You want to watch Reseune lose everything it's got—"

"Old news. Murder-suicide. You couldn't stand the notoriety that would come with a trial. You thought you could shut it up. You didn't know there were tapes. You didn't know Ari recorded her little parties. And people will be shocked. But only for a while. People have always liked scandal around the rich and famous. It's all lost in the glitter. Who knows, maybe your boy will take to the life. Or come to some tragic end. Drug overdose. Tape-tripping. A waste. But the one thing you know he won't get is a post at Reseune. Or anywhere else our influence reaches. Not mentioning the other boy. The azi. It's probably a mistake to put him under interrogation. He's so fragile right now. But we have to get to the facts."

Jordan did not so much as move for a long while.

"There's also, of course," Giraud said, "Paul."

Jordan shut his eyes.

"Defeat?" Giraud asked.

"I'm sure," Jordan said, looking at him, "you mean to make me a proposition. You've put this together so carefully. Their safety for my silence?"

Giraud smiled without humor. "You know we can take them. You just gave us too many hostages, Jordie, and you can't protect a one of them, except by following orders. You don't want your boy to live with that tape. You don't want him prosecuted, you don't want the Krugers up on charges, and your friend Merild dragged into court, and all your friends in Council tied to it, one string after another. There's just no place an investigation like this ends once you start it moving. You don't want Grant or Paul subject to interrogation after interrogation. You know what that would do. *We* don't want an investigation getting out of bounds and *I* don't want scandal touching Reseune. Let me tell you how it'll be. You give us a detailed confession. Nothing's going to happen to you: you know that. You'll even get your dearest wish: a transfer out of here. We'll insist your work is important. And you'll go on with it, in a quiet, comfortable place without cameras, without microphones, without visitors. Isn't that better than the alternatives?"

"Except I didn't do it. I don't know what happened. I walked out of there. Ari and I quarreled. I accused her of blackmailing my son. She laughed. I left. I didn't threaten her. I didn't say a thing. You know I'd be a damn fool to tell Ari what I intended. And it didn't include murder. I didn't know. That's the plain truth. I hadn't made up my mind to go to the Bureau. I wasn't sure if there wasn't a way to buy her off."

"Now we have a different truth. Do we get one an hour?"

"It *is* the truth."

"But *you* can't be psychprobed. *You* can't prove what you witnessed. Or did. *You* can't prove a damned thing. So we're back where we started. Frankly, Jordie, I don't care whether you did it. You're our chief problem in the mop-up. You'd *like* to have done it, you're number one on my agenda, and if you're not the one who did it, you're more dangerous than the one who did, because if someone else killed Ari, it was personal. If you did it, it was something else. So we'll examine hell out of those pipes, the valves, the whole system. If we don't find evidence, we'll make it, quite frankly. And I'll give you the whole script you can use for the Bureau. You stick to that story and I'll keep my end of the bargain. Just *ask* for what you want. Anything within reason. You plead guilty, you take the hit, you just retire to a comfortable little enclave, and everything will be fine. If not—I'm really afraid we'll have to take measures of our own.''

"I want them transferred out of here. Justin. Grant. Paul. That's my price.''

"You can't get that much. You can get their safety. That's all. They'll stay right here. If you change your mind, so can we. If you attempt escape, if you suicide, if you talk to anyone or pass a message of any kind—they'll pay for it. That's the deal. It's just that simple.''

A long, long silence. "Then put them with me.''

Giraud shook his head. "I'll be generous. I don't have to be, understand. I'll give you Paul. I have *some* sympathy for you. Paul, of course, will be under the same restrictions.''

"You won't touch him.''

"What do you think? That I'd set him to spy on you? No. Not him. Not your son. Not the azi. You keep your bargain, I'll keep mine. Do we have a deal?''

Jordan nodded after a moment. His mouth trembled, only slightly.

"You'll stay here,'' Giraud said, "pending the Internal Affairs investigation. You'll be in detention. But you'll have reasonable comforts. Access to Paul—we can manage that. Access to your son—only under very restricted circumstances. Let me advise you on that: that boy will try to help you. For his sake, you'd better stop it cold. You're probably the only one who can. Do we agree?''

"Yes.''

"I want to show you that tape I promised you.''

"No.''

"I think you should see it. I think you really should. I want you to think about it—what we can use if you can't provide political motives for your crime. I'm sure you can be convincing. I'm sure you can suggest radical connections. Centrist connections. Because there has to be a motive. Doesn't there?'' He pressed a button. The wall-screen lit. It was Jordan's face he watched. Jordan with his eyes fixed on the corner, not the screen. Jordan, with a face like a carved image in the dimmed light, the flashes from the screen. Voices spoke. Bodies intertwined. Jordan did not look. But he reacted. He heard.

Giraud had no doubt of it.

"Did Jordan Warrick ever discuss in your presence his opinion of Ariane Emory?"

"Yes, ser," Grant answered. He sat still at the desk, his hands folded in front of him, and watched the light on the Scriber flicker, the little black box between himself and this man who said he was from the Bureau of Internal Affairs. He answered question after question.

Justin had not come back. They had fed him and let him take a shower, and told him that a man would be interviewing him that afternoon. Then they had put him back to bed and put the restraints back on. So he supposed it was afternoon. Or it was whatever they wanted it to be. He could become very angry at what they had done to him, but there was no use in it; it was what they wanted to do, and he had no way to prevent it. He was frightened; but that did no good either. He calmed himself and answered the questions, not trying to make a logic structure out of them yet, because that would affect his responses and they would lead him then; and he would lead them; and it would become adversarial. Which he did not want. He wanted to understand, but when he caught himself wanting it too much, he turned everything off, in that way he had learned when he was very, very small—azi tactic. Perhaps it helped him. Perhaps it was another of the differences between himself and Justin, between himself and a born-man. Perhaps it made him less than human. Or more. He did not know. It was only useful, sometimes, when he knew that someone wanted to manipulate him.

He just became *not-there*. The information flowed. They would take it when he was unconscious if he did not give it freely; and he expected they would check it by psychprobe anyway, no matter.

He would put it together later, recalling the questions, just what he had been asked and what the answers were. Then he might be able to think. But not now.

Not-there, that was all.

Eventually the man from Internal Affairs was *not-there* too. Others appeared and the illusions of doors opened.

The next place was the psych-lab. Then was the hardest thing, to flow with it, to be *not-there* through the interrogation under drugs. To walk the line between *there* and *not-there* took a great deal of concentration, and if he began to wobble and went too far into *not-there* and stayed too long, then it would be hard to find his way back again.

There tried to find its way into his thinking, with doubt that Justin had ever come to his room, with suspicion that, if he had, Ari's wrath had finally come down on them, and Justin and Jordan were being charged with his abduction. . . .

But he drove that out. He did not fight the techs as he had the men—if ever they had been real. The techs were Reseune techs and they had the keys to every smallest thought he owned.

The first rule said: It is always right to open to your key-command.

The second rule said: A key-command is absolute.

The third rule said: An operator with your keys is always right.

No Reseune operator, he believed with all his heart, would create an illusion of Reseune operators. No one *but* a Reseune operator held his keys. The whole universe might be flux of particles and dissolve about him: but in it, he existed, and the operator who had his keys existed.

Justin might never have existed at all. There might be no such place as Reseune and no such world as Cyteen. But the one who whispered correct numbers and code-phrases to him could enter his mind at will, and leave without a trace; or pick up this or that and look at it—not change it: a vase set on a table stayed a moment and sought its old position, not violently, just persistently—*the other face belongs out*. It would take many such entries, many rotations of the same vase, many distractions, like moving another table, shifting the couch about, before the vase would stay awhile in its new orientation. Even then it would tend to go back—over time.

Easier if the visitor said: we're going to rearrange this one room; and showed him the key. And ordered him to stand aside and watch. And then explained how all of it was going to fit together with the rest of the house, after which, if it truly worked, he would have less and less apprehension about it.

As it was, this visitor was rough, and knocked things about and then cornered him and asked him questions. Which made him anxious, because he was smart enough to know that occasionally tactics like that could be a distraction to get that vase on the table moved. Or to avoid that obvious temptation and go for something he might not notice for a while.

The visitor hit him once or twice and left him dazed. When he knew the door was closed he lay there awhile, and the vase that was in pieces picked itself up and mended itself; and the furniture straightened itself, and all the pieces started to go back again.

He had to lie there a long time being sure that everything really *was* in its right place. The stranger could have done worse. The stranger could have gone a level deeper, and chased him through deeper and deeper rooms, until the stranger cornered him where there was no retreat. Then the stranger would have found a way into *him*, whereafter he would have been dragged inside himself, into dark territory the invader knew and he would probe only reluctantly.

That was not the way it was, of course. It was only the image he had, a child's picture, that a tech had helped him build. The vase was the tamper-gate. The yes-no/are-you-safe gate. It was right at the entry and any operator who tried to reassure him always rotated it just a little.

This visitor had thrown it to the floor.

He came out again in a room far more bleak and blank. Shadows came and went and spoke to him. But he was still largely *not-there*. He was exhausted, and the rooms kept coming disarranged, the furniture flying about at random, requiring him to order it again, which meant he had to go inside a great deal, and these people kept hitting him, blows on the cheek which felt like the flesh was deadened there. They spoke to him, but the words flew apart in pieces. He had no time for them. He was coming apart inside and if they woke him up he was not sure things would go back where they belonged.

Someone gave him the key-words the last visitor had left. And insisted he wake up. After which he was looking at Petros Ivanov sitting on his bed.

"They're going to take you in the chair. Will you let them do that?"

"Yes," he said. He would let them do anything. Whoever they were. He was much too busy putting things back on shelves and watching them fall off again.

The room became a different room. There were flowers. There was a waterfall. It made a rhythmical sound that had no rhythm. Of course. It was a fractal. Fractals were common in nature. He tried obligingly to discover the pattern. They had handcuffed him to the chair. He was not sure what that datum had to do with anything. He worked at the math since that was the problem they had given him. He did not know why.

He slept, perhaps. He knew they had done something to his mind because the tamper-gate was unstable: the vase kept tottering off the table by the door. Not safe. Not safe.

But of a sudden he remembered that Justin was supposed to come. That had been true before. He violated the cardinal rule and cautiously, examining the cost of it carefully, took something other than the operator's truth as valid.

If he was wrong there was no way back from this, and he had no map.

If he was wrong he would not readily be able to reconstruct himself.

. He put the vase back. He sat down to wait.

Justin would come. If not—nothing had ever existed.

He could see and taste and walk in their world. But not really. They would make wreckage of him. But not really. Nothing was—

—real.

Anyway.

---

vi

The lying-in-state was barbaric, the Hall of State echoing with somber funeral music and cloyed with flowers and greenery—a spectacle right out of old Earth, some commentator had remarked, while other news analysts compared it to the similar display at the death of Corey Santessi, chief architect of the Union, whose forty-eight-year tenure on Council first in the Internal Affairs seat and then in the Citizens Bureau, had set the precedent for inertia in the electorates—then too, there had been a need, considering the far-flung colonies and the degree to which a rumor could travel and grow, to demonstrate indisputably that Santessi was dead, to have a decorous passing-of-the-torch and allow all the colleagues who had fought Santessi's influence to get up in public, shed sufficient tears, and deliver pious speeches that stifled speculation by endless repetition.

Much more so, when the deceased was synonymous with Reseune and resurrection, and the victim of assassination.

"We had our differences," Mikhail Corain said in his eulogy, "but Union has suffered an inestimable loss in this tragedy." It would be tasteless to mention that it was a double loss, counting the presumed murderer. "Ariane Emory was a woman of principle and vision. Consider the arks that preserve our genetic heritage, in orbit about distant stars. Consider the rapprochement with Earth and the agreements which have made possible the preservation and recovery of rare species—"

It was one of his better speeches. He had sweated blood over it. There were worrisome mutterings about suppression of evidence in the case, about the unexplained order which Reseune had claimed was buried in the House computers by Emory herself, calling for the termination of Emory's personal guards, a termination carried out by staff without question. There was the notorious case of the Warrick azi kidnapped and tampered with by Rocher extremists, then returned to Reseune. There was the fact of Rocher himself making inflammatory speeches, publicly rejoicing in the assassination, a newsworthy item that got far more press than the legitimate Centrist-affiliated Abolitionists like Ianni Merino regretting the taking of a life, then going on to decry the termination of the azi, all of which was too complicated for the news-services: Ianni never *had* learned the technique of one-issue-at-a-time, and it echoed too closely what Rocher had said. The reporters swarmed the stairways and office doorways like predators staking out a reef, darting out, Scribers running, to ask every Centrist in the Council and Senate: "Do you think there was a conspiracy?" and: "What's your reaction to the Rocher speech?"

Which was a damned narrow line for some Centrists to walk.

He hoped to hell he had defused some of it. That he had been quotable.

Never say that the news-services were a function of the Bureau of Information, whose elected Councillor was Catherine Lao, Ariane Emory's reliable echo on Council: never say that promotions could be had and careers could be made—if reporters came up with material that would make Upper Management happy. It was not the reporters' fault if they sensed that Upper Management wanted more, more and more on the Conspiracy theory: it sure as hell was good theater.

Corain sweated every time he saw a Scriber near one of his party. He had tried to talk to each one of them, personally, urging circumspection and decorum. But cameras were an intoxicant, the schedule of meetings around the funeral was harried and high-pressure, and not every Councillor and not every staffer in the party agreed with the party line.

There were faces for the cameras that had never been available before: the director of Reseune, Giraud Nye, for one. The reporters took endless pains to explain to the viewing public that, contrary to the general assumption, Ariane Emory had not been the Administrator of Reseune, had in fact held no administrative post in Reseune at all for the last fifty-odd years. There were new names to learn. Giraud Nye. Petros Ivanov. Yanni Schwartz.

Nye, damn him, had a certain flair in interviews.

And when a Council seat fell vacant and the Councillor in question had appointed no proxy, then the Bureau Secretary of that particular electorate appointed a proxy. Which in this case was Giraud Nye.

Who might well resign his post in Reseune to run for Emory's seat.

That meant, Corain thought bleakly, Nye would win. *Unless* Jordan Warrick's trial brought up something explosive. Unless Warrick used the trial for a podium, and leveled charges. But Corain's own informants in the Bureau of Internal Affairs said that Warrick was still under house arrest; Merild, in Novgorod, himself under investigation by the Bureau as a possible conspirator, was *not* the lawyer to undertake Warrick's defense, and, God, an Abolitionist lawyer had tried to contact Warrick.

Warrick had sensibly refused, but he had told Internal Affairs to appoint one to advise him—which made a major stir in the news: a man with Warrick's resources, a Special going before a Council hearing with a Bureau-appointed lawyer, like a virtual indigent, because his credit accounts in Reseune were frozen and Reseune could not with any propriety handle both prosecution and defense out of its own legal department.

Solemn music played. The family members gathered for a final moment at the coffin. Then the military honor guard closed it and sealed it. The military escort and Reseune Security waited outside.

Ariane Emory was going to space. No monuments, she had said. Cremation and transport into space, where the carrier *Gallant*, happening to be in Cyteen System, would use one of its missiles to send Emory's ashes sunward. Which was the final extravagance she had asked of the Union government.

The bitch was determined to make sure nobody made off with a sample, that was what. And chose the whole damn sun for a cenotaph.

——————————— vii ———————————

Assassination meant a funeral on too short notice to muster the whole Council—but the Bureau Secretaries were in Novgorod or on the Station; the Cyteen senate had been in session; the Council of Worlds had been in session. And the ambassadors from Earth and Alliance had come down from Cyteen Station. Three Councillors had been accessible: Corain of the Bureau of Citizens, resident on Cyteen; Ilya Bogdanovitch of the Bureau of State; and Leonid Gorodin, of Defense.

An actual two-thirds majority of Centrists, Corain reflected. Damned little good it did at a funeral.

One was expected, of course, to offer Nye welcoming courtesies on his appointment as proxy. No reception: the solemnity of the occasion forbade, even if he had not been Emory's cousin. But one did drop by the offices that had been Emory's. One did present one's respects. One did meet with Nye, however briefly, and offer condolences. And study this man and judge this man and try, in the few moments one was likely to get, to estimate what sort of man this was, who came out of complete shadow inside the enclave of Reseune, to assume the mantle of Ariane Emory. . . .

To judge in five minutes, if it were possible, whether this man, who was a Special, could possibly take up all the linkages of power that Emory had, give the bitch credit, wielded all too well.

"Ser," Nye said, on that meeting, took his hand. "I feel I know you, after all the dinner discussions Ari and I had. She respected you."

That put a body at immediate disadvantage, first because if Nye knew him, it was not mutual; and second, because he remembered what Nye was, and thought how Ariane Emory would react to that description of the situation.

For a half second he felt halfway nostalgic for the bitch. Ariane *had* been a bitch, but he had spent twenty years learning to read her. This man was a total blank. And that gave him a lost and frustrated feeling.

"We opposed each other on issues," Corain murmured, as he had murmured similar things to other successors in his long tenure, "but not in our desire to see the best for the state. I find myself at a loss, ser. I don't think I ever expressed that to her. But I don't think any of us realize even yet what Union will be without her."

"I have serious things to discuss with you," Nye said, not having released his hand. "Concerns that would have been foremost in her mind."

"I'd be pleased to meet with you, at your convenience, ser."

"If you have time in your schedule now—"

It was not the sort of thing Corain liked, abrupt meetings, without briefings. But it was a new relationship, an important relationship. He hated to start it off with an excuse and a refusal to talk.

"If you prefer," he said; and ended up in the office that had been Emory's, with Nye behind the desk, no Florian and Catlin, but an azi staffer named Abban, whose rejuv-silvered hair had no dye, no pretenses, less than Nye, whose hair was silvered brown, who was easily a hundred, and probably the azi was no less than that. Abban served them both coffee, and Corain sat there thinking of the journalistic and political eyes watching every move outside these offices, marking who called, who stayed, and how long.

There was no graceful way to hasten matters.

"I think you know," Nye said quietly, over the coffee, "that a great deal has changed. I'm sure you know that I *will* stand for election."

"I wouldn't be surprised, no."

"I'm a good administrator. I'm not Ari. I don't know how to be. I would like to see the Hope project through: it was very dear to her heart. And I believe in it, personally."

"You know my opinion, I think."

"We will have our differences. Philosophical ones. If I'm the choice of the Science electorate." A sip of coffee. "But the most urgent thing—I think you understand—is the Warrick case."

Corain's heart increased its beats. Trap? Proposition? "It's a terrible tragedy."

"It's a devastating blow to us. As head—ex-head of Reseune Security, I've talked with Dr. Warrick, extensively. I can tell you that it was personal, that it was a situation that had arisen—"

"You're saying he's confessed?"

Nye coughed uncomfortably and sipped at his coffee, then looked up into Corain's eyes. "Ari had trouble keeping her hands off her lab assistants. That was what happened. Justin Warrick, Jordan's son, is a parental replicate. There was old business between Dr. Emory and Jordan Warrick."

More and more tangled. Corain felt an irrational unease at this honesty from a stranger. And did not say a word in the gap Nye left for him.

"Ari transferred an Experimental who was virtually Warrick family," Nye said, "to put pressure on the boy—to put pressure on Jordan. This much we understand now. The boy acted on his own to protect his companion, sent the azi out to people he understood as friends of his father. Unfortunately—the issue isn't presently clear—there were further links that led to the Rocher party. And extremists."

Damn. An evidence-trail like that was trouble. Of course he was supposed to feel the threat.

"We got the azi out, of course," Nye said. "That's what was behind it. There's no way the azi got to Ari: he was under observation at the hospital. But Jordan Warrick found out what Ari had done—to his son. He confronted her in the lab, alone. They quarreled. Ari hit him; he hit her; her head hit the counter-edge. That wasn't murder. It became murder when he took a lab-stool and used it to damage the conduits, shut the cold-lab door and upped the pressure in that line. Unfortunately that kind of damage didn't look like an accident to the engineers.''

"Council will determine that." Murder, between two Specials. And too much entrusted to him by a very dangerous third. Corain warmed his hand with the tiny cup, feeling a certain chill.

"Warrick doesn't want this to go to trial."

"Why?"

"The law has limited power over him; but reputations can be harmed. The son, in particular."

"Meaning—forgive me—someone's made that clear to him."

Nye shook his head gravely. "Motive is going to come out in a trial. There's no way to avoid it. There are other considerations, for us. We *are* going to withhold information in this case. That's why I wanted to talk to you—because it's important that you understand. We know about your interview with Dr. Warrick. We both know that the inquiry could range far afield if it got started. A political free-for-all. Damned little justice. Merino may restrain himself, but Rocher won't, if the case comes before Council, and what could come out at that point isn't in our interest, your interest, certainly not in the interest of the Defense Bureau or our national security; it's not even in Jordan Warrick's interest. He's given us a confession. He doesn't want to testify, —he can't testify, you understand, by psychprobe; and young Justin's evidence under probe is damning. We don't want to use it against his father. The boy's been through enough and it's meaningless cruelty in a case where the murderer has legal immunity."

The room seemed very close of a sudden. Corain thought of recorders. Was damned sure that one was running, somewhere. "What are you asking me?"

"We don't want Ari's problems made public. We don't think that would serve any useful purpose. On the one hand we understand very well what provoked Dr. Warrick; and we have utmost sympathy for him; on the other hand, we very much fear that questioning is going to involve a conspiracy theory. Much as we'd like to get Rocher—that line of questioning is only going to give him a forum he couldn't get otherwise, worse, it'd give him a right-of-discovery in this. I don't think you want that any more than we do.''

Recorders. Dammit. "We have nothing to hide.''

"We're not talking about a cover-up. We're talking about saving an innocent boy unnecessary grief. Jordan Warrick has already confessed. He doesn't want to have his personal life and his son's dragged through a public hearing. The law can't mindwipe him. The worst he can get is close confinement, removal from his work—which in my estimation, would be as tragic as the act he committed.''

Corain thought it through a moment, knowing there was a hook in it somewhere, in the situation or in the proposal, one, but he could not see where. "You mean a non-adversarial settlement. This is a murder case—''

"A case with security implications. A case in which the murderer and the victim's family and resident territory are equally willing to ask for a non-adversary proceeding. If the aim here is justice instead of a political forum—justice would be better served by a settlement in closed Council.''

"There's no precedent for this.''

"Precedent has to be set somewhere—in this case, on the side of humanity. There are no losers by this procedure. Except Rocher loses his forum. Even Ari gains by it. The last thing she would want is to have her death give Rocher a chance to damage the institution she devoted her life to. We can establish a separate facility for Dr. Warrick, provide him everything he needs to continue his work. We don't want a vendetta. We will insist on his retirement—his complete retirement from public life, because we don't want *him* taking advantage of this once the settlement is made. Very plainly, ser, *both* of us have to refrain from making this a political issue. And that includes Dr. Warrick. The settlement will *postpone* trial indefinitely. In case he breaks his silence. We don't want to have our hands tied.''

"I have to think about this. Before I agree to anything, frankly, I'd like the option of talking to Dr. Warrick on neutral ground. Matter of conscience, you understand. A lot of us, who might be the natural opposition—will feel that way."

"Of course. Damn, I hate to have to deal with this on the day of Ari's funeral. But business goes on. It has to."

"I understand you, ser Nye." Corain finished the little cup, made up the nethermost recesses of his mind that he *had* to find out what the going rate was on real coffee, that it was worth the extravagance, that he could afford it, even at two hundred a half kilo, which was the freight from Earth to Cyteen. Another level of his mind was saying that there was a camera somewhere, and still another that all the advantages he had seen in Ariane Emory's death were there—

If a deal could be worked out, if a compromise could be made. Nye was damned sharp. He had to start all over learning his signals the way he had learned Emory's. The man was a cipher, an unknown quantity out of a territory none of his observers could penetrate. Only Warrick. And Warrick was lost to them. That much was clear.

Things were different in Union. From the time that pipe in the laboratory had exploded, the course of history had shifted.

They were entering a period in which the Centrist party might make rapid gains, if they could avoid getting bogged down in wrangling that won no one anything and would not unseat the Expansionists.

The Rubin project and the Fargone project were presumably on hold. The Hope project might be funded, but further expansions and colonizations might be subject to more intense debate. One could look forward to a period of adjustment inside Reseune as well as out, while personalities inside Reseune held in check during the nearly sixty years of Emory's autocratic regime (there was no question who in Reseune had directed the director even after she had resigned the post) were likely to break out and grab for power within the administrative structure.

That also went for other alliances, like those on Council.

Ludmilla deFranco was a freshman Councillor. Nye would be. Powerful Science . . . was going to have a novice at the helm—a damned smart one, but still, a novice who did not have the network to support him. Yet. Two of the five Expansionists were successors this year and Ilya Bogdanovitch was a hundred thirty-two years old and tottering.

Corain murmured the courtesies, thanked the proxy from Reseune, expressed condolences to the family, and walked out with his mind busy with the possibility, the very real possibility, of a Centrist majority in the Council.

It occurred to him that he had not raised the issue of the terminated azi. Merino's issue. He could hardly go back and do it. In fact, he was reluctant to do it, because very possibly that order had come from Reseune Security, for exactly the reasons Nye gave. It was morally repugnant. But it was not, not *quite* as if azi who had served Ariane Emory for most of her hundred and twenty years were harmless. There were, he understood, severe psychological consequences of such a loss; no human reared as CIT could possibly understand the impact of it, except perhaps the staff who routinely worked with azi. He would raise the issue with Warrick. Ask Warrick whether it was warranted. Or whether Warrick thought it had in fact been Emory who had put that instruction in the system.

Damn, he had rather not bring it up at all. The azi were dead. Like Emory. That closed the book. There was no use for that issue; instinct had kept him from raising it.

It was the old proverb. Deal with the devil if the devil has a constituency. And don't complain about the heat.

<hr />

viii

Adm. Leonid Gorodin settled uncomfortably into the chair and took the offered cup. He had come in to pay the requisite courtesy, and Nye had said: "There's something I have to discuss with you. About the Fargone facility. About the Rubin project. And Hope. Have you got a moment?"

It was not Gorodin's habit to discuss any issue with the opposition or with reporters—without his aides, without references, in an office his own staff had not vetted. But the same instinct for intrigue that said it was dangerous also said it was the one chance he might have without having Corain aware that he was in serious conference with the opposition.

And the names were the names he wanted to hear.

"I truly hate to get to business on the day of Ari's funeral," Nye said. "But there's really no choice. Things can slip out of control so quickly." He took a sip of coffee. "You know I'm going to run for Ari's seat."

"I expected," Gorodin said. "I expect you'll win."

"It's a critical time for us. Ari's death—the potential loss of Warrick on top of it—it's a double blow. Not only to us. To Union. To our national interests. You understand that I have a top-level security clearance. Equal to Ari's. I have to have. I won't ask you for answers; but I *am* associated with your projects— I worked with your predecessor during the war—"

"I'm aware you have the clearance. And that you're privy to those files. And you're keeping them out of the investigation."

"Absolutely. No discussion of those files and no interview with a staffer on those projects, except by personnel with equivalent clearance. You don't need to worry about leaks, admiral. *Or* a trial."

Gorodin's heart jumped. He wished he had not heard that. There was the likelihood of recorders, and he had to make his reaction clear. "What are you saying?"

"Non-adversary settlement. Warrick did it. He's confessed. The motive was blackmail and sexual harassment. His son, you understand. With a complicated situation that—between you and me—could do the boy great harm. Warrick's deal is simple: a facility where he can continue his work. We won't agree to Fargone. It'll have to be on Cyteen. But I've talked to Corain."

"Already."

"An hour ago. I didn't mention the security aspects of this. We talked politics. You know and I know, admiral, that there are radical elements involved on the fringes of this case. There are people going to be going over the testimony of witnesses that *can* be psychprobed, and going over it, and going over it. There are elements of Justin Warrick's testimony that involve the Fargone project, that are going to have to be classified."

"Warrick discussed it with his *kid?*"

"The motive for the transfer was the boy. Justin Warrick knows—more than he ought to know. If there have been leaks in this, admiral, they've all come from Jordan Warrick. And frankly, if it gets to trial, I'm afraid the threads of motivation—run into some very sensitive areas. But if we black out too much of the transcript, that raises other suspicions—in some minds, —doesn't it?"

"My God, what's your fucking security worth? Who else knows?"

"Very likely the azi that was kidnapped. He's Justin's."

"My God."

"It's not likely that Rocher's boys cracked him. He's Alpha and he's a tape designer—the azi is, understand. Not an easy subject. But there is the possibility that he wasn't aware of having classified information. That's why we went to Lu's office when we needed help breaking him out of there. We needed to get hold of him alive and debrief him, in the case we missed someone. Fortuitously and fortunately, the action took care of the kidnappers. All of them. We think. But we weren't overusing our authority when we told Lu that azi was a security risk. I suppose the rush of events has been too rapid for all of us. Ari was going to send me to the city with the report for Lu. Unfortunately—"

"You don't think there was any possible motivation on Warrick's part, involving the azi and Rocher—"

"When he killed Ari? A crime of anger that didn't start out that way: he hit her, that was all. But when she turned out to be seriously injured he realized he'd just killed his chance of appointment at Fargone. So he killed her and tried to make it look like an accident. It wasn't quite in cold blood; it wasn't quite otherwise either. He hated her. I'm afraid Ari had serious weaknesses when it came to adolescent boys. A great mind. Correspondingly eccentric vices. Frankly, we're anxious to avoid having that aspect of Ari put out in public view. Conspiracies—no. There weren't. You can interview Warrick yourself if you like. Or his son. We have his deposition under psychprobe. Not Jordan Warrick's, of course, but the son's indicates fairly well what was going on. There are also some vids that are—very explicit. We don't intend to erase them. But they don't have to go out to the news-services. It's a very old story, I'm afraid. Blackmail. Outraged parent. A cover-up that turned into murder."

"Damn." *Get my son out of there*, Warrick had said. Had meant it, evidently. "Damn."

"We want to honor our commitments. The arrangement we have in mind puts Jordan Warrick in a facility of his own, under guard. And he can go on doing work for you. We'll do the testing. You won't have to worry about its integrity. It's altogether a humane solution, one that conserves a talent we can't afford to lose.''

"You've talked to Corain."

"He says he's got to study the idea. I tried to point out, there are no disadvantages to him in supporting a settlement. What does anyone gain from a prosecution of this case? What does anyone gain, except Rocher and his cronies? —And we've lost terribly by this. Not only the mind. You understand . . . we're still committed to the projects.''

"The Fargone facility.''

"We assume that will go forward. Perhaps—the military can make use of more of it than we planned.''

"Meaning the Rubin project is going under.''

"No. We're still committed to that.''

"Without Dr. Emory?'' Gorodin drew a large breath. ''You think you can succeed.''

Nye was silent for a moment. ''Refill,'' he said to the azi who served them, and that man, gray and silent, came and poured in both cups.

Nye sipped thoughtfully. Then: ''Do you want the technical details?''

"I leave that to the scientists. My interest is practical. And strategic. Can you go on from Emory's notes?''

"Which had you rather have duplicated? A chemist who is, admittedly, extraordinary in potential. Or Emory herself?''

Gorodin swallowed down a mouthful. ''You're serious.''

"Let me go into some of the surface technicalities, at least. The project demands a subject with an extraordinary amount of documentation—on the biochemical level. There aren't many subjects of the quality we want, who have that kind of documentation. Both Ari and Rubin have it: Rubin because of his medical problems, Ari because she was born to Emory and Carnath when they were both above a century in age. Born in Reseune labs, of course. By a process we ran, on which our records are immaculate. Her father was dead when she was born; her mother died when she was seven. Her uncle Geoffrey brought her up beyond that. She succeeded Geoffrey Carnath as director of Reseune when she was sixty-two. And she was Olga Carnath's own prize project, the subject of intensive study and recording first by her mother and then by Geoffrey Carnath. Suffice it to say, her documentation is equal to Rubin's, if not more extensive. More than that—Ari always *intended* that she eventually be one of the Specials affected by this project. She left abundant notes—for her successor.''

''My God.''

''Why not? She has the value. Now that she's gone, granted her theories are valid—we have a choice between recovering a chemist who, frankly, means nothing to us, or Ari—whose mind, I don't hesitate to say—is on a level with Bok or Strehler, whose research has had profound effect on national security. And we *can* do it.''

''You're serious.''

''Absolutely. We see no reason to abandon the project. There are essentials: Warrick is one. You understand—as many of the elements of Ari's life we can study, the better our chances of success.''

''What—about Rubin?''

''It would still be possible to go ahead with that. It would be useful as a control. And a cover under the cover, so to speak. I don't want the Rubin project in Reseune. I don't want it impacting what we plan to do. You understand—the name of the game is re-tracing. Intensive monitoring—Ari was used to that, but her successor ought not to have direct contact with someone else undergoing the same thing. We'd have to run both halves of the Rubin project at Fargone.''

''You imply you intend to do this—whether or not you have official support.''

''I'm seeking that support. I want to save Warrick. I want to cooperate fully with the military. We need the kind of security and cover you can provide us—at least until the new Ari can surface. Then it appears as a Reseune project—a thoroughly *civilian* project. That's useful, isn't it?''

''God.'' Gorodin drank down the other half of his coffee. And held out his cup to the azi.

''Abban,'' Nye said. The azi came and filled the cup—while Gorodin used the delay to do some fast adding.

''What,'' he said then, carefully, ''does this have to do with Warrick?''

''We need him. We need him to go on with his work.''

''Him? To reconstruct *her*? Working on *her* tapes?''

''No. That wouldn't be wise. I'm talking about Reseune. Remember—we have to think in twenty-, fifty-year terms.

He's still young. He's only now showing what he *can* do. His own research interlocks with Ari's. Let me be honest with you: Ari's notes are extremely fragmentary. She was a genius. There are gaps of logic in her notes—sort of an *of course* that Ari could bridge and didn't need to write down. We can't guarantee success: no program of this sort can. We only know that we have a better chance with Ari, that we knew intimately, than with a stranger that we don't. She coded a great deal. Her leaps from point to point, the connections . . . in a field she damned near built . . . make her notes a real maze. If we lose the principals of Ari's life—if we can't recover something like the life Ari lived—if certain people aren't available to consult, then I think our chances of seeing this project work go down and down. Ultimately Ari's notes could become meaningless. The matrix becomes lost, you see, the social referent irrecoverable. But we have it now. I think we can do it. I *know* we can do it.''

"But what damn use is all of this, then—beyond recovering Emory herself? How many people are we going to have that kind of record on? What can it apply to? It can't get us Bok."

"Emory herself is not negligible. Emory able to take up her work where she left off—but at about age twenty. Maybe younger. We don't know. We'll find out. Understand: *what we learn* doing this will tell us how much data we have to have with other projects. Like Bok. We just have to be damned careful this round. Because if the worst-case holds, *every* precaution is necessary: *every* influence is irreplaceable. Getting Ari back is step one. If there's going to be an amplification of her work on personality formation—*Ari* is the key to it. We have a chance with her. We *know* her. We can fill in the gaps in the information and make corrections if it looks necessary. We don't know Rubin to that extent. We don't have the headstart even with him we do with her, do you see? Rubin has become a luxury. Retrieving Ari Emory is a necessity. We can try it on our own, but it would be a hell of a lot easier—with Defense Bureau support.''

"Meaning money."

Nye shook his head. "Cover. The ability to hold on to Warrick. The ability to shield what we're doing. The authority to protect our research—and our subject—from Internal Affairs."

"Ah." Gorodin drew a deep breath. "But money—it always comes to money."

"We can bear our end of it if you fund the Rubin project. But the necessity to protect our subjects is absolute. Success or failure hinges on that."

Gorodin leaned back in his chair and chewed his lip. And thought again about recorders. "Have you talked to Lu?"

"Not yet."

"You haven't mentioned this to anyone outside Reseune."

"No. I don't intend to. We had one security breach—with the azi. We've covered it. There won't be another."

Gorodin thought about it—civilians running their own affairs under military cover. One breach and God knew what else. Too many amateurs.

Reseune wanted to start a close cooperation, on a project Gorodin, dammit, saw shifting the balance of power irrevocably toward Union—

Ariane Emory experimenting with a kid on Fargone had seemed a hell of a lot safer. Reseune trying to raise the dead seemed—

—hell, go for the big gain. Go for everything.

It was a pittance, to the Defense budget.

"I don't think there's much problem," Gorodin said. "We just appropriate the Fargone facility. We invoke the Military Secrets Act. We can cover any damn thing you need."

"No problem," Nye said. "No problem in that. As long as it stays classified."

"No problem with that," Gorodin said.

"So we stamp everything Rubin project," Nye said. "We build the Fargone facility; we work the Rubin project under deep secrecy out there; we get deeper cover for our work on Cyteen."

"Two for the price of one?" It struck Gorodin after he had said it that the expression was a little coarse, on the day of Emory's funeral. But, hell, it was her resurrection they were talking about. Not identity, Warrick had said. *Ability*. That was close enough.

He was damned sure Giraud Nye had the inclination to keep Reseune's control over the project. The Project, meaning an embryo in a womb-tank and a kid growing up in Reseune. Twenty years.

He suddenly added that to his own age. He was a hundred twenty-six, ground time. A hundred forty-six by then. And Nye—was not young.

It was the first time it had ever really hit him—what Warrick had meant about the time factor in Reseune. He was used to time-dilation—in a spacer's sense: that hundred forty-six ground-time would lie far lighter on him, who lost months of ground-time in days of jump. But Reseune's kind of time meant lifetimes.

"We'd like that second project full-scale," Nye said. "Having a comparative study could save us in a crisis, and we're beyond any tentative test of theories. Comparison is going to give us our answers. It's not a luxury."

Part of the Rubin project at Fargone meant part of the data within easy reach. And meant a fail-safe. Gorodin always believed in fail-safes—in equipment; or in planning. Spacer's economy. Two was never too many of anything.

"Do it," he said. "Makes cover a hell of a lot easier." There was the matter of clearing it with Lu, and the chiefs of staff. But Lu and the chiefs of staff would go with anything that promised this kind of return and put Emory's work at the disposal of Defense.

Defense took a lot of projects under its wing. Some were conspicuous failures. Those that worked—paid for all the rest.

ix

Steps passed the door continually. More than usual. There were voices. Some of them Justin thought he knew; someone had stopped outside the door, a group of people talking.

Please, he thought. *Please. Somebody stop here.* He hoped for a moment; and feared. He listened, sitting on the sleeping mat that was all the furniture in the room. He clenched his hands together in the hollow of his crossed legs.

"Call Ari," he kept saying to anyone who dealt with him. "Tell her I want to talk with her."

But they were azi. They had no authority to go above their Supervisor. And as many times as he asked, the Supervisor never came.

It was a suicide cell he was in, padded walls and door, just a sink and the toilet and the sleeping mat. The light was always on. Food came in water-soluble wrappers little more substantial than toilet paper, without utensils. They had taken his clothes and given him only hospital pajamas, made of white paper. They had not questioned him any more. They had not spoken to him again. He did not know how much time had passed, and his sleeping was erratic with depression and lack of cues from lights or activity outside. And the tape-flashes, seductive and destructive. He refused to let the flashes take hold in the isolation. He refused it even when it would have been consolation.

Not me, he kept thinking, keeping himself awake, away from the dreams. Not my choice. I'm not hers. I won't think her thoughts.

Ari was holding him hostage, he thought. She was holding him and maybe Grant against some threat of Jordan's to go to the Bureau with charges. Maybe she had arrested Jordan too. Maybe Jordan could *not* help him. But in any case—the police would come. And they had not psychprobed him again; they could not psychprobe Jordan.

It was Grant who was vulnerable. She would use Grant against Jordan—and use him too. He had no doubt of it.

He hoped for the police to come. Internal Affairs. Science Bureau. Anyone.

He hoped that was the small commotion outside.

But he had hoped that—time after time.

Grant would have been waiting for him to come back; but instead it was security that would have come in on him, hauled him off for more questions—

He heard the electronic lock tick. The door opened.

"Ser Nye wants to talk to you," one of two azi said; both Security. "Please come."

He got up. His knees went to jelly. He walked out into the light, knowing it was another psychprobe session; but at least he would get a chance to say something to Giraud, at least he would have a chance for a half-dozen words before they put the drug into him.

That they just let him walk loose was the last thing he was prepared for. He felt himself dizzy, his knees aching and shaking so it was hard to navigate.

Tape-flash again. And Florian—

Down the hall to the barren little interview room he had seen before. He reached the open door and stopped, dazed and disoriented by the realization it was not Giraud Nye at the table. It was a stout round-faced man that for a bewildered second his mind insisted to make into Giraud's lean form.

Not Giraud.

Denys Nye, rising from his chair with a distressed look.

"Where's Grant?" Justin demanded. "Where's my father? What's going on?" His voice gave way on him. His legs shook as he reached the narrow table and leaned on it in Denys' face. "I've got the right to talk to my family, dammit! I'm a minor! *Remember?*"

"Sit down," Denys said, fluttering a hand. "Sit. Please. —Get him something to drink."

"I don't want anything! I want to know—"

"Please," Denys said in his quiet, distressed way, and made a second appeal with his hand. "Please sit down. —Get him something. —Please, sit down."

Justin fell into the chair, feeling a crying jag coming on. He clamped his jaw and drew breaths until he had it under control; and Denys sank into his seat, folded his hands on the table in front of him and let him calm down while one of the azi brought back a soft drink and set it down on the table.

"What's in it?"

"Nothing. Nothing. Poor boy. Damn this all anyway. Have they told you about Ari?"

It was a strange thing to say. It made no sense. It fluttered like a cold chill through his nerves. "What *about* Ari? Where's my father?"

"Ari's dead, Justin."

It was like the world jolted sideways. For a moment everything went out of focus. Then where he was came crashing in on him. Where he was and what they were doing and the silence all around him.

Dead. Like not-natural-dead. Like—

—the plane crashed?

—some crazy person—in Novgorod?

"Jordan found out what she was doing to you," Denys said in the gentlest voice Justin had ever heard him use, "and he killed her. Locked her into the cold-lab and killed her."

He just sat there a moment. It was not true. It was not true.

Jordan had no idea what Ari had done. He had covered everything. And Ari was not dead. Ari could not be—dead.

"Jordan admits it," Denys said in that quiet tone. "You know they can't do anything. Legally. The law can't touch him for—questioning, or anything like that. Not psychprobe. Certainly not mindwipe. Jordie's all right. He's safe. I promise you."

He was shaking. He picked up the cup and slopped it carrying the drink to his mouth. He slopped it again setting it down. The icy liquid soaked his knee. There was no sense to things. He could not get his mind to function. "What about Grant? I told him I was going to come back. I didn't come back—"

"Grant's still in hospital. He's safe. Jordan's been to see him. Jordan's flying to Novgorod this afternoon. They're working out an arrangement for him to leave Reseune."

"That's a damned lie!" They were starting to work psych games with him. He saw it coming. He flung himself up and came face to face with the two azi that moved to stop him. He froze. They froze.

"Boy. Justin. Please. Please, sit down. Listen to me."

"Ari's not dead!" he yelled at Denys. "It's a damned lie! What are you trying to do? What is *she* trying to do?"

"Oh, God, boy, sit down. Listen to me. Your father won't have much time. Please. *Damn* that brother of mine! So damned afraid of putting you in hospital— Look. Sit down."

He sat. There was nothing else to do. They could do anything they wanted to.

"Listen to me, Justin. Internal Affairs has been questioning Jordie; Jordie begged Giraud to keep you out of it. He didn't want the story out, do you understand? He didn't want them psychprobing you. Giraud just flat refused them permission. Jordie backed him on it. But my damn brother went off to the capital and kept the lid on, and they kept saying you were all right—" Denys drew a small breath, reached across and laid his hand on Justin's on the table. "You're not all right. Dammit, it wasn't like Giraud's was the first psychprobe you'd had in the last few weeks, is it?"

He jerked his hand from under Denys'. "Let me alone!"

"Do you want a sedative?"

"I don't want anything. I want out of here! I want to talk to my father!"

"No. You don't. Not in that tone of voice. Understand me? He's leaving. He won't be back."

He stared at Denys. *Not be back—*

"Council's drawn up a plan," Denys said, "to allow him a facility over in Planys. He *won't* be able to travel. He won't be able to call you—for quite a while. I don't want you to upset him, son. He's got to meet with a Council inquiry tomorrow. He's got to get through that in one piece. Are you understanding me? It's very important."

It was real. It had happened. He stared into Denys Nye's worried eyes with the feeling that the whole world was chaos, except it was going to sort itself out again in some terrible new shape no one he loved lived in.

"Do you want the sedative? No tricks, Justin. I promise you. Just enough to let you rest awhile before you talk with him."

. He shivered. And controlled it. "No," he said. "Let me get dressed. Let me clean up."

"Absolutely." Denys patted his hand. "You can use the shower down the hall. I've told them to bring clothes for you."

He nodded.

"I'm going to have Petros have a look at you."

"No!"

"When you get through this. When you're satisfied everything's all right. No one's going to touch you. You've had enough of that. God knows. Are you getting tape-flashes?"

The question triggered one. Or simple memory. It shamed him. Like some dark, twisted side of himself that was always—very like Ari. That—dammit—had learned what she did—felt good. He never wanted a psychtech wandering through that. He never wanted Jordan to know, he never wanted to let it show on his face what was going on in the dark inside him. And maybe everyone knew.

Ari had said—she had pictures. If Ari was dead—the House investigators had them. Had everything.

There was no dignity left him then, except to keep from noticing they knew, or admitting the truth to anyone.

"Listen to me, son." Denys' hand closed on his again. It was soft and warm and any human contact affected him in terrible ways. "Son, I can't excuse what Ari did. But there was more to her than—"

He jerked back.

He saw Denys read him. Saw the thinking going on in Denys' eyes and tried to keep the color from his face. "—than you want to hear about," Denys concluded. "I know. Listen. *Listen to me. Make this register*— All right?"

"All right. I'm with you."

"Brave lad. Listen now. Jordie's covering—for us and for you. He's lying to the press, *and* the Council. He's telling them it was Ari standing in the way of his transfer. Every reason in the world but the truth—and they can't psychprobe him. You have to understand, Justin—you're . . . *him*, as much as you're his son. That puts a freight on everything that happened between you and Ari that—that pushed him beyond the limit. It was old business—between him and Ari. He understands what happened to you. Yes. You know what I'm telling you. And he loves you very much. But part of it is his own pride. Do you understand? Those of us who work inside these walls—know how tangled and complicated even a parent's love can be . . . in a moment when he was pushed too far. Everything he wants is gone, except you. And *you* can take everything else he's got—if you go in there with your emotions out of control. I want you to get control of yourself. Let him take a little peace of mind out of here with him. Let him see his son's all right. For his sake."

"*Why won't they let me go with him?*"

"Because you're a minor. Because of the security arrangements. Because, truthfully, I couldn't get Giraud to agree to it. Security, they keep saying."

"That's a damn lie!"

"Listen, now. I'm going to get some arrangement where you *can* get visiting privileges. Not right away. Maybe not even this year. But time and quiet can do a lot for this situation. They're scared as hell there's a conspiracy—the Winfield-Kruger mess, you know."

O God. My fault. My fault. "They *can't* think Jordan was in on that. *I* was. Giraud ran the psychprobe. Run it again! I can swear he didn't know a damn thing—"

"Unfortunately, son, that's exactly the kind of thing Jordie wants to prevent—getting you involved in the investigation. There *is* fire under that smoke. I'm afraid Jordie was meeting with a man called Merild, who had connections that are run-

ning into some very dark corners. He was also meeting in secret with a number of very high-up Centrists who are linked to
Ianni Merino—the Abolitionists. And Rocher has come out
with a very inflammatory statement about Ari's death that Merino hasn't quite repudiated. A lot of people in the government
are running scared, scared of investigations, scared of guilt by
association. Internal Affairs demanded to get hold of Grant.
Giraud had to do a probe to satisfy them—''

"Oh, my God—''

"He *had* to. I know. I *know*, son. But they could have
learned too much from you. Justin, the shock waves Ari's
death has generated—are enormous. You can't imagine how
enormous. The government is in crisis. Careers are in jeop-
ardy. Lives are. There's an almost universal conviction that
this *had* to be political; that the reasons for what's changed
their lives has some meaning beyond a dissatisfied scientist
breaking Ari's skull. It's human to think like that. And Jordie's
testimony—the fact that he can't testify under probe—the fact
that Florian and Catlin were put down—some posthumous order of Ari's, they think. . . . Yes. They're gone too. —People
sense something else going on. They *want* to think something
else is going on. Crime of passion, from an education tape-
designer, you know, gives people cold chills. We're supposed
to be too rational. Jordie's going to have to do the best damn
psych-out in front of the Council committee he's ever done in
his life. And for Jordie's own sake, the quieter things stay for
the next few years, the better. Just be patient. Jordie's not
without friends. He's not old. Forty-six isn't old. He can
outlast the furor, if you don't do something that blows the lid
off everything we've arranged.''

He found enough air to breathe finally. He tried to think that
through. He tried to think—what was the safest thing for his
father and what his father would want. Tried *not* to think—O
God!—that it was his own mistakes that had caused it.

"Can you get yourself together?'' Denys pressed him.

"I'm together. I'm all right. What about Grant?'' *Oh, God,
they could mindwipe him. Florian dead! And Catlin—*

"Giraud is assigning Grant back to you.''

Good things no longer happened to him. He did not believe
them. He did not trust them.

"He *has*,'' Denys said, "because I just signed the papers.

Get through this business with Jordan and you can get him out of hospital. —Do you want that sedative, son?"

Justin shook his head. Because Jordan would know if there was any drug involved. He had read him all along. Jordan must have. He hoped—

He hoped he could keep from tape-flashes if Jordan hugged him. That was how bad it was. That was what Ari had done to him. He was losing his father. He was not going to see him again. And he could not even tell Jordan goodbye without feeling Ari's hands on him.

"I'm all right," he said. If he could not lie to Denys and make it credible, he had no hope of lying to Jordan. Getting himself together had to start now. Or he was not going to make it.

———————————— X ————————————

Mikhail Corain looked anxiously at the aide who had laid the fiche-card on his desk. "Dell's?" he asked.

The aide nodded.

Corain waved a hand, dismissing the aide, slid the card into the desktop viewer and tilted the screen.

Dell Hewitt was a member of Internal Affairs. She happened to be a Centrist who was a friend of Ginny Green, who had been the Centrist candidate in Internal Affairs in the last election. And in this nervous time of investigations and committees rummaging into every dark corner in Novgorod, she had laid more than her own career on the line with what she had leaked to Yvonne Hahner, who she knew would leak it to Dellarosa in his staff. As good as wrap it up and mail it.

Regarding the azi Catlin and Florian: no conclusion. Perhaps the termination was ordered outside the system. Perhaps inside, by persons unknown. Perhaps Ariane Emory did order the termination, not wanting them interviewed. Perhaps she felt it was humane. Perhaps it was some kind of death pact the azi themselves had asked for: Reseune says they would have been very profoundly affected by the thought of losing her. Also, Reseune says, they were Security, but with a fix on Emory. They were therefore capable of harm to Reseune, and retraining would be difficult if not impossible without

*mindwipe, which their age precluded. Giraud Nye refuses to
open the books on their psychsets. The order did come under
Emory's personal code. Giraud Nye cites security considerations in refusing to allow Internal Affairs technicians to examine the computers.*

Corain sipped the coffee warmed by the desk-plate. Two
hundred fifty cred the half-kilo. They were damned small sips.
But, a man was due a little luxury, who had been a scratch-
and-patch outback farmer most of his life.

No *new* news. That was disappointing. He traced down the
long list of things Reseune had refused to allow Internal Affairs to do, and read the legal justifications. Reseune's legal
staff was winning every round. And Internal Affairs, at the up-
permost administrative level, was not hitting back.

Then:

*Internal Affairs is investigating the rumor at Reseune that
certain genesets were checked out and not logged. This means
someone could have duplicated genesets that ought not to exist. . . .*

Azi-running? God, you can get a geneset from a blood
sample. From anything. Why would anyone steal one from
Reseune?

*. . . such as Experimentals and Special material which can-
not otherwise be obtained.*

*Smuggling actual genesets prepared for use by Reseune re-
quires cryogenics which would be detected in shipment unless
simply omitted from manifests. However—the digitalized
readout of a geneset is another story. Reseune in the person of
administrator Nye denies that there is any such activity, or that
documentation could have been released without record.*

*Also there is some rumor on staff that there have been
unwarranted terminations. Reseune is blocking this inquiry.*

Corain gnawed his lip. And thought: *I don't want to know
this. Not right now. Things are too delicate. My God, if this
hits the streets—all the arrangements can come unglued.*

A side note from Dellarosa: *What about the chance Emory
was running the genesets herself? Or ordered it? What's a
Special worth, to someone who has access to a birth-lab?*

Votes. A Council seat. Support from the very, very rich.
Corain took a swallow of coffee. And sweated.

Physical evidence suffered from inexpert handling from the

Moreyville police. Certain surfaces in the outer lab and the cold-lab have Jordan Warrick's fingerprints, Emory's fingerprints, the prints of the azi attendants, of certain of the other regular users of the lab, and a number of students who have come forward to be printed. The door bears a similar number of prints. No presence-tracers were available to the Moreyville police who did the preliminary investigation. Subsequent readings would have been meaningless due to the traffic in and out of the lab by police and residents. The security door records were released and corroborate the comings and goings given in verbal testimony. Again, Reseune will not allow Internal Affairs technicians access to the computers.

The autopsy results say that Emory froze to death, that the skull fracture was contributory, in that she was probably unconscious at the time of the pipe rupture. She was suffering from extremely minor rejuv failure and had arthritis of the right knee and mild asthma, all of which were known to her doctors. The only unexpected finding was a small cancer in the left lung, localized, and unknown to her physician at the time: it is a rare type, but less rare among early pioneers on Cyteen. The treatment would have been immediate surgery, with drug therapy. This type of cancer does respond to treatment but frequently recurs, and the prognosis combined with other immune-system problems due to the rejuv difficulty would have been less than favorable.

God.

She was dying anyway.

---

xi

Justin composed himself with several deep breaths as he walked down the hall beside Denys Nye. He had showered, shaved, was dressed in his ordinary work-clothes, blue sweater, brown pants. He was not shaking. He had asked for three aspirin and made sure that that was all he had gotten before he swallowed them. As a tranquilizer it was at least enough, with his exhaustion, to dull the nerves.

Jordan *looked* all right. He would. Jordan was like that.

God, he couldn't have killed her. He couldn't. They're making him say these things. Someone is lying.

"Hello, son."

It was not one of the cold little interview rooms. It was an administrative office. Denys was not going to leave. He had explained that. Neither were the azi guards going to leave. And a recorder was running, because no one trusted anything, and they wanted to be able to prove to investigators that nothing had gone on in the meeting.

"Hello," he said back. And thought he ought to go and put his arms around his father at a time like this, in front of all the people who would see the tape, but, dammit, Jordan was not inviting it, Jordan was being reserved and quiet and had things to say to him Jordan needed to get in order. All he had to say was goodbye. All he *could* say was goodbye. Anything else— *anything* else—and he could make a mistake that would go on that tape and ruin everyone's life worse than he had already done.

Things like: *I'm sorry I tried to deal with Ari. I'm sorry I didn't tell you. I'm sorry you had to find it out yourself.*

It's all my doing. All of it.

Don't bring up Grant, Denys had warned him. Don't bring it up at all. The committees could want to talk to him if you do. Let them forget about him.

"Are you all right?" Jordan asked him.

"I'm fine. Are you?"

"Son, I—" Jordan's mouth trembled.

O God, he's going to lose it. In front of all of them.

"They told me everything. You don't have to tell me. Please."

Jordan drew a deep breath and eased it out again. "Justin, I want you to know *why* I did it. Because Ari was an influence this world didn't need. I did it the same way I'd try to fix a bad tape. I don't have any remorse for it. I won't ever have. It was a perfectly logical decision. Now someone else is running Reseune and I'm transferred, which is exactly what I wanted, where I won't have Ari changing my designs and using her name on my work she's done over. I'm free. I'm just sorry— sorry it blew up like this. I'm a better scientist than I am a plumber. That's what the investigators said. I backed up the pressure and they caught it in the monitor records."

The anger had been there at the start, real anger, profound, shattering anger. It cooled at the last. It became a recitation, a learned part, an act meant to look like an act. He was grateful for that last coolness, when Jordan threw the ball to him.

I know why you did it, he almost said, then thought that that could come out wrong. Instead he said: "I love you."

And nearly lost control. He bit his lip till it bled. Saw Jordan with his own jaw clenched.

"I don't know if they'll let me write to you," Jordan said.

"I'll write."

"I don't know if they'll give me the letters." Jordan managed a small laugh. "They imagine we can pass messages in *hello, how's the weather?*"

"I'll write anyway."

"They think—they think there's some damn conspiracy. There isn't. I promise you that, son. There isn't anyone who knew and there wasn't supposed to be anyone who knew. But they're afraid out there. People think of Ari as political. That's how she was important to them. They don't think of her first as a scientist. They don't understand what it means when someone takes your work and turns it inside out. They don't understand the ethics that were violated."

Ethics that were violated. God. He's playing for the cameras. The first was a speech to the committee but the last was a code to me. If he goes on any longer they're going to catch him at it.

"I love you," Jordan said then. "More than anything."

And held out his arms. It was over. The play was over. The actors had to embrace. It was all right to cry now.

He would not see Jordan after this. Not hear from him. Maybe forever.

He crossed the little space like an automaton. He hugged Jordan and Jordan hugged him hard, a long time. A long time. He bit his lip through, because the pain was all that helped keep him focused. Jordan was crying. He felt the sobs, quiet as they were. But maybe that would help Jordan's case. Maybe they had done all right, in front of the cameras. He wished he could cry. But for some reason he was numb, except the pain, and the taste of blood.

Jordan had played it too hard, had sounded too cold-blooded, too dangerous. He should not have done that. They might play that tape on the news. People would be afraid of him. They might think he was crazy. Like the Alphas that went over the edge. Like Bok's clone. They might stop him from his work.

He almost shouted: *He's lying. My father is lying.* But Jordan was holding on to him. Jordan had done exactly what Jordan wanted to do. Jordan had not been locked in a room for a week. He knew what was going on in the world, he had been talking to the investigators. Jordan was playing a part, running psych on all of them, that was what he was doing: Jordan was going to go to that Senate committee and get himself the best deal he could; and maybe that bit would keep the tape off the news, because Jordan's work was very important to Defense and the military could silence anything it wanted.

"Come on," Denys said.

Jordan let him go and let him leave. Denys walked him out the door.

Then Justin cried. Leaned against the wall outside after the door had shut and cried until his gut ached.

xii

He had thought there could be no more shocks.

But Petros Ivanov met him at the door of the hospital, took him away from his Security escort and walked with him to Grant's room.

"How is he?" he asked before they got there.

"Not doing well," Ivanov said. "I wanted to warn you." Ivanov said other things, how they had had to put Grant under probe again; and how he had gone into shock; how they took him out to the garden in a chair every day, how they massaged him and bathed him and waited on treatment because Denys had kept telling them Justin was going to come, this day, and the next day and the next—they were *afraid* to probe Grant again, because he was right on the edge, and they thought there might be illegal codewords, words not in the psych record.

"No," he said before he pushed Grant's door open. And wanted to kill Ivanov. Wanted to beat him to a bloody pulp and go for the staff next and Giraud Nye into the bargain. "No. There aren't any codewords. Dammit, I *told* him I'd come back. And he was waiting."

Grant was still waiting. Right now he had his hair combed,

looked comfortable enough unless you knew he did not move on his own. Unless you knew he had lost weight and the skin was too transparent and you saw the glassiness in the eyes and took his hand and felt the lack of muscle tone.

"Grant," he said, sitting down on the edge of the bed. "Grant, it's me. It's all right."

Grant did not even blink.

"Get out of here," he said to Ivanov, with a glance over his shoulder; and did not try to be polite.

Ivanov left.

He shifted over and gently unfastened the restraints they kept on him. He was calmer than he had thought he could be. He picked up Grant's arm and laid it across him so he had room to sit, and raised the head of the bed a little. He reached then and with two fingers along Grant's jaw, turned his face toward him. It was like moving a mannequin. But Grant blinked.

"Grant? It's Justin."

Another blink.

O God, he had thought Grant would be gone. He had thought he was coming in here to find a half-corpse that they could not do anything with except put down. He was prepared for that . . . in five minutes from the front door to Grant's room he had gone from the hope of recovering Grant to the expectation of losing him. Now it was full circle.

Now he was scared. He was *safe* if Grant was dead.

O God! Damn *me for thinking like that! Where did I learn to think like that? Where did I learn to be that cold?*

Is it tape-flash too?

What did she do *to me?*

He felt like he was coming apart—felt hysteria welling up like a tide; and Grant did not need that. His hand was shaking when he took Grant's hand in his. And even then he thought of Ari's apartment, how the room had looked. He began talking to distract himself, not knowing what he was saying, not wanting to think again the thought that had flashed through his mind, like it was somebody else's. He knew that he could not touch people anymore without it being sexual. He could not hold on to a friend. Or embrace his father. He kept remembering, day and night; and he knew that it was dangerous to love anyone because of the ugliness in his mind, because he was always thinking thoughts that would horrify them if they knew.

And because Ari was right, if you loved anyone They could get to you, the way They had gotten to Jordan. Grant was the way to him. Of course. That was why They had let him have Grant back.

He was not on his own now. Someday Grant was going to lay him wide open to his enemies. Maybe get him killed. Or worse—do to him what he had done to Jordan.

But until then he was not alone, either. Until then, for a few years, he could have something precious to him. Until Grant found out what kind of ugliness he had in him. Or even after Grant found out. Grant, being azi, would forgive anything.

"Grant, I'm here. I told you I'd come. I'm here."

Perhaps for Grant it was still that night. Perhaps he could go back to that, and pick it up again at the morning after.

Another blink, and another.

"Come on, Grant. No more nonsense. You fooled them. Come on. Squeeze my hand. You can do that."

Fingers tightened. Just slightly. The breathing rate increased. He shook at Grant slightly, reached up and flicked a finger against his cheek.

"Hey. Feel that? Come on. I'm not taking any of this. It's me. Dammit, I want to talk to you. Pay attention."

The lips acquired muscle tone. Relaxed again. The breaths were hard now. Several rapid blinks.

"Are you listening?"

Grant nodded.

"Good." He was shaking. He tried to stop it. "We've got a problem. But I've got permission to get you out of here. If you can wake up."

"Is it morning?"

He drew a quick breath, thought at first to say yes, then thought that disorientation was dangerous. That Grant was wary. That Grant might pull back at a lie. "A little later than that. There was a glitch-up. A bad one. I'll explain later. Can you move your arm?"

Grant moved it, a little twitch. A lift of the hand, then. "I'm weak. I'm awfully weak."

"That's all right. They're going to take you over in the bus.

You can sleep in your own bed tonight if you can prove you can sit up.''

Grant's chest rose and fell rapidly. The arm moved, dragged over, fell at his side like something dead. He gulped air and made a convulsive move of his whole body, lifting his shoulders barely enough to let the pillow slip before he fell back.

"Close enough," Justin said.

Food tasted very strange to him. Too strong. Even soggy cereal was work, and made his jaws ache. He ate about half the bowl that Justin spooned into his mouth and made a weak movement of his hand. " 'Nough.''

Justin looked worried when he set the bowl aside.

"It's a lot for me," Grant said. Talking was an effort too, but Justin looked so scared. Grant reached out and put his hand on Justin's because that was easier than talking. Justin still looked at him with all hell in his eyes. And he wished like hell he could take that pain away.

Justin had told him everything last night, poured it on him while he was still groggy and exhausted, because, Justin had said, *that's the way they hit me with it, and I guess it hurts less while you're numb*.

Grant had cried then. And Justin had cried. And Justin had been so tired and so unwilling to leave him that he had stretched himself out on Grant's bed beside him, still dressed and on top of the covers, and fallen to sleep.

Grant had struggled to throw the bedspread over him, had not had the strength in his arm; so he had rolled over, left the spread with Justin and rolled back again.

And lay there with just the sheet, too cold until Justin woke up midway through the night and got a blanket for him. And hugged him and cried on his shoulder, a long, long time.

"I need you so much," Justin had said.

Perhaps because he was azi, perhaps because he was human, he did not know—that was the most important thing anyone had ever said to him. He had wept too. He did not know why, except Justin was his life. Justin was everything to him. "I need you too," he had said. "I love you."

In the dark hours. In the hours before morning. When people could say things that were too real to say by daylight.

Justin had fallen to sleep by his side a second time. Grant

had waked first, and lain there a long time, content to know Justin was there. Until Justin had waked and gotten up, apologizing for having slept there.

As if he had not wanted Justin there, all night. As if Justin was not the most important thing in the world to him, who made him feel safe. Who was the one he would do anything for.

Whom he loved, in a way that no woman and nothing he had ever longed for could matter to him.

xiii

"Ari's set is positive," the voice from the lab informed Giraud Nye, and he drew a long breath of relief.

"That's wonderful," he said. "That's really wonderful. How are the other two?"

"Both positive. We've got a take on all three in all the tanks."

"Wonderful."

Schwartz signed off. Giraud Nye leaned back with a sigh.

There were nine womb-tanks active on the Rubin project. Triple redundancy on each of the subjects, over Strassen's loud complaints. It was rare that Reseune ran any backups at all on a CIT replication; if a set failed to implant or had some problem, the restart just put it a few weeks late, that was all, and the recipient could wait, unless the recipient wanted to pay double the already astronomical cost to have a backup. In the case of a contracted run of azi sets, or somebody's project, the normal rule was one spare for every pair, the spares to be voided after six weeks.

This one was going to tie up nine tanks for three weeks, and six for six weeks, before they made a final selection and voided the last backups.

Reseune was taking no chances.

Everyone who has ever taken a tape with prescriptive drugs is familiar with the sensor patch. The simplest home-use machines use a one-way cardiac sensor, a simple patch which monitors pulse rate. Any tape, whether entertainment or informational, when taken with a prescription cataphoric, has the potential to produce severe emotional stress where the content triggers memory or empathy. In experiencing the classic play Othello, *for instance, a certain individual, viewing a certain performance, and bringing to it his own life experience, may empathize with one or the other characters to an extent no mass-production tape can anticipate.*

This viewer is undergoing stress natural to the drama. The heart rate increases. The sensor picks it up and carries it to the machine's monitor-circuits. If it rises above the level set by the tape-technician the tape will automatically switch to a different program, a small tape-loop that provides only relaxing music and sound.

This young boy has come to a learning clinic to acquire a skill—improvement in penmanship. As he tenses muscles in his hand and lower arm his clinical technician's skilled fingers locate the muscles and place the numbered patches precisely on the skin. More are added to the muscles about the eye. Others go beneath the arm, over the heart, and over the carotid artery.

These small gray strips have two contacts: this much more advanced machine has a biofeedback loop. The numbers on the patches correspond to the numbers the tape-manual gives to the technician, who need not, for this kind of manual skill tape, be a licensed psychotherapist. Attaching these to the skin above the muscles indicated in the manual makes it possible for the machine to sense the activity of an individual muscle or muscle group and immediately send or cease sending impulses.

This woman, skilled in penmanship, wears identical sensors as she writes the exercise. Her muscle actions are being recorded. This is the actual recording of the tape.

The young student is somewhat anxious as he waits for the cataphoric to take effect. This is his first experience with prescriptive tape. The technician reassures him that this is very little different from the entertainment tapes. The patches are uncomfortable, but only for the moment. The drug takes effect and the technician tests to be sure the boy is ready. The tape begins, and the boy experiences stress as he sees the exercise. The technician quietly reassures him. In a moment, through the output-input function of the patches, the boy feels the muscle action of the skilled penman as she takes up the pen and begins to write. He experiences the success, sees the shape of the letters, feels the small precise movements of the hand and fingers, and feels the relaxation of the calligrapher at her work.

It may take several sessions, but the improvement is already evident as the boy writes the exercise immediately after waking. He holds the pen easily and comfortably, no longer cramps his fingers with a hard grip, and his entire posture has improved as he has found the proper pivot point on which to rest his hand. He is amazed and delighted at the result. He will practice the exercise several times during the day, to reinforce the pattern. He will do it again just after breakfast, and several times the following day. His enthusiastic practice will set the *habit. He may repeat the tape until he and his parents are satisfied with the result.*

This Beta-class azi is assigned to the special forces. He stands patiently, tensing muscles in his back at the technician's request. He shuts his eyes, quite evidently bored by the procedure which caused the young student such anxiety. He looks forward to the tape, but the skill he is learning requires the entire body. He has been through this twice a month for much of his life, and the biofeedback patches are more important in his estimation than the cataphoric. He has acquired a skill at tape-learning: his concentration is much more skilled than the student's. He knows the names of the muscles, knows how to attach the patches himself, and does a great deal of optional study in his own quarters, under a cataphoric dose hardly more than you might use in your own home for an entertainment tape, because he has learned how to induce a learning-state without the use of the drug.

At the end of the month, he receives another kind of tape, which citizens do not receive: it is a very private experience, which he cannot describe in words, because much of it is non-verbal. He calls it good tape. The term frequently heard at Reseune is reward tape.

The woman who administers the tape is not a technician. She is a Beta-qualified supervisor, and she uses a much more complex machine. This one has a blood-chemistry loop: it analyzes the blood it receives and injects natural mood-elevators—a procedure used in the general population only when psych-adjustment is called for.

For the azi, who has taken this sort of tape all his life, it is a pleasant experience, which he values more than the other rewards the service provides. This one is internal, and profound.

Unlike an intervention in a citizen patient, which depends heavily on the psychologist's investigative skills to tailor a tape, this tape is precisely targeted, prepared by the same designers who prepared the azi's psychset. It has an accuracy virtually impossible with a non-azi patient whose life has been shaped by unrecorded experiences in a random world. This azi, cloistered from birth and given his psychset by tape, is a much more known quantity, even after he has served in the armed forces and lived with naturally born citizens.

Everyone who has ever held authority over him has had special training in dealing with azi. No azi Supervisor is permitted to raise his voice with his charges. Reward or the withholding of reward is the rule of discipline; and the trust between this man and any psychologist-supervisor is more profound than that between parent and child. That this is a different Supervisor than last month does not trouble him. He has absolute confidence in her once he is sure that she is licensed.

People who have had their first experience working with unsocialized azi generally comment first that they feel they have to whisper; and then that they find themselves overwhelmed by the emotional attachment the azi are instantly ready to give them.

They trust me too much, is the almost universal complaint.

But this man is a soldier and works regularly with unlicensed citizens. He has developed emotional defenses and interacts freely with his citizen comrades. His commanding officer has had a training course and passed a test that qualifies him to deal with azi, but he holds no license and does not treat this man any differently than the others in his command. The commanding officer is only aware that a request from this man to undergo counseling has to be honored immediately, and if the azi requests the intervention of a Beta-supervisor, he must be sedated and sent to hospital without delay, because while problems in azi are very rare and a socialized azi's emotional defenses are generally as strong as any citizen's, an azi's psychset is not built by experience, but by instruction, and the defenses are not a network of social reliances as they are in a normal human mind. An azi who feels that shield weakened is vulnerable to everyone around him. He has entered something very like a cataphoric-induced learning-state, in which he is less and less capable of rejecting stimuli that impinge on him. The result is very like taking a cataphoric in a crowded room, intensely uncomfortable for the azi and potentially damaging.

The tape this man is enjoying is more than pleasurable for him. It is also reaffirming his values and reinforcing his self-esteem. His trust right now is absolute. He experiences what

*no citizen will experience in a random world: he is in touch
with absolute truth and agrees perfectly with what he is.*

This is Reseune, where our soldier was born. This three-
year-old azi, much younger than our student, is preparing
himself for what is commonly called deep-tape. He is anxious
not about the procedure, which he has had before, but about
the machine, which he has finally begun to notice as significant
in the room. The psychsurgeon hugs him and reassures him,
and finally makes a face and gets a laugh from him. He helps
the surgeon attach the patches.

The dosage of cataphoric he receives is very heavy. His
thresholds are completely flat and his blood chemistry is constantly monitored.

The tape is reinforcing his value-sets in words he is capable
of understanding.

It tells him how to win approval. It tells him what his talents
are and what his strengths are.

It may remind him that he has tendencies to avoid, much in
the same way a parent may tell a child he must mind and not
sulk. But the tape dwells continually on positive things and
praise, and always ends that way.

As it closes the Supervisor tells him a word he must lock this
up with; and he will remember it. The next time the Supervisor
will access that set of instructions with that particular key,
which is recorded in the azi's file, with his tapes. As he grows,
his deep-tape will become more abstract. The verbal keys will
be integrated into larger and larger complexes as his
psychstructures are merged into complete sets, and he will accept the values he is given with an azi's complete openness to a
licensed Supervisor.

Because the child has shown distress at the machine the Supervisor remembers to reassure him about the equipment while
he is still receptive to instruction. Any distress the azi may feel
with any of these procedures, no matter how minor, is carefully traced for cause and dealt with seriously. At no time does
a Supervisor wish one of his charges to fear these procedures.

All the azi tape is designed here, in these ordinary-looking
offices, by designers some of whom are azi themselves. Much
of it is done with the help of computers, which analyze the ex-

tremely meticulous physiological testing done on azi types . . . such things as hand-eye coordination in a particular azi geneset, reaction time, balance, vision, hearing, physical strength, hormonal activity, Rezner scores, reaction to stress. The designer takes all of these things into account in making a tape specifically for that geneset, tailored precisely to that geneset's strengths and weaknesses, and linking into a particular pyschset.

It is a designer who consults Reseune's library to select a geneset which can be given the special skills necessary to a new technology.

It is a designer who attends an azi returned to the labs by his Supervisor for what the report calls severe problems. It is a designer who will order the tests and interview the azi to discover whether the problem lies with the Supervisor or the azi. It is a designer who will prepare a tape to cure the problem—or issue a binding order regarding the handling of all azi of that geneset, restricting them from certain duties.

It is a designer who has destined this boy for civilian security duties, a change from the military training his genotype generally gets. Designers are usually conservative in shifting a genotype into new applications, because they, as much as their subjects, want to assure success. At Reseune, where azi test subjects are used, a keyword procedure creates a retrieval tab on the test set so that a psychsurgeon can maintain it separate for a considerable time before integrating it into the psychset. The few azi who run what are called short-term tests are specially trained in isolating and handling the interventions, and are themselves the judges of whether they should accept a particular test. Reseune's rule is to experiment slowly, and to deal with only one change at a time.

Occasionally an azi, like any member of the general public, develops severe psychological problems.

Many of these are sent to Reseune, where designers and psychsurgeons work with them, attempting to devise solutions to the psychological difficulties, solutions which also benefit science and find their way into general psychotherapy.

In some instances the solution has to be retraining, which necessitates mindwipe and a long period of recovery. In an azi of proven genotype and psychset a problem of this magnitude is always due to extreme trauma, and Reseune will take legal measures on the azi's behalf in the event of negligence or mistreatment.

In other instances the solution is only in the genetics wing; Reseune forbids reproduction of a genotype that has met difficulty until the designers working with the afflicted azi can find a fix for the problem.

In very, very few cases, there is no fix, no remedial psychset to install even with mindwipe, and a panel of qualified staff members can find no humane solution, except to terminate. The azi's quality of life is the main consideration, and Reseune, which has made the rules which forbid a Supervisor to speak sharply to one of its azi in the workplace, likewise must take the decision any next of kin must face when a body functions after reasoning, meaningful life has ceased. . . .

CHAPTER 4

The womb-tank tilted, spilled its contents into the fluid-filled receiving tank, and Ariane Emory struggled and twisted, small swimmer in an unfamiliar dim light and wider sea.

Until Jane Strassen reached down into the water and took her up, and the attendants tied off the cord and took her to a table for a quick examination while Jane Strassen hovered.

"She's perfect, isn't she?" There was worry in that question. An hour ago it would have been clinical worry, professional worry, anxiety about a project which could go very wrong if there was something wrong with the baby. But there was a certain personal anguish involved of a sudden, which she would not have expected to feel.

You're the closest match to Olga Emory's tests, her cousin Giraud had said; and Jane had thrown a tantrum, refused, protested that her management of Wing One labs did not include time to take on motherhood at a slightly fragile, overworked one hundred and thirty-two years of age.

Olga took it on at eighty-three, Giraud had said. *You're a strong-minded woman, you're busy as hell—so was Olga—you have Olga's interest in art, you were born in space, and you've got the professional skill and the brains. You're the best match we've got. And you're old enough to* remember *Olga.*

I hate kids, she had retorted, *I had Julia by immaculate conception, and I resent any comparison to that obnoxious nit-picking bitch!*

Giraud, damn him, had smiled. And said: *You're on the project.*

Which brought her to this, this room, this hour, agonizing while the medical experts looked over a squirming newborn, and the thoughts of personal responsibility took hold.

She had never involved herself much with her genetic daughter, who was her personal concession to immortality, conceived with the unknowing help of a Pan-paris mathematician who had made his donation to Reseune, because she had thought a random chance and new blood might be preferable. Too much planning, she had maintained, made bad gene pools; and Julia was the result of her personal selection, not bad, not good either. She had entrusted Julia mostly to nurses, and dealt with her less and less as Julia proved a sweet, sentimental space-brain—no, *bright,* in any less demanding environment, but overwhelmed right now by the discovery of her own biology and as feckless in her personal life as one of the azi.

But *this,* Ari's replicate, this end-of-life adopted daughter, was what she had hoped for. The ideal student. This was a mind that could take anything she could throw at it and throw it back again. And she was forbidden to do it.

She had done tape of Olga with the child. Hand on Ari's shoulder. Sharp tug at Ari's sweater, straightening it. Ari's angry, desperate wince. That was the pair she damned well remembered. It brought back everything.

For eighteen years of her life she had listened to that voice. Olga had carped at everyone on staff. Olga had carped at the kid, what time Olga had had time, till it was a wonder the kid was sane, in between which the kid had been totally on her own with the azi. Olga had taken all those damned blood-samples and psych-tests and more psych-tests, because Olga had theories that led to theories Ari had worked on. Olga had gotten Ari's earliest Rezner tests, which damned near hit the top of the scale, and from that time on it had been a case of blood in the water: Olga Emory, with her pet theories of scientific child-rearing, had believed that she had an Estelle Bok on her hands, destined for centuries of immortality via Reseune labs. And every other kid in Reseune's halls had heard that Ari was brilliant and Ari was special because mothers and fathers on staff knew their professional heads would roll if their kid blacked the deserving eye of Olga's precious Ari.

In those pioneering days on Cyteen, when intellectuals running from the Earth Company visa laws had gathered at what had then been the far end of space and founded Cyteen Station, renegade political theorists, famous physicists, chemists and legendary explorers had been thicker in the station mess hall than people who could fix the toilets; rejuv was a new development, Reseune was being founded to work with it, Bok's physics was rewriting the textbooks, and speculations and out-there theories had possessed people who should have known better. And Olga Emory had been a brilliant intellect with an instinct for cross-disciplinary innovation, but she had entertained some real eetees in her mental basement.

Never mind James Carnath, who had more of them, and determined he and Olga were going to make a baby to outdo Bok the day he found out he was terminal.

Which had led them all to this room and this project.

So she had to do everything Olga's way. *Straighten up, Ari. Stand still, Ari. Do your homework, Ari*— Twitch and bitch.

Between that and throwing Ari at azi nurses, the same way she had done with Julia. She had considerable remorse for that, in retrospect.

Changing that parental disinterest would change Ari. Benign neglect. It was a terrible thing to recognize her own personal mistakes retroactively. Studying up on Olga had been like looking in a too-revealing mirror. Giraud had been right. A hell of a thing to find out, at a hundred and thirty-two.

To this day she had no more maternal feeling for Julia than for any other product of the labs . . . or for the two azi the attendants were busy birthing over on the other side of the room. In the case of Ari, never mind the experience with one daughter and fifty-two years' experience with students, it had to be a question of following program. For the kid's own good. She had *respected* Ari Emory, and dammit, if she failed with her, that was all the reputation she was going to leave in Reseune. At a hundred and thirty-two. She *hated* fuck-ups. She hated personal indulgence and fuzzy thinking.

It was still damned hard to look at Julia and see what a meek thing she had come to be—constantly fouling up at work, spoiling her new baby beyond bearing, dependent on an endless succession of lovers—and know that it was partly genes and partly her fault. The same neglect, the same carping she had now to admit she had done with Julia, was part and parcel of what made Ari run. Psychsets and genetics at work.

Wrong kid, right parent, maybe. And vice versa.

Hell of a hand nature dealt out.

_____ ii _____

"They're all in good shape," Petros Ivanov said.

"That's wonderful. Really wonderful." Denys took a bite of fish and another one. Private lunch, in the executive dining room, with the curtains back on the seal-windows of the observation deck. The weather-makers were giving them a rain, as requested, a major blow, water sheeting down the windows. The atmosphere was going to be compromised for a day or so. "Damn Giraud. Of *course* it'll go all right, he says, and runs off to the capital. And damn if he's called!"

"Everything's right on the profile so far. The azi are absolutely norm. They're already on program."

"So's Ari."

"Strassen's bitching about the head nurse."

"What else is new?"

"Says she's opinionated and she upsets her staff."

"*An azi is opinionated.* That means the azi is going exactly down the instructions and Jane's mad because she's got new staffers in her apartment. She'll survive." He poured more coffee. "Olga's azi is still a damn worry. Ollie's younger, he's a hell of a lot tougher-minded than that poor sod Olga had, by all accounts, and Jane's got a good point: run tape on Ollie to soften him up and Jane's temper will crack him. Her style with the kid she can manage; changing Ollie and changing the way she deals with him is further than Jane's going to go without exploding. If that kid's got even an ordinary baby's instincts she'll pick up on adult tensions right from the cradle. Figuring she's got Ari's sensitivity, God knows *what* she can pick up on. So what do you do?''

Petros grinned. ''Run tape on Jane?''

Denys snorted into his coffee and sipped. ''I sure as hell wish. No. Jane's a professional. She knows what this is worth. We've got a bargain. We keep hands off Ollie and she cues Ollie how to play this. We just trust an azi that can make our Janie happy can cope with anything.''

Laughter.

He was mad as hell at Giraud. There was a good deal of this Giraud could have taken off his shoulders, but Giraud had a tendency to kite off to the capital whenever things got tense on the Project.

It's all yours, Giraud had said. *You're the administrator. And welcome to it.*

It had taken most of a year sifting through Ari's notes, that small initial part of the computer record the technicians could get at easily. Reseune's records computers had run for three weeks just compiling the initial mass of data on Ari. Thank God Olga had archived everything with cross-referencing and set it up in chronological order. The tapes had to be located, all this not only on Ari, but on two azi who had been protosets and unique. There was a tunnel under the hills out there and there were three more under construction, because that enormous vault was full, absolutely full to capacity, with workers beginning to divide tape into active, more active and most active, so more of it could be put in the House itself.

And when the data-flood from the Project came rolling out in full operation it would be a tidal wave in the House Archives. One of those tunnels was specifically to house the physical records of the Project; and that included software design for some of the things Ari had halfway worked out and someone else was going to have to finish before that baby was talking.

Reseune was *not* going to farm out anything to do with the Project. It was farming out some of the azi production runs, to clear personnel time. It would have been an economic crisis, except the military had thrown money at Reseune's extension at Fargone and Reseune's extension in Planys, money which funded more tanks, more computers, more production *and* those tunnels. Meanwhile Jordan Warrick was doing everyone a favor by actually handling the physical set-up over in Planys, which had Warrick happier than he had been since Ari's demise, turning out real work again—no small gain in itself, since it made Defense happy. They had lost Robert Carnath from House Operations and promoted him over the Planys lab: Robert was no friend of Warrick's and a sharp enough administrator to keep all the reins in his hands. They had lost other staff out to the Fargone lab construction and they were going to lose more, when that lab went active and the Rubin project kicked in. Reseune had been overstaffed when the thing began and now it was actually buying azi contracts from hackers like Bucherlabs and Lifefarms, rejuving every azi over forty and driving staff berserk with retraining tapes. Fifteen barracks were empty down in the Town, and they had just signed a buy-back deal with Defense for certain Reseune azi approaching retirement: it saved Defense expensive retraining and pensioning, it made certain azi damned happy when they learned they were going on working and getting staff positions at RESEUNEAIR and in freight and production and wherever else an azi whose outlook otherwise was transfer to some dull government work center could fill a slot and look forward instead of back. It gave Reseune a large pool of discipline-conscious, security-conscious personnel—instantly. Mistakes and glitches were bound to proliferate in Reseune's smooth operations, but *not* on the Project, where there were no new faces, and where the top talent could consequently pay full attention to their jobs.

The military buy-back had saved them. Denys was proud of that stroke. It *took* something to multiply a Project designed for one subject into four—counting Rubin and the two azi. And to coordinate the project-profile *and* the finance *and* the covert aspects of it. Giraud handled the latter. Denys had had the rest in his lap for long enough he felt *he* had just given birth.

"It's not easier from here," he told Petros. "From here on, it's going to be a race between that kid and profile-management. If anyone fouls up, *I* want to know about it. If she gets an unscheduled sniffle, I want to know about it. Nothing's minor until we've got results to check against profile.''

''Hell of a way to go, developing the profile while it's running.''

''We'd have to anyway. There are *going* to be differences. We'd always be altering it. And we'd never know where we're going anyway. If that kid *is* Ari in any measurable degree, we'll never damn well know, will we?''

No laughter at all.

iii

Justin poured, wine swirling into Grant's many times emptied glass. Poured another for himself and set the dead bottle down. Grant looked at his glass with a slightly worried look.

Duty. Grant was getting drunk and thinking about the fact. He knew. He knew the way he could tell that Grant was not going to say a thing, Grant had just decided that duty was not the operative word tonight.

They talked about the office. They talked about a design sequence they had been working on. A bottle of wine apiece did not do much for the design—the connections were getting fuzzy.

But Justin felt better for it.

He felt a strange dissatisfaction with himself. A baby arrived and he went through the day in a state of unreasoning depression. Reseune was aflutter with: ''Is she cute?'' and ''How is she doing?'' and he felt as if someone had a fist closed around his heart.

Over a baby being born, for God's sake. And while a kind of a party was going on in the techs' residencies, and another one over in Wing One residency, he and Grant held their own morose commemoration.

They sat in the pit in the apartment that had been home when they were both small, the apartment that had been Jordan's, crackers and drying sausage slices on the plate, two dead wine bottles standing in cracker crumbs and moisture-rings on the stone table, and a third bottle a third gone. And that was finally enough to put him at distance from things.

Wish a little baby would die? God, what kind of thinking is that?

He lifted his next glass when he had filled it, and touched it to Grant's with labored cheerfulness. "Here's to the baby."

Grant frowned and did not drink when he did.

"Come on," Justin said. "We can be charitable."

Grant lifted his eyes and made a small motion of his fingers. *Remember they could have us monitored.*

That was always true. They played games with the House monitors, but they had to go outside to have a word or two they did not have to worry about.

"Hell, let them listen. I don't care. I feel sorry for the kid. She didn't ask for this."

"No azi does," Grant said sharply. Then a frown made a crease between his brows. "I guess no one does."

"No one does." The depression settled back over the room. He did not know what was going to happen to them, that was what. Reseune was changing, full of strange faces, assignment shifts, the azi were—unsettled by the rejuv order. Elated by that, elated by the fact that they must have pleased someone, and distressed at the reassignments and the transfers and the arrival of strangers. Not harmfully distressed, just—having more change fall on them than they had ever had to cope with: Supervisors' interview schedules were overcrowded and Supervisors themselves were asking for relief that did not exist.

While over in Wing One residency there was an apartment shut up like a mausoleum. Not dusted, not touched, not opened.

Waiting.

"I don't think they'll have any better luck than they did with Bok," Justin said finally. "I really don't. *Jane Strassen*, for God's sake. The endo—" Endocrinology was not a thing one could say after a bottle and a half of wine. "Damn chemistry. Works fine on the machines. Just nature's way of getting at the thresholds. Nice theory. But they'll end up driving her crazier than Bok. They'd have better luck if they outright ran deep-tape on her. The creativity factor's a piece of garbage. Bring her up to *like* Ari's work, deep-tape a little *empathy*, for God's sake, and turn her loose. The whole project's a damn lunatic obsession. It's not Ari's talent they want, not a nice bright kid, it's Ari! It's the *power* they want back, it's personality! It's a clutch of rejuved relics staring at the great The End and having Reseune's budget to squander. That's what's going on. It's a damn disaster. It's too many people's lives and too damn little caring upstairs, that's what they're doing. I feel sorry for the kid. I really feel sorry for her."

Grant only stared at him a long while. Then: "I think there *is* something about creativity and tape—that we *don't* have it to the same degree—"

"Oh, hell." Sometimes he trod on Grant without knowing he had done it. Sometimes he opened his mouth and forgot with Grant the sensitivity he made his living using with azi down in the Town. And hated himself. "That's a lot of garbage. I damn sure don't believe it when you fix a design a dozen senior designers have been sweating on for a month."

"I'm not talking about that. I *am* azi. Sometimes I can see a problem from a vantage they don't have. Frank is azi too, but he's not what I am. I can get a little arrogant. I'm entitled. But every time I have to argue with Yanni I feel it right in the gut."

"Everybody feels it in the gut. Yanni's a—"

"Listen to me. I don't think you feel this. I can do it. But I know every bit of what makes me tighten up fits right in that book in the bedroom, and what makes you do it wouldn't fit in this apartment. Look at what they're doing with Ari. They had to build a damn tunnel in the mountain to hold what she was."

"So what's it mean that at lunch the day the war started she had fish and she was two days into her cycle? That's crap, Grant, that's plain crap, and that's the kind of thing they built that tunnel to hold." *Along with those damn tapes, that's there. Till the sun freezes over. That's what people will remember I was.* "You choke up with Yanni because he's got a three-second fuse, that's all. It's his sweet nature, and losing the Fargone post didn't improve it."

"No. You're not listening to me. There is a difference. The world is too complicated for me, Justin. That's the only way I can explain it. I can see the microstructures much better than you. My concentration is all on the fine things. But there's something about azi psychsets—that can't cope with random macrostructures. That whole tunnel, Justin. Just to hold her psychset.''

"Psychset, hell, it's full of what she *did*, and who she hurt, and she was a hundred twenty years old! You want to go to Novgorod and buy councillors, you'd fill that tunnel up too, damn fast.''

"I couldn't. I couldn't see behind me. That's what it feels like.''

"You've lived in these walls all your life. You could learn.''

"No. Not the same things. That's what I'm saying. I could learn everything Ari knew. And I'd still focus too tight.''

"You don't either! *Who* saw the conflict in the 78s? *I* didn't!''

Grant shrugged. "That's because born-men make most of their mistakes by rationalizing a contradiction. I don't make that leap without noticing it.''

"You read *me* with no trouble at all.''

"Not always. I don't know what Ari did to you. I know *what* happened. I know I wouldn't have been affected the same way.'' They could talk about that now. But rarely did. "She could have re-structured me. She was very good. But she couldn't do that to you.''

"She did a damn lot.'' It hurt. Especially tonight. He wanted off the topic.

"She couldn't. Because you don't have a psychset that only fills one book. You're too complicated. You can change. And I have to be very *careful* of change. I can see the inside of my mind. It's very simple. It has rooms. Yours is Klein bottles.''

"God,'' Justin snorted.

"I'm drunk.''

"We're drunk.'' He leaned forward and put his hand on Grant's shoulder. "And we're both Klein-spaced. Which is why we're back where we started and I'm willing to bet my psychset is no more complicated than yours. You want to work it out?''

"I—'' Grant blinked. "You want an example? My heart just skipped. That embarrasses hell out of me. It's that Supervisor trigger. I don't want to do that because I don't think it's smart to mess with your mind; and I jump inside like it was an order.''

"Hell, I hate it when you go self-analytical. You don't want to do it because you don't know when Security is listening; and it's personal and you've got manners. All your deep-sets just describe the same thing I feel. Which is why I stay out of your head.''

"No." Grant held up a finger. Earnest. A near hiccup. "The profound reason why we're different. Endo-endo—hell! hormones work—in learning—Blood chemistry reacts—to the environment. A given stimulus—sometimes adrenaline is up— sometimes down—sometimes some other thing—shades of gray. Variability—in a random environment. You remember some things right, some wrong, some light, some heavy. We—" Another near hiccup. "—start out from the cradle— with cataphorics. Knock the damn thresholds flatter than anything in nature. That means—no shades in our original logic set-up. Things are totally true. We can trust what we get. *You* take your psychset in through your senses. Through natural cataphorics. You get your *informational* learning through tape and your psychset through senses. Chancy as hell what you get out of anything you see or hear. You learn to average through the flux because you know there'll be variances. But *we've* had experts eliminate all logical incon-inconsistencies. We *can* take in every detail; we have to, that's the way we process— right. That's why we're damn good at seeing specific detail. That's why we process faster on some problems you can't hold in your head. We go learning-state without kat and our early memories didn't come from endocrine-learning; we have no shades of truth. You're averaging and working with a memory that has a thousand shades of value and you're better at averaging shades than you are at remembering what really happened, that's how you can process things that come at you fast and from all sides. And that's what we're worst at. You can come up with two contradicting thoughts and believe both of them because there's flux in your perceptions. I can't.''

"Oh, we're back to that again! Hell, you work the same as I do. *And* you forget your keycard *more* than I do.''

"Because I'm processing something else.''

"So do I. Perfectly normal.''

"Because I have a dump-reflex just like you: I can go through ac-actions that are purely body-habit. But I'm socialized, I rarely take tape, and I've got two processing systems. The top level I've learned in the real world; endocrine system learning. The bottom, where my reactions are, is simple, damn simple, and merci-mercilessly logical. An azi isn't a human *lacking* a function. He's got the logical function underneath and the random function on top. And you're backwards. You get the random stuff first."

"*I'm* backwards."

"Whatever."

"God. An Emoryite. You *test* that way because the cataphorics engrave the pathways they establish so damn deep they're the course of least resistance and they're so damn structured they *trigger* the endo-en—do-crine system in Pavlovian patterns that experience alone wouldn't. For every test that supports Emory there's another one that supports Hauptmann-Poley."

"Hauptmann was a social theorist who wanted his results to support his politics."

"Well, what in hell was Emory?"

Grant blinked and took a breath. "Emory asked *us*. Hauptmann socialized his subjects till they'd figured out what he wanted them to say. And how he wanted them to test. And an azi *always* wants to please his Supervisor."

"Oh, *shit*, Grant. So would Emory's."

"But Emory was *right*. Hauptmann was wrong. *That's* the difference."

"Tape affects how your endo-crine system responds. Period. You give me enough tape and I'll jump every time you tell me to. And my pulse will do exactly what yours does."

"I'm one hell of a tape designer. When I'm old as Strassen I'll be damn good. I'll have all this endocrine learning. That's why some old azi get more like born-men. And some of us get to be real eetees. That's why old azi have more problems. Wing Two's going to be damn—damn busy with a yardful of annies on rejuv."

Justin was shocked. They were words staff meticulously avoided using. Born-men. Annies. The Yard. It was always CITs; azi; the Town. Grant was pronouncedly drunk.

"We'll see whether it makes any difference," Justin said, "whether Ari Emory had whitefish or ham for breakfast on her twelfth birthday."

"I didn't say I thought the Project would work. I say I think Emory's right about what azi are. They didn't start out to invent us. They just needed people. Fast. So start with tape in the cradle. Perfectly benign accident. Now we're eco-economic."

Back in the pre-Union days.

"Hell."

"I didn't say I minded, ser. We already outnumber you. Soon we'll establish farms where people can grow up like weeds and commune with their glands. There's bound to be a use for them."

"Hell with you!"

Grant laughed. He did. Half of it was an argument they had had a dozen times in different guises; half of it was Grant trying to psych him. But the day fell into perspective finally. It was only a memory tick-over. A jolt backward. Done was done. There was no way to get those damned blackmail tapes out of Archive, since they were Ari's and Ari was sacred. But he had learned to live with the prospect of all of it turning up someday on the evening news.

Or finding that no bargains held forever.

Jordan had killed a dying woman for reasons the Project was going to immortalize in the records anyway—if it worked. If it worked, every hidden detail of Ari's personal life was going to have scientific significance.

If it worked to any degree, and the Project went public, there was the chance Jordan could seek a re-hearing and release maybe to Fargone—after twenty years or so of the Project itself; which would mean all the people who had conspired to cover what Ari had done and all the Centrists who had been embarrassed by potential connections the case had had to the radical underground—were going to resist it. Reputations were going to be threatened all over again. Merino and the Abolitionists. Corain. Giraud Nye. Reseune. The Defense Bureau, with all its secrets. There might be justice in the courts, but there was none among the power brokers that had put Jordan where he was. The walls of secrecy would close absolutely, to keep silent a man they could no longer control. And his son—

who had set everything in motion by a kid's mistake, a kid's bad judgment.

If the Project failed it would be a failure like the Bok clone, which had done nothing but add a tragic and sordid little footnote to a great woman's life—a very expensive failure, one Reseune would never publicize, the way to this day the outside world had heard a totally different story about the murder, heard a different story about the changes at Reseune, and knew nothing about the Project: administrative reorganization, the news-services said, in the wake of Ariane Emory's death.

And went on with some drivel about Ari's will having laid out far-reaching plans and the lab being beneficiary of her considerable investments.

If it failed—it had political consequences, particularly between Reseune Administration and the Defense department, which was *inside* the wall of secrecy. Then there was no predicting what Giraud Nye would do to protect himself: Giraud *had* to carry this off to prove himself, and in the meanwhile dangling the Project in front of Defense let Giraud grab power in some ways greater than Ari had had. Power to silence. Power to use the covert agencies. If Giraud was halfway clever, and if the Project did not fail conspicuously and definitively, he was going to be older than Jane Strassen before he had to admit the Project was not working. He could even re-start, and run the whole scam again, at which point Giraud was certainly going to be looking at the end of his need for any kind of power. After Giraud, the Deluge. What should Giraud care?

Justin only hoped it failed. Which meant a poor kid who only happened to have Ari's geneset ended up a psych case, mindwiped or worse. Maybe an endless succession of babies. A power as big and a man as smart as Giraud would not fail all at once. No. There would be studies of the study of the study. Unless there was a way to make sure it failed in public.

Sometimes he had thoughts that scared him, like finding some article of Ari's lying on his bed. He would never in his life be able to know if certain thoughts were his, just the natural consequence of a deep-seated anger, of himself growing older and harder and more aware how business was done in the world; or whether it was Ari still in control of him.

Worm was an old joke between him and Grant.

He had to go on making nothing of it. Because that was all that kept it isolated.

———————————— iv ————————————

"Get down from there!" Jane snapped, startled into a snarl, and her gut tightened as the two-year-old trying for the kitchen countertop leaned and stretched, reckless of her light weight, the tile floor and the metal-capped chair legs. Ari reacted, the chair slipped a fraction, she snatched the box of crackers and turned; the chair tipped and Jane Strassen grabbed her on the way down.

Ari yelled with outrage. Or startlement.

"If you want the crackers you ask!" Jane said, tempted to give her a shake. "You want to ouch your chin again?"

Hurt-Ari was the only logic that made a dent in Ari-wants. And a universally famous genetic scientist was reduced to baby-babble and a helpless longing to smack a small hand. But Olga had never believed in corporal punishment.

And if Olga had been human Ari had picked up rage and frustration and resentment in the ambience with her the same as a genetic scientist who wanted to take her out to the river and drown her.

"Nelly!" Jane yelled at the nurse. And remembered *not* to shout. In her own apartment. She left the chair on the floor. No. Nit-picking Olga could never have left a chair on the floor. She stood there with her arms full of struggling two-year-old waiting on Nelly, who had damn well better have heard her. Ari struggled to get down. She set Ari down and held on to her hand when Ari wanted to sit down and throw a tantrum. "Stand up!" Holding a small hand hard. Giving an Olga-like jerk. "Stand up! What kind of behavior is that?"

Nelly showed up in the doorway, wide-eyed and worried.

"Straighten that chair up."

Ari jerked and leaned to reach after the cracker box that was lying with the chair, while adults were busy. Damned if she was going to forget what she was after.

Does she or doesn't she get the cracker? No. Bad lesson. She'd better not *get away with it, she'll break her neck.*

Besides, Olga was a vengeful bitch.

"Stand still. Nelly, *put* those crackers up where she *can't* get them. Shut *up*, Ari. —You take her. I'm going to the office. And if there's a scratch on her when I come back I'll—"

Wide azi eyes stared at her, horrified and hurt.

"Dammit, *you* know. What am I going to do? I can't watch her every damn minute. Shut *up*, Ari." Ari was trying to lie down, hanging off her hand with her full weight. "You don't understand how active she *is*, Nelly. She's tricking you."

"Yes, sera." Nelly was devastated. She was out-classed. She had had all the tape showing her what a two-year-old CIT could do. Or get into. Or hurt herself with. Don't stifle her, Nelly. Don't hover. Don't *not* watch her. The azi was on the verge of a crisis. The azi needed a Supervisor to hug her and tell her she was doing better than the last nurse. It was not Olga's style. Jane-type shouts and Olga-type coldness were driving the more vulnerable azi to distraction. And she was spending half her time keeping the kid from killing herself, half keeping the azi from nervous collapse.

"Just get a lock installed on the damn kitchen," Jane said. Ari howled like hell if she was shut into the playroom. She *hated* the playroom. "Ari, *stop* it. Maman can't hold you."

"Yes, sera. Shall I—"

"Nelly, you know your job. Just take Ari and give her a bath. She's worked up a sweat."

"Yes, sera."

The azi took Ari in hand. Ari sat down and Nelly picked her up and carried her.

Jane leaned back against the counter and stared at the ceiling. At the traditional location of God, no matter what the planet.

And Phaedra came in to say that daughter Julia was in the living room.

A second time Jane looked ceilingward. And did not shout. "Dammit, I'm a hundred thirty-four and I don't deserve this."

"Sera?"

"I'll take care of it, Phaedra. Thank you." She pushed herself away from the counter. "Go help Nelly in Ari's bath-room." She *wanted* to go to the office. "No. Find Ollie. Tell him calm Nelly down. Tell Nelly I shout. It's all right. Get!"

Phaedra got. Phaedra was one of *her* staff. Phaedra was competent. Jane walked out of the kitchen, down the hall in Phaedra's wake, and took the left turn, the glass-and-stone walk past the dining room and the library to the front living room.

Where Julia was sitting on the couch. And three-year-old Gloria was playing on the long-pile rug.

"*What* in hell are you doing here?" Jane asked.

Julia looked up. "I took Gloria to the dentist. Routine. I thought I'd drop by for a minute."

"You know better."

Julia's soft mouth hardened a little. "That's a fine wel-come."

Jane took a deep breath and went over and sat down with her hands locked between her knees. Gloria sat up. Another baby. Meditating destruction of something. The apartment was safed for a two-year-old's reach. Gloria was a tall three. "Look, Julia. You know the situation. You're *not* supposed to bring Gloria in here."

"It's not like the baby was going to catch something. I was just passing by. I thought we could go out for lunch."

"That's not the *point*, Julia. We're being taped. You know that. I don't want any question of compromise. You under-stand me. You're not a child. You're twenty-two years old, and it's about time—"

"I said we could go out for lunch."

With Gloria. God. Her nerves were at the breaking point. "We'll go out for lunch—" Gloria was over at the bookcase. Gloria was after a piece of pottery. "*Gloria, dammit!*" No platythere and no three-year-old ever turned from an objective. She got up and snatched the kid back, dragged her toward the couch and Gloria started to scream. Which could carry all the way down the damn hall where another little girl was trying to drown her nurse. Jane shifted her grip and clamped her hand over Gloria's mouth. "Shut that up! *Julia, dammit, get this kid out of here!*"

"*She's your granddaughter!*"

"I don't care what *she is, get her out of here!"* Gloria was struggling hysterically and kicking her shin. *"Out, dammit!"*

Julia got that desperate, offended, out-of-breath look; came and snatched Gloria away, and Gloria, uncorked, screamed as if she was being skinned.

"Get out!" Jane shouted. "Dammit, shut her up!"

"You don't care about your own granddaughter!"

"We'll go to lunch tomorrow! *Bring* her! Just shut her up!"

"She's not one of the damn azi!"

"Watch your mouth! What kind of language is that?"

"You've got a granddaughter! You've got *me*, for God's sake, and you don't bloody care!"

Hysterical howls from Gloria.

"I'm not going to talk about it now! *Out!"*

"Damn you then!" Julia started crying. Gloria was still screaming. Julia grabbed Gloria up and hauled her to the door and out it.

Jane stood in the quiet and felt her stomach profoundly upset. Julia had finally got some guts. And damn near sabotaged the Project. There was not *supposed* to be another little girl. They were still feeling their way. Little changes in self-percept while it was forming at incremental rates could have big effects down the line. If the start was true, Ari would *handle* course deviations at the far end just fine.

Ari did not need to be wondering, Maman, who was that?

Ari had been an only child.

So now the damn Project had Julia's nose out of joint. Because *mother* was one of Julia's triggers, *mother* was the root of all Julia's problems, *mother* was what Julia was determined to succeed in being, because Julia knew that that was the one place where the great and famous Jane Strassen had messed up and Julia was sure she could do it right. Julia felt deprived in her childhood so she was going to the other extreme, ruining her own kid with smothering: *that* little brat knew exactly how to get everything from mama but consistency, and she needed a firm hand and a month away from mama before it was too late.

Amazing how accurate hindsight could be.

V

It was patches again. Florian felt himself a little fluttery, fluttery like when things got confused. The big building and sitting on the edge of the table always made him feel that way, but he could answer when the Super asked him where the One patch went. Right over his heart. He knew that. He had a doll he could patch. But it didn't have so many.

"That's right," the Super said, and patted him. "You're an awfully good boy, Florian. You're very smart and you're very quick to do things. Can you tell me how old you are?"

Old meant big and as he got bigger and smarter the right answer meant more fingers. Right now he got to hold up the first and the next and the next, and stop. Which was hard to do without letting them all come up. When he did it right he felt good all over. The Super gave him a hug.

When he got through there was always a sweet. And he knew all the answers to everything the Super asked. He felt fluttery but it was a good fluttery.

He just wished they would give him the sweet now and forget about the patches.

vi

Ari was tremendously excited. She had a new suit—red, with a glittery pattern on the front and on one sleeve. Nelly had brushed her hair till it crackled and flew, all black and shiny, and then Ari, all dressed, had had to dither about the living room till maman and Ollie were ready. Maman looked very tall and very beautiful, glittery with silver, and the silver in her hair was pretty. Ollie went too, handsome in the black the azi wore. Ollie was a special azi. He was always with maman, and if Ollie said something Ari had to do it. She did, or at least she did today, because maman and Ollie were going to take her to a Party.

There were going to be a lot of big people there. She would go there and then Ollie would take her to Valery's to a children's party.

Valery was a boy. He was sera Schwartz's. Azi would watch them and they would play games and there would be ices, on a table their size. And other children. But mostly she liked Valery. Valery had a spaceship that had red lights. He had a glass thing you could look through and it made patterns.

Most of all she hoped there would be presents. Sometimes there were. Since everyone was dressed up, there might be.

But it was special, to go where the big people were. To walk down the hall holding maman's hand, dressed up and acting nice, because you were supposed to, and not make trouble. Especially when there could be presents.

They rode the lift downstairs. She saw a lot of tall azi in the hall: azi wore black more than they wore other colors; and even if they didn't, she could always tell them. They were not like maman or uncle Denys, they looked like azi. Sometimes she pretended to be them. She walked very quiet and stood straight and looked very straight like Ollie and said yes, sera to maman. (Not to Nelly. To Nelly you said, yes.) Sometimes she pretended to be maman and she told Nelly, make my bed, Nelly, please. (And to Ollie, once: Ollie, dammit, I want a drink. But that had not been a good idea. Ollie had brought her the drink and told maman. And maman had said it was not nice and Ollie was not going to do things for her when she was rude. So she said dammit to Nelly instead.)

Maman led her down the hall through the azi and through a doorway where there were a lot of people in the doorway. One woman said: "Happy new year, Ari." And bent over in her face. She had a pretty necklace and you could see way down her blouse. It was interesting. But Ollie picked her up. That was better. She could see people's faces.

The woman talked to maman, and people crowded in, all talking at once, and everything smelled like perfume and food and powder.

Someone patted her on the shoulder as Ollie held her. It was uncle Denys. Denys was fat. He made a lot of room around him. She wondered whether he was solid all the way through or sort of held his breath more than regular people to keep him so round.

"How are you, Ari?" uncle Denys yelled at her in all the racket, and all of a sudden the people stopped talking and looked at them. "Happy new year."

She was puzzled then, but interested. If it was her new year it was a birthday, and if it was a birthday party people were supposed to come to her apartment and bring her presents. She didn't see any.

"Happy new year," people said. She looked at them hopefully. But there were no presents. She sighed, and then as Ollie brought her through the crowd, she caught sight of the punch and the cake.

Ollie knew. "Do you want some punch?" he asked.

She nodded. There was a lot of noise. She was not sure she liked this many big people. The party did not make sense. But punch and cake was looking better. She clung to Ollie's strong shoulder and felt a good deal more cheerful, because Ollie could carry her right through to the table with the punch bowl and Ollie understood very well what was important. Punch, especially in a pretty bowl and with a big cake, was almost as good as presents.

"I've got to set you down," Ollie said. "All right? You stand right there and I'll get your punch."

That was not all right. Everyone was tall, the music was awfully loud, and when she was standing on the floor she could not see anything but people's legs. Somebody might step on her. But Ollie set her down, and maman was coming, with uncle Denys. And the crowd did not step on her. A lot of people looked at her. Some smiled. So she felt safe.

"Ari." Ollie gave her the cup. "Don't spill."

The punch was green. She was not altogether sure of it, but it smelled good and it tasted better.

"You're getting too big to carry," uncle Denys said. She looked up and wrinkled her nose at him. She was not sure she liked that idea. Maman said the same thing. But Ollie didn't. Ollie was big and he was very strong. He felt different than anyone. She liked him to carry her: she liked to put her arms around his neck and lean on him, because he was like a chair you could climb on, and you couldn't feel his bones, just a kind of solid. He was warm, too. And smelled good. But Ollie was getting punch for maman and uncle Denys from another bowl, and she just kept close to him and drank her punch while Denys and maman talked and loud music played.

Ollie looked down at her when maman and Denys had their punch. "Do you want some cake?" Ollie asked, talking loud. "They're going to have cake at the children's party."

That promised better. "I want some more punch," she said,

and gave Ollie her cup. "And cake, please." She stood there in a little open space to wait. She put her hands behind her, and remembered maman said not to rock back and forth, it was stupid-looking. People she did not know came up and said she was pretty, and wished her happy new year, but she was ready to leave, except for the punch and cake Ollie was getting. She was going to stay for that.

Children's party sounded a lot better.

Maybe there would be presents *there*.

"Come on over and sit down," Ollie said, not giving her the cake or the punch. He carried it for her. There were chairs along the wall. She was relieved. If she got punch on her new suit she would look bad and maman would scold her. She climbed up onto a chair and Ollie set the dish in her lap and set the cup on the seat beside her. She had the whole row to herself.

"I'm going to get mine," Ollie said. "Stay there. I'll be back."

She nodded, with cake in her mouth. White cake. The nice kind. With good icing. She was much happier. She swung her feet and ate cake and licked her fingers while Ollie waited at the punch bowl and maman talked with Denys and Giraud.

Maybe they waited about the presents. Maybe something interesting was going to happen. They all glittered. Some of them she had seen at home. But a lot were strange. She finished her cake and licked her fingers and slid off the chair to stand, because most of the people were around the tables and the floor was mostly clear.

She walked out to see how far Ollie had got in the line. But someone had distracted Ollie. That was a chance to walk around.

So she walked. Not far. She did not want maman and Ollie to leave and lose her. She looked back to see if she could still see maman. Yes. But maman was still busy talking. Good. If maman scolded her she could say, I was right here, maman. Maman could not be too mad.

A lot of the clothes were pretty. She liked the green blouse you could see through. And the black one a man was wearing, all shimmery. But maman's jewelry was still the best.

There was a man with bright red hair.

In black. Azi. She watched him. She said hello when somebody said hello to her, but she was not interested in that. She had always thought her hair was pretty. Prettier than anybody's. But his was *pretty*. *He* was. It was not fair. If there was hair like that *she* wanted it. She was suddenly dissatisfied with her own.

He looked at her. He was not azi. No. Yes. His face went all straight and he turned his chin, so, and pretended he did not see her looking at him. He was with a dark-haired man. That man looked at her, but the azi did not want him to.

He looked at her anyway. He was handsome like Ollie. He looked at her different than grown-ups and she thought he was not supposed to do that, but she did not want to look anywhere else, because he was different than everyone. The azi with red hair was by him, but he was not the important one. The man was. The man was looking at her, and she had never even seen him. He had never come to visit. He had never brought presents.

She went closer. The azi didn't want her to be close to his friend. He had his hand on the man's shoulder. Like she was going to get him. But the man watched her like she was maman. Like he had done something bad and she was maman.

He was being her. And she was being maman. And the azi was being Ollie, when maman was yelling.

Then the azi saw something dangerous behind her. She looked.

Maman was coming. But maman stopped when she looked.

Everyone was stopped. Everyone was watching. They had stopped talking. There was just the music. Everyone was afraid.

She started toward maman.

Everyone twitched.

She stopped. And everyone twitched again. Even maman. *She* had done that.

She looked back at maman. Twitch.

She looked back at the man.

Twitch. Everybody.

She didn't know she could do that.

Maman was going to be mad, later. Ollie was.

If maman was going to shout she might as well *do* something first.

The azi and the man looked at her when she walked up to them. The man looked like she was going to get him. The azi thought so too.

The man had pretty hands like Ollie. He was a lot like Ollie. People all thought he was dangerous. That was wrong. She knew it was. She could scare them good.

She came up and took his hand. Everyone was doing what she wanted. Even he was. She had maman good. The way she could do Nelly.

She *liked* that.

"My name's Ari," Ari said.

"Mine's Justin," Justin said quietly. In all that quiet.

"I'm going to a party," she said. "At Valery's."

Jane Strassen came to collect the child. Firmly. Grant got between them, and put his hand on Justin's shoulder, and turned him away.

They left. That was all there was to do.

"Damn," Grant said, when they were back in the apartment, "if no one had moved it would have been nothing. Nothing at all. She picked up on it. She picked up on it like it was broadcast."

"I had to see her," Justin said.

He could not say why. Except they said she *was* Ari. And he had not believed it until then.

―――――――――――――― vii ――――――――――――――

"Night, sweet," maman said; and kissed her. Ari put her arms up and hugged maman and kissed her too. Smack.

Maman went out and it was dark then. Ari snuggled down in bed with Poo-thing. She was full of cake and punch. She shut her eyes and all the people were glittery. Ollie got her cake. And all the people looked at her. Valery's party was nice. They played music-chairs and had favors. Hers was a glittery star. Valery's was a ball. They were real sorry about sera Schwartz's lamp.

New year was fun.

"Is she all right?" Ollie asked in the bedroom. And Jane nodded, while he unhooked her blouse. "Sera, I am sorry—"

"Don't talk about it. Don't fret about it. It's all right." He finished; she slid the silver blouse down her arms and threw it on the chair back. Ollie was still shaken.

So, in fact, was she. Not mentioning it was Denys' and Giraud's damn idea.

Olga had had the kid up in front of visitors, hauled her around like a little mannequin—subjected her to the high-pressure social circuit in which Ari's sensitive nerves must have been raw.

They could not take the curtain of secrecy off. There was only one part of that high-tension atmosphere they could access, that inside Reseune itself.

The Family. In all its multifarious, *ne*farious glory.

Enough sugar in her often-tested metabolism, enough no-don't and behave-Ari and promised rewards to be sure a four-year-old was going to be hyper as hell.

She felt, somehow, sick at her stomach.

viii

Justin hugged his coat about him as he and Grant took the outside walk between Residency and the office, and jammed his hands into his pockets. Not a fast walk, despite the morning chill, on a New Year's morning where everyone was slow getting started.

He stopped at the fishpond, bent and fed the fish. The koi knew him. They expected him and came swimming up under the brown-edged lotus. They ruled their little pool between the buildings, they entertained the children of the House and begat their generations completely oblivious to the fact that they were not on the world of their origin.

Here was here. The white old fellow with the orange patches had been taking food from his hand since he was a young boy, and daily, now, since Jordan had gone and he and Grant had sought the outside whenever they could. Every morning.

Spy-dishes could pick up their voices from the House, could pick them up anywhere. But surely, surely, Security just did the easy thing, and caught the temperature of things from time to time by flipping a monitor switch on the apartment, not wasting overmuch time on a quiet pair of tape-designers who had not made the House trouble in years. Security could bring them in for psychprobe anytime it wanted. That they had not—meant Security was not interested. Yet.

Still, they were careful.

"He's hungry," Justin said of the white koi. "Winter; and children don't remember."

"One of the differences," Grant said, sitting on the rock near him. "Azi children would."

Justin laughed in spite of the distress that hovered over them. "You're so damn superior."

Grant shrugged cheerfully. "Born-men are so blind to other norms. We aren't." Another piece of wafer hit the water, and a koi took it, sending out ripples that disturbed the lotus. "I tell you, all the trouble with alien contacts is preconceptions. They should send us."

"This is the man who says Novgorod would be too foreign."

"Us. You and me. I wouldn't worry then."

A long pause. Justin held the napkin of wafers still in his hands. "I wish to hell there was a place."

"Don't worry about it." It was not Novgorod Grant meant. Of a sudden the shadow was back. The cold was back in the wind. "Don't. It's all right."

Justin nodded, mute. They were so close. He had had letters from Jordan. They looked like lace, with sentences physically cut from the paper. But they said, in one salutation: *Hello, son. I hear you and Grant are well. I read and re-read all your letters. The old ones are wearing out. Please send more.*

His sense of humor is intact, he had commented to Grant. And he and Grant had read and re-read that letter too, for all the little cues it had given him about Jordan's state of mind. Read and re-read the others that got through. Page after page of how the weather was. Talk about Paul—constantly, *Paul and I.* That had reassured him too.

Things are moving, Denys had said, when he brought up the subject of sending voice tapes. Or making phone calls, carefully monitored.

And they had been so close to getting that permission.

"I can't help but worry," Justin said. "Grant, we've got to be so damn clean for the next little while. And it won't finish it. It won't be the last time. You or I don't have to have done anything.''

"They brought the girl there. They didn't stop us from coming. Maybe they didn't expect what happened, but it wasn't our doing. A roomful of psychologists—and they froze. They cued the girl. She was reading *them*, not us. It's that flux-thinking again. Born-men. They didn't want what happened; and they *did* want it, they set up the whole thing to show Ari off, and she was *doing* it—she was proving what they've worked to prove. And proving nothing. Maybe we cued her. We were watching her. I got caught at it. Maybe that made her curious. She's four years old, Justin. And the whole room jumped. What's any four-year-old going to do?''

"Run to her mother, dammit. She started to. Then everybody relaxed and she picked that up too. And got this look—'' He twitched his shoulders as a sudden chill got down his neck. Then shoved his imagination back down again and tried to think. The way no one had, last night.

"Does it occur to you,'' Grant said, "the fallibility of CIT memory? Flux-thinking. You have prophetic dreams, remember? *You* can dream about a man drinking a glass of milk. A week later you can see Yanni drinking tea at lunch and if seeing him do that has a high shock-value, you'll super the dream-state right over him, you'll swear you dreamed about him doing that, exactly at that table, and even psychprobe can't sort it out after that. It's happened to me twice in my life. And when it does, I take my tape out of the vault and betake myself to the couch for a session until I feel better. Listen to me: I'll concede the child's behavior may have been significant. I'll wait to see how it integrates with other behavior. But if you want my analysis of the situation, every CIT in that room went dream-state. Including you. Mass hallucination. The only sane people in that room for thirty seconds were the azi and that kid, and most of us were keyed on our CITs and bewildered as hell.''

"Except you?''

"I was watching you *and* her.''

Justin gave a heavy sigh and some of the tension went out of him. It was nothing, God knew, he did not *know*. It was what Grant said, a roomful of psychologists forgot their science. Flux-thinking. Shades of values. "Hell with Hauptmann,'' he muttered. "I'm becoming an Emoryite." Two more quiet breaths. He could remember it with less emotional charge now and see the child—instead of the woman. *I'm going to a party at Valery's.*

Not a touch of maliciousness in that. She had not been playing her game then. She had looked up with a face as innocent as any child's and offered a let's-be-friends opening. Them and Us. Peace-making, maybe. He was not in touch with his own four-year-old memories. Jacobs, who worked that level in citizen psych, could tell him what a four-year-old CIT was like. But he could haul up a few things out of that dark water: Jordan's face when he was in his thirties.

Himself and Grant feeding the pond-fish. Four or five or six. He was not sure. It was one of his oldest memories and he could not pin it down.

And he sweated, suddenly, shying off.

Why? Why do I do that?

What's wrong with me?

Walls.

Children—had not been an interest of his. Emphatically— not an interest of his. He had mentally shied off every chance to learn, fled his own childhood like a territory he was not going back to; and the preoccupation of Reseune with the Project had disgusted him.

Twenty-three years old and a fool, doing routine work, wasting himself, not thinking to left and right. Just straight down a track. Not checking out much tape because tape meant helplessness; because tape opened up areas he did not want opened.

Throwing down those walls to *then,* to Jordan, to anything that had been—brought the anger up, made his palms sweat. Getting involved—

But they had *become* involved.

"It's a trap, isn't it?" he said to Grant. "Your psychset won't let you see what I saw. But is it valid for *her,* Grant? She has that flux-dimension, and so do all us CITs."

Grant gave a humorless laugh. "You're conceding I'm right."

"It was a roomful of CITs being fools. But maybe we saw something you didn't."

"Flux. Flux. Klein bottles. True and not-true. I'm *glad* I

know what planet I'm standing on, all the time. And I saw what I saw without supering the past *or* the future."

"Damn. Sometimes I wish I could borrow your tape."

Grant shook his head. "You're right too. About seeing things I don't. I know you do. I'm worried. I'm worried because I know I can't see the situation the way a CIT does. I can logic my way through what you'll do, but damned if I can understand the flux."

"You mean your pathways are so down azi-tracks you don't see it." He could not let the Hauptmann-Emory debate pass; Grant nattered at him with it all the time, and Grant was trying him with it now. Under the other things, a little touch of clinical perspective: *get out of it, Justin. Don't react. Think.*

"I mean," Grant said, "if we were all azi we wouldn't *have* this problem. And *she* wouldn't: they could install the damn psychset and she'd be exactly what they wanted. But she isn't. They aren't. Rationality isn't what they're after, it's not what they're practicing. From where I stand, you're as upside down as they are, and I wish to hell you'd listen to me and keep your head down, throw out the hallucinations, and don't react. Any possible trouble is years away. There's time to prepare for it."

"You're absolutely right: we're not dealing with azi mindset here. They're not a hell of a lot careful. If anything goes wrong with their precious project next week they'll know it was my fault. Anytime that kid crosses my path—there's no way I can be innocent. Facts have nothing to do with it. She's just damn well killed any chance of getting any give in Jordan's situation; hell, they may not even let the letters through—"

"Don't *look* for blame. Don't act as if you have it. Mark me: if you go around reacting, they'll react."

Ari's voice. Out of the past. *Sweet, get control of yourself. Boy, I do appreciate your distress, but get a grip on it. Are you afraid of women, sweet? Your father is. Family is such a liability.*

He rested his head in his hands and knew even when he did it that he had lost his edge, lost everything, scattered it as thoroughly as he could manage it—all the fine-edged logic, all the control, all the defensive mechanisms. He walked Reseune's corridors like a ghost, laid himself open to everyone, shielded no reactions. *See, I'm harmless.*

No one had to worry about him. He was all nerves and reactions. He detected everyone's vague distaste and their caution around him. Jordan's calamity and his own guilt over precipitating it had taken the fight out of him, maybe made him half crazy, that was what they had to think.

Except the handful who had seen the tapes. Who had seen those damnable tapes and knew what Ari had done, knew why he waked in cold sweats and why he shied off from people touching him or being near him. Especially Petros Ivanov knew, having probed his mind after Giraud and everyone had done with him. *I'm going to do a little intervention*, Petros had said, patting his shoulder while he was going under; it had taken three large Security men to get him over there to hospital and several interns to get the drug into him. Giraud's orders. *I'm just going to tell you it's all right. That you're safe. You've been through trauma. I'm going to close off that time. All right? Relax. You know me, Justin. You know I'm on your side. . . .*

O God, what did they do to me? Ari, Giraud, Petros—

He wept. Grant put a hand on his arm. Grant was the only one, the only one who could. The child had touched his hand. And he had flashed-back. It was like touching a corpse.

He sat like that for a long time. Until he heard voices, and knew other people were on the walk, far across the quadrangle. There was a hedge to hide them. But he made the effort to pull himself together.

"Justin?" Grant said.

"I'm all right. Dammit." And, which he had never said to Grant: "Petros did something to me. Or Giraud did. Or Ari. Don't you see it? Don't you see a difference?"

"No."

"Tell me the truth, dammit!"

Grant flinched. A strange, distant kind of flinching. And pain, after that. Profound pain.

"Grant? Do *you* think they did something to me?"

"I don't understand born-men," Grant said.

"Don't give me that shit!"

"—I was about to say—" Grant's face was white, his lips all but trembling. "Justin, you people—I don't understand."

"Don't lie to me. What were you going to say?"

"I don't know the answer. God, you'd been shocked over and over; if you were azi you'd have gone like I did. Better if you could have. I don't know what's going on inside you. I see—I see you—"

"Spit it out, Grant!"

"—You're not—not like you would have been if it hadn't happened. Who could be? You learn. You adjust."

"That's not what I'm asking. *Did they do anything?*"

"I don't know," Grant said. All but stammered. "I don't know. I can't judge CIT psychsets."

"You can judge *mine*."

"Don't back me into a corner, Justin. I *don't know*. I don't know and I don't know how to know."

"I'm psyched. Is that what you see? Come on. Give me some *help*, Grant."

"I think you've got scars. I don't know whether Petros helped or hurt."

"Or knocked me the rest of the way down and did it to me like Ari did. The kid—" It had been a jolt. A severe jolt. Time-trip. *I'm afraid of the tape-flashes. I shut them out. I warp myself away from that time. That in itself is a decision, isn't it?*

Petros: "I'm going to close it down."

Wall it off.

God. It's a psychblock. It could be.

They weren't my friends. Or Jordan's. I know that.

He drew a deep, sudden gulp of air. *I'm blocking off everything I learned from her. I'm scared stiff of it.*

"Justin?"

The kid's shaken it loose. The kid's thrown me back before Petros. Before Giraud. Back when there was just Ari.

Back when I didn't believe anything could get to me. I walked in her door that night thinking I was in control.

Two seconds later I knew I wasn't.

Family is a liability, sweet.

What was she telling me?

"Justin?"

Would she want *what Reseune is becoming? Would she* want *that kid in Giraud's hands? Damn, he was in Ari's pocket while she was alive. But after she died—*

"Justin!"

He became aware of Grant shaking at him. Of real fear. "I'm all right," he mumbled. "I'm all right."

He felt Grant's hand close on his. Grant's hand was warm. The wind had gone through him. What he was looking at, he did not know. The garden. The pond. "Grant, —whether or not that kid's Ari reincarnate, she's smart. She's figured out how to psych *them*. Isn't that what it's all about? She's figured out what they want, isn't that what you say about Hauptmann's subjects? She's got them believing all of it. Denys and Jane and Giraud and all of them. *I* don't have to believe in it to believe what can happen to us if Giraud thinks we're a threat."

"Justin. Let it alone. Let's go. It's cold out here."

"*Do* you think they ran a psychblock on me?" He dragged himself back from out-there; looked at Grant's pale, cold-stung face. "Give me the truth, Grant."

A long silence. Grant was breathing hard. Holding back. It took no skill to see that.

"I think they could have," Grant said finally. The grip on his hand hurt. There was a tremor in Grant's voice. "I've done whatever I could. I've tried. Ever since. Don't slip on me. Don't let them get their hands on you again. And they can—if you give them any excuse. You know they can."

"I'm not going under. I'm not. I *know* what they did." He took a deep breath and drew Grant closer, hugged him, leaned against him, exhausted. "I'm doing all right. Maybe I'm doing better than I have been in the last six years."

Grant looked at him, pale and panicked.

"I swear," Justin said. He was beyond cold. Frozen through. Numb. "Damn," he said. "We've got time, don't we?"

"We've got time," Grant said. And pulled at him. "Come on. You're freezing. So am I. Let's get inside."

He got up. He threw the rest of the food to the fish, stuffed the napkin into his pocket with numb fingers, and walked. He was not thoroughly conscious of the route, of all the automatic things. Grant had no more to say until they got to the office in Wing Two.

Then Grant lingered at the door of his office. Just looked at him, as if to ask if he was all right. "I've got to run to library."

He gave Grant a silent lift of the chin. I'm all right. "Go on, then."

Grant bit his lip. "See you at lunch."

"Right."

Grant left. He sat down in the disordered little office, logged on to the House system, and prepared to get to work. But a message-dot was blinking on the corner of his screen. He windowed it up.

See me first thing, my office, it said. *Giraud Nye*.

He sat there staring at the thing. He found his hand shaking when he reached to punch the off switch.

He was not ready for this. Psychprobe flashed into his mind; all the old nightmares. He needed all his self-control.

All the old reflexes were gone. Everything. *He* was vulnerable. Grant was.

He had whatever time it took to walk over there to pull himself together. He did not know what to do, whether to route himself past the library and try to warn Grant—but that looked guilty. Every move he could make could damn him.

No, he thought then, and bit his lip till it bled. It flashed back to another meeting. A taste of blood in his mouth. Hysteria jammed behind his teeth.

It's started, he thought. *It's happened*.

He turned the machine on, sent a message over to Grant's office: *Giraud wants to see me. I may be held up on the lunch. —J*. It was warning enough. What Grant could do about it, he had no idea.

Worry. That was what.

He shut down again, got up, locked the office, and walked down the corridor, still tasting the blood. He kept looking at things and people with the thought that he might not be back. That the next thing he and Grant might see might be an interview room in the hospital.

---

ix

Giraud's office was the same he had always had, in the Administrative Wing, the same paneled and unobtrusive entry with the outside lock—more security than Ari had ever used. Giraud was no longer official head of Security. He was *Councillor* Nye these days—for outsiders' information. But everyone in the House knew who was running Security—still.

Justin slid his card into the lock, heard it click, set for his

CIT-number. He walked into the short paneled hall and opened the inside door, on the office where Giraud's azi Abban was at his accustomed desk.

That was the first thing he saw. In the next split-second he saw the two Security officers and Abban was rising casually from his chair.

He stopped cold. And looked at the nearer of the azi officers, eye to eye, calmly: *Let's be civilized.* He took the next quiet step inside and let the door shut at his back.

They had a body-scanner. "Arms out, ser," the one on the left said. He obliged them, let them pass the wand over him. It found something in his coat pocket. The officer pulled out the paper napkin. Justin gave him a disparaging look in spite of the fact that his heart was going like a hammer and the air in the room seemed too thin.

They satisfied themselves he was not armed. Abban opened the door and they took him through it.

Giraud was not the only one there. Denys was. And Petros Ivanov. He felt his heart trying to come up his throat. One of the officers held him lightly by the arm and guided him to the remaining chair, in front of Giraud's desk. Denys sat in a chair to the left of the desk, Petros to the right.

Like a tribunal.

And the Security men stayed, one with his hand on the back of Justin's chair, until Giraud lifted a hand and told them to leave. But Justin's ears told him someone had stayed when the door had shut.

Abban, he thought.

"You understand why you're here," Giraud said. "I don't have to tell you."

Giraud wanted an answer. "Yes, ser," he said in a muted voice.

They'll do what they damned well please.

Why have they got Petros here? Unless they're going to run a probe.

"Have you got anything to say?" Giraud asked.

"I don't think I should have to." He found a tenuous control of his voice. *Dammit, get a grip on things.*

And like a wind out of the dark: *Steady, sweet. Don't give everything away.*

"I didn't provoke that. God *knows* I didn't want it."

"You could have damn well left."

"I left."

"After." Giraud's face was thin-lipped with anger. He picked up a stylus and posed it between his fingers. "What's your intention? To sabotage the project?"

"No. I was there like everyone else. No different. I was minding my own business. What did you do, prime her for that show? Is *that* it? A little show? Impress the Family? Con the press? I'll *bet* you've got tape."

Giraud had not expected that. He gave away very little. Denys and Petros looked distressed.

"The child wasn't prompted," Denys said quietly. "You have my word, Justin, it wasn't prompted."

"The hell it wasn't. It's a damn good show for the news, isn't it—just the sort of thing that makes great fodder for the eetees out there. The kid singles out the killer's replicate. God! what a piece of science!"

"Don't bother to play for a camera," Giraud said. "We're not being taped."

"I didn't expect." He was shaking. He shifted his foot to relax his leg, to keep it from trembling. But, God, the brain was working. They were going to haul him off for another session, that was what they were working up to; and somehow that shook the fog out of his mind. "I imagine you'll work me over good before I get to the cameras. But it'd be sloppy as hell to have me on the tape in that party and dropping right out again. Or turning up dead. Makes a problem for you, doesn't it?"

"Justin," Petros said, a tone of appeal. "No one's going to 'work you over.' That's not what we're about here."

"Sure."

"What we're about," Giraud said in a hard, clipped voice, "is one clear question. Did *you* cue her?"

"You find your own answers. Write down whatever you want. Look at the damn tape."

"We have," Giraud said. "Grant had eye contact with her. So did you, right before she moved."

Attack on a new target. Of course they got around to Grant. "What else were people looking at? What else were we *there* to look at? I looked at her. Did you think I'd come there and *not*? You saw me there. You could have told me to leave. But of course you didn't. You set me up. You set up the whole thing. How many people in there knew it? Just you?"

"You maintain you didn't cue her."

"Dammit, no. Neither of us did. I asked Grant. He wouldn't lie to me. He admits the eye contact. He was looking at her. 'I got caught at it,' was the way he put it. It wasn't his fault. It wasn't mine."

Petros stirred in his chair. Leaned toward Giraud. "Gerry, I think you have to take into account what I said."

Giraud touched the desk control. The screen tilted up out of the surface; he typed something with his right hand, likely a file-scan. Dataflow reflected off the metal on his collar, a flicker of green.

Manipulation of more than data. Orchestrated, Justin told himself. The whole play. A little moment of suspense now. Secrets.

And he still could not keep himself from reacting.

Giraud read or mimed reading. His breathing grew larger. His face was no friendlier when he looked up. "You don't like tapestudy. Odd, in a designer."

"I don't damn well trust it. Can you blame me?"

"You don't even do entertainment tapes."

"I work hard."

"Let's not have that kind of answer. You skipped out on your follow-ups with Petros. You don't take tape more than once every month or so. That's a damned strange attitude in a designer."

He said nothing. He had used all the glib answers.

"Even Grant," Giraud said, "doesn't go into the lab for his. He uses a home unit. Not at all regulation."

"There's no rule about that. If that satisfies him, it satisfies him. Grant's bright, he's got good absorption—"

"It's not your instruction to do that."

"No, it's not my instruction."

"You know," Petros said, "Grant's self-sufficient, completely social. He doesn't need that kind of reinforcement as often as some. But considering what he's been through, it would be better if he took it deep. Just as a checkup."

"Considering what you put him through? No!"

"So it is your instruction," Giraud said.

"No. It's his choice. It's his choice, he's entitled, the same as I am, the last I heard."

"I'm not sure we *need* a designer-team that's phobic about tape."

"Go to hell."

"Easy," Denys said. "Take it easy. Giraud, there's nothing wrong with his output. Or Grant's. That's not at issue."

"There was more than one victim in Ari's murder," Petros said. "Justin was. Grant was. I don't think you can ignore that fact. You're dealing with someone who was a boy when the incident happened, who was, in fact, the victim of Ari's own criminal act, among others. I haven't wanted to press the issue. I've been keeping an eye on him. I've sent him requests to come in to talk. Is that true, Justin?"

"It's true."

"You haven't answered, have you?"

"No." Panic pressed on him. He felt sick inside.

"The whole situation with the Project," Petros said, "has bothered you quite a bit, hasn't it?"

"Live and let live. I'm sorry for the kid. I'm sure you've got all the benefit of Security's eavesdropping in my apartment. I hope you get a lot of entertainment out of the intimate bits."

"Justin."

"You can go to hell too, Petros."

"Justin. Tell me the truth. *Are* you still getting tape-flashes?"

"No."

"You're sure."

"Yes, I'm sure."

"You felt a lot of stress when you walked into the party, didn't you?"

"Hell, no. Why should I?"

"I think that's your answer," Petros said to Giraud. "He came in there stressed. Both of them did. Ari had no trouble picking up on it. That's all there is to it. I don't think it was intended. I'm more disturbed about Justin's state of mind. I think it's just best he go back to his wing, and show up at family functions, and carry on as normally as he can. I don't think anything useful is served by a probe. He's carrying enough stress as it is. I do want him to come in for counseling."

"Giraud," Denys said, "if you *believe* young Ari's

sensitivities, bear in mind she wasn't afraid of Justin. Stressed as he was, she wasn't afraid of him. Quite the opposite.''

"I don't like that either." Giraud drew a breath and leaned back, looking at Justin from under his brows. "You'll take Petros' prescription. If he tells me you're not cooperating, you'll be tending a precip station before sundown. Hear me?''

"Yes, ser."

"You'll go on working. If something takes you across Ari's path, you speak to her or not according to your judgment, whichever will provoke the least curiosity. You'll show up at Family functions. If she speaks to you, be pleasant. No more than that. You stray off that line, you'll be in here again and I won't be in a good mood. And that goes for Grant, just the same. You make it clear to him. Do you understand me?''

"Yes, ser." Like any azi. Quiet. Respectful. *It's a trap. It'll still close. There's something more to this.*

"You can go. Open the door, Abban."

The door did open. He shoved himself out of his chair. Denys did the same. He made it as far as the door and Denys went out it with him, caught his arm, steered him past Security out into the small box of the entry hall and out again into the main corridor.

Then Denys tugged him to a stop. "Justin."

He stayed stopped. He was shaking, still. But defiance did not serve anything.

"Justin, you're under a lot of pressure. But you know and I know—there's no memory transfer. It's *not* the old Ari. We don't want, frankly, another case of animosity with the Warricks. We don't *want* you taking Jordan's part in this. You know what's at stake.''

He nodded.

"Justin, listen to me. Giraud did the probe on you. He knows damned well you're honest. He's just—"

"A bastard."

"Justin. Don't make things hard. Do what Giraud says. Don't make a mistake. You don't want to hurt the little girl. I know you don't. What Ari did to you—has nothing to do with her. And you wouldn't hurt her.''

"No. I never did anything to *Ari*, for God's sake. You think I'd hurt a kid?"

"I know. I know that's true. Just think about that. Think

about it the next time you have to deal with her. Ari tore you up. You can do the same thing to that child. You can hurt her. I want you to think seriously about that."

"I didn't do anything to her!"

"You didn't do anything. Calm down. Calm down and take a breath. Listen to me. If you can handle this right, it could help you."

"Sure."

Denys took his arm again, faced him closer to the wall as Security left the office. Held on to him. "Justin. I wanted to tell you—the request that's on my desk, the phone link: I'm going to give it a few weeks and then allow it. You'll be on some kind of delay—Jordan's clever, and Security has to have time to think. That's the best I can do. Does that make you feel better?"

"What's it cost me?"

"Nothing. Nothing. Just don't foul it up. Stay out of trouble. All right?"

He stared at the wall, at travertine patterns that blurred in front of his eyes. He felt Denys pat his shoulder.

"I'm damn sorry. I'm damn sorry. I know. You haven't had a day of peace. But I want you *on* the Project. That's why I fought Giraud to keep you here. Ari liked you—no. Listen to me. Ari *liked* you. Never mind what she did. I know her—posthumously—as well as I know myself. Ari's feud with Jordan was old and it was bitter. But she got your test scores and made up her mind she wanted you."

"They were faked!"

"No, they weren't. Not outstandingly high, *you* know that. But scattered through half a dozen fields. You had the qualities *she* had. Not her match, but then, you hadn't had Olga Emory pushing you. She told me—personally—and this is no lie, son, that she *wanted* you in her wing, that you were better than the tests showed, a damned lot better, she said, than Jordan. Her words, not mine."

"Science wasn't what she had in mind, you know that."

"You're wrong. It's not what you want to hear, God knows. But if you want to understand why she did what she did— that's something you *should* know. I have one interest in this. Ari. Understand—she had cancer. Rejuv breakdown. The doctors argue whether the cancer kicked the rejuv or whether the rejuv was failing naturally and let the cancer develop. Whatever was going on, she *knew* she was in trouble and the timing couldn't have been worse. Surgery would have delayed the project, so she put Petros and Irina under orders and covered it up. She set the whole project up, so that when she had to go for surgery—I'm sure she didn't rule that out: she wasn't a fool; but so when she did, it wouldn't leave the subject without support, you understand, and it could run a few months with a light hand. Understand: I knew, because I was her friend, Justin. I was the one she allowed access to her notes. Giraud's damn good at the money end of this. But my concern is her concern: the Project. I think you have your sincere doubts about it. No controls, no duplicatable result— But it's founded on two centuries of duplicatable results with the azi. And of course it's not the kind of thing that we can quantify: we're dealing with a human life, an emotional dimension, a subjective dimension. We may disagree like hell, Justin, in there, in private, and I respect you for your professional honesty. But if you try to sabotage us, you'll have me for an enemy. Do you understand me?''

"Yes, ser.''

"I'll tell you another thing: Ari did some very wrong things. But she was a great woman. She *was* Reseune. And she was my friend. I've protected you; and I've protected her reputation by the same stroke; and *damned* if I'll see some sordid little incident destroy that reputation. I'll keep you from that. You understand me?''

"You've got the tapes in the archives! If this poor kid halfway follows in Ari's track, researchers are going to want every last detail—and that's no small one.''

"No. That won't matter. That's from the *end* of her life, beyond the scope of their legitimate interest. And even so, that's why we're working with Rubin. Rubin's the one the military can paw over. Ari is *our* project. *We* keep title on the techniques. Did Reseune ever release anything—it has a financial interest in?''

"My God, you can run that scam on the military for years. Admit it. It's Giraud's damn fund-raiser. His bottomless source of military projects.''

Denys smiled and shook his head. "It's going to *work*, Justin. We didn't prompt her.''

"Then tell me this: are you sure *Giraud* didn't?"

Denys' eyes reacted minutely. The face did not. It went on smiling. "Time will prove it, won't it? In your position, rather than be made a public fool, I'd keep my mouth shut, Justin Warrick. I've helped you. I've spoken for you and Jordan and Grant when no one else did. I've been your patron. But remember I was Ari's friend. And I *won't* see this project sabotaged."

The threat was there. It was real. He had no doubt of it. "Yes, ser," he said in half a voice.

Denys patted his shoulder again. "That's the only time I'm going to say that. I don't want ever to say it again. I want you to take the favor I'm doing you and remember what I told you. All right?"

"Yes, ser."

"Are *you* all right?"

He drew a breath. "That depends on what Petros is going to do, doesn't it?"

"He's just going to talk to you. That's all." Denys shook at him gently. "Justin, —are you getting tape-flashes?"

"No," he said. "No." His mouth trembled. He let it. It made the point with Denys. "I've just had enough hell. The hospital panics me, all right? Do you blame me? I don't trust Petros. Or anyone on his staff. I'll answer his questions. If you want my cooperation, keep him away from me and Grant."

"Is that blackmail?"

"God, I couldn't have learned anything about that, could I? No. I'm asking you. I'll do anything you want me to. I've got no percentage in hurting the kid. I don't want that. I just want my job, I want the phone-link, I want to—"

He lost his composure, turned and leaned against the wall until he had gotten his breath.

Hand them all the keys, sweet, that's right.

Damn stupid.

"You've got all that," Denys said. "Look. You answer Petros' questions. You try to work this thing out. You were a scared kid yourself. You're still scared, and I'm terribly afraid all this did you more damage than you're willing to have known—"

"I can do my job. You said that."

"That's not in question. I assure you it's not. You don't

know who to trust. You think you're all alone. You're not. Petros does care. I do. I know, that's not what you want to hear. But you can come to me if you feel you need help. I've told you my conditions. I want your help. I *don't* want any accusations against Ari, the project, or the staff.''

''Then keep Petros' hands off me and Grant. Tell Security to take their damn equipment out. Let me live my life and do my work, that's all.''

''I want to help you.''

''Then help me! Do what I asked. You'll get my cooperation. I'm not carrying on a feud. I just want a little peace, Denys. I just want a little peace, after all these years. Have I—ever—done anyone any harm?''

''No.'' A pat on his shoulder, on his back. ''No. You haven't. Never anything. The harm was all against you.''

He turned, leaning against the wall. ''Then leave me *alone*, for God's sake, let me talk to my father, let me do my work, I'll be all right, just let me alone and *get Security out of my bedroom!*''

Denys looked at him a long time. ''All right,'' he said. ''We'll try that awhile. We'll try it, at least on the home front. I don't say we won't notice who comes and goes through your door. If something looks suspicious they'll be on you. Not otherwise. I'll give that order. Just don't give me any cause to regret it.''

''No, ser,'' he said, because it was all he could get out.

Denys left him then.

When he got back to the office Grant met him in the doorway—Grant, scared and silent, asking questions just by being there.

''It's all right,'' he said. ''They asked if we meant to do it. I said no. I said some other things. Denys said they were going to get Security off our tails.''

Grant gave him a look that wondered who was listening and who he was playing for.

''No, it's what he said,'' he answered Grant. And shut the door for what privacy they had. He remembered the other thing, the important thing, then, the back and forth of promises and threats like so many hammer-blows, and he leaned on the back of the work-station chair, finding himself short of breath. ''He said they were going to let us talk to Jordan.''

"Is that true?" Grant wondered.

That was the thing that threw him off his balance, that they suddenly promised him favors when they had least reason. When they could haul him off to hospital by force and they had just demonstrated that.

Something was going on.

_____ X _____

"Music," he told the Minder that night, when they walked in the door. It started the tape at the cutoff point. It reported on calls. There were none. "We're not popular," he said to Grant. There was usually at least one, something from the lab, somebody asking about business, who had failed to catch them at the office.

"Ah, human inconstancy." Grant laid his briefcase on the accustomed table, shed his coat into the closet, and walked over to the sideboard and the liquor cabinet while Justin hung his up. He mixed two drinks and brought them back. "Double for you. Shoes off, feet up, sit. You can use it."

He sat down, kicked the shoes off, leaned back in the cushions and drank. Whiskey and water, a taste that promised present relief for frayed nerves. He saw Grant with the little plastic slate they used—writing things they dared not say aloud; and Grant wrote:

Do we believe them about dropping the bugging?

Justin shook his head. Set the glass down on the stone rim of the cushioned pit-group and reached for the tablet. *We feed them a little disinformation and see if we can catch them.*

Back to Grant; a nod. *Idea?*

To him. *Not yet. Thinking.*

Grant: *I suppose I have to wait till fishfeed to find out what happened.*

Himself: *Complicated. Dangerous. Petros is going to do interviews with me.*

Grant: a disturbed look. Unspoken question.

Himself: *They suspect about the flashes.*

Grant: underline of word *interviews.* Question mark.

Himself: *Denys said. No probe.* Then he added: *They've realized I have a problem with tape. I'm scared. I'm afraid they*

*were doing a voice-stress. If so, I flunked. Will flunk Petros'
test worse. Long time—I tried to think the flashes were trauma.
Now I think maybe a botched-up block: deliberate. Maybe they
want me like this.*

Grant read it with a frown growing on his face. He wrote
with some deliberation. Cleared the slate and tried again. And
again. Finally a brief: *I think not deliberate block. I think too
many probes.*

Himself: *Then why in hell are we writing notes in our own
living room?* Triple underlined.

Grant reacted with a little lift of the brows. And wrote: *Because
anything is possible. But I don't think deliberate block.
Damage. Giraud came in asking questions on top of an intervention
Ari was running and hadn't finished. If that isn't
enough, what is? Whatever Ari did would have been extensive
and subtle. She could run an intervention with a single sentence.
We know that. Giraud came breaking in and messed
something up.*

Justin read that and felt the cold go a little deeper. He
chewed the stylus a moment and wrote: *Giraud had seen the
tapes. Giraud knew what she did. Giraud may work more with
military psychsets, and that doesn't reassure me either. They
got him that damn Special rating. Politics. Not talent. God
knows what he did to me. Or what Petros did.*

Grant read and a frown came onto his face. He wrote: *I can't
believe it of Petros. Giraud, yes. But Petros is independent.*

Himself: *I don't trust him. And I've got to face those interviews.
They can take me off job. Call me unstable, suspend
Alpha license. Transfer you. Whole damn thing over again.*

Grant grabbed the slate and wrote, frowning: *You're Jordan's
replicate. If you show talent matching his without psychogenics
program at same time they're running Rubin Project
you could call their results into question. Also me. Remember
Ari created me from a Special. You and I: possible controls on
Project. Is that why Ari wanted us? Is that why Giraud
doesn't?*

The thought upset his stomach. *I don't know*, he wrote.

Grant: *Giraud and Denys run the Project without controls
except Rubin himself, and there's no knowing how honest
those results will be. We are inconvenient. Ari wouldn't ever*

have worked the way they're working. Ari used controls, far as you can with human psych. I think she wanted us both.

Himself: *Denys swears the Project is valid. But it's compromised every step of the way.*

Grant: *It's valid if it works. Like you've always said: They don't plan to release data if it does work. Reseune never releases data. Reseune makes money off its discoveries. If Reseune gets Ari back, an Ari to direct further research, will they release notes to general publication? No. Reseune will get big Defense contracts. Lot of power, power of secrecy, lot of money, but Reseune will run whole deal and get more and more power. Reseune will never release the findings. Reseune will work on contract for Defense, and get anything Reseune wants as long as Defense gets promises of recovering individuals—which even Reseune won't be able to do without the kind of documentation under that mountain out there. That takes years. Takes lifetimes. In the meantime, Reseune does some things for Defense, lot of things for itself. Do I read born-men right?*

He read and nodded, with a worse and worse feeling in his gut.

Grant: *You're very strange, you CITs. Perhaps it goes with devising your own psychsets—and having your logic on top. We know our bottom strata are sound. Who am I to judge my makers?*

---- xi ----

Jane sat down on the edge of the bed and pulled her hair out of the way as Ollie sat down by her and brushed his lips across her nape.

The Child, thank God, was asleep, and Nelly had won the battle of wills for the night.

Ari was hyper—*had* been hyper, all day, wanting to go back to Valery's place and play.

Time for *that* to change. Valery had become a problem, as she had predicted. Time for Ari to have another playmate. There had never been only one.

Damn. Hell of a thing to do to the kid.

Ollie's arms came around her, hugged her against him. "Is something the matter?" Ollie asked.

"Do something distracting, Ollie dear. I don't want to think tonight."

Damn. I'm even beginning to talk *like Olga.*

Ollie slid a hand lower and kissed her shoulder.

"Come on, Ollie, dammit, let's get rough. I'm in a mood to kill something."

Ollie understood then. Ollie pushed her down on the bed and made himself a major distraction, holding her hands because Ollie had no particular desire to end up with scratch marks.

Ollie was damned good. Like most azi who took the training, he was very, very good, and trying to keep him at bay was a game he won only slowly and with deliberation, a game precisely timed to what would work with her.

Work, it did. Jane sighed, and gave herself up after a while to Ollie's gentler tactics. Nice thing about an azi lover—he was always in the mood. Always more worried about her than about himself. She had had a dozen CIT lovers. But funny thing . . . she cared more about Ollie. And he would never expect that.

"I love you," she said into his ear, when he was almost asleep, his head on her shoulder. She ran her fingers through his sweat-damp hair and he looked at her with a puzzled, pleased expression. "I really do, Ollie."

"Sera," he said. And stayed very still, as if she had lost her mind after all these years. He was exhausted. She was still insomniac. But he was going to stay awake if his eyes crossed, if she wanted to talk, she knew that. She had his attention.

"That's all," she said. "I just decided to tell you that."

"Thank you," he said, not moving. Looking as if he still thought there was more to this.

"Nothing else." She rubbed his shoulder. "You ever wanted to be a CIT? Take the final tape? Go out of here?"

"No," he said. Sleep seemed to leave him. His breathing quickened. "I really don't. I don't want to. I couldn't leave you."

"You could. The tape would fix that."

"I don't want it. I truly don't want it. It couldn't make me not want to be here. Nothing could do that. Don't tell me to take it."

"I won't. No one will. I only wondered, Ollie. So you don't want to leave here. But what if I have to?"

"I'll go with you!"

"Will you?"

"Where will we go?"

"Fargone. Not for a while yet. But I really want to be sure you're all right. Because I do love you. I love you more than I do anyone. Enough to leave you here if that's what you want, or to take you with me, or to do anything you want me to. You deserve that, after all these years. I want you to be happy."

He started to answer, hitching up on one elbow. Facile and quick, an azi's ready and sincere protest of loyalty. She stopped him with a hand on his lips.

"No. Listen to me. I'm getting older, Ollie. I'm not immortal. And they're so damn scared I won't turn Ari loose when I have to— That's coming, Ollie. Two more years. God, how fast it's gone! Sometimes I could kill her; and sometimes— sometimes I feel so damn sorry for her. Which is what they don't want. They're afraid I'll break the rules, that's at the center of it. They—Giraud and Denys, damn their hearts, have decided she's too attached to you. They want that to stop. No more contact with her. Cold and critical. That's the prescription. Sometimes I think they earnestly hope I'll drop dead on cue, just like the damn script. I had a talk with Giraud today—" She drew a deep breath and something hurt behind her eyes and around her heart. "They offered me the directorship at RESEUNESPACE. Fargone. The Rubin Project, with bows and ribbons on it."

"Did you take it?" he asked, finally, when breath was too choked in her to go on.

She nodded, bit her lip and got it under control. "I did. Sweet Giraud. *Oh, you just withdraw to Wing One when she's seven*, that was what they told me when I took this on. Now they've got the nervies about it and they want me the hell out of reach. *It's not enough*, Giraud says. *Olga died when Ari was seven. Being over in Wing One, just walking out of her life, that's too much rejection, too attainable an object*. Dammit. So they offer me the directorship. Morley's out, I'm in, dammit."

"You always said you wanted to go back to space."

Another several breaths. "Ollie, I wanted to. I've wanted to for years and years. Until—somewhere I just got old. And they offered me this, and I realized I don't want to go anymore. That's a terrible thing to realize, for an old spacer brat. I've gotten old on the ground, and all the things I know are here, everything that's familiar, and I want it around me, that's all—'' Another breath. ''Not the way I'm going to have it, though. They can promote me. Or they can retire me. Damned if I'll take retirement. That's the trouble of doing your job and never bothering to power-grab. That upstart Giraud can fire me. That's what it comes down to. Damn his guts. So I go to Fargone. And start the whole thing over with another damn brat, this one with medical problems. Shit, Ollie. Do somebody a favor and look at what they do to you.''

Ollie brushed at her hair.. Stroked her shoulder. Ached his heart out for her, that was what Ollie would do, because she was his Supervisor, and god was in trouble.

''Well, hell if I want to drag you into the same mess. Think what it'll be, if you go out there. I'll die on you in not so many years—add it up, Ollie; and there you are, twenty lightyears from civilization. What kind of thing is that to do to somebody who's got less choice than I do? Huh? I don't want to put you in that kind of position. If you like it here at Reseune, I can get you that CIT tape and you can stay here where it's civilized, no take-hold drills and no Keis and fishcakes and no corridors where people walk off the ceiling . . .''

''Jane, if I tell you I want to go, what will you tell me? That I'm a stupid azi who doesn't know what he wants? I know. Am I going to let you go off with some damn azi out of the Town?''

''I'm a hundred and—''

''—I don't care. I don't care. Don't make us both miserable. Don't playact with me. You want me to tell you I want to be with you, I'm telling you. But it's not fair to hold this over me. I can hear it. *Dammit, Ollie, I'll leave you behind, I will*— I don't want to listen to that for two years. I don't even want to think about it.''

Ollie was not one to get upset. He was. She saw that finally and reached up and brushed his cheek with her fingertips. ''I won't do that. I won't do it. Damn, this is too much seriousness. Damn Giraud. Damn the project. Ollie, they don't want you to touch Ari after this.''

His brow furrowed in distress. "They blame me."

"It's not a question of blame. They see she likes you. It's the damn program. They wanted to take you out of here right away and I told them go to hell. I told them I'd blow it, right then. Tell the kid everything. And *they'll* walk a narrow line, damn right they will. So they had a counteroffer ready. One they thought I'd jump at. And a threat. Retirement. So what could I do? I took the directorship. I get myself and you—you—out of here. I should be glad of that."

"I'm sorry if I did this."

"Dammit, no, you didn't. I didn't. No one did it. Olga never beat the kid. Thank God. But I can't stand it, Ollie. I can't stand it anymore."

"Don't cry. I can't stand that."

"I'm not about to. Shut up. Roll over. It's my turn. Do you mind?"

xii

"Of course not," he said to Petros, across the desk from him, while the Scriber ran, and he knew well enough they had a voice-stress running, that was probably reading-out to Petros on that little screen. Petros glanced from it often and sometimes smiled at him in his best bedside manner.

"You're involved in an intimate relationship with your companion," Petros said. "Don't you have any misgivings about that? You know an azi really can't defend himself against that kind of thing."

"I've really thought about that. I've talked with Grant about it. But it's the pattern we were brought up with, isn't it? And for various reasons, you know what I'm talking about, we both have problems that cut us off from the rest of the House, and we were both—let's call it—in need of support."

"Describe these problems."

"Oh, come on, Petros, you know and I know we're not on top of the social set. Political contagion. I don't have to describe it for you."

"You feel isolated."

He laughed. "My God, were you at the party? I thought you were."

"Well, yes." A glance at the monitor. "I was. She's a nice little kid. What do you think?"

He looked at Petros, raised an eyebrow at Petros' dour drollery, and gave a bitter laugh. "I think she's a bit of a brat, and what kid isn't?" He made it a quiet smile, catching Petros' eye. "Thank God *I* couldn't get pregnant. You might have a kid of mine to play with. Put that in your tapes and file it. How am I doing on voice-stress?"

"Well, that was tolerably stressed."

"I thought it was. You're trying to get me to react, but do we have to be grotesque?"

"You consider the child grotesque."

"I consider the kid charming. I think her situation is grotesque. But evidently your ethics can compass it. They're holding my father at gunpoint as far as I'm concerned, so I'm damn well not going to make a move. Those are my ethics. Am I lying?"

Petros was not smiling. He was watching the monitor. "Nice. Nice reaction."

"I'm sure."

"Annoyed as hell, are you? What do you think of Giraud?"

"I love him like my own father. How's that for comparisons? True or false?"

"Don't play games with this. You can do yourself harm."

"Register a threat to the patient."

"I'm sure that's not what I intended. I am going to insist you undergo some therapy. Mmmmn, got a little heartbeat there."

"Of course you did. I'll do your therapy, in your facility. As long as my azi sits through it with me."

"Irregular."

"Look, Petros, I've been through hell in this place. Are you trying to drive me crazy or are you going to give me a reasonable safeguard? Even a non-professional has a right to audit a psych procedure if the patient requests it. And I'm requesting a second opinion. That's all. Do it right and you won't even need Security to bring me in. Do it wrong and I'll consider other options. I'm not a panicked kid anymore. I know where I can file a protest, unless you plan to lock me up and have me disappear—damned bad for your tape record, isn't it?"

"I'll do better than that." Petros flipped switches and the

monitor swung aside, dead. "I'll give you the tape and you can take it home. I just want your word you're going to use it."

"Now you've got real surprise. Pity you cut the monitor."

"You're scared out of good sense," Petros said. "I don't blame you. Good voice control, but your pulse rate is way up. Psyched yourself for this, have you? I could order a blood test. Verbal intervention? Grant try to prep you?"

"I have to sign a consent."

Petros let out a slow breath, arms on the desk. "Keep yourself out of trouble, Justin. This is off the record. Keep yourself out of trouble. Take the orders. They *are* going to put off the phone calls."

"Sure." The disappointment made a lump in his chest. "I figured. It's all a game, anyway. And I believed Denys. I knew better."

"It's not Denys. Military security nixed it. Denys is going to put together a file that may convince them. Just cooperate for a while. You can't improve things by the show you just put on. You understand me. Keep out of trouble. You will go on getting the letters." Another sigh, an intensely unhappy look. "I'm going to see Jordan. Is there anything you want to tell him?"

"What are they doing with him?"

"Nothing. Nothing. Calm down. I'm just going over there to check out some equipment. Supering my techs. I just thought I'd offer. I thought it might make you feel better. I'm going to take him a photo of you. I thought he'd like that. I'm going to bring one back—or try."

"Sure."

"I'm going to. For his sake, as much as yours. I was his friend."

"The number of my father's friends amazes me."

"I won't argue with you. Any message?"

"Tell him I love him. What else won't be censored?"

"I'll tell him as much as I can. This is still off the record. I have a job here. Someone else would do it worse. Think about that for yourself. Go home. Go to your office. Don't forget to pick up the tape at the counter."

He was not sure, when he had left, when he was walking back across the quadrangle toward the House with the tape and a prescription, whether he had won or lost the encounter. Or what faction in the House had won or lost.

But he had not known that for years.

```
┌─────────────────────────────────────────────────┐
│                                                   │
│            Verbal Text from:                      │
│        PATTERNS OF GROWTH                         │
│     A Tapestudy in Genetics: #1                   │
│         "An Interview with                        │
│          Ariane Emory": pt. 1                     │
│                                                   │
│   Reseune Educational Publications: 8970-8768-1   │
│              approved for 80+                     │
│                                                   │
└─────────────────────────────────────────────────┘
```

Q: Dr. Emory, thank you for giving us the chance for a few direct questions about your work.

A: I'm glad to have the opportunity. Thank you. Go on.

Q: Your parents founded Reseune. Everyone knows that. Are you aware some biographers have called you the chief architect of Union?

A: I've heard the charge. [mild laughter] I wish they'd wait till I'm dead.

Q: You deny your effect—politically as well as scientifically?

A: I'm no more the architect than Bok was. Science is not politics. It may affect it. We have so little time. Could I interject an observation of my own—which may answer some of your questions in one?

Q: By all means.

A: When we came out from Earth we were a selected genepool. We were sifted by politics, by economics, by the very fact that we were fit for space. Most of the wave that reached the Hinder Stars were colonists and crews very care-

fully vetted by Sol Station, the allegedly unfit turned down, the brightest and the best, I think the phrase was then, sent out to the stars. By the time the wave reached Pell, the genepool had widened a bit, but not at all representative of Sol Station, let alone Earth—we did get one large influx when politics on Earth took a hand, and the wave that founded Union ended up mostly Eastern bloc, as they used to call it. A lot of chance entered the genepool in that final push—before Earth slammed the embargo down and stopped genetic export for a long time.

Cyteen was the sifting of the sifting of the sifting . . . meaning that if there was one population artificially selected to the extreme, it was Cyteen—which was mostly Eastern bloc, mostly scientists, and very, very small, and very far, at that time, from trade and the—call it . . . pollination . . . performed by the merchanters. That was a dangerous situation. Hence Reseune. That's where we began. That's what we're really for. People think of Reseune and azi. Azi were only a means to an end, and one day, when the population has reached what they call tech-growth positive, meaning that consumption will sustain mass production—azi will no longer be produced in those areas.

But meanwhile azi serve another function. Azi are the reservoir of every genetic trait we've been able to identify. We have tended to cull the evidently deleterious genes, of course. But there's a downside to small genepools, no matter how carefully selected, there's a downside in lack of resiliency, lack of available responses to the environment. Expansion is absolutely necessary, to avoid concentration of an originally limited genepool in the central locus of Union. We are not speaking of eugenics. We are speaking of diaspora. We are speaking of the necessary dispersion of genetic information in essentially the same ratios as that present on ancestral Earth. And we have so little time.

Q: Why—so little time?

A: *Because population increases exponentially and fills an ecosystem, be it planet or station, in a relatively short time. If that population contains insufficient genetic information, that population, especially a population at greater density than the peripheries of the system—we are of course speaking of Cyteen—and sitting at the cultural center of Union, which is another dimension not available to lower lifeforms, but very significant in terms of a creature able to engineer its own systems in all senses—if that population, I say, in such power, contains inadequate genetic information, it will run into trouble and confront itself with emergency choices which may be culturally or genetically radical. In spreading into space at much lesser density and with such preselection at work, humankind faces potential evolutionary catastrophe in a relatively small number of generations—either divergence too extreme to survive severe challenge or divergence into a genetic crisis of a different and unpredictable outcome— certainly the creation of new species of* genus homo *and very probably the creation of genetic dead ends and political tragedy. Never forget that we are more than a social animal, we are a political animal; and we are capable of becoming our own competitor.*

Q: You mean war.

A: Or predation. Or predation. Never forget that. Dispersion is absolutely essential, but so are adequately diverse genepools in the scattered pockets that result. That is the reason azi were created and continue to be created. They are the vectors of that diversity, and that some economic interests have found them—profitable—is understandable but overall repugnant to me personally and to everything Reseune stands for. History may accuse me of many things, ser, but I care profoundly what becomes of the azi, and I have exerted every influence to assure their legal protection. We do not create Thetas because we want cheap labor. We create Thetas because they are an essential and important part of human alternatives. The ThR-23 hand-eye coordination, for instance, is exceptional. Their psychset lets them operate very well in environments in which CIT geniuses would assuredly fail. They are tough, ser, in ways I find thoroughly admirable, and I recommend you, if you ever find yourself in a difficult situation in Cyteen's wilderness, hope your companion is a ThR azi, who will survive, ser, to perpetuate his type, even if you do not. That is genetic alternative at work.

Someday there will be no more azi. They will have fulfilled their purpose, which is to increase, and multiply, and fill the gaps in the human record as the original genepool disperses to a mathematically determined population density—as it must disperse, for its own future well-being, its own genetic health.

I say again: azi are genetic alternative. They are the vector for change and adaptation in the greatest challenge the human species has yet faced. They are as they are precisely because the time within which this can be accomplished is so very brief. Reseune has not opposed the creation of additional labs, simply because its interests are primarily scientific and because the task of maintaining the impetus to expansion requires vast production and education facilities. But Reseune has never relinquished its role in the creation and selection of new genesets: no other laboratory has the right to originate genetic material.

While you're being patient, let me make two most essential points: one—Reseune insists on the full integration of all azi genesets into the citizen population in any area of Union that has achieved class one status: in practical terms—azi are ideally a one-generation proposition: their primary purpose is not labor, but to open a colonial area, bring it up to productivity, and produce offspring who will enter the citizen genepool in sufficient numbers to guarantee genetic variety. The only azi who should be produced for any other purpose are those generated as a stopgap measure for defense and other emergencies in the national interest; those engaged in certain critical job classifications; and those generated for appropriate research in licensed facilities.

Two—Reseune will oppose any interest which seeks to institutionalize azi as an economic necessity. In no wise should the birthlabs be perpetuated as a purely profit-making operation. That was never their purpose.

Q: Are you saying you have interests in common with the Abolitionists?

A: Absolutely. We always have had.

CHAPTER
5

Florian ran along the sidewalk that crossed the face of Barracks 3, remembered politeness when he met a handful of adults coming the other way, stopped, stood aside, panting, and gave a little bow that the adults returned with the slightest nods of their heads. Because they were older. Because Florian was six and because it was natural for a boy to want to run but it was also natural for adults to have serious business on their minds.

So, this time, did Florian have business. He was fresh from tapestudy. He had an Assignment, a real, every-morning Assignment. It was the most important thing that had ever happened to him, he loved everything about it, and he had been so excited he had begged the Super twice to let him go there and not to the Rec Hall where he was supposed to go after tape.

"What," the Super had said, with a smile and a little twinkle in her eye that he was sure meant she was going to let him, "no Rec? Work and Rec are both important, Florian."

"I've had Rec before," he had said. *"Please."*

She had given him the chit then, *and* the Rec chit, for later, she had said, as long as he showed it to the Work Super first.

And held out her arms. Hug the Super, the very *nice* Super, and *don't* run in the hall, walk, walk, and walk, as far as the door, walk down the sidewalk until he hit the downhill road, and then *run*, fast as he could.

Which was fast, because he was not only Alpha-smart, he was good at running.

Down the shortcut between Barracks 4 and 5, zip across the road, and shortcut again to the path that led to the AG building. He slowed down finally because his side was hurting, and he hoped in the way of things that moved everybody around all the time, Olders with younger boys, they were going to check him into a bunk a little closer to AG next month: it was *far* from Barracks 104.

Olders with jobs had priority on the bunks nearest. That was what he had heard from an Older, who was Kappa, who said he was always in the same barracks-group.

He caught his breath as he walked up to AG-100. He had been near here before. He had seen the pens. He liked the smell. It was—it was the way AG smelled, that was all, and there was nothing like it.

It was a kind of an Ad place in front. All white, with a seal-door, of course. You were supposed to go to Ad. He knew that the way tape showed you things. He pulled down the door-latch and it let him into a busy office, where there was a counter he was supposed to go to.

He could lean on counters lately. Just barely. He was not as tall as other sixes. Taller than some, though. He waited till a Worker turned around and came to see what he wanted.

"I'm Florian AF-9979," he said, and held up the red chit. "I'm Assigned here."

She gave him a polite nod and took the chit. He waited, licking dry lips, not fidgeting while she put it in the machine.

"You certainly are," she said. "Do you know how to follow the colors?"

"Yes," he said with no doubt at all.

And didn't ask questions because she was a Worker doing her Job and she would probably say. If you didn't get everything you needed when she was finished then you asked. That way you didn't make people make mistakes. Which was a Fault on your side. He knew.

She sat down at a keyboard, she typed, and the machine put

out a card she took and added a clip to. He watched, excited because he knew it was a keycard, and it was probably his because she was working on his Business.

She brought it to him and leaned over the counter to show him things about it; he stood on tiptoe and twisted around so they could both see.

"There's your name, there are your colors. This is a keycard. You clip it to your pocket. Whenever you change clothes you clip it to your pocket. That's very serious. If you lose it come to this office immediately."

"Yes," he said. It all clicked with things tape said.

"Have you any questions?"

"No. Thank you."

"Thank you, Florian."

Little bow. *Walk*, then, back out the door and onto the walk and look up at the corner of the building where the color-codes started, but he could read all the words on the card anyway: and on the building.

Walk. No running now. This was Business and he was important. Blue was his color and white inside that and green inside the white, so he went the blue direction until he was inside blue and then inside blue's white zone. The squares told him. More and more exciting. It was the pens. He saw green finally on a sign at the intersection of the gravel walks and followed that way until he saw the green building, which also said AG 899. That was right.

It was a barn of sorts on one side. He asked an azi for the Super, the azi pointed to a big bald man talking to someone over in the big doorway, and he went there and stood until the Super was clear.

"Florian," the Super said when he had seen the card. "Well." Looking him up and down. And called an azi named Andy to take him and show him his work.

But he knew that, from tape. He was supposed to feed the chickens, make sure all the water was clean, and check the temperature on the brooders and the pig nursery. He knew how important that was. "You're awfully young," Andy said of him, "but you sound like you understand."

"Yes," he said. He was sure he did. So Andy let him show him how much he was to feed, and how he was to mark the chart every time he did, and every time he checked the water;

and how you had to be careful not to frighten the chicks because they would hurt each other. He loved how they all
bunched up like a fluffy tide, and all went this way or that way;
and the piglets squealed and would knock you down if you let
them get to swarming round you, which was why you carried a
little stick.

He did everything the best he could, and Andy was happy
with him, which made him the happiest he had ever been in his
life.

He carried buckets and he emptied water pans and Andy said
he could try to hold a piglet as long as he was there to watch. It
wiggled and squealed and tramped him with its sharp little feet
and it got away while he was laughing and trying to protect
himself; Andy laughed and said there was a way to do it, but he
would show him later.

It was a nice feeling, though. It had been warm and alive in
his arms, except he knew pigs were for eating, and for making
other pigs, and you had to keep that in mind and not think of
them like people.

He dusted himself off and he went out to catch his breath a
minute, leaning on the fence rail by the side of the barn.

He saw an animal in that pen that he had never seen, so
beautiful that he just stood there with his mouth open and never
wanted to blink, it was like that. Red like the cattle, but shiny-
pelted, and strong, with long legs and a way of moving that
was different than any animal he had ever seen. This one—
didn't walk; it—went. It moved like it was playing a game all
by itself.

"What's that?" he asked, hearing Andy come up by him.
"What kind is that?"

"AGCULT-894X," Andy said. "That's a horse. He's the
first ever lived, the first ever in the world."

———————————— ii ————————————

Ari *liked* the playschool. They got to go out in the open air and
play in the sandbox every afternoon. She liked to sit barefoot
and make roads with the graders and Tommy or Amy or Sam
or Rene would run the trucks and dump them. Sometimes they
pretended there were storms and all the toy workers would run

and get in the trucks. Sometimes there was a platythere and it tore up the roads and they had to rebuild them. That was what Sam said. Sam's mother was in engineering and Sam told them about platytheres. She asked maman was that so and maman said yes. Maman had seen them big as the living room couch. There were really big ones way out west. Big as a truck. The one they had was only a middle-sized one, and it was ugly. Ari liked being it. You got to tear up the roads and the walls, just push it right through under the sand and there it all went.

She took it and shoved it along with the sand going over her hand. "Look out," she said to Sam and Amy. "Here it comes." She was tired of Amy building her House. Amy had a big one going, sand all piled up, and Amy made doors and windows in the House, and fussed and fussed with it. Which was no fun, because Sam put a tower on Amy's house and Amy knocked it off and told him go make a road up to her door, *she* was making a house and *her* house didn't have towers. Amy got a spoon and hollowed out behind the windows and put plastic in so you couldn't see inside anyway. She made a wall in front and hollowed out an arch for the road. And they both had had to sit and wait while Amy built. So Ari looked at that arch where the road was supposed to come and thought it would be just the place, and the sand would all come down. "Look out!"

"No!" Amy yelled.

Ari plowed right through it. Bang. Down came the wall. The sand came down on her arm and she just kept going, because platytheres did, no matter what. Even if Amy grabbed her arm and tried to stop her.

Sam helped her knock it down.

Amy yelled and shoved her. She shoved Amy. Phaedra got there and told them they mustn't fight and they were all going inside.

Early.

So that was nasty Amy Carnath's fault.

Amy was not back the next day. That was the way with people she fought with. She was sorry about that. You fought with them and they took them away and you only saw them at parties after. There had been Tommy and Angel and Gerry and Kate, and they were gone and couldn't play with her anymore.

So when Amy was gone the next day she moped and sulked and told Phaedra she wanted Amy back.

"If you don't fight with her," Phaedra said. "We'll ask sera."

So Amy did come back. But Amy was funny after that. Even Sam was. Every time she did something they let her.

That was no fun, she thought. So she teased them. She stole Sam's trucks and turned them over. And Sam let her do that. He just sat there and frowned, all unhappy. She knocked Amy's house down before she was through with it. Amy just pouted.

So she did.

Sam turned his trucks back over and decided they had had a wreck. That was an all-right game. She played too, and set the trucks up. But Amy was still pouting, so she ran a truck at her. "Don't," Amy snapped at her. "Don't!"

So she hit her with it. Amy scrambled back and Ari got up and Amy got up. And Amy shoved her.

So she shoved her harder, and kicked her good. Amy hit her. So she hit. And they were hitting each other when Phaedra grabbed her. Amy was crying, and Ari kicked her good before Phaedra snatched her out of reach.

Sam just stood there.

"Amy was a baby," Ari said that night when maman asked her why she had hit Amy.

"Amy can't come back," maman said. "Not if you're going to fight."

So she promised they wouldn't. But she didn't think so.

Amy was out for a couple of days and she came back. She was all pouty and she kept over to herself and she wasn't any fun. She wouldn't even speak when Sam was nice to her.

So Ari walked over and kicked her good, several times. Sam tried to stop her. Phaedra grabbed her by the arm and said she was wrong and she had to sit down and play by herself.

So she did. She took the grader and made sad, angry roads. Sam came over finally and ran a truck on them, but she still hurt. Amy just sat over in the other corner and sniveled. That was what maman called it. Amy wouldn't even play anymore. Ari felt a knot in her throat that made it hard to swallow, but she was not baby enough to cry, and she hated Amy's sniveling, that hurt her and made nothing any fun anymore. Sam was sad too.

After that Amy wasn't there very often. When she was she just sat to herself and Ari hit her once, good, in the back.

Phaedra took Amy by the hand and took her to the door and inside.

Ari went back to Sam and sat down. Valery wasn't there much at all. Pete wasn't. She liked them most. That left just Sam, and Sam was just Sam, a kid with a wide face and not much expression on it. Sam was all right, but Sam hardly ever talked, except he knew about platytheres and fixing trucks. She liked him all right. But she lost everything else. If you liked it most, it went away.

It was not Amy she missed, it was Valery. Sera Schwartz had gotten transferred, so that meant Valery was. She had asked him if he would come back and see her. He had said yes. Maman had said it was too far. So she understood that he was really gone and he would not come back at all. She was mad at him for going. But it was not his fault. He gave her his space-ship with the red light. That was how sorry he was. Maman had said that she had to give it back, so she had to, before she left the Schwartzes' place and said goodbye.

She did not understand why it was wrong, but Valery had cried and she had. Sera Schwartz had been mad at her. She could tell, even if sera Schwartz was being nice and said she would miss her.

Maman had taken her home and she had cried herself to sleep. Even if maman was mad at something and told her stop crying. She did for a while. But for days after she would snivel. And maman would say stop it, so she did, because maman was getting upset and things were getting tight around the apartment—tight was all she could call it. That made everything awful. So she knew she was upsetting maman.

She was scared sometimes. She could not say why.

She was unhappy about Amy, and she tried to be good to Sam and Tommy, when he came, but she thought if she got Amy back she would hit her again.

She would hit Sam and Tommy too, but if she did she would not have anybody at all. Phaedra said she had to be good, they were running out of kids.

"This is the Room," the Instructor said.

"Yes, ser," Catlin said. She was nervous and anxious at the same time. She had heard about the Room from Olders. She heard about the things they did to you, like turning the lights on and off and sometimes water on the floor. But her Instructor always had the Real Word. Her Instructor told her she had to get through a tunnel and do it fast.

"Are you ready?"

"Yes, ser."

He opened the door. It was a tiny place with another door. The one behind her shut and the lights went out.

The one in front of her opened and cold wet air hit her in the face. The place had echoes.

She moved, not even sure where the tunnel was or whether she was in it.

"Stop!" a voice yelled. And a red dot lit the wall and popped.

It was a shot. She knew that. Her body knew what to do; she was tumbling and meaning to roll and find cover, but the whole floor dropped, and she kept rolling, down a tube and splash! into cold water.

She flailed and got up in knee-deep water. You never believed a Safe. Someone had shot. You ran and got to cover.

But: *Get through*, the Instructor had said. *Fast as you can.*

So she got, fast as she could, till she ran into a wall and followed it, up again, onto the dry. In a place that rang under her boots. Noise was bad. It was dark and she was easy to see in the dark because of her pale skin and hair. She did not know whether she ought to sneak or run, but *fast* was *fast*, that was what the Instructor said.

She ran easy and quick, fingers of one hand trailing on the wall to keep her sense of place in the dark and one hand out ahead of her so she wouldn't run into something.

The tunnel did turn. She headed up a climb and down again onto concrete, and it was still dark.

Something—! she thought, just before she got to it and the Ambush grabbed her.

She elbowed it and twisted and knew it was an Enemy when

she felt it grab her, but it only got cloth and twisting got her away, fast, fast, hard as she could run, heart hammering.

She hit the wall where it turned, bang! and nearly knocked herself cold, but she scrambled up and kept going, kept going—

The door opened, white and blinding.

Something made her duck and roll through it, and she landed on the floor in the tiny room, with the taste of blood in her mouth and her lip cut and her nose bleeding.

One door shut and the other opened, and the man there was not the Instructor. He had the brown of the Enemy and he had a gun.

She tried to kick him, but he Got her, she heard the buzz.

The door shut again and opened and she was getting up, mad and ashamed.

But this time it was her Instructor. "The Enemy is never fair," he said. "Let's go find out what you did right and wrong."

Catlin wiped her nose. She hurt. She was still mad and ashamed. She had gotten through. She wished she had got the man at the end. But he was an Older. That was not fair either. And her nose would not stop bleeding.

The Instructor got a cold cloth and had her put it on her neck. He said the med would look at her nose and her mouth. Meanwhile he turned on the Scriber and had her tell what she did and he told her most Sixes got stopped in the tunnel.

"You're exceptionally good," he said.

At which she felt much, much better. But she was not going to forget the Enemy at the end. They Got you here even when the lesson was over. That was the Rule. She hated being Got. She hated it. She knew when you grew up you went where Got was dead. She knew what dead was. They took the Sixes down to the slaughterhouse and they saw them kill a pig. It was fast and it stopped being a pig right there. They hauled it up and cut it and they got to see what dead meant: you just stopped, and after that you were just meat. No next time when you were dead, and you had to Get the Enemy first and make the Enemy dead fast.

She was good. But the Enemy was not fair. That was a scary thing to learn. She started shaking. She tried to stop, but the

Instructor saw anyhow and said the med had better have a look at her.

"Yes, ser," she said. Her nose still bubbled and the cloth was red. She blotted at it and felt her knees wobble as she walked, but she walked all right.

The med said her nose was not broken. A tooth was loose, but that was all right, it would fix itself.

The Instructor said she was going to start marksmanship. He said she would be good in that, because her genotype was rated that way. She was expected to do well in the Room. All her genotype did. He said genotypes could sometimes get better. He said that was who she had to beat. That was who every azi had to beat. Even if she had never seen any other AC-7892.

She got a good mark for the day. She could not tell anyone. You were never supposed to. She could not talk about the tunnel. The Instructor told her so. It was a Rule.

It was only the last Enemy that worried her. The Instructor said a gun would have helped and size would have helped, but otherwise there was not much she could have done. It had not been wrong to roll at the last. Even if it put her on the floor when the door opened.

"I could have run past him," she said.

"He would have shot you in the back," the Instructor said. "Even in the hall."

She thought and thought about that.

---

iv

"Vid off," Justin said, and the Minder cut it. He sat in his bathrobe on the couch. Grant wandered in, likewise in his bathrobe, toweling his hair.

"What's the news tonight?" Grant asked, and Justin said, with a little unease at his stomach:

"There's some kind of flap in Novgorod. Something about a star named Gehenna."

"Where's that?" There *was* no star named Gehenna in anybody's reckoning. Or there had not been, until tonight. Grant looked suddenly sober as he sat down on the other side of the pit.

"Over toward Alliance. Past Viking." The news report had

not been entirely specific. "Seems there's a planet there. With humans on it. Seems Union colonized it without telling anybody. Sixty years ago."

"My God," Grant murmured.

"Alliance ambassador's arrived at station with an official protest. They're having an emergency session of the Council. Seems we're in violation of the Treaty. About a dozen clauses of it."

"How *big* a colony?" Grant asked, right to the center of it.

"They don't know. They don't say."

"And nobody *knew* about it. Some kind of Defense base?"

"Might be. Might well be. But it isn't now. Apparently it's gone primitive."

Grant hissed softly. "Survivable world."

"Has to be, doesn't it? We're not talking about any ball of rock. The news-service is talking about the chance of some secret stuff from back in the war years."

Grant was quiet a moment, elbows on knees.

The war was the generation before them. The war was something no one wanted to repeat; but the threat was always there. Alliance merchanters came and went. Sol had explored the other side of space and got its fingers burned—dangerously. Eetees with a complex culture and an isolationist sentiment. Now Sol played desperate politics between Alliance and Union, trying to keep from falling under Alliance rule and trying to walk the narrow line that might leave it independent of Alliance ships without pushing Alliance into defending its treaty prerogatives or bringing Alliance interests and Union into conflict. Things were so damned delicate. And they had gotten gradually better.

A generation had grown up thinking it was solving the problems.

But old missiles the warships had launched a hundred years ago were still a shipping hazard. Sometimes the past came back into the daily news with a vengeance.

And old animosities surfaced like ghosts, troubling a present in which humans knew they were not alone.

"It doesn't sound like it was any case of finding three or four survivors," he said to Grant. "They're saying 'illegal colony' and they admit it's ours."

"Still going? Organized?"

"It's not real clear."

Another moment of silence. Grant sat up then and remembered to dry his hair before it dried the way it was. "Damn crazy mess," Grant said. "Did they say they got them off, or are they going to? Or what are they going to do about it?"

"Don't know yet."

"Well, we can guess where Giraud's going to be for the next week or so, can't we?"

V

Ari was bored with the offices. She watched the people come in and out. She sat at a desk in back of the office and cut out folded paper in patterns that she unfolded. She got paper and drew a fish with a long tail.

Finally she got up and slipped out while Kyle wasn't looking, while maman was doing something long and boring in the office inside; and it looked like maman was going to be talking a long time.

Which meant maman would not mind much if she walked up and down the hall. It was only offices. That meant no stores, no toys, nothing to look at and no vid. She liked sitting and coloring all right. But maman's own offices were best, because there was a window to look out.

There was nothing but doors up and down. The floor had metal stripes and she walked one, while she looked in the doors that were open. Most were.

That was how she saw Justin.

He was at a desk, working at a keyboard, very serious.

She stood in the doorway and saw him there. And waited, just watching him, for the little bit until he would see her.

He was always different from all the rest of the people. She remembered him from a glittery place, and Grant with him. She saw him only sometimes, and when she asked maman why people got upset about Justin, maman said she was imagining things.

She knew she was not. It was a danger-feeling. It was a worried feeling. She knew she ought not to bother him. But it was all right here in the hall, where there were people going by. And she just wanted to look at him, but she did not want to go inside.

She shifted to her other foot and he saw her then.

"Hello," she said.

And got that fear-feeling again. His, as he looked up. And hers, as she thought she could get in trouble with maman.

"Hello," he said, nervous-like.

It was always like that when she was around Justin. The nervous-feeling went wherever he did, and got worse when she got close to him. From everybody. It was a puzzle she could not work out, and she sensed by the way maman shut down on questions about Justin that he was a puzzle maman did not approve of. Ollie too. Justin came to parties and she saw him from across the room, but maman always came and got her if she went to say hello. So she thought that Justin was somebody in a lot of trouble for something, and maybe there was something Wrong with him, so they were not sure he was going to behave right. Sometimes azi got like that. Sometime CITs did. Maman said. And it was harder to straighten CITs out, but easier to make azi upset. So she mustn't tease them. Except Ollie could take it all right.

There was a lot about Justin that said azi, but she knew that he wasn't. He was just Justin. And he was a puzzle that came and went and no one ever wanted kids around.

"Maman's down there with ser Peterson," she said conversationally, also because she wanted him to know she was not running around where she had no business to be. So this was Justin's office. It was awfully small. Papers were everywhere. She leaned too far and caught her balance on the door. Fool, maman would say. Stand up. Stand straight. Don't wobble around. But Justin never said much. He left everything for her to say. "Where's Grant?"

"Grant's down at the library," Justin said.

"I'm six now."

"I know."

"How do you know that?"

Justin looked uncomfortable. "Isn't your maman going to be wanting you pretty soon?"

"Maman's having a meeting. I'm tired of being down there." He was going to ignore her, going back to his work. She was not going to have him turn his shoulder to her. She walked in and up to the chair by his desk. She leaned on the arm and looked up at him. "Ollie's always working."

"So am I. I'm busy, Ari. You go along."

"What are you doing?"

"Work."

She knew a go-away when she heard one. But she did not have to mind Justin. So she leaned on her arms and frowned and tried a new approach. "I go to tapestudy. I can read that. It says *Sub—*" She twisted around, because it was a long word on the screen. *"Sub-li-min-al mat—ma-trix."*

He turned the screen off and turned around and frowned at her.

She thought maybe she had gone too far, and oughtn't to be leaning on her elbows quite so close to him. But backing up was something she didn't like at all. She stuck out her lip at him.

"Go back to maman, Ari. She's going to be looking for you."

"I don't want to. What's a sub-liminal matrix?"

"A set of things. A special arrangement of a set." He shoved his chair back and stood up, so she stood up and got back. "I've got an appointment. I've got to lock up the office. You'd better get on back to your mother."

"I don't want to." He was awfully tall. Like Ollie. Not safe like Ollie. He was pushing her out, that was what. She stood her ground.

"Out," he said, at the door, pointing to the hall.

She went out. He walked out and locked the door. She waited for him. She had that figured out. When he walked on down the hall she went with him.

"Back," he said, stopping, pointing back toward where maman was.

She gave him a nasty smile. "I don't have to."

He looked upset then. And he got very quiet, looking down at her. "Ari, that's not nice, is it?"

"I don't have to be nice."

"I'd like you better."

That hurt. She stared up at him to see if he was being nasty, but he did not look like it. He looked as if he was the hurt one.

She could not figure him. Everybody, but not him. She just stared.

"Can I go with you?" she asked.

"Your maman wouldn't like it." He had a kind face when he talked like that. "Go on back."

"I don't want to. They just talk. I'm tired of them talking."

"Well, I've got to go meet my people, Ari. I'm sorry."

"There aren't any people," she said, calling his bluff, because he had not been going anywhere until she bothered him.

"Well, I still have to. You go on back."

She did not. But he walked away down the hall like he was really going somewhere.

She wished she could. She wished he would be nice. She was bored and she was unhappy and when she saw him she remembered the glittery people and everybody being happy, but she could not remember when that was.

Only then Ollie had been there all the time and maman had been so pretty and she had played with Valery and gotten the star that hung in her bedroom.

She walked back to ser Peterson's office very slow. Kyle didn't even notice. She sat down and she drew a star. And thought about Valery. And the red-haired man, who was Grant. Who was Justin's.

She wished Ollie and maman had more time for her.

She wished maman would come out. And they would go to lunch. Maybe Ollie could come.

But maman did not come anytime soon, so she drew lines all over the star and made it ugly.

Like everything.

---

vi

The documents show, the report came to Mikhail Corain's desk, *the operation involved a clandestine military operation and the landing of 40,000 Union personnel, the majority of them azi. The mission was launched in 2355, as a Defense operation.*

There was no further support given the colony. The operation was not sustained.

The best intelligence Alliance has mustered says that there are thousands of survivors who have devolved to a primitive lifestyle. Beyond question they are descended of azi and citi-

zens. The assumption is that they had no rejuv and that after sixty years the survivors must be at least second and third generation. There are ruins of bubble-construction and a solar power installation. The world is extremely hospitable to human life and the survivors are in remarkably good health considering the conditions, practicing basic agriculture and hunting. The Alliance reports express doubt that the colonists can be removed from the world. The ecological damage is as yet undetermined, but there is apparently deep penetration of the colony into the ecosystem, and certain of the inhabitants have retreated into areas not easily accessible. It is the estimate of Alliance that the inhabitants would not welcome removal from the world and Alliance does not intend to remove the colony, for whatever reason.

The estimation within the Defense Bureau is that Alliance is interested in interviewing the survivors. Defense however will oppose any proposal to retrieve these Union nationals as an operation which Alliance will surely reject and which would be in any case counter-productive.

The azi were primarily but not exclusively from Reseune military contracts.

See attached reports.

The majority of citizens were military personnel.

Nye will offer a bill expressing official regret and an offer of cooperation to the Alliance in dealing with the colonists.

The Expansionist coalition will be unanimous in that vote.

Corain flipped through the reports. Pages of them. There was a sub-sapient on the world the colonists called Gehenna. There were a great many things that said Defense Bureau, and Information Unavailable.

There was no way in hell Alliance or Union was going to be able to retrieve the survivors, for one thing because they were scattered into the bush and mostly because (according to Alliance) they were illiterate primitives and Alliance was going to resist any attempt to remove them, that much was clear in the position the Alliance ambassador was taking.

Alliance was damned mad about the affair, because it had been confronted with a major and expensive problem: an Earth-class planet in its own sphere of influence with an ecological disaster and an entrenched, potentially hostile colony.

So was Corain angry about it, for reasons partly ethical and partly political outrage: Defense had overstepped itself, Defense had covered this mess up back in the war years, when (as now) Defense was in bed with Reseune and gifted with a blank credit slip.

And if Corain could manage it, there was going to be a light thrown on the whole Expansionist lunacy.

<hr>

vii

Gorodin—was not accessible. That was not entirely a disaster, in Giraud Nye's estimation. Secretary of Defense Lu had sat proxy so often in the last thirty years he had far more respect on Council and far more latitude in voting his own opinion than a proxy was supposed to have, the same way the Undersecretary of Defense virtually merged his own staff with Lu's and Gorodin's on-planet office: it was in effect a troika at the top of Defense and had been, *de facto*, since the war years.

And in Giraud's unvoiced opinion it was better that the proxy was in and Gorodin was somewhere classified and inaccessible at the other end of Union space: Lu, his face a map of wise secrets as rejuv declined, his dark eyes difficult even for a veteran of Reseune to cipher, was playing his usual game of *no authority to answer that* and *I don't feel I should comment*, while reporters clamored for information and Corain called for full disclosure.

Full disclosure it had to be, at least among political allies.

And Giraud had heard enough to upset his stomach all the way from Reseune to this sound-secure office, the sound-screening working at his nerves and setting his teeth off.

"It is absolutely true," Lu said, without reference to the folio that lay under his hands. "The mission was launched in 2355; it reached the star in question and dropped the colonists and the equipment. There was never any intention to return. At the time, we knew that the world was there. We knew that Alliance knew, that it was within their reach, or Earth's, and by the accident of its position and its potential—it would be of major importance." Lu cleared his throat. "We knew we couldn't hold it in practicality, we couldn't defend it, we couldn't supply it. We did in fact purpose to remove it from profitability."

Remove it from profitability. Alliance had sent a long-prepared and careful survey to the most precious find yet in near space—and found it, to its consternation, inhabited, inhabited by humans not their own and not plausibly Earth's—leaving the absolutely undeniable conclusion, even without the ruined architecture and the fact that the survivors were azi-descended—

Union had sabotaged a living planet.

"Forty thousand people," Giraud said, feeling an emptiness at the pit of his stomach. "Dropped onto an untested planet. Just like that."

Lu blinked. Otherwise he might have been a statue. "They were military; they were expendables. It was not, you understand, my administration. Nor was there, in those days, the—sensitivity to ecological concerns. So far as anyone then was reckoning, we were in a difficult military position, we had to reckon that a Mazianni strike at Cyteen was a possibility. There were two possibilities in such a move: first, the colony would survive and maintain Union principles should we meet with disaster, should Earth have launched some suicide mission at Cyteen itself. The secrecy of the colony was important in that consideration."

"It was launched in *2355*," Giraud said. "A year after the war ended."

Lu folded his hands. "It was planned in the closing years of the war, when things were uncertain. It was executed after we had been confronted with general calamity, and that disastrous treaty. It was a hole card, if you like. To let either Earth or Alliance have a world potentially more productive than Cyteen—would have been disastrous. That was the second part of the plan: if the colony should perish, it would still contribute its microorganisms to the ecology. And in less than a century—present Alliance or whatever new owner—with a difficult problem, which our science could handle and theirs couldn't. I might say—some native microorganisms were even—engineered to accept our own engineered contributions. At your own facility. As I'm sure your records will say. Not mentioning the azi and the tape-tailoring."

"You're damn right the records show it." Giraud found his breath difficult. "My God, we never knew the thing was actually *launched*! You know what kind of a security problem we've got? This isn't the 2350s. We're not at war. Your damn little timebomb's gone off in a century when we've got aliens stirred up on Sol's far side, we've got ecological treaties—we've got our own *position*, for God's sake, on ecological responsibility, the genebanks, the arks, the—''

''It was, of course, the architect of the genebanks and the treaty and the arks who actually administered Reseune during the development of the Gehenna colony. Councillor Emory was signatory to all contracts with Defense.''

''—the Abolitionists, my *God*, we've handed them the best damn *issue* they could have dreamed of! It was a study project. God, Jordan Warrick's *father* worked on those Gehenna tapes.''

''We trust Reseune security procedures didn't tell the project members what they were working on.''

''Trust, hell! It's on the *news*, general. The news gets to Planys, eventually. You want to gamble Jordan Warrick won't know who in what department might have been working on those tapes, and what names and what specifics to hand to investigators if they get to him?''

''Damage his own father's reputation?''

''To *protect* his father's reputation, dammit; and blast Reseune's. You spent forty thousand azi to sabotage a *planet*, for God's sake, you linked the research to the Science Bureau, and it couldn't have picked a worse time to surface.''

''Oh,'' Lu said quietly, ''I can imagine worse times than this. This is a quiet time, a time when humanity—especially Alliance—has many other worries. In fact Gehenna's done exactly what it was designed to do: there *is* ecological calamity, Alliance *is* holding off development. The course of development of the Alliance has been irrevocably altered: if they absorb that population they will absorb an ethnically unique community with Union values, if you believe in the validity of your own taped instructions. In any case, we forestalled either Alliance or Earth getting a very valuable resource—and a stepping-stone to further stars. Now Alliance will either track down a scattered lot of primitives and remove them by force—a logistic nightmare—or Alliance will have to take them into account in its own settlement of the world. If they choose to settle. Intelligence informs us they're having second thoughts. They perceive a possible difficulty if they entangle themselves with this—ground-bound culture. There was always a vocal opposition to their colonization effort. The spacers who are far and away the majority in Alliance are quite doubtful about any move that puts power in the hands of the ground-bound—blue-skyers, as spacers call them, and a pre-industrial constituency—or another, much more problematical protectorate—is more than the Council of Captains wants to take on . . . not mentioning of course, *their* science bureau, which bids fair to study it to death, while the construction companies scheduled to build a station there are holding off their creditors. The Alliance ambassador demands information for their Science people and an apology; cheap at the price. There'll be a little coolness—ultimately cooperation. I assure you, they're much more scared at what Sol has poked into than *we* are—only natural considering they're much closer to the problem. All in all, it's an excellent time for it to surface: we watched their preparations, we weren't taken by surprise—that's why Adm. Gorodin is inaccessible, as it happens. We knew this was coming.''

"And kept it from us!''

Lu maintained an icy little silence. Then: "Us—meaning Science; or us, meaning Reseune?''

"Us, Reseune, dammit! Reseune has an interest in this!''

"A past interest,'' Lu said. "The child is far from adult. She can ride out this storm. Emory is beyond reach of any law, unless you are religious. Let them subpoena a few documents. Warrick is in quarantine, thoroughly discredited as far as testimony before the Council might go. If his father was working on the project, it can only harm the Warrick name. What is there to concern Reseune?''

Giraud shut his mouth. He was sweating. Bogdanovitch was dead four years ago, Harad of Fargone was in the seat of State and making common cause with Gorodin of Defense and deFranco of Trade, and Lao of Information. Damn them. The Expansionist coalition held firm, the Abolitionists were in retreat and Corain and the Centrists had lost ground, losing Gorodin to the Expansionist camp where he had always belonged, but Nasir Harad, damn him, snuggled close to Gorodin, the source of the fat Defense contracts for his station, and State and Defense and Information were the coalition within the Expansionist coalition—the secret bedfellows.

Reseune did not have the influence it had had. That was the bitter truth Giraud had to live with. It gave him stomach upsets and kept him awake at night. But Ari had been—so far as they understood—unique.

"Let me tell you," Giraud said, "there are things within our files which are very sensitive. We do not want them released. More, we don't want any chance of Warrick being called out of Planys to testify. You don't understand how volatile that situation is. He has to be kept quiet. His recall of small detail, things he might have heard, things he might have discussed with his father down the years—will be far better than you or I want. His memory is extremely exact. If you don't want Alliance to be able to unravel what you've done in specific detail, *keep Warrick quiet*, can I be more clear?"

"Are you saying present administration can be compromised?"

Dangerous question. Dangerous interest. Giraud took another breath. "I'm only asking you to listen to me. Before you discover that the threads of this lead, yes, under closed doors. You want the Rubin project blown to hell—you let Warrick get loose, and there won't *be* a Rubin project."

"Sometimes we're not sure there *is* a Rubin project," Lu said acidly, "since RESEUNESPACE has yet to do more than minor work. Tests, you say. Data collation. *Is* there a director?"

"There is a director. We're about to transfer the bank. It's not a small operation. This inquiry is not going to help us. We're strained as it is. There's an enormous amount of data involved. That's the nature of the process. We are in operation. We have been in operation for six years. We do not intend to waste resources in a half-hearted effort, general." Damn. It's a tactic. Distract and divert. "The point is Warrick. The point is that the Planys facility is under your security and we have to rely on it. We hope we *can* rely on it."

"Absolutely. As we hope to rely on your cooperation on the Gehenna matter, Councillor Nye."

Blackmail. Plain and simple. He saw Harad's hand in this. "To what extent?"

"Agreement to cooperate with Alliance scientists. We'll swear it was a lost operation, one concealed behind the secrecies of war. Something no one knew had been done. No one in office now. That a communications screw-up saw it launched.''

"Ariane Emory's name has to be kept out of it."

"I don't think that's possible. Let the dead bear the onus of responsibility. The living have far more at stake. I assure you—far more at stake. We want to keep an active channel into this situation on Gehenna. Descendants of Union citizens are still legally our citizens. *If* we choose to take that view. We may not. In any case—Science should be interested in the impact on the ecology; and the social system. We stand to gain nothing by withholding an apparent cooperation. *Not* the actual content of the tapes, to be sure. But at least the composition of the colony, the ratio of military personnel to azi. The personal histories of some of the military. Conn, for instance. Distinguished service. They should have some recognition, after all these years.''

Sentiment. Good God.

"Reseune," Giraud said, "equally values Emory's distinguished record.''

"I'm afraid that part will get out. The azi, you know. Once the public knows that, there's hardly any way you can hide it. But damage control is already in operation. State is onto it.''

"Harad *knew* about this operation?"

"It does fall within State's area of responsibility. Science doesn't make foreign policy. *Our* obligation in that consideration is quite different. I do urge you to think—what your contracts are worth. We do *not* contract primarily with Bucherlabs. We continue to work with you. We continue to support RESEUNESPACE—even at a cost disadvantage. We expect that relationship to be a mutually satisfactory one—one we hope we can continue.''

"I see," Giraud said bitterly. "I see." And after a breath or two: "Ser Secretary, we need that data protected—for more than a dead woman's reputation. To keep Council from blowing this wide open—and destroying any chance of success.''

"Now you want our help. You want me to throw myself and my Bureau on the grenade. Is that it? —Let me explain to you, ser, we *have* other considerations right now, primarily among them a rampant anti-militarism that's feeding on this scandal as it is—which is a critical danger to our national defense, at a time when we're already under budget constraints, at a time when we can't get the ships we need and we can't get the problem of expanded perimeters through the heads of the public or the opposition of Finance in Council. We have a major problem, ser, your project has become a sink into which money goes and nothing emerges, and, dammit, you want us to stand and shield you from inquiry while you refuse our requests for records. I suggest you defend *yourself*, ser—with Reseune's well-known resources. Maybe it's time to bring this project of yours out. Make a choice. Give me a *reason* I can *use* to maintain that data as Classified—or give me the records I need.''

"She's not ready, my God, not *now*, in the middle of scandal that touches her predecessor. She's a six-year-old kid, she can't handle that kind of attack—''

"It's your problem,'' Lu said, folding his hands, settling into that implacable, bland stare. "We don't know, frankly, ser, if we *have* anything to protect. For all you've been willing to demonstrate to us, it *is* another Bok clone.''

"I'll show you records.''

"Bok's clone was quite good as a child. It was later the problems manifested. Wasn't it? And unless you're willing to go public with the child and give me a reason to clamp down on the records—I can't extend that protection any further than I have.''

"Dammit, you leave us vulnerable and they'll find us the door that leads to your own territory.''

"Through *yours*, I think. You were very active in Reseune administration in those years. Can it be—those records you defend—lay the blame to you, ser?''

"That's your guess. It may shine light where a good many people don't want it.''

"So we direct the strike, don't we? It's always useful to know what you've left open for attack. I'm sorry it has to be in your territory. But I certainly won't leave it in mine.''

"If you'll apply a little patience—''

"I prefer the word *progress*, which, quite truthfully, I find lacking in Reseune lately. We can discuss this. I am prepared to discuss it. But I think you'll understand I am inflexible on certain points. Cooperation is very essential just now. If we do not have a reason to withhold those records, we must provide those records. You must understand—we have to provide something to the inquiry. And soon.''

One did. One sat and one listened while the Defense *proxy*, damn him to hell, laid out Gorodin's program for, as he called it, damage control.

A proposal for scientific and cultural cooperation with Alliance. Coming from Defense via the Science Bureau.

An official expression of regret from the Council in joint resolution, made possible by the release of selected documents by the present administration of Reseune, indicating Bogdanovitch, Emory, and Azov of Defense, all safely deceased, collaborated in the planning of the Gehenna operation.

Damn him.

"We'll see to Warrick," Lu said. "Actually—allowing him conference with his son might have some benefit right now. Monitored, of course."

---------------------- viii ----------------------

"*Justin?*" The voice came from the other end, Jordan's voice, his father's voice, after eight years; and Justin, who had steeled himself not to break down, *not* to break down in front of Denys, on whose desk-phone the call came, bit his lip till it bled and watched the image come out of the break-up on the screen—a Jordan older, thinner. His hair was white. Justin stared in shock, in the consciousness of lost years, and mumbled: "Jordan—God, it's good to see you. We're fine, we're all fine. Grant's not here for this one, but they'll let him next time. . . ."

". . . *You're looking fine,*" Jordan's voice overrode him, and there was pain in his eyes. "*God, you've grown a bit, haven't you? It's good to see you, son. Where's Grant?*"

Time-delay. They were fifteen seconds lagged, by security at either end.

"You're looking good yourself." O *God*, the banalities they had to use, when there was so little time. When there was everything in the world to say, and they could not, with security waiting to break the connection at the first hint of a breach of the rules. "How's Paul? Grant and I are living in your apartment, doing real well. I'm still in design—"

A lift from Denys' hand warned him. No work discussions. He stopped himself.

"*. . . A little grayer. I know. I'm not doing badly at all. Good health and all that. Paul too. Damn, it's good to see your face. . . .*"

"You can do that in a mirror, can't you?" He forced a little laugh. "I hope I do look that good at the same age. Got a good chance, right? —I can't report much—" They won't let me. "—I've been keeping busy. I get your letters." Cut to hell. "I really look forward to them. So does—"

His father grinned as the joke got through. "*You're my time machine. You've got a good chance. . . . I get your letters too. I keep all of them.*"

"So does Grant. He's grown too. Tall. You could figure. We're sort of left hand and right. We look out for each other. We're doing fine."

"*You weren't going to catch him. Not the way he was growing. Paul's gone gray too. Rejuv, of course. I'm sorry. I was absolutely certain I'd told you in the letters. I forget about it. I'm too damn lazy to dye it.*"

Meaning the censors had cut the part it was in, damn them.

"I think it looks pretty good. Really. You know everything looks pretty much the same at home—" Not elsewhere. "Except I miss you. Both of you."

"*I miss you too, son. I really do. They're signing me I've got to close down now. Damn, there's so much to say. Be good. Stay out of trouble.*"

"You be good. We're all right. I love you."

The image broke up and went to snow. The vid cut itself off. He bit his lips and tried to look at Denys with dignity. The way Jordan would have. "Thanks," he said.

Denys' mouth made a little tremor of its own. "That's all right. That went fine. You want a tape? I ran one."

"Yes, ser, I would like it. For Grant."

Denys ejected it from the desk recorder and gave it to him. And nodded to him. Emphatically. "I'll tell you: they're watching you very closely. It's this Gehenna thing."

"So they want a good grip on Jordan, is that it?"

"You understand very well. Yes. That's exactly what they want. That's exactly why Defense suddenly changed its mind about priorities. There's even a chance—a chance, understand—you may get an escorted trip to Planys. But they'll be watching you every time you breathe."

That shook him. Perhaps it was meant to. "Is that in the works?"

"I'm talking with them about it. I shouldn't tell you. But, God, son, don't make any mistakes. Don't do anything. You've done spectacularly well, since you—got your personal problem worked out. Your work's quite, quite fine. You're going to be taking on more responsible things—you know what I mean. More assignments. I want you and Grant to work together on some designs. Really, I want you to work into a staff position here. Both of you."

"Why? So you've got something to take away?"

"Son,—" Denys gave a deep sigh and looked worried. "No. Precisely the opposite. I want you to be necessary here. Very necessary. They're setting up the Fargone facility. And that's a hell of a long way from Planys."

A cold feeling crept about his heart, old and familiar.

"For God's sake," Denys said, "*don't* give them a chance. That's what I'm telling you. We're not totally in control of what's happening. Defense has gotten its hands on your father. It's not going to let go. You understand, it's Gehenna that got you what you've gotten this far: it's Gehenna and the fallout from that, that's made them think they have to give your father something to lose. But we haven't released you to them. We've kept you very quiet. The fact that you were a minor protected you and Grant from some things: but without their noticing—you've gotten old enough to mess with. And the RESEUNESPACE facility at Fargone has a military wing, where you'd make a hell of a hostage."

"Is that a threat?"

"Justin, —give me at least a little respite. Give me as much credit as I give you. And your father. I'm trying to warn you about a trap. *Think* about it, if nothing else. I truly don't trust this sudden beneficence on the part of Defense. You're right not to. And I'm trying to warn you of a possible problem. If you're essential personnel we have a hold on you, and whatever you think, you're a hell of a lot safer if we have that hold, now. Draw your own conclusions. You know damn well what an advantage it would be for them if they could have you under their hand out at Fargone and Jordan in their keeping at Planys. That's what I'm trying to tell you. Use that information any way you see fit. But I'll give you what chance I can."

He took the tape. He thought about it. "Yes, ser," he said finally. Because Denys was right. Fargone was not where he wanted to be sent, not now, not any longer. No matter what Jordan might have wanted.

---

ix

I thought this might handle some of your objections on MR-1959, Justin typed at the top of his explanation of the attachment to the EO-6823 work, *—JW.* And pulled the project files up and sent them over to Yanni Schwartz's office.

With trepidations.

He was working again. Working overtime and very hard, and earnestly trying, because he saw where he had gotten to. He took the tapes. He assimilated things. He tried the kind of designs he had been working on in his spare time eight years ago and tried to explain to Yanni that they were only experimental alternates to the regular assignments.

Which for some reason made Yanni madder than hell.

But then, a lot of things did.

"Look," Justin had said when Yanni blew up about the MR-1959 alternate, "Yanni, I'm doing this on my own time. I did the other thing. I just thought maybe you could give me a little help on this."

"No damn way you can *do* a thing like this," Yanni had said. "That's all there is to it."

"Explain."

"You can't link a skill tape into deep-sets. You'll turn out rats on a treadmill. That's what you're doing."

"Can we talk about this? Can we do this at lunch? I really want to talk about this, Yanni. I think I've got a way to avoid that. I think it's in there."

"I don't see any reason to waste my time on it. I'm busy, son, I'm *busy*! Go ask Strassen if you can find her. If anybody can find her. Let her play instructor. For that matter, ask Peterson. He's got patience. I don't. Just do your job and turn in your work and don't give me problems, for God's sake, I don't need any more problems!"

Peterson handled the beginners.

That was what Yanni meant.

He did not object with the fact that Denys Nye had urged him to take up his active studies. He did not object with the fact Ariane Emory had had time to look at his prototype designs. He swallowed it and told himself that Yanni always hit below the belt when he was bothered, Yanni was a psych designer, Yanni was right up there with the best they had, and Yanni working with an azi was patience itself; but Yanni arguing with a CIT cut loose with every gun he had, including the psych-tactics. Of course it stung. That was because Yanni was damned good and he was firing away at a psychological cripple who was trapped and frustrated at every turn.

So he got out of there with a quiet Yes, ser, I understand. And ached all night before he got his mental balance again, gathered up his shattered nerves, and decided: *All right, that's Yanni, isn't it? He's still the best I've got. I can wear him down. What can he do to me? What can words do?*

A hell of a lot, from a psychmaster, but living in Reseune and aiming to *be* what Yanni was, meant taking it and gathering himself up and going on.

"Don't take him so seriously," was Grant's word on the fracas—Grant, who went totally business and very shielded when he was within ten feet of Yanni Schwartz, because Yanni scared him out of good sense.

"I don't," Justin said. "I won't. He's the only one who *can* teach me anything, except Jane Strassen and Giraud and Denys, and hell if I'll go to the Nyes. Let's don't even think about hanging around Strassen."

"No," Grant said fervently. "I don't think you'd better do that."

Considering what else hung around Strassen's office, to be sure.

He did not consciously set up war with Yanni. Only he hurt inside, he was unsure of himself, he tried to do his best work and Yanni wanted him to design with tabs so a surgeon could pull it out again, because, as Yanni had said on a quieter day, when pressed a second time to be specific on the MR-1959 problem: "You're not that good, dammit, and a skill tape isn't a master-tape. Quit putting feathers on a pig. Stay out of the deep-sets, or haven't you got brains enough to see where that link's going? I haven't got time for this damn messing around.

You're wasting your time and you're wasting mine. You might be a damn fine designer if you got a handle on your own problems and quit fucking around with things they learned eighty years ago wouldn't fucking *work*! You haven't invented the wheel, son, you've just gone down an old dead end.''

"Ari never said that," he offered finally, which was like pulling his guts up. It came out in a half-breath and much too emotional.

"What did she say about it?"

"She just critiqued the design and said there were sociological ramifications I didn't have—"

"Damn right."

"She said she was going to think about it. Ari—was going to *think* about it. She didn't say she could answer me right then. She didn't say *I* should think about it. So I don't think you can toss me off like that. I can show you the one I was working on, if that makes a difference."

"Son, you'd better wake up to it, Ari was after one thing with you, and you damn well know what that was. Don't go off on some damn mental tangent and fuck yourself up six, eight years later because you're so damn sure you were better at seventeen than you are now. That's crap. Recognize it. You got fucked up in several senses, it's natural you want to try to pick up where you left off, but you'd do yourself a better service if you picked up where you *are*, son, and realized that it wasn't your *ideas* that made Ari invite you into her office and spend all that time with you. All right?"

For a moment he could hardly get his breath. They were private, in Yanni's office. No one could hear but them. But no one, *no one*, in all these years, had ever said to him as bluntly what Yanni said, not even Denys, not even Petros, and he got a fight-flight flash that shoved enough adrenaline into his system that he reacted, he knew he was reacting: he wanted to be anywhere else but trapped in this, with a man he dared not hit— God, they would have him on the table inside the hour, then—

"Fuck *you*, Yanni, what are you trying to do to me?"

"I'm trying to help you."

"Is that your best? Is that the way you deal with your patients? God help them."

He was close to breaking down. He clenched his jaw and

held it. *You know I've been in therapy, you unprincipled bastard. Get off me.*

And Yanni took a long time about answering him, much more quietly. "I'm trying to tell you the truth, son. No one else is. Don't corner him, Petros says. What do you want? Petros to put a fresh coat of plaster on it? He can't lay a hand on you. *Denys* won't let him do an intervention. And that's what you fucking *need*, son, you need somebody to cut deep and grab hold of what's eating at you and show it to you in the daylight, I don't care how you hate it. I'm not your enemy. They're all so damn scared how it'll look if they bring you in for major psych. They *don't* want that for fear it'll leak and Jordan will blow. But I care about *you*, son, I care so damn much I'll rip your guts out and give them to you on a plate, and trust the old adage doesn't hold and that you *can* put yourself back together. Ari's in the news right now and it's not good; and there's too damn much media attention hovering around the edges of our security. We *can't* arrest you and haul you in for the treatment you need. You listen to me. You listen. Everybody else is saving their ass. And you're bleeding, while Petros does half-hearted patches on a situation all of us can see: Denys tried to talk to you. You won't cooperate. Thank God you *are* trying to wake up and get to work. If I did what I wanted, son, I'd have shot you full of juice before I had this little talk with you and maybe it'd sink in. But I want you to look real hard at what you're doing. You're trying to go back to where you were. You're wasting time. I want you to accept what happened, figure the past is the past, and turn me in the kind of work you're capable of. *Fast* work. You're slow. You're damned slow. You muddle along with checks and rechecks like you're scared shitless you're going to fuck up, and you don't need to do that. You're not the final checker, you don't have to work like you are, because I'm sure as hell not going to let you do that for a long while yet. So just relax, *put the work out*, and do the best you can on your own level. Not—" He made a careless flip at the pages. "Not this stuff."

He sat there in silence a while. Bleeding, like Yanni said. And because he was stubborn, because there was only one thing he wanted, he said: "Prove to me I'm wrong. Do me a critique. Run it past Sociology. Show me what the second and third generation would do. Show me how it integrates. Or doesn't.''

"Have you looked around you? Have you seen the kind of schedules we've been running? Where do you think I've got the time to mess with this? Where do you think I'm going to budget Sociology to solve a problem that's been solved for eighty years?''

"I'm saying it's solved here. I'm saying I've got it. *You* critique my designs, then. You want to tell me I'm crazy, *show* me where I'm wrong.''

"*Dammit*, I won't help you wallow in the very thing that's the matter with you!''

"I'm Jordan's son. I was good enough—''

"Was, was, *was*, dammit! Stop looking at the past! Six years ago wasn't worth shit, son!''

"Prove it to me. *Prove* it, Yanni, or admit you can't.''

"Go to Peterson!''

"Peterson can't prove anything to me. I'm better than he is. I started that way.''

"You arrogant little bastard! You're *not* better than Peterson. Peterson pays his way around here. If you weren't Jordan's son, you'd be living in a one-bedroom efficiency with an allotment your work entitles you to, which won't pay for your fancy tastes, son. Grant and you together don't earn that place you're living in.''

"What does my father's work pay for, and what does he get? Send my designs to him. He'd find the time.''

Yanni took in a breath. Let it out again. "Damn. What do I do with you?''

"Whatever you want. Everyone else does. Fire me. You're going to get these designs about once a week. And if you don't answer me I'll ask. Once a week. I want my education, Yanni. I'm due that. And you're the instructor I want. Do whatever you like. Say whatever you like. I won't give up.''

"Dammit—''

He stared at Yanni, not even putting it beyond Yanni to get up, come around the desk and hit him. "I'd ask Strassen,'' he said, "but I don't think they want me near her. And I don't think she's got the time. So that leaves you, Yanni. You can fire me or you can prove I'm wrong and teach me why. But do it with logic. Psyching me doesn't do it.''

"I haven't got the time!"

"No one does. So make it. It doesn't take much, if you can see so clearly where I'm wrong. Two sentences are all I need. Tell me where it'll impact the next generation."

"Get the hell out of here."

"Am I fired?"

"No," Yanni snarled. Which was the friendliest thing staff had said to him in years.

So he did two tapes. One for Yanni. One the one he wished they would let him use. Because it taught him things. Because it let him see the whole set.

Because, as Grant said, a skill was damned important to an azi.

And he still could not work out the ethics of it—whether it was right to make a Theta get real pleasure out of the work instead of the approval. There was something moral involved. And there were basic structural problems in linking that way into an azi psychset, that was the trouble with it, and Yanni was right. An artificial psychset needed simple foundations, not complicated ones, or it got into very dangerous complexities. Deep-set linkages could become neuroses and obsessive behavior that could destroy an azi and be far more cruel than any simple boredom.

But he kept turning in the study designs for Yanni to see, when Yanni was in a mellow mood; and Yanni had been, now and again.

"You're a fool," was the best he got. And sometimes a paragraph on paper, outlining repercussions. Suggesting a study-tape out of Sociology.

He cherished those notes. He got the tapes. He ran them. He found mistakes. He built around them.

"You're still a fool," Yanni said. "What you're doing, son, is making your damage slower and probably deeper. But keep working. If you've got all this spare time I can suggest some useful things to do with it. We've got a glitch-up in a Beta set. We've got everything we can handle. The set is ten years old and it's glitching off one of three manual skills tapes. We think. The instructor thinks. You've got the case histories in this fiche. Apply your talents to that and see if you and Grant can come up with some answers."

He went away with the fiche and the folder, with a trouble-shoot to run, which was hell and away more real work than Yanni had yet trusted him with.

Which was, when he got it on the screen, a real bitch. The three azi had had enough tape run on them over the years to fill a page, and each one had been in a different application. But the glitch was a bad one. The azi were all under patch-tape, a generic calm-down-it's-not-your-fault, meaning three azi were waiting real-time in some anguish for some designer to come up with something to take their nameless distress and deal with it in a sensible way.

God, it was months old. They were not on Cyteen. Local Master Supervisors had all had a hand in the analysis, run two fixes on one, and they had gone badly sour.

Which meant it was beyond ordinary distress. It was not a theoretical problem.

He made two calls, one to Grant. "I need an opinion."

One to Yanni. "Tell me someone else is working on this. Yanni, this is a probable wipe, for God's sake, give it to someone who knows what he's doing."

"You claim you do," Yanni said, and hung up on him.

"Damn you!" he yelled at Yanni after the fact.

And when Grant got there, they threw out everything they were both working on and got on it.

For three damnable sleep-deprived weeks before they comped a deep-set intersect in a skills tape. In all three.

"Dammit," he yelled at Yanni when he turned it in, "this is a mess, Yanni! You could have found this thing in a week. These are human beings, for God's sake, one of them's running with a botch-up on top of the other damage—"

"Well, you manage, don't you? I thought you'd empathize. Go do a fix."

"What do you mean, 'do a fix'? Run me a check!"

"This one's all yours. Do me a fix. You don't need a check."

He drew a long, a desperate breath. And stared at Yanni with the thought of breaking his neck. "*Is* this a real-time problem? Or is this some damn trick? Some damn exercise you've cooked up?"

"Yes, it's real-time. And while you're standing here

arguing, they're still waiting. So get on it. You did that fairly fast. Let's see what else you can do."

"I know what you're doing to me, dammit! Don't take it out on the azi!"

"Don't you," Yanni said. And walked off into his inner office and shut the door.

He stood there. He looked desperately at Marge, Yanni's aide.

Marge gave him a sympathetic look and shook her head.

So he went back and broke the news to Grant.

And turned in the fix in three days.

"Fine," Yanni said. "I hope it works. I've got another case for you."

X

"This is part of my work," maman said, and Ari, walking with her hand in maman's, not because she was a baby, but because the machinery was huge and things moved and everything was dangerous, looked around at the shiny steel things they called womb-tanks, each one as big as a bus, and asked, loudly:

"Where are the babies?"

"Inside the tanks," maman said. An azi came up and maman said: "This is my daughter Ari. She's going to take a look at a few of the screens."

"Yes, Dr. Strassen," the azi said. Everyone talked loud. "Hello, Ari."

"Hello," she yelled up at the azi, who was a woman. And held on to maman's hand, because maman was following the azi down the long row.

It was only another desk, after all, and a monitor screen. But maman said: "What's the earliest here?"

"Number ten's a week down."

"Ari, can you count ten tanks down? That's nearly to the wall."

Ari looked. And counted. She nodded.

"All right," maman said. "Mary, let's have a look. —Ari, Mary here is going to show you the baby inside number ten, right here on the screen."

"Can't we look inside?"

"The light would bother the baby," maman said. "They're like birthday presents. You can't open them till it's the baby's birthday. All right?"

That was funny. Ari laughed and plumped herself down on the seat. And what came on the screen was a red little something.

"That's the baby," maman said, and pointed. "Right there."

"Ugh." It clicked with something she had seen somewhere. Which was probably tape. It was a kind of a baby.

"Oh, yes. Ugh. All babies look that way when they're a week old. It takes them how many weeks to be born?"

"Forty and some," Ari said. She remembered that from down deep too. "Are they all like this?"

"What's closest to eight weeks, Mary?"

"Four and five are nine," Mary said.

"That's tanks four and five, Ari. Look where they are, and we'll show you—which one, Mary?"

"Number four, sera. Here we are."

"It's still ugly," Ari said. "Can we see a pretty one?"

"Well, let's just keep hunting."

The next was better. The next was better still. Finally the babies got so big they were too big to see all of. And they moved around. Ari was excited, really excited, because maman said they were going to birth one.

There were a lot of techs when they got around to that. Maman took firm hold of Ari's shoulders and made her stand right in front of her so she would be able to see; and told her where to look, right there, right in that tank.

"Won't it drown?" Ari asked.

"No, no, babies live in liquid, don't they? Now, right now, the inside of the tank is doing just what the inside of a person does when birth happens. It's going to push the baby right out. Like muscles, only this is all pumps. It's really going to bleed, because there's a lot of blood going in and out of the pumps and it's going to break some of the vessels in the bioplasm when it pushes like that."

"Does the baby have a cord and everything?"

"Oh, yes, babies have to have. It's a real one. Everything is real right up to the bioplasm: that's the most complicated thing—it can really grow a blood system. Watch out now, see the light blink. That means the techs should get ready. Here it comes. There's its head. That's the direction babies are supposed to face.''

"Sploosh!" Ari cried, and clapped her hands when it hit the tank. And stood still as it started swimming and the nasty stuff went through the water. "Ugh."

But the azi techs got it out of there, and got the cord, and it did go on moving. Ari stood up on her toes trying to see as they took it over to the counter, but Mary the azi made them stop to show her the baby making faces. It was a boy baby.

Then they washed it and powdered it and wrapped it up, and Mary held it and rocked it.

"This is GY-7688," maman said. "His name is August. He's going to be one of our security guards when he grows up. But he'll be a baby for a long time yet. When you're twelve, he'll be as old as you are now."

Ari was fascinated. They let her wash her hands and touch the baby. It waved a fist at her and kicked and she laughed out loud, it was so funny.

"Say goodbye," maman said then. "Thank Mary."

"Thank you," Ari said, and meant it. It was fun. She hoped they could come back again.

"Did you like the lab?" maman asked.

"I liked it when the baby was born."

"Ollie was born like that. He was born right in this lab."

She could not imagine Ollie tiny and funny like that. She did not want to think of Ollie like that. She wrinkled her nose and made Ollie all right in her mind again.

Grown up and handsome in his black uniform.

"Sometimes CITs are born out of the tanks," maman said. "If for some reason their mamans can't carry them. The tanks can do that. Do you know the difference between an azi and a CIT, when they're born the same way?"

That was a hard question. There were a lot of differences. Some were rules and some were the way azi were.

"What's that?" she asked maman.

"How old were you when you had tape the first time?"

"I'm six."

"That's right. And you had your first tape the day after your birthday. Didn't scare you, did it?"

"No," she said; and shook her head so her hair flew. Because she liked to do that. Maman was slow with her questions and she got bored in between.

"You know when August will have his first tape?"

"When?"

"Today. Right now. They put him in a cradle and it has a kind of a tape going, so he can hear it."

She was impressed. Jealous, even. August was a threat if he was going to be that smart.

"Why didn't I do that?"

"Because you were going to be a CIT. Because you have to learn a lot of things the old-fashioned way. Because tapes are good, but if you've got a maman or a papa to take care of you, you learn all kinds of things August won't learn until he's older. CITs get a head start in a way. Azi learn a lot about how to be good and how to do their jobs, but they're not very good at figuring out what to do with things they've never met before. CITs are good at taking care of emergencies. CITs can make up what to do. They learn that from their mamans. Tape-learning is good, but it isn't everything. That's why maman tells you to pay attention to what you see and hear. That's why you're supposed to learn from that first, so you know tape isn't as important as your own eyes and ears. If August had a maman to take him home today he'd be a CIT."

"Why can't Mary be his maman?"

"Because Mary has too many kids to take care of. She has five hundred every year. Sometimes more than that. She couldn't do all that work. So the tape has to do it. That's why azi can't have mamans. There just aren't enough to go around."

"*I* could take August."

"No, you couldn't. Mamans have to be grown up. *I'd* have to take him home, and he'd have to sleep in your bed and share your toys and have dirty diapers and cry a lot. And you'd have to share maman with him forever and ever. You can't send a baby back just because you get tired of him. Would you like to have him take half your room and maman and Nelly and Ollie have to take care of him all the time? —because he'd be the baby then and he'd have to have all maman's time."

"No!" That was not a good idea. She grabbed onto maman's hand and made up her mind no baby was going to sneak in and take half of everything. Sharing with nasty friends was bad enough.

"Come on," maman said, and took her outside, in the sun, and into the garden where the fish were. Ari looked in her pants-pockets, but there was no crumb of bread or anything. Nelly had made her put on clean.

"Have you got fish-food?"

"No," maman said, and patted the rock she sat on. "Come sit by maman, Ari. Tell me what you think about the babies."

Lessons. Ari sighed and left the fish that swam up under the lilies; she squatted down on a smaller rock where she could see maman's face and leaned her elbows on her knees.

"What do you think about them?"

"They're all right."

"You know Ollie was born there."

"Is that baby going to be another Ollie?"

"You know he can't. Why?"

She screwed up her face and thought. "He's GY something and Ollie's AO. He's not even an Alpha."

"That's right. That's exactly right. You're very smart."

She liked to hear that. She fidgeted.

"You know, you were born in that room, Ari."

She heard that again in her head. And was not sure maman was not teasing her. She looked at maman, trying to figure out if it was a game. It didn't *look* like a game.

"Maman couldn't carry you. Maman's much too old. Maman's been on rejuv for years and years and she can't have babies anymore. But the tanks can. So she told Mary to make a special baby. And maman was there at the tank when it was birthed, and maman picked it up out of the water, and that was you, Ari."

She stared at maman. And tried to put herself in that room and in that tank, and be that baby Mary had picked up. She felt all different. She felt like she was different from herself. She did not know what to do about it.

Maman held her hands out. "Do you want maman to hold you, sweet? I will."

Yes, she wanted that. She wanted to be little and fit on maman's lap, and she tried, but she hurt maman, she was so big, so she just tucked up beside maman on the rock and felt big and clumsy while maman hugged her and rocked her. But it felt safer.

"Maman loves you, sweet. Maman truly does. There's nothing wrong at all in being born out of that room. You're the best little girl maman could have. I wouldn't trade you for anybody."

"I'm still yours."

Maman was not going to answer/maman was, so fast a change it scared her till maman said: "You're still mine, sweet."

She did not know why her heart was beating so hard. She did not know why it felt like maman was not going to say that at first. That scared her more than anything. She was glad maman had her arms around her. She was cold.

"I told you not everybody has a papa. But you did, Ari. His name was James Carnath. That's why Amy's your cousin."

"Amy's my cousin?" She was disgusted. People had cousins. It meant they were related. Nasty old Amelie Carnath was not anybody she wanted to be related to.

"Where *is* my papa?"

"Dead, sweet. He died before you were born."

"Couldn't Ollie be my father?"

"Ollie can't, sweet. He's on rejuv too."

"He doesn't have white hair."

"He dyes it, the same as I do."

That was an awful shock. She couldn't think of Ollie being old like maman. Ollie was young and handsome.

"I want Ollie to be my papa."

Maman made that upset-feeling again. She felt it in maman's arms. In the way maman breathed. "Well, it was James Carnath. He was a scientist like maman. He was very smart. That's where you get half your smart, you know. You know when you're going on rejuv and you know you might want a baby later you have to put your geneset in the bank so it's there after you can't make a baby anymore. Well, that was how you could be started even if your papa died a long time ago. And there you waited, in the genebank, all the years until maman was ready to take care of a baby."

"I wish you'd done it sooner," Ari said. "Then you wouldn't be so old."

Maman cried.

And she did, because maman was unhappy. But maman kissed her and called her sweet, and said she loved her, so she guessed it was as all right as it was going to get.

She thought about it a lot. She had always thought she came out of maman. It was all right if maman wanted her to be born from the tanks. It didn't make her an azi. Maman saw to that.

It was nice to be born where Ollie was born. She liked that idea. She didn't care about whoever James Carnath was. He was *Carnath*. Ugh. Like Amy.

She thought when Ollie was a baby he would have had black hair and he would be prettier than August was.

She thought when she grew up to be as old as maman she would have her own Ollie. And she would have a Nelly.

But not a Phaedra. Phaedra bossed too much.

You didn't have to have azi if you didn't want them. You had to order them or they didn't get born.

That, for Phaedra, who tattled on her. She would get August instead when he grew up, and he would be Security in their hall, and say *good morning, sera* to her just like Security did to maman.

She would have a Grant too. With red hair. She would dress him in black the way a lot of azi did and he would be very handsome. She did not know what he would do, but she would like to have an azi with red hair all the same.

She would be rich like maman.

She would be beautiful.

She would fly in the plane and go to the city and she would buy lots and lots of pretty clothes and jewels like maman's, so when they went to New Year they would make everybody say how beautiful they all were.

She would find Valery and tell him come back. And sera Schwartz too.

They would all be happy.

Verbal Text from:
PATTERNS OF GROWTH
A Tapestudy in Genetics: #1
"An Interview with
Ariane Emory": pt. 2

Reseune Educational Publications: 8970-8768-1
approved for 80+

Q: Dr. Emory, we have time perhaps for a few more questions, if you wouldn't mind.

A: Go ahead.

Q: You're one of the Specials. Some people say that you may be one of the greatest minds that's ever lived, in the class of da Vinci, Einstein, and Bok. How do you feel about that comparison?

A: I would like to have known any one of them. I think it would be interesting. I think I can guess your next question, by the way.

Q: Oh?

A: Ask it.

Q: How do you compare yourself to other people?

A: Mmmn. That's not the one. Other people. I'm not sure I know. I live a very cloistered life. I have great respect for anyone who can drive a truck in the outback or pilot a starship. Or negotiate the Novgorod subway. [laughter] I suppose that I could. I've never tried. But life is always complex. I'm not sure whether it takes more for me to plot a genotype than for some-

one of requisite ability to do any of those things I find quite daunting.

Q: That's an interesting point. But do you think driving a truck is equally valuable? Should we appoint Specials for that ability? What makes you important?

A: Because I have a unique set of abilities. No one else can do what I do. That's what a Special is.

Q: How does it *feel* to be a Special?

A: That's very close to the question I thought you'd ask. I can tell you being a Special is a lot like being a Councillor or holding any office: very little privacy, very high security, more attention than seems to make sense.

Q: Can you explain that last—than seems to make sense?

A: [laughter] A certain publication asked me to detail a menu of my favorite foods. A reporter once asked me whether I believed in reincarnation. Do these things make sense? I'm a psychsurgeon and a geneticist and occasionally a philosopher, in which consideration the latter question actually makes more sense to me than the first, but what in hell does either one matter to the general public? More than my science, you say? No. What the reporters are looking for is an equation that finds some balance between my psyche and their demographically ideal viewer—who is a myth and a reality: what they ask may bore everyone equally by pleasing no one exactly, but never mind: which brings us finally to the question I expect you're going to ask.

Q: That's very disconcerting.

A: Ask it. I'll tell you if we've found it yet.

Q: All right. I think we've gotten there. Is this it? What do you know that no one else does?

A: Oh, I like that better. What do I know? That's interesting. No one's ever put it that way before. Shall I tell you the question they always ask? What it feels like to have a Special's ability. What do I know is a much wiser question. What I feel, I'll answer that quite briefly: the same as anyone—who is isolate, different, and capable of understanding the reason for the isolation and the difference.

What do I know? I know that I am relatively unimportant and my work is vastly important. That's the thing the interviewer missed, who asked me what I eat. My preference in wines is utter trivia, unless you're interested in my personal biochemistry, which does interest me, and does matter, but certainly that has very little to do with an article on famous people and food, whatever that means. If that writer discovered a true connection between genius and cheeses, I am interested, and I want to interview him.

Fortunately my staff protects me against the idly curious. The state set me apart because in the aggregate the state, the people, if you will, know that given the freedom to work, I will work, and work for the sake of my work, because I am a monomaniac. Because I do have that emotional dimension the other reporters were trying to reach, I do have an aesthetic sense about what I do, and it applies to what one very ancient Special called the pursuit of Beauty— I think everyone can understand that, on some level. On whatever level. That ancient equated it with Truth. I call it Balance. I equate it with Symmetry. That's the nature of a Special, that's what you're really looking for: a Special's mind works in abstracts that transcend the limitations of any existing language. A Special has the Long View, and equally well the Wide View, that embraces more than any single human word will embrace, simply because communicative language is the property of the masses. And the Word, the Word with a capital W, that the Special sees, understands, comprehends in the root sense of the term, is a Word outside the experience of anyone previous. So he calls it Beauty. Or Truth. Or Balance or Symmetry. Frequently he expresses himself through the highly flexible language of mathematics; or if his discipline does not express itself readily in that mode, he has to create a special meaning for certain words within the context of his work and attempt to communicate in the semantic freight his language has accumulated for centuries. My language is partly mathematical, partly biochemical, partly semantics: I study biochemical systems— human beings—which react predictably on a biochemical level to stimuli passing through a system of receptors—hardware—of biochemically determined sensitivity; through a biochemical processor of biochemically determined efficiency— hardware again—dependent on a self-programming system which is also biochemical, which produces a uniquely tailored software capable of receiving information from another human being with a degree of specificity limited principally by its own hardware, its own software, and semantics. We haven't begun to speak of the hardware and software of the second human being. Nor have we addressed the complex dimension of culture or the possibility of devising a mathematics for social systems, the games statisticians and demographers play on their level and I play on mine. I will tell you that I leave much of the work with microstructures to researchers under my direction and I have spent more of my time in thinking than I have in the laboratory. I am approaching a degree of order in that thought that I can only describe as a state of simplicity. A very wide simplicity. Things which did not seem to be related, are related. The settling of these things into order is a pleasurable sensation that increasingly lures the thinker into dimensions that have nothing to do with the senses. Attaching myself to daily life is increasingly difficult and I sometimes find myself needing that, the flesh needs affirmation, needs sensation— because otherwise I do not, personally, exist. And I exist everywhere.

At the end I will speak one Word, and it will concern humanity. I don't know if anyone will understand it. I have a very specific hope that someone will. This is the emotional dimension. But if I succeed, my successor will do something I can only see in the distance: in a sense, I am doing it, because getting this far is part of it. But the flesh needs rest from visions. Lives are short-term, even one extended by rejuv. I give you Truth. Someone, someday, will understand my notes.

That is myself, speaking the language not even another Special can understand, because his Beauty is different, and proceeds along another course. If you're religious you may think we have seen the same thing. Or that we must lead to the same thing. I am not, myself, certain. We are God's dice. To answer still another Special.

Now I've given you more than I've given any other interviewer, because you asked the best question. I'm sorry I can't answer in plain words. By now, the average citizen is capable of understanding Plato and some may know Einstein. The majority of scientists have yet to grasp Bok. You will know, in a few centuries, what I know right now. But humanity in the macrocosm is quite wise: because in the mass you are as visionary as any Special, you give me my freedom, and I prove the validity of your judgment.

Q: You can't interpret this thing you see.

A: If I could, I would. If words existed to describe it, I would not be what I am.

Q: You've served for decades in the legislature. Isn't that a waste? Isn't that a job someone else could do?

A: Good question. No. Not in this time. Not in this place. The decisions we make are very important. The events of the last five decades prove that. And I need contact with reality. I benefit in—a spiritual way, if you like. In a way that affects my personal biochemical systems and keeps them in healthy balance. It's not good for the organism, to let the abstract grow without checking the perceptions. In simpler terms, it's a remedy against intellectual isolation and a service I do my neighbors. An abstract mathematician probably doesn't have anywhere near our most junior councillor's understanding of the interstellar futures market or the pros and cons of a medical care system for merchanters on Union stations. By the very nature of my work, I do have that understanding; and I have a concern for human society. I know people criticize the Council system as wasting the time of experts. If providing expert opinion to the society in which we all live is a waste of time, then what good are we? Of course certain theorists can't communicate out-field. But certain ones can, and should. You've seen the experts disagree. Sometimes it's because one of us fails to understand something in another field. Very often it's because the best thinking in two fields fails to reconcile a question of practical effects, and that is precisely the point in which the people doing the arguing had better be experts: some very useful interdisciplinary understandings are hammered out in Council and in the private meetings, a fusion of separate bodies of knowledge that actually sustains this unique social experiment we call Union.

That's one aspect of the simplicity I can explain simply: the interests of all humans are interlocked, my own included, and politics is no more than a temporal expression of social mathematics.

CHAPTER
6

"This bell has to ring once when you push the left-hand button and twice when you push the right-hand button," the Super said, and Florian listened as the problem clicked off against the things he knew. So far it was easy to wire. "But—" Here came the real problem, Florian knew. "But you have to fix it so that if you push the left-hand button first it won't work at all and if you push the right-hand button twice it won't work until you push the left-hand button. Speed does matter. So does neatness. Go."

Parts and tools were all over the table. Florian collected what he needed. It was not particularly hard.

The next job was somebody else's project. And you had to look at the board and tell the instructor what it would do.

His fingers were very fast. He could beat the clock. Easy. The next thing was harder. The third thing was always to make up one for somebody else. He had fifteen minutes to do that.

He told the Instructor what it was.

"Show me how you'd build that," the Instructor said. So he did.

And the Instructor looked very serious and nodded finally and said: "Florian, you're going to double up on tape."

He was disappointed. "I'm sorry. It won't work?"

"Of course it'll work," the Instructor said, and smiled at him. "But I can't give that to anybody on this level. You'll do double-study on the basics and we'll see how you do with the next. All right?"

"Yes," he said. Of course it was yes. But he was worried. He was working with Olders a lot. It was hard, and took a lot of time, and they kept insisting he take his Rec time, when he had rather be at his job.

He was already late a lot, and Andy frowned at him, and helped him more than he wanted.

He thought he ought to talk to the Super about all of it. But he made them happy when he worked hard. He could still do it, even if he was tired, even if he fell into his bunk at night and couldn't even remember doing it.

The Instructor said he could go and he was late again. Andy told him the pigs didn't understand his schedule and Andy had had to feed them.

"I'll do the water," he said, and did it for Andy's too. That was fair. It made Andy happy.

It made Andy so happy Andy let him curry the Horse with him, and go with him to the special barn where they had the baby, which was a she, protected against everything and fed with a bucket you had to hold. He wasn't big enough to do that yet. You had to shower and change your clothes and be very careful, because they were giving the baby treatments they got from the Horse. But she wasn't sick. She played dodge with them and then she would smell of their fingers and play dodge again.

He had been terribly relieved when Andy told him that the horses were not for food. "What *are* they for?" he had asked then, afraid that there might be other bad answers.

"They're Experimentals," Andy had said. "I'm not sure. But they say they're working animals."

Pigs were sometimes working animals. Pigs were so good at smelling out native weeds that drifted in and rooted and they were so smart at not eating the stuff that there were azi who did nothing but walk them around, every day going over the pens and the fields with the pigs that nobody would ever make into bacon, and zapping whatever had sneaked inside the fences. The machine-sniffers were good, but Andy said the pigs were better in some ways.

That was what they meant in the tapes, Florian thought, when they said one of the first Rules of all Rules was to find ways to be useful.

_____ ii _____

Ari read the problem, thought into her tape-knowing, and asked maman: "Does it matter how many are boys and how many are girls?"

Maman thought a moment. "Actually it does. But you can work it as if it doesn't."

"Why?"

"Because, and this is important to know, certain things are less important in certain problems; and when you're just learning how to work the problem, leaving out the things that don't matter as much helps you to remember what things are the most important in figuring it. Everything in the world is important in that problem—boys and girls, the weather, whether or not they can get enough food, whether there are things that eat them—but right now just the genes are going to matter. When you can work all those problems, then they'll tell you how to work in all the other things. One other thing. They'd hate to tell you you knew everything. There might be something else no one thought of. And if you _thought_ they'd told you everything, that could trick you. So they start out simple and then start adding in whether they're boys and girls. All right?"

"It _does_ matter," Ari said doggedly, "because the boy fish fight each other. But there's going to be twenty-four blue ones if nobody gets eaten. But they will, because blue ones are easy to see, and they can't hide. And if you put them with big fish there won't be any blue fish at all."

"Do you know whether a fish sees colors?"

"Do they?"

"Let's leave that for a moment. What if the females like blue males better?"

"Why should they?"

"Just figure it. Carry it another generation."

"How much better?"

"Twenty-five percent."

"All those blue ones are just going to make the big fish fatter and *they'll* have lots of babies. This is getting complicated."

Maman got this funny look like she was going to sneeze or laugh or get mad. And then she got a very funny look that was not funny at all. And gathered her up against her and hugged her.

Maman did that a lot lately. Ari thought that she ought to feel happier than she was. She had never had maman spend so much time with her. Ollie too.

But there was a danger-feeling. Maman wasn't happy. Ollie wasn't. Ollie was being azi as hard as he could, and maman and Ollie didn't shout at each other anymore. Maman didn't shout at anybody. Nelly just looked confused a lot of the time. Phaedra went around being azi too.

Ari was scared and she wanted to ask maman why, but she was afraid maman would cry. Maman always had that look lately. And it hurt when maman cried.

She just held on to maman.

Next morning she went to playschool. She was big enough to go by herself now. Maman hugged her at the door. Ollie came and hugged her too. He had not done that in a long time.

She looked back and the door was shut. She thought that was funny. But she went on to school.

---

iii

RESEUNE ONE left the runway and Jane clenched her hands on the leather arms of the seat. And did not look out the window. She did not want to see Reseune dwindle away. She bit her lips and shut her eyes and felt the leakage down her face while the gentle acceleration pressed her into the seat.

She turned her face toward Ollie when they reached cruising altitude. "Ollie, get me a drink. A double."

"Yes, sera," Ollie said, and unbelted and went to see to it.

Phaedra, sitting in front of them, had turned her chair around to face her across the little table. "Can I do something for you, sera?"

God, she needs to, doesn't she? Phaedra's scared. "I want you to make out a shopping list. Things you think we'll need on-ship. You'll have to place some orders when we make station. There's an orientation booklet in the outside pocket. It'll review you on procedures."

"Yes, sera."

That put a patch on Phaedra's problems. Ollie was walking wounded. He had asked her for tape. He—had asked her for tape, azi to Supervisor; and she had refused him.

"Ollie," she had said. "You're too much a CIT. I need you to be. Do you understand what I'm saying?"

"Yes," he had said. And held up better than she had.

"One for yourself too," she yelled at him, over the engine noise; and he looked around and nodded understanding. "And Phaedra!"

Peggy came up to Ollie's side at the bar, wobbled as the plane hit a little chop and then ducked down and took out a pair of glasses.

For Julia. Back in the back. Julia and Gloria.

"You've ruined my life!" Julia had screamed at her in the terminal. Right in front of Denys, the azi, and the Family that had come to see them off. While poor Gloria stood there with her chin quivering and her eyes running over. Not a bad kid. A kid who had had too much of most things, too little of what mattered, and who stared at the grandmother she had hardly ever seen and probably looked for signs of ultimate evil about her person. Gloria had no idea in the world what she was going to. No idea in the world what ship discipline meant, or the closed steel world of a working station.

"Hello, Gloria," she had said, nerving herself, trying not—God, not ever—to compare the kid against Ari—against Ari, who might hear a plane take off and might look up and realize it was *RESEUNE ONE*. Nothing more than that.

Gloria had run over to her mother. Who was about to hyperventilate. Who managed, atop it all, to impart a sense of the ridiculous to their departure. It was probably just as well they were traveling with Reseune Security. There was no trusting Julia not to bolt and run in Novgorod.

Irrationally afraid of the shuttle, the void, the jumps, all the things that involved a physics Julia had never troubled herself to learn and now decided she could not personally rely on.

Too bad, kid. I wish I could make a bubble for you where things work the way you want. I'm sorry it all overwhelms you.

It did from the moment you were born. Sorry, daughter. I'm really sorry about that.

Sorry you're going with me.

Ollie brought back the drinks. He was pale, but he was doing quite well, considering. She managed to smile at him when he handed her hers, and he looked at her again when he sat down with his own drink in hand.

She had taken half of hers down without noticing it. "I'll be all right," she said, and lifted the glass. "Skoal, Ollie. Back where I came from. Going home, finally."

And on her second double: "It feels like I was twenty again, Ollie, like nothing of Reseune ever happened."

Or she had gotten that part of her numb for a while.

---------------------- iv ----------------------

Phaedra was not at the playschool. Nelly was. Nelly was easy to get around. Sam could push her in the swing really high. Nelly worried, but Nelly wasn't going to stop them, because she would be mad at Nelly and Nelly didn't like that.

So Sam pushed her and she pushed Sam. And they climbed on the puzzle-bars.

Finally Jan came after Sam and Nelly was walking her home when uncle Denys met them in the hall.

"Nelly," Denys said, "Security wants to talk to you."

"Why?" Ari asked. Of a sudden she was afraid again. Security and Nelly were as far apart as you could think of. It was like everything else recently. It was a thing that didn't belong.

"Nelly," Denys said. "Do what I say."

"Yes, ser," Nelly said.

And Denys, big as he was, got down on one knee and took Ari's hands while Nelly was going. "Ari," he said, "something serious has happened. Your maman has to go take care of it. She's had to leave."

"Where's she going?"

"Very far away, Ari. I don't know that she *can* come back. You're going to come home with me. You and Nelly. Nelly's going to stay with you, but she's got to go take some tape that will make her feel better about it.''

''Maman can too come back!''

''I don't think so, Ari. Your maman is an important woman. She has something to do. She's going—well, far as a ship can take her. She knew you'd be upset. She didn't want to worry you. So she said I should tell you goodbye for her. She said you should come home with me now and live in my apartment.''

''No!'' *Goodbye*. Goodbye was nothing maman would ever say. Everything was wrong. She pulled away from Denys' hands and ran, ran as hard as she could, down the halls, through the doors, into their own hall. Denys couldn't catch her. No one could. She ran until she got to her door, her place; and she unclipped her keycard from her blouse and she put it in the slot.

The door opened.

''Maman! Ollie!''

She ran through the rooms. She hunted everywhere, but she knew maman and Ollie would never hide from her.

Maman and Ollie would never leave her either. Something bad had happened to them. Something terrible had happened to them and uncle Denys was lying to her.

Maman's and Ollie's things were all off the dresser and the clothes from the closet.

Her toys were all gone. Even Poo-thing and Valery's star.

She was breathing hard. She felt like there was not enough air. She heard the door open again and ran for the living room.

''Maman! Ollie!''

But it was a Security woman who had come in; she was tall and she wore black and she had got in and she shouldn't have.

Ari just stood there and stared at her. The woman stared back. The uniformed woman, in her living room, who wasn't going to leave.

''Minder,'' Ari said, trying to be brave and grown-up, ''call maman's office.''

The Minder did not answer.

''Minder? It's Ari. Call maman's office!''

''The Minder is disconnected,'' the Security woman said. And it was true. The Minder hadn't said a thing when she had come in. Everything was wrong.

"Where's my mother?" she asked.

"Dr. Strassen has left. Your guardian is Dr. Nye. Please be calm, young sera. Dr. Nye is on his way."

"I don't want him!"

But the door opened and uncle Denys was there, out of breath and white-faced. In maman's apartment.

"It's all right," Denys panted. "Ari. Please."

"Get out!" she yelled at uncle Denys. "Get out, get out, get out!"

"Ari. Ari, I'm sorry. I'm terribly sorry. Listen to me."

"No, you're not sorry! I want maman! I want Ollie! Where are they?"

Denys came and tried to take hold of her. She ran for the kitchen. There were knives there. But the Security woman dived around the couch and caught her, and picked her up while she kicked and screamed.

"Careful with her!" Denys said. "Be careful. Put her down."

The woman set her feet back on the floor. Denys came and took her from the woman and held her against his shoulder.

"Cry, Ari. It's all right. Get your breath and cry."

She gasped and gasped and finally she could breathe.

"I'm going to take you home now," Denys said gently, and patted her face and her shoulders. "Are you all right, Ari? I can't carry you. Do you want the officer to? She won't hurt you. No one's going to hurt you. Or I can call the meds. Do you feel like you want me to do that?"

Take you home was not her home anymore. Something had happened to everyone.

Denys took her hand and she walked. She was too tired to do anything else. She was hardly able to do that.

Uncle Denys took her all the way to his apartment, and he set her down on his couch and he had his azi Seely get her a soft drink.

She drank it and she could hardly hold the glass without spilling it, she was shaking so.

"Nelly is staying here," uncle Denys said to her, sitting down on the other side of the table. "Nelly will be your very own."

"Where's Ollie?" she asked, clenching the glass in her lap.

"With your maman. She needed him."

Ari gulped air. It was a good thing, she thought, if maman had to go somewhere, maman and Ollie ought to be together.

"Phaedra's gone with them," Denys said.

"I don't care about Phaedra!"

"You want Nelly, don't you? Maman left you Nelly. She wanted Nelly to go on taking care of you."

She nodded. There was a large knot in her throat. Her heart was ten times too big for her chest. Her eyes stung.

"Ari, I don't know much about taking care of a little girl. Neither does Seely. But your maman sent all your things here. You'll have your very own suite, you and Nelly, right in there, do you want to go see where your room is?"

She shook her head; and tried not to cry. She tried to get a good mad. Like maman.

"We won't talk about it now. Nelly's going to be here tonight. She'll be a little upset. You know she can't take much upset. Promise me you'll be good to her, Ari. She's your azi and you have to be kind to her, because she really ought to stay in the hospital, but she's so worried about you, and I know you need her. Nelly's going to come home every night between her sessions—they're going to give her tape, you know, they have to, because she's terribly upset; but she loves you and she wants to come take care of you. I'm afraid it's you who'll have to take care of her. You understand me? You can hurt her very, very badly."

"I know," Ari said, because she did.

"There you are. You're a brave little girl. You aren't a baby at all. It's very hard, very hard. —Thank you, Seely."

Seely had brought her a glass of water and a pill, and expected her to take it. Seely was a nobody. He wasn't like Ollie. He wasn't nice, he wasn't mean, he wasn't anything but azi all the time. And he took her glass and put it on his tray and offered her the water.

"I don't want any tape!" she said.

"It's not that kind of pill," uncle Denys said. "It'll make your head stop hurting. It'll make you feel better."

She didn't remember telling him her head hurt. Maman always said don't take other people's pills. Never, never take azi-pills. But maman was not here to tell her what this one was.

Like Valery. Like sera Schwartz. Like all the Disappeareds. Maman and Ollie had gotten caught too.

Maybe I can Disappear next. And find them.

"Sera," Seely said. "Please."

She took the pill off the tray. She put it in her mouth and drank it down with the water.

"Thank you," Seely said. He was so smooth he wasn't there. He took the glass away. You would never notice Seely.

Uncle Denys sat there so fat he made the whole chair go down, with his arms on his knees and his round face upset and worried. "You won't have to go to playschool for a few days. Until you want to. You don't think you can feel better. I know. But you will. You'll feel better even tomorrow. You'll miss your maman. Of course you will. But you won't hurt as much. Every day will be a little better."

She didn't want it to be better. She didn't know who made people Disappear. But it wasn't maman. They could offer her whatever they wanted. It wouldn't make her believe what they said.

Maman and Ollie had known there was trouble. They had been terribly upset and kept hiding it from her. Maybe they thought they could take care of it and they couldn't. *She* had felt it coming and hadn't understood.

Perhaps there was a place people went to. Perhaps it was like being dead. You got in trouble and you got Disappeared somewhere in some way even maman couldn't stop it happening.

So she knew she couldn't either. She had to push and push, that was what, and get in trouble until there wasn't anybody. Maybe it was her fault. She had always thought so. But when they ran out of people to Disappear she had to find out what was going on.

Then maybe she could go.

She was Wrong, of a sudden. She couldn't feel her hands or her feet, and she felt a burning in her stomach.

She was having trouble. But Seely picked her up in his arms and the whole room swung and became the hall and became the bedroom. Seely laid her gently on the bed and took her shoes off, and put a blanket over her.

Poo-thing was beside her on the bedspread. She put out her hand and touched him. She could not remember where she had gotten Poo-thing. He had always been there. Now he was here. That was all. Now Poo-thing was all there was.

—————————————— v ——————————————

"Poor kid," Justin said, and poured more wine into the glass. "Poor little kid, dammit to *hell*, couldn't they let her come down to the airport?"

Grant just shook his head. And drank his own wine. He made a tiny handsign that warned of eavesdroppers.

Justin wiped his eyes. He never forgot that. Sometimes he found it hard to care.

"Not our problem," Grant said. "Not yours."

"I know it."

That for the listeners. That they never knew, one way or the other, whether they were there. They thought of ways to confound Security, even thought of devising a language without cognates, with erratic grammar, and using tape to memorize it. But they were afraid of the suspicion their using it might raise. So they went the simplest route: the tablet. He reached for it and scrawled: *Sometimes I'd like to run off to Novgorod and get a job in a factory. We design tape to make normal people. We build in trust and confidence and make them love each other. But the designers are all crazy.*

Grant wrote: *I have profound faith in my creators and my Supervisor. I find comfort in that.*

"You're sick," Justin said aloud.

Grant laughed. And Grant went serious again, and leaned over and took hold of Justin's knee, the two of them sitting cross-legged on the couch. "I don't understand good and evil. I've decided that. An azi has no business tossing words like that around, in the cosmic sense. But to me you're everything good."

He was touched by that. And the damned tape-flashes still bothered him. Even after this many years, like an old, old pain. With Grant it never mattered. That, as much as anything, gave him a sense of comfort. He laid his hand on Grant's, pressed it slightly, because he could not say anything.

"I mean it," Grant said. "You hold a difficult place. You

do as much good as you can. Sometimes too much. Even I can rest. You should."

"What can I do when Yanni loads me down with—"

"No." Grant shook at his knee. "You can say no. You can quit working these hours. You can work on the things you want to work on. You've said yourself—you know what he's doing. Don't let them give you this other thing. Refuse it. You don't need it."

There was a baby in process on Fargone, replicate of one Benjamin Rubin, who lived in the enclave on the other side of an uncrossable wall, and worked in a lab Reseune had provided.

It provided something visible for Defense to hover over. And Jane Strassen, when she arrived, would find herself mother to another of the project's children.

He knew. They gave him Rubin's interviews. They let him do the tape-structures. He had no illusions they would run them without checks.

Not, at least, these. And that was a relief, after running without them for a year.

"It's a degree of trust, isn't it?" His voice came out hoarse, showing the strain he had not wanted to show.

"It puts another kind of load on you, a load you don't need."

"Maybe it's my chance to do something worthwhile. It's a major project. Isn't it? It's the best thing that's happened in a long time. Maybe I can make Rubin's life—better or something." He leaned forward to pour more wine. Grant moved and did it for him. "At least Rubin had some compassion in his life. His mother lives on-station, he sees her, he's got something to hold on to."

Give or take the guards that attended a Special. Justin knew all these things. A confused, remote intellectual whose early health problems had been extreme, whose attachment to his mother was excessive and desperate; whose frail body had made health a preoccupation for him; whose various preoccupations had excluded adolescent passions, except for his work. But nothing—nothing of what had shaped Ari Emory.

Thank God.

"I can do something with it," he said. "I'm going to take

some work in citizen psych. Do me some good. It's a different methodology.''

Grant frowned at him. They could talk work at home, without worrying about monitors. But their line of conversation had gotten dangerous, maybe already gone over the line. He was not sure anymore. He was exhausted. Study, he thought, would take him off real-time work. Study was all he wanted. Grant was right, he was never cut out for trouble-shooting real-time situations. He cared too damn much.

Yanni had yelled at him: ''Empathy is fine in an interview. It's got no place in the solution! Get it straight in your head who you're treating!''

Which made sense to him. He was not cut out for clinical psych. Because he never could get it straight, when he felt the pain himself.

By Yanni's lights, even, he thought, by Denys'—because there was no way this could have come to him without Denys working at Giraud—it was the most generous thing they could have done for him, putting him back in work that took a security clearance, re-establish his career in a slightly different field, in work very like Jordan's, let him work on a project where he could gain some reputation—CIT work was something the military would notice without actually giving the military an excuse to move on him, and it might clear him and do some good for Jordan. That was at least a possibility.

It was a kind of ultimatum, he thought, a kindness that could go entirely the other way if he tried to avoid the honor. That was always what he had to think about. Even when they were doing him favors.

vi

Ari woke with someone close to her, and remembered waking halfway through the night when someone got into bed with her, and took her in her arms and said in Nelly's voice, ''I'm here, young sera. Nelly's here.''

Nelly was by her in the morning, and maman was not, the bedroom was strange, it was uncle Denys' place, and Ari wanted to scream or to cry or to run again, run and run, until no one could find her.

But she lay still, because she knew maman was truly gone. And uncle Denys was right, she was better than she was, she was thinking about breakfast in between thinking how much she hurt and how she wished Nelly was somewhere else and maman was there instead.

It was still something, to have Nelly. She patted Nelly's face hard, until Nelly woke up, and Nelly hugged her and stroked her hair and said:

"Nelly's here. Nelly's here." And burst into tears.

Ari held her. And felt cheated because she wanted to cry, but Nelly was azi and crying upset her. So she was sensible like maman said, and told Nelly to behave.

Nelly did. Nelly stopped snuffling and sniveling and got up and got dressed; and gave Ari her bath and washed her hair and dressed her in her clean blue pants and a sweater. And combed and combed her hair till it crackled.

"We're supposed to go to breakfast with ser Nye," Nelly said.

That was all right. And it was a good breakfast, at uncle Denys' table, with everything in the world to eat. Ari did eat. Uncle Denys had seconds of everything and told her she and Nelly could spend the day in the apartment, until Nelly had to go to hospital, and then Seely would come and take care of her.

"Yes, ser," Ari said. Anything was all right. Nothing was. After yesterday she didn't care who was here. She wanted to ask Denys where maman was, and where maman was going. But she didn't, because everything was all right for a while and she was so tired.

And if Denys told her she wouldn't know the name of that place. She only knew Reseune.

So she sat and let Nelly read her stories. Sometimes she cried for no reason. Sometimes she slept. When she woke up it was Nelly telling her it would be Seely with her.

Seely would get her as many soft drinks as she wanted. And put on the vid for her. And do anything she asked.

She asked Seely could they go for a walk and feed the fish. They did that. They came back and Seely got her more soft drinks, and she wished she could hear maman telling her they weren't good for her. So she stopped on her own, and asked Seely for paper and sat and drew things.

Till uncle Denys came back and it was time for supper, and uncle Denys talked to her about what she would do tomorrow and how he would buy her anything she wanted.

She thought of several things. She wanted a spaceship with lights. She wanted a new coat. If uncle Denys was going to offer, she could think of things. She could think of really expensive things that maman never would get her.

But none of them could make her happy. Not even Nelly. Just when they were going to give you things, you took them, that was all, and you asked them for lots and lots to make it hard for them, and make them think that was important to you and you were happier with them, —but you didn't forget your mad. Ever.

vii

Grant sweated, waiting in Yanni Schwartz's outer office, with no appointment and only Marge's good offices to get him through the door. He heard Yanni shouting at Marge. He could not hear what he said. He imagined it had to do with interruptions and Justin Warrick.

And for a very little he would have gotten up and left, then, fast, because from moment to moment he knew he could bring trouble down on Justin by coming here. He was not sure that Yanni would not shake him badly enough to make him say something he ought not. Yanni was the kind of born-man he did not like to deal with, emotional and loud and radiating threat in every move he made. The men who had taken him to the shack in the hills had been like that. Giraud had been like that when he had questioned him. Grant sat there waiting and not panicking only by blanking himself and not thinking it through again until Marge came back and said:

"He'll see you."

He got up and made a little bow. "Thank you, Marge."

And walked into the inner office and up to the big desk and said: "Ser, I want to talk to you about my CIT."

Azi-like. Justin said Yanni could be decent enough to his patients. So he took the manner and stood very quietly.

"I'm not in consultation," Yanni said.

Yanni gave him no favors, then. Grant dropped the dumb-annie pose, pulled up the available chair and sat down. "I still want to talk to you, ser. Justin's taking the favor you're doing him and I think it's a bad mistake."

"A mistake."

"You're not going to let him have anything but the first-draft work, are you? And where does that leave him after twenty years? Nowhere. With no more than he had before."

"Training. Which he badly needs. Which you should know. Do we have to discuss your partner? You know his problems. I don't have to haul them out for you."

"Tell me what you think they are."

Yanni had been relaxed, mostly. The jaw clamped, the chin jutted, the whole pose shifted to aggression as he leaned on his desk. "Maybe you'd better have your CIT come talk to me. Did he send you? Or is this your own idea?"

"My own, ser." He was reacting, dammit. His palms were sweating. He hated that. The trick was to make the CIT calm down instead. "I'm scared of you. I don't want to do this. But Justin won't talk to you, at least he won't tell you the truth."

"Why not?"

The man *had* no quiet-mode. "Because, ser, —" Grant took a breath and tried not to pay attention to what was going on in his gut. "You're the only teacher he has. If you discard him, there's no one else good enough to teach him. You're like his Super. He has to rely on you and you're abusing him. That's very hard for me to watch."

"We're not talking azi psych, Grant. You *don't* understand what's going on, not on an operational level, and you're on dangerous personal ground—it's your own mindset I'm talking about. Don't identify. You know better. If you don't, —"

"Yes, ser, you can recommend I take tape. I know what you can do. But I want you to listen to me. *Listen!* I don't know what kind of man you are. But I've seen what you've done. I think you may be trying to help Justin. In some ways I think it has helped. But he can't go on working the way he is."

Yanni gave a growl like an engine dying and slowly leaned back on the arm of his chair, looking at him from under his brows. "Because he's not suited to real-time work. I know it. You know it. Justin knows it. I thought maybe he'd calm down, but he hasn't got the temperament for it, he can't get the perspective. He hasn't got the patience for standard design work, repetition drives him crazy. He's creative, so we put him in on the Rubin project. Denys got him that. I seconded it. It's the best damn thing we can do for him—put him where he can do theoretical work, *but not that damn out-there project of his*, and he won't concentrate on anything else, I know damn well he won't! He's worse than Jordan with an idea in his head, he won't turn it loose till it stinks. Have you got an answer? Because it's either the Rubin project or it's rot away in standard design, and I haven't got time on my staff to let one of my people take three weeks doing a project that should have been booted out the door in three days, you understand me?''

He had thought down till then that Yanni was the Enemy. But of a sudden he felt easier with Yanni. He saw a decent man who was not good at listening. Who was listening for the moment.

''Ser. Please. Justin's not Jordan. He doesn't work like Jordan. But if you give him a chance he *is* working. Listen to me. Please. You don't agree with him, but he's learning from you. You know that an azi designer has an edge in Applications. I'm an Alpha. I can take a design and internalize it and tell a hell of a lot about it. I've worked with him on his own designs, and I can tell you—I can tell you I believe in what he's trying to do.''

''God, that's all I need.''

''Ser, I know what his designs *feel* like, in a way no CIT can. I have the logic system.''

''I'm not talking about his ability. He's fixed his rat-on-a-treadmill problems. He's got that covered. I'm talking about what happens when his sets integrate into CIT psych. Second and third and fourth generation. We don't want a work-crazy population. We don't want gray little people that go crazy when they're not on the assembly line. We don't want a suicide rate through the overhead when there's job failure or a dip in the economy. We're talking CIT psych, and that's exactly the field he's weakest in and exactly what I think he ought to go study for ten or twenty years before he does some real harm. You know what it *feels* like. Let me tell you I know something about CIT psych from the inside, plus sixty years in this field, and I trust a junior designer can appreciate that fact.''

''I respect that, ser. I earnestly assure you. So does he. But

his designs put—put *joy* into a psychset. Not just efficiency.
The designs you say will cause trouble are their own reward
tape. Isn't it true, ser, that when an azi has a CIT child, and he
teaches that child as a CIT, he teaches *interpretively* what he
understands out of his pyschset. And an azi with one of
Justin's small routines somewhere in his sets, even if he was
never as lucky as I am, to be socialized as I am, to be Alpha
and have one lifelong partner, would get so much sense of purpose out of that, so much sense of purpose, he would think
about his job and get better at it. And have pride in that, ser.
Maybe there are still problems in it. But it's the emotional
level he reaches. It's the key to the logic sets themselves. It's a
self-programming interaction. That's what no one is taking
into account.''

''Which create a whole complex of basic structural problems in synthetic psychsets. Let's talk theory here. You're a
competent designer. Let's be real blunt. They tried this eighty
years ago.''

''I'm familiar with that.''

''And they hung a few embellishments onto the psychsets
and they ended up with neuroses. Obsessive behaviors.''

''You say yourself he's avoided that.''

''*And it's self-programming*, do you hear yourself talking?''

''Worm,'' Grant said. ''But a benign one.''

''That's just about where that kind of theory belongs.
Worm. God! If it is self-programming, you *have* created a
worm of sorts, and you're playing with people's lives. If it
isn't, you've got a delayed-action problem that's going to crop
up in the second or third generation. Another kind of worm, if
you want to put it that way. Hell if I want to give research time
to it. I've got a budget. You two are on my departmental budget and you're a hell of an expense with no damned return that
justifies it.''

''We have justified it this last year.''

''Which is killing Warrick. Isn't that your complaint? He
can't go on outputting at that level. He can't take it. Psycho-
logically he can't take it. So what are you going to do? Carry it
by yourself, while Justin lives in the clouds somewhere designing sets that won't work, that I'm damned well not going to let
him install in some poor sod of a Tester. No!''

''I'll do the work. Give him the freedom. Lighten the load.

A little. Ser, give him the chance. He has to rely on you. No one else can help him. He is good. You know he is.''

"And he's damned well wasting himself."

"What were you doing at the start? Teaching him, while you took his designs apart. Do that for him. Lighten the load a little. The work will get done. You just can't pressure him like that, because he'll do it if he thinks someone is suffering, he just won't stop, he's like that. Give us things we can handle and we'll handle them. Justin has a talent at integration that can get more out of a genotype than anyone ever did, because he does get into the emotional level. Maybe his ideas won't work, but, for God's sake, he's still studying. You don't know what he can be. Give him a chance.''

Yanni looked at him a long time, upset, unhappy, with his face red and his teeth working at his lip. "You're quite a salesman, son. You know what's the matter with him on this? Ari got hold of a vulnerable kid with an idea that was real advanced for a seventeen-year-old, she flattered hell out of him, she fed him full of this crap, and psyched him right into her bed. You're aware of that?''

"Yes, ser. I'm well aware of it.''

"She did a real job on him. He thinks he was brilliant. He thinks there was more there than there was, and you don't do him any service by feeding that. He's bright, he's not brilliant. He'd be damn good on the Rubin project. I've seen what he can do, and there *is* a lot in him. I respect hell out of that. I don't like to feed a delusion. I spend my life trying to make normal people and you're asking me to humor him in the biggest delusion of his poor fucked-up life. I hate that like hell, Grant. I can't tell you how much I hate it.''

"*I'm* talking to a man who's the nearest thing to a Supervisor Justin's got; the man Justin fought to get to help him; who's going to take a talent that's been fucked-up and kill it because it's a drain on the teacher. What kind of man is that?''

"Dammit.''

"Yes, ser. Damn *me* all you like. It's Justin I'm talking about. He trusts you and he doesn't trust many people. Are you going to damn *him* because he's trying to do something you think will fail?''

Yanni chewed on his lip. "You're one of Ari's, aren't you?''

"You know I am, ser."

"Damn, she did good work. You remind me what she was. After all that's happened."

"Yes, ser." It stung. He thought that it was meant to.

But Yanni gave a great sigh and shook his head. "I'll do this. I'll put him on the project. I'll keep the work light. *Which means, dammit, that you're going to carry some of it.*"

"Yes, ser."

"And if he does his damn designs I'll rip them apart. And teach him what I can. Everything I can. Has he got his problem with tape solved?"

"He has no problem with tape, ser."

"If you're in the room with him. That's what Petros says."

"That's so, ser. Can you blame him?"

"No. No, I can't. —I'll tell you, Grant, I *respect* what you're doing. I'd like to have a dozen of you. Unfortunately—you're not a production item."

"No, ser. Justin as much as Ari and Jordan—had a hand in my psych-sets. But you're welcome to analyze them."

"Stable as hell. Good. Good for you." Yanni got up and came around the desk as Grant got up in confusion. And Yanni put his hand on his shoulder and took his hand. "Grant, come back to me if you think he can't handle things."

That affected him, when before, he doubted everything about this man's goodwill. "Yes, ser," he said, thinking that if Yanni was telling the truth, and if there was anything of himself he could give that Yanni could not have out of library and lab, he would give it. Freely.

"Out," Yanni said brusquely. "Go."

Azi-like, simple, equal to equal. When he knew that Yanni was upset about Strassen, and about everything that was going on, and it had been the worst of times to go to him.

He went, with a simplicity of courtesies he had not felt with anyone but Justin and Jordan, since he was very young.

And with an anguish over what he might have done in his presumption, adding stress to what he knew was a delicate tolerance for Justin in the House, at a delicate time and a delicate balance in Justin's own mind. He had not known, from the time he determined to go to Yanni, whether Justin would forgive him—or whether he would deserve forgiveness.

So that was where he had to go first.

*　　*　　*

"You did *what?*" Justin cried, from the gut; and felt a double blow, because Grant reacted as if he had hit him, flinched and turned his face and turned it back again, to look at him helplessly, without any of Grant's accustomed defenses.

That took the wind out of him. There was no way to shout at Grant. Grant had acted because Grant had been forced into a caretaker role by his behavior, that was what his knowledge of azi told him; and he had misread that, an Alpha Supervisor's worst mistake, and leaned on Grant for years in ways that, God help him, he had needed.

Grant going azi on him—was his fault. No one else's.

He reached out and patted Grant's shoulder and calmed himself down as much as he could, while he was shocked full of adrenaline and he could hardly breathe, as much from what he had done to Grant as from the fact that Grant might well have damned him.

So. That was not Grant's fault. Everything would be all right, if Grant had not exposed himself to Giraud's attention again. Just go back to Yanni and try to recover things without the emotionalism that would finish the job in Yanni's eyes.

He just wanted to sit down a moment. But he could not even do that without letting Grant know how badly he was upset.

"Yanni wasn't mad," Grant pleaded with him. "Justin, he wasn't mad. It wasn't like that. He just said he would lighten up."

He gave Grant a second pat on the arm. "Look, I'm sure it's all right. If it isn't, I'll fix it. Don't worry about it."

"Justin?"

There was pain in Grant's voice. His making. Just like the crisis.

"Yanni's going to have my guts for shoving you in there," Justin said. "He ought to. Grant, you don't have to go around me. I'm all right. Don't worry."

"Stop it, dammit." Grant grabbed him and spun him around, hard, face to face with him. "Don't go Supervisor on me. I knew what I was doing."

He just stared in shock.

"I'm not some dumb-annie, Justin. You can hit me, if you like. Just don't pull that calm-down routine on me." Anger. Outright anger. It shocked hell out of him. It was rescue when he thought there was none. He was shaking when Grant let go his arm and put his hand on the side of his face. "God, Justin, what do you think?"

"I put too much on you."

"No. They put too much on *you*. And I told Yanni that. I'm not plastic. I know what I'm doing. What have *you* been doing all these years? I used to be your partner. What do you think I've gotten to be? One of the psych-cases you deal with? Or what do you think I am?"

Azi, was the obvious answer. Grant challenged him to it. And he froze up inside.

"Dumb-annie, huh?"

"Cut it, Grant."

"Well?"

"Maybe—" He got his breath and turned away. "Maybe it's pride. Maybe I've been taught all my life to think I'm the stronger one. And I know I've been fractured for years. And leaning on you. Hell if I don't feel guilty about that."

"Different kind of pressure," Grant said. "Mine can't come from anywhere but you. Don't you know that, born-man?"

"Well, I sure as hell pushed you into Yanni's office."

"Give me a *chance*, friend. I'm not a damn robot. Maybe my feelings are plastic, but they're sure as hell real. You want to yell at me, yell. *Don't* pull that Supervisor crap."

"Then don't act like a damn azi!"

He could not believe he had said that. He stood there in shock. So did Grant for a moment. With that hanging in the air between them.

"Well, I am," Grant said then, with a little shrug. "But I'm not guilty about it. How about you?"

"I'm sorry."

"No, go ahead. Damn-azi all you like. I'd rather that than watch you bottle it up. You work till you're dropping, you're eating your gut out, and one more aberrant azi psychset is going to push you over the edge. So damn-azi all you like. I'm glad you've gotten self-protective. It's about time."

"God, don't psychoanalyze me."

"Sorry, can't help that. Thank God *I* only have one born-man to worry about. Two would drive me into the wards. So damn born-men too. They cause a hell of a lot of trouble. You were right about Yanni. He's quite reasonable with azi. It's other born-men he pours it out on, everything he stores up. Question is whether he was telling me the truth. But if you'll calm down and listen to me, nothing about the fact you can't handle real-time is news to him. I only pointed out you were wasted in the Rubin project, and that if he wanted motivated work, he'd do well to put up with your doing design in your spare time. Which you're damn well due. I don't think I was at all unreasonable.''

Eavesdroppers, Justin thought with a jolt, and sorted back wildly to remember what they had said. He signed Grant to be careful, and Grant nodded.

"I'm sorry," Justin said then, calmer. And wishing he could find a dark place to hide him. But Grant was doing all right. Grant was holding up fine, with a dignity he could not manage. "Grant, I—just react to things. Flux-thinking. You've got to understand."

"Hey," Grant said. "I *don't* understand. I marvel at it. The number of levels you can react on is really amazing. The number of things you can believe at one time is incredible. I don't understand it. I'm going to spend days figuring that reaction and I'll probably still miss nuances."

"Real simple. I'm scared as hell. I thought I knew where things were and all of a sudden even you went sideways on me. So everything shifted to polar-opposite values. Born-men are real logical."

"God. Life would be so dull if there weren't born-men. Now I wonder which pole Yanni was at while I was talking to him. That's enough to worry hell out of you."

"Was he calm?"

"Very."

"Then you got the main set, didn't you?"

"We just have to learn not to agitate you people. I think they ought to put that in the beginning tape-sets. 'Excited born-men go to alternate programming sets. Every born-man is schiz. And he hates his alter ego.' That's the whole key to CIT behavior."

"You're not far wrong."

"Hell. I've been endocrine-learning for years. I'm really amazed. I went right over to it. Dual and triple opinions, the whole thing. I must say I prefer my natural psychset. My *natu-*

ral psychset, thank you. A lot easier on the stomach. Do you want to go to lunch?"

He looked at Grant, at Grant with the shields up again, with that slight, mocking smile that was Grant's way of defying fate, the universe, and Reseune Administration. For a moment he felt both fortunate and terrified.

As if for the first time everything that had been going away from him had stopped and trembled on the edge of reversing itself.

"Sure," he said. "Sure." He caught Grant's arm and steered him out the door. "If you could make headway with Yanni Schwartz you could hire out by the hour. Probably everybody in the Wing could use your services."

"Un-unh. No. I'm in regular employment, thanks."

People were staring. He dropped Grant's arm. And realized half the Wing must have heard him shouting at Grant. And was looking for signs of damage.

They were a source of gossip for a whole host of reasons. And now there was a new one.

That would get back to Yanni too.

viii

There were new things all the time. Nelly took Ari to the store in the North Wing, and they came back with packages. That was fun. She bought Nelly things too, and Nelly was so happy it made her feel good, to see Nelly with a new suit and looking pretty and so proud.

But Nelly was not maman. She liked it at first when Nelly put her arms around her, but Nelly always was Nelly, that was all, and all at once one night she felt so empty when Nelly did that. She didn't tell Nelly, because Nelly was telling her a story. But after that it was harder and harder to put up with Nelly holding her, when maman was gone. So she fidgeted down and sat on the floor for her stories, which Nelly seemed to think was all right.

Seely was just nobody. She teased Seely sometimes, but Seely never laughed. And that felt awful. So she left Seely alone, except when she asked him for a soft drink or a cookie. Which she got more of than maman would like. So she tried to be good and not to ask, and to eat vegetables and not have so much sugar. It's not good for you, maman would say. And anything maman said was something she tried to remember and keep doing, because everything of maman's she forgot was like forgetting maman. So she ate the damn vegetables and got a lump in her throat because some of them tasted awful, all messed up with white creamy stuff. Ugh. They made her want to throw up. But she did it because of maman and it made her so sad and so mad at the same time she felt like crying.

But if she did cry she went to her room and shut the door, and wiped her eyes and washed her face before she came out again, because she was not going to snivel.

She wanted somebody to play with but she didn't want it to be Sam. Sam knew her too well. Sam would know about her maman. And she would beat his face in, because she couldn't stand him looking at her with his face that never showed anything.

So when Nelly asked did she want to go back to playschool she said all right if Sam wasn't there.

"I don't know who there is, then," Nelly said.

"Then I'll go by myself," she said. "Let's go do the gym. All right?"

So Nelly took her. And they fed the fish and she played in the sandbox, but the sandbox was no fun by herself; and Nelly was not good at making buildings. So they just fed the fish and took walks and played on the playground and in the gym.

There was tapestudy. And a lot of the grown-ups did lessons with her. She learned a lot of things. She lay there in her bed at night with her head so full of new things she had trouble thinking of maman and Ollie.

Uncle Denys was right. It hurt less, day by day. That was the thing that scared her. Because if it didn't hurt the mad was harder to keep. So she bit her lip till it hurt and tried to keep it that way.

There was a children's party. She saw Amy there. Amy ran and got behind sera Peterson and acted like a baby. She remembered why she had wanted to hit Amy. The rest of the kids just stared at her a lot and sera Peterson told them they had to play with her.

They weren't happy about it. She could tell. There was Kate and Tommy and a kid named Pat, and Amy, who cried and snuffled over in the corner. Sam was there too. Sam came out from the others and said Hello, Ari. Sam was the only friendly one. So she said Hello, Sam. And wished she could go home, but Nelly had gone in the kitchen to have tea with sera Peterson's azi, and Nelly was having a good time.

So she went over and sat down and played their game, which was a dice game, and you moved around a board, which was Union space. You got money. All right. She played it, and everybody got to arguing and laughing and teasing each other again. Except Amy. Except they teased each other and not her. But that was all right. She learned their game. She started getting money. Sam was the luckiest one with the dice, but Sam was too careful with his money and Tommy was too reckless. "I'll sell you a station," she said. And Amy bought it for most of what Amy had. So Amy charged a lot and Ari just charged less. And what Amy had bought was off at the edge anyway. So Ari got more money and Amy got mad. And nobody wanted to trade for Amy's station, but Ari offered to buy it back, not for what Amy wanted for it.

So Amy took it and bought ships. And Ari raised her prices a little.

Amy sniveled. And pretty soon she was in trouble again, because Ari kept beating her by using her money to buy up cargoes and keeping a surplus of the only things Amy could get because stupid Amy kept coming to *her* stations instead of sticking to Tommy's. Amy wanted a fight. Amy got a fight. But she didn't want Amy to lose real soon and ruin the game, so she told Amy what she ought to do.

Amy got real mad then. And sniveled some more.

She didn't take the advice either.

So Ari got her in trouble and took all but one of her ships. Then the last one. By that time she had a way to win. But everybody else was looking unhappy and nobody was teasing anybody, except Amy left the table crying.

Nobody said anything. They all looked at Amy. They all looked at her like they wanted not to be there.

She was going to win. Except Sam didn't know it. So she said, "Sam, you can have my pieces."

And she went and got Nelly in the kitchen and said she wanted to go home. Nelly looked worried, then, and stopped having fun with Corrie, and they went home.

She moped around the rest of the day, being lonely. And mad. Which was fine. She thought of maman then. And missed Ollie. Even Phaedra.

And thought if Valery had been there he would not have been so stupid.

"What's the matter?" uncle Denys asked that evening. He was very kind about it. "Ari, dear, what happened at the party? What did they do?"

She could Disappear them all if she said they had a fight. Maybe they would anyway. She wasn't sure. At least Amy and Kate were still around, even if they were stupid.

"Uncle Denys, where did Valery go?"

"Valery Schwartz? His maman got transferred. They moved, that's all. You still remember Valery?"

"Can he come back?"

"I don't know, dear. I don't think so. His maman has a job to do. What happened at the party?"

"I just got bored. They're not much fun. Where did maman and Ollie go? What station?"

"To Fargone."

"I'm going to send maman and Ollie a letter." She had seen mail in maman's office. She had never thought of doing that. But she thought that would get to maman's office at the other place. At Fargone.

"All right. I'm sure they'd like that."

Sometimes she thought maman and Ollie weren't really anywhere. But uncle Denys talked like they were, and they were all right. That made her feel better, but it made her wonder why maman never even called on the phone.

"Can you call Fargone?"

"No," uncle Denys said. "It's faster for a ship to go. A letter gets there much faster than a phone call. In months, not years."

"Why?"

"You say hello, and it takes twenty years to get there; and they say hello and it takes twenty years to get here. And then you say your first sentence and they don't hear it for years. You could take hundreds of years having a conversation. That's why letters are faster and a whole lot cheaper, and they don't use phones and radios between any two stars. Ships carry everything, because ships go faster than light. There are more complications to the question, but that's more than you really want to know to get a message to your maman. It's just a long way. And a letter is the way you do things.''

She had never understood how far far could be. Not when they were jumping ships around the board. She felt cold and lonely then. And she went to her room and wrote the letter.

She kept tearing it up because she didn't want to make maman worry about her being miserable. She didn't want to say: *maman, the kids don't like me and I'm lonely all the time.*

She said: *I miss you a lot. I miss Ollie. I'm not mad at Phaedra anymore. I want you and Ollie to come back. Phaedra too. I'll be good. Uncle Denys gives me too many cookies, but I remember what you said and I don't eat too much. I don't want to be fat. I don't want to be hyper, either. Nelly is very good to me. Uncle Denys gives me his credit card and I buy Nelly lots of things. I bought a spaceship and a car and puzzles and story tapes. And a red and white blouse and red boots. I wanted a black one but Nelly says that's for azi until I'm older. Little girls don't wear black, Nelly says. I could too, but sometimes I do what Nelly says. I mind everybody. I saw Amy Carnath today and I didn't hit her. She still snivels. I study a lot of tapes. I can do math and I can do chemistry. I can do geography and astrography and I'm going to study about Fargone because you're there. I want to go to Fargone if you can't come here. Are there any kids there? Have you got a nice place? Tell uncle Denys I can come. Or you come home. I'll be very good. I love you. I love Ollie. I am going to give this to uncle Denys to send to you. He says it takes a long time to get there and your letter will take a long time to get to me so please write to me as soon as you can. I think it will be almost a year. By then I will be eight. If you tell Denys to let me come real soon I guess I will be almost nine. Tell him I can bring Nelly too. She'll be scared but I'll tell her it's all right. I'm not afraid of jumps. I'm not afraid to come by myself. I do a lot of things by myself now. Uncle Denys doesn't care. I know he would let me come if you said yes. I love you.*

ix

Florian was late again. There was a shortcut along between

240 and 241 and he took it, dodging out between two groups of Olders and skipping backward to nod a courtesy and murmur: "Excuse me, please," before he turned and sprinted across the road and up to Security.

"I'm very sorry," he said, arriving at the desk inside Square One. He was trying not to pant as he handed his chit to the azi at the desk. The man looked at the chit and put it in his machine.

"Blue to white to brown," the man said. "Change in brown. Instructions there."

"Yes," he said, and looked where the man pointed. Blue started with that door and he went, not running, but going in a great hurry.

He knew he was still late when he got to brown. The azi in charge was waiting for him. "I'm sorry," he said. "I'm Florian AF-9979."

The man looked him over and said: "Size 6M, cabinets on the wall, go change. Hurry."

"Yes," he said, and went into the changing room, hunted quickly for 6M, pulled out the plastic packet and threw it onto the bench while he peeled out of his clothes. He put the black uniform on, sat down quick to pull on the socks and put on the slippers, then hung his AG uniform on the pegs beside uniforms of all sizes and colors. He was so nervous he almost forgot his new keycard, but he got it off his other coveralls and clipped it to the black ones, then raked a hand through his hair and hurried outside again.

"Down the hall," the azi with the clipboard said. "Brown to green. Run!"

He ran. And followed the halls till he found a door marked with green-in-brown. Inside, then, into a gym. He came bursting in where there was a man with a clipboard, and another Younger, who was dressed like him, in black coveralls. Who was a *girl*. He felt a shock, but gut-level, reacted to the Super and made a little bow. "Sorry I'm late, ser."

The Super looked at him just long enough to keep him worried, and he did not dare look back at the girl who was, he was sure now, here just like he was, to find her partner for this Assignment.

Then the Super made a mark on his board and said: "Florian, this is Catlin. Catlin is your partner."

Florian looked at the girl again, his heart beating hard. It was a mistake. It must be. He was late. He got a girl partner. He was supposed to change bunks and he had thought he was supposed to bunk with his partner. Wrong, then. He did not know where he was going to sleep.

He wanted his classes back. He had been upset about the new Assignment even if his old Super told him he could still have AG on his Rec hours. He wanted—

But the girl bothered him. She looked—

She was blonde, blue-eyed, a scab on her chin. She was taller than he was, but that was nothing unusual. She had a thin, very serious face. He thought he had seen her before. She stared at him, the way you weren't supposed to stare. Then he realized he was doing it too.

"Catlin," the Super said, "you know the way from here. Take Florian over to Staging, talk to the Super there."

"Yes, ser," she said, and Florian almost asked the Super to look and check if there was some mistake, but he was late, he had gotten a bad start with this man, and he did not know why he was as upset as he was, but he was panicked. Catlin was already going. He caught up with her as she walked toward another door behind the hanging buffer-mats at the end of the gym. She used her keycard, held the door for him, and led the way into another long cement hallway.

Down stairs then. And another cement hall.

"I'm supposed to have a bunk assignment?" he said finally, behind her.

She looked back on the stairs and he caught up with her in the long concrete hall at the bottom.

"22. Like me," she said. "We're going in with Olders. Partners room together, two and two."

He was shocked. But she seemed to know what was right, and *she* was not upset. So he just walked behind her, wondering if somehow the Computers had glitched up and he was supposed to have gotten tape to explain all this and help him not make mistakes. He had, he thought, to talk to the Super where they were going.

They got to the other place. Catlin keyed in, and there was a Super sitting at a desk. "Ser," Catlin said. "Catlin and Florian, ser."

"Late," the Super said.

"Yes, ser," Catlin said.

"My fault," Florian said. "Ser, —"

"Excuses don't matter. You're Assigned to Security. You go into Staging, you pick out what you think you might need. And both of you will be right. All right. Fifteen minutes to get your equipment. You do mess, you've got this evening to plan it out, you'll do a Room tomorrow morning. It's a one-hour course, you can talk about it. You're supposed to. Go."

"I—" he said. "Ser, I have to feed the pigs. I— Am I supposed to have gotten tape about this? I haven't."

The Super looked straight at him. "Florian, you'll do AG when you aren't doing Security. This is your Assignment. You can go to AG in your Rec time. Four hours Rec time for every good pass through the Room. There isn't any tape for this. It's up at 0500, drill at 0530, breakfast at 0630, then tape, Room, or Rec, whatever the schedule calls for; noon mess as you can catch it, follow your schedule; evening mess at 2000, follow your schedule, in bunks at 2300 most nights. If you've got any problems you talk to your Instructor. Catlin knows. Ask her."

"Yes, ser," Florian breathed, thinking: *What about Andy? What about the pigs? They said I could go to AG.* And because the Super had answered and he was terribly afraid this *was* the right Assignment, he caught up with Catlin.

It was a Staging-room, like in the Game he knew. His old Super had said it was an Assignment, there would be Rooms, all of this he knew: it would be like Rooms he had done before and he would be more out of Security than AG after this.

But it was not right. He was supposed to bunk with a girl. He was put into a place she knew and he didn't. He was going to make more mistakes. They always said a Super would never refuse to talk to you, but the one back there made him afraid he was already making mistakes.

Like being late to start with.

He came into the Staging-room behind Catlin; he knew it was going to be a Security kind of Room, and he was not terribly shocked to find guns and knives on the table with the tools, but he didn't even want to touch them, and there was a queasy feeling in his stomach when Catlin picked up a gun. He grabbed pliers and a circuit-tester; Catlin took a length of fine cord and he started through the components tray, grabbing things and stuffing them into his pockets by categories.

"Electronics?" she asked.

"Yes. Military?"

"Security. You know weapons?"

"No."

"Better not have one, then. What kind are your Rooms?"

"Traps. Alarms."

Catlin's pale brows went up. She nodded, looking more friendly. "Ambushes. There's usually an Enemy. He'll kill you."

"So will traps."

"Are you good?"

He nodded. "I think so."

And he was staring again. Her face had been bothering him all along. It was like he knew her. He knew her the way you knew things from tape. Maybe she was remembering him too just then, the way she was staring. He was not completely surprised, except that it had happened at all: tape never surprised him. He knew it was not a mistake if he knew her from tape. She was supposed to be important to him, if that was the case, the way his studies were important, and he had never thought that was supposed to happen until he was Contracted to somebody.

But she was azi. Like him.

And she knew all about her Assignment and he was new and full of mistakes.

"I think I'm supposed to know you," he said, worried.

"Same," she said.

No one had ever *paid* that much attention to him. Not even Andy. And he felt shaky, to know he had run into someone tape meant for him.

"Why are we partners?" he asked.

"I don't know," she said. Then: "But electronics is useful. And you know a different Room. Come on. Tell me what you know."

"You go in," he said, trying to pull up everything, fast and all of it, the way he would do for a Super. "There's a door. There can be all kinds of traps. If you make one go off you lose. Sometimes there's noise. Sometimes the lights go out. Sometimes there's someone after you and you have to get through and rig traps. Sometimes there's an AI lock. Sometimes there's water and that's real dangerous if there's a line loose. But it's pretend, you don't really get electrocuted.''

"Dead is dead,'' she said. "They shoot at you and they trap the doors and if you don't blow them up they'll blow you up; and sometimes all the things you said. Sometimes gas. Sometimes Ambushes. Sometimes it's outside and sometimes it's a building. Some people get killed for real. I saw one. He broke his neck.''

He was shocked. And then he thought it could be him. And he thought about door traps. He took a battery and a coil of wire and a penlight, and Catlin gave him a black scarf—for your face, she said. She took a lot of other things, like face-black and cord and some things that might be weapons, but he didn't know.

"If they have gas masks in Staging it's a good idea to have one,'' Catlin said, "but there aren't. So they probably won't do gas, but you don't know. They aren't fair.''

A bell rang.

Time was up.

"Come on,'' Catlin said, and the door opened and let them out with what they had.

Down a hall and through more doors. And upstairs again, until they came out in another concrete hall.

With a lot of doors.

"We're looking for 22,'' Catlin said.

That was two more. Catlin opened the door and let them into a plain little room with a double bunk.

"Top or bottom?'' Catlin asked.

"I don't care,'' he said. He had never thought about a room all his own. Or even half his. There was a table and two chairs. There was a door.

"Where does that go?''

"Bathroom,'' Catlin said. "We share with the room next door. They're Olders. You knock before you go in. That's their Rule. If they're Olders you take their Rules.''

"I'm lost,'' he said.

"That's all right,'' Catlin said, emptying her pockets onto the table. "I've been here five days. I know a lot of the Rules. The Olders are pretty patient. They tell you. But you better remember or they'll tell the Instructor and you're in trouble.''

"I'll remember.'' He looked at her emptying her pockets

and thought how his stuff was right where he wanted it. "Do we have to change clothes for the Room?"

"In the morning, always."

He emptied his pockets, but he put everything together the way he wanted it. Catlin looked at what he was doing.

"That's smart," she said. "You always know where all that stuff is."

He looked at her. She was serious. "Of course," he said.

"You're all right," she said.

"I think you must be pretty good," he said.

"They don't Get me often," she said. And pulled back the chair and sat down with her arms on the table while he was emptying his pockets. "Do they you?"

"No," he said.

She looked quite happy in her sober way. And picked up the gun and flipped up the panel on the grip and snapped it shut again. "The gun's real," she said. "But the charges aren't. You still have to check, though. Rounds can get mixed up. Once somebody's did. You always think about that. The Enemy could have mixed-up rounds. And blow you to bits. The practice rounds have a big black band. The real ones don't. But these can still kill you if you get hit close up. You have to be careful when you're working partners. More people get killed with practice rounds than anything else in training."

Catlin knew more stories about how people got killed than he had ever heard in his life. He felt his stomach upset.

But Catlin wanted to know all about the traps, all about the things he had seen. She was full of questions and with everything he said he saw her strange eyes concentrate in the way people would if they were smart and they were going to remember. So he asked about Ambushes, and she told him a lot of things she had seen.

She *was* smart, he thought. She sounded like she could do the things she said. He had never planned to be in Security. He had never planned to have a girl for a partner and he never imagined anyone like Catlin. She did sort of smile. It lit up her eyes, but her mouth hardly moved. She made him so nervous he was gladder when she did that than when most people smiled wide open. A smile out of Catlin was hard to get. You had to really tell her something that impressed her. And when you got one you wanted another one because in between there was just nothing.

They went to mess, which was what they called the dining hall here. They all had to stand and wait till they could sit, and they were years younger than anyone. Most were boys, very tall, a few were girls, all of them were in their teens and everybody was on strict manners. He would have been terribly nervous if Catlin had not known when to stand and when to sit and tugged at his sleeve to cue him. But it was very good food, and as much as you wanted, and when the near-grown boys around them talked they were polite and didn't act annoyed that they were there. Who's your partner? one asked Catlin, and she said: Florian AF, ser. Like talking to a Super.

Welcome in, that boy said. And they made him stand up so people could see him. He was nervous. But the boy stood up beside him and introduced him as Florian AF, Catlin's partner, a tech. He wasn't sure he was, but it was something like; and they all looked at him a moment, then they gave a kind of Welcome In and he could sit down. It was not too different from a dorm, except there they never made you stand up at table, because your dining hall was a whole lot of dorms. Green Barracks had its own kitchen, and there were seconds and thirds if you wanted them, you didn't have to have a med's order.

The Instructor said they had two hours for Rec then and then they had to have lights out by 2300.

But Catlin thought they ought to go back to their quarters—that was what they called it in Green Barracks—and figure out about the Room, because the Instructor said they could do that; and they asked each other questions about the Room until just before their lights-out.

He was anxious about undressing. He had never undressed around girls, just the meds and the techs, and they had always been careful to give him something to put on and to turn their backs or leave the room till he had. Catlin said it was all right if they were roommates, everybody else did; so she took off her shirt and pants, he took off his, and she went to take a shower first. She came back in her clean underwear and threw the dirty clothes in the hamper.

She was like he thought she would be under her clothes, all bones and skinny muscle that would have made him think they didn't feed you much in Security, except he had just had one of their meals. She was shaped different, all right, thinner around the chest—her ribs showed—and flat where boys weren't. He had never seen a girl in her underwear. It was thin and didn't hide much, and he tried not to stare or to think about her staring at him. He wasn't sure *why* it was bad, it still didn't feel right. But that was the way it had to be, because sleeping in their clothes would make them a mess.

So they had to be polite with each other and get along with the situation.

He took his shower fast, like Catlin said, because the Olders would want it soon; and he put on his clean underwear and came and got in the bottom bunk, because Catlin had the top. He got in fast, because she was under her covers and he was out there all alone in his underwear.

"Last one," Catlin said from up above, "has to turn the lights out. It's *my* Rule. All right?"

He looked for the switch from where he was lying. He had never been in a place where the lights didn't just go out at the right time. He had never slept anywhere but a barracks with fifty or so boys in the same room. He slithered out of the covers again and dived over and hit the switch and dived back again, remembering the straight line to the bunk, so hard it made the bed shake.

He realized he had shaken up Catlin too. "Sorry," he said, and tried to be quieter getting under the covers again. He was very conscious he was with a stranger, who might be a seven, but they were different from each other, she was Security and Security was very stiff and cold. He didn't want to do wrong or make her annoyed with him. He lay there in the dark in a place with only one person in it, worse than being in a new dorm, very much worse. He felt cold and it was only partly because the sheets were. All the sounds were gone, except one of the Olders starting up the shower.

He wondered where Catlin had lived before this. She didn't seem nervous. Somebody had told her everything that would happen. Or she was just able to *do* everything. Having a boy for a partner didn't bother *her*. She was glad about him being good at traps. He hoped he was as good as she expected. He would be terribly embarrassed if he got them Blown Up in the first doorway.

And he was terribly afraid he was going to have to do Traps

in the dark, which was the hardest, and that meant he was going to need the penlight. Catlin said he could hide that with his coat, they usually let you have one. Because working against the light he was a target for sure.

Don't make noise, she had said. I'll watch your back; you just work; but noise is going to help the Enemy. We can try to Get one that way, but that depends on how much time we have. Or whether it's a speed run or a kill run. They'll tell us that.

What's a kill run? he had asked.

Where you get most of your points for Getting the Enemy.

Like where you have to *set* the Traps, he had said, relieved he understood. Sometimes we do it both ways—you have to take one apart and leave one for the Enemy following you. You get extra points if he misses it. Sometimes they make you go back through right away, and you don't know whether it's your Trap or his or whether he got stopped. The blow-ups show, but you can't trust those either, because he could touch it off and set another one.

That's sneaky, she had said, her eyes lighting the way they could. That's *good*.

He wanted to go blank so that he could go to sleep: there was a Room to do in the morning; and he knew he had to rest, but that was hard to do, his mind was so full of things without answers.

The Room did not make him half so anxious as this place did.

Why are they doing this? he wondered. And thinking of the gun on the table and about the too-quiet mess hall and all of Catlin's stories about people shooting each other in the Game: *Are they sure I belong here?*

It's not a Game, Catlin had said sternly when he had called it that. A game is what you do on the computers in Rec. This is real, and they cheat.

He really wanted to go back to AG. He wanted to see the Horse. He wanted to feed the baby in the morning.

But you had to survive the Room to do that for just four hours.

From now on.

He really tried to go blank. He tried hard.

Why don't they give me tape? Why don't they make it so I know what to do?

Why don't they make it so I feel better about this?

Has the Computer forgotten about me?

———————————— X ————————————

Ari thought every night how her letter was on its way now and she figured out where it had to be if it took so many months. Maman and Ollie would be at Fargone now. She felt a lot better to know where they were. She looked at pictures of Fargone and she could imagine them being there. Uncle Denys brought her a publicity booklet for RESEUNESPACE that had maman's name in it. And pictures of where maman would be working. She kept it in her desk drawer and she liked to look at it and imagine herself going there. She wrote another letter every few days, and she told maman how she was doing. Uncle Denys said he would have to save up a packet of her letters and send them in a bundle because it was awfully expensive and maman wouldn't care if she got them all at once, all in one envelope. She wanted to address it to maman and Ollie, but uncle Denys said that would confuse the postal people, and if she was going to write to Ollie, maman would give it to him: the law said an azi couldn't receive any mail except through his Supervisor, which was silly for Ollie, nothing could upset him; but it was the law.

So the address had to be:

Dr. Jane Strassen
Director
RESEUNESPACE
Fargone Station

And her return address was:

Dr. Denys Nye
Administrator
Reseune Administrative Territory
Postal District 3
Cyteen Station

She wanted to put her own name on the letter, but uncle Denys said she would have to wait until she was grown up and had her own address. Besides, he said, if it was from the Administrator of Reseune to the Director of RESEUNESPACE it looked like business and it would get right to maman's desk without anybody waiting.

She was in favor of that.

She asked why their address was Cyteen Station when they lived on Cyteen, and he said mail didn't go to planets without going through stations; and if you wanted to write to somebody on Earth the address was always Sol Station, but because there was Mars and the Moon you had to put Earth, then the name of the country.

Uncle Denys tried to explain what a country was and how they started. That was why he got her the *History of Earth* tape. She wanted to do that one again. It had a lot of really strange pictures. Some were scary. But she knew it was just tape.

She went to tapestudy. She studied biology and botany, and penmanship and history and civics this week. She got Excellent on her exams and uncle Denys gave her a nice holo that was a Terran bird. You turned it and the bird flapped his wings and flew. It came all the way from Earth. Uncle Giraud had got it in Novgorod.

But there was only Nelly for playschool. And it was boring doing the swings and the puzzlebars with just Nelly. So she didn't go every day anymore. She got tired of going everywhere with Nelly, because Nelly worried about everything and Nelly was always worrying about her. So she told uncle Denys she could go to tapestudy by herself, and she could go to library by herself, because people knew her, and she was all right.

She took a lot of time getting back from tapestudy. Sometimes she stopped and fed the fish, because there was a Security guard right at the door and uncle Denys had said she could do that. Today she went down the tunnel because there had been a storm last night and you had to stay indoors for a few days.

So she got to thinking how she and maman had come this way once when she went to see ser Peterson. You took the elevator. Dr. Peterson was boring as Seely was; but that hall was where Justin's office was.

Justin would be interesting, she thought. Maybe he would at least say hello. And so many people had Disappeared that she liked to check now and again to see if people were still there. It always made her feel safer when she found they were. So if she got a chance to see an old place, she liked to.

She took the lift up to the upstairs hall, and she walked the metal strips she remembered: that was nice too, like once upon a time, when maman had been down the hall in that very office; but it made her sad, too, and she stopped it and walked the center of the hall.

Justin's office door was open. It was messy as the last time. And she was happy of a sudden, because Justin and Grant were both there.

"Hello," she said.

They both looked at her. It was good to see someone she knew. She really hoped they would be glad to see her. There weren't many people who would talk to her that weren't uncle Denys's.

But they didn't say hello. Justin got up and looked unfriendly.

She felt lonely all of a sudden. She felt awfully lonely. "How are you?" she asked, because that was what you were supposed to say.

"Where's your nurse?"

"Nelly's home." She could say that now about uncle Denys's place without it hurting. "Can I come in?"

"We're working, Ari. Grant and I have business to do."

"Everybody's working," she complained. "Hello, Grant."

"Hello, Ari," Grant said.

"Maman went to Fargone," she said. In case they hadn't heard.

"I'm sorry," Justin said.

"I'm going to go there and live with her."

Justin got a funny look. A real funny look. Grant looked at her. And she was scared because they were upset, but she didn't know why. She sat there looking up and wishing she knew what was wrong. Of a sudden she was real scared.

"Ari," Justin said, "you know you're not supposed to be here."

"I can be here if I want. Uncle Denys doesn't mind."

"Did uncle Denys say that?"

"Justin," Grant said. And gently: "Ari, who brought you here?"

"Nobody. I brought myself." She pointed. "I came from tapestudy. I'm taking a shortcut."

"That's nice," Justin said. "Look, Ari. I'll bet you're supposed to go straight home."

She shook her head. "No. I don't have to. Uncle Denys is always late and Nelly won't tell him." She kept getting this upset-feeling, no matter how she tried to be cheerful. It was not them being bad to her. It was not a mad either. She tried to figure out what it was, but Grant was worried about Justin and Justin was worried about her being there.

Hell with Them, maman would say. Meaning the Them that kept things messed up.

"I'm going," she said.

But she did it again the next day, sneaked up and popped sideways around the doorframe and said: "Hello."

That scared them good. She laughed. And came out and was nice then. "Hello."

"Ari, for God's sake, go home!"

She liked that better. Justin was mad like maman's mad. She liked that a lot better. He wasn't being mean. Neither was Grant. She had got them and they were going to yell at her.

"I did Computers today," she said. "I can write a program."

"That's nice, Ari. Go home!"

She laughed. And tucked her hands behind her and rocked and remembered not to. "Uncle Denys got me a fish tank. I've got guppies. One of them is pregnant."

"That's awfully nice, Ari. Go home."

"I could bring you some of the babies."

"Ari, just go home."

"I have a hologram. It's a bird. It flies." She pulled it out of her pocket and showed how it turned, and came inside to do it. "See?"

"That's fascinating. Please. Go home."

"I'll bet you haven't got one."

"I know I don't. Please, Ari, —"

"Why don't you want me here?"

"Because your uncle is going to get mad."

"He won't. He never knows."

"Ari," Grant said.

She looked at him.

"You don't want us to *call* your uncle, do you?"

She didn't. It wasn't very nice. She frowned at Grant.

"Please," Justin said. "Ari."

He was halfway nice. And she was out of tricks. So she went outside, and looked back and smiled at him.

He was sort of a friend. He was her secret friend. She wasn't going to make him mad. Or Grant. She would come by just a second every day.

But they were gone the next day: the door was shut and locked.

That worried her. She figured they had either figured out she was coming at the same time every day or they were truly Disappeared.

So she sneaked over on her way to tape the next morning and caught them.

"Hello!" she said. And scared them.

She saw they were mad, so she didn't laugh at them too much. And she just waved them goodbye and went on.

She caught them now and again. When her guppy had babies she brought them some in a jar she had. Justin looked like that made him feel better about her. He said he would take care of them.

But when she took the lid off they were dead. She felt awful.

"I guess they were in there too long," she said.

"I guess they were," Justin said. He smelled nice when she leaned on the desk near him. A lot like Ollie. "I'm sorry, Ari."

That was nice anyway. It was the first time he had really been just Justin with her. Grant came and looked and he was sorry too.

Grant took the jar away. And Justin said, well, sometimes things died.

"I'll bring you more," she said. She liked coming by the office. She thought about it a lot. She was leaning up by Justin's desk now and he had stopped having that bad feeling. He was just Justin. And he patted her on the shoulder and said she had better go.

He had never been that nice since a long, long time ago. So she was winning. She thought he would be awfully nice to talk to, but she wasn't going to push and make everything go wrong. Not with him and not with Grant. He was her friend.

And when maman sent for her she would ask him and Grant if they wanted to go with her and Nelly.

Then she would have all the special people and she would be all right on the ship, because Justin was a CIT and he was grown-up and he would know how to do everything you had to do to get to Fargone.

She had a birthday coming. She had not even wanted a kids' party. Just the presents, thank you.

Even that hadn't made her happy. Until now.

She skipped down the hall, playing step-on-the-metal-line. And got Nelly's keycard out of her pocket and used it on the lift.

Because she knew how Security worked.

---

xi

"You damn fool," Yanni yelled, and threw the papers at him. And Justin stood there, paralyzed in shock as the sheets of his last personal project settled on the carpet around them. "You damned *fool*! What are you trying to do? We give you a chance, we do everything we fucking *can* to get you a chance, I sweat my *ass* off on my own fucking *time* working up critiques on this shit you dream up to prove to a hardheaded juvenile-fixated *fool* that his brilliant junior study project was just that, a fucking *junior study project* that Ari Emory would have dismissed with a *Thanks, kid, but we tried that*, if she hadn't been interested in getting her hands on your juvenile body and fucking over your *father*, son, *which you've just done all by yourself, you damned fool! Get this shit out of here! Get yourself back to your office, and you keep that kid out, you hear me?*"

It hit him in the gut, and paralyzed him between wanting to kill Yanni and believing for a terrible moment that it was over, that a little girl's spite had ruined him, and Jordan, and Grant.

But then he heard it all the way to the end and realized it was not entirely that, it was not doomsday.

It might as well be.

"What did she say?" he asked. "What did she say about it? *The kid brought me a damn jar of fish, Yanni, what am I going to do, throw her out of the office? I tried!*"

"*Get out of here!*"

"What did she *say?*"

"She asked her uncle Denys to invite you to her fucking *birthday* party. That's all. That's all. You've got yourself a *situation*, son. You've got yourself a real situation. Seems she's been coming by the office a lot. Seems she's been dodging Security through the upstairs, seems she's been using her azi's keycard to get up and down the lift, seems she's just real attracted to you, son. What in hell do you think you're doing?"

"Is this a psych? Is that it? Denys asked you to run a psych and see what falls out?"

"*Why didn't you report it?*"

"Well, hell, I have a few reasons, don't you think?" He got his breath back. He got his balance back and stared at Yanni hard and straight. "It's your security she outflanked. How am I to know Reseune Security can't track a seven-year-old kid? I'm not going to be rude to her. No, thanks. I don't want any part of it. *I* don't want to be the one to ring up Denys Nye and tell him he's lost track of his ward. You want a kid to get determined about something, you just tell her I'm forbidden territory. No, thanks. Denys said be polite, make nothing of it, avoid her where I can—hell, I started shutting my office when I knew she was due back from tape, what else can I do?"

"You could report it!"

"And get in the middle of it again? Get myself yanked in for another inquisition? I followed orders. I figured you were bugging my office. I *figured* Security knew where she was. I *figured* you knew exactly what I said, which was nothing. *Nothing*, Yanni, except Go home, Ari. Go home, Ari. *Go home, Ari.* And I got her out. It's a juvenile behavior. She's found an adult to tease. She's being an ordinary brat kid. For God's sake, you make something out of this, you'll *fix* it, Yanni, does a damned juvenile-fixated *fool* have to tell you calm down with this kid and just let her pull her little prank? She can read you. She can read the tension you're pouring on her, I know damned well she can, because I have to fight like hell to keep her from reading *me* in the two or three minutes she comes past and says hello, and you and Denys must be doing real well, the way you're coming through to me. Get off her! Just let the whole thing *alone*, for God's sake, or what in hell are you trying to *do*, push her at me till it *takes?*" A second pause for breath, while Yanni just stood there and stared at him in a way that raised the hair on his neck. "Is that what you're trying to *do*? Is that what's behind this? Are you helping her do this?"

"You're paranoid."

"Damned right. Damned *right*, Yanni. What are you trying to do to me?"

"Get out of here! Get the fuck out of here! I got you off. I got you off with Administration. I spent the fucking morning on you, *Petros* wasted a day covering your ass, and you're damn right this is a psych and you just flunked it, son, you just flunked it! I don't trust you. I don't trust you further than I can see where you are. You walk a tight line, a damned tight line. If she shows up again you get her out of there and you phone Denys before her steps are cool!"

"What about Jordan?"

"Now you want favors."

"What about Jordan?"

"I don't hear anything about them cutting the phone calls. But you're playing with it, son. You're really playing with it. *Don't* push. Don't push any further."

"What are you putting in that report?"

"That you're not real casual around that kid. That you've got yourself some real hostilities about that kid."

"Not about that kid! About the lousy things you're doing to her, Yanni, about your whole damned *program*, your whole damned *project*! You're going to drive her crazy, shooting her full of stuff and jerking everything human away from her, Yanni. You're not a human being any longer!"

"And you've lost your perspective, boy, you've damned well lost your professional perspective! You're feeding your own damn insecurities into the situation. You're *interpreting*, son, you're not observing, you're not functioning, you've lost your objectivity, and you're off the project, son, you're *off the project* until you come back here with your head back together. Now get out of here! And don't bother me with these damn play-time projects of yours until you *get* your problem fixed. *Get out!*"

"I don't know what I could have said."

He was shaking. He was shaking all over again when Grant came over to the couch and handed him a glass. The ice rattled. He drank a gulp, and Grant settled down beside him with the tablet.

Give it a few days. Yanni explodes. He calms down.

He shook his head. Made a helpless gesture with the glass and rested his eyes against his hand a moment while the whiskey hit his bloodstream and the cold hit his stomach. "Maybe," he said finally, "maybe Yanni's right. Maybe I'm what he said, an assembly-line designer making an ass out of myself."

"That's not so."

"Yanni ripped me to shreds the last two designs. He was *right*, dammit, the whole thing would have blown up, they'd have had suicides."

Grant grabbed the tablet next to him, and wrote:

Don't give up. And went on writing: *Denys said once Ari didn't fake your Aptitudes. You've taken it as an article of faith that she did. You've always thought you belonged in Education. You do. But Ari wanted you in Design. I wonder why.*

His gut went queasy when he read that.

Grant wrote: *Ari did a hell of a lot to you. But she never refused to look at your work.*

"I'm off the project," he said. Because that was no news to Security and their eavesdroppers. "He says I hate the kid. It's not true, Grant. It's not true. It's not true."

Grant gripped his shoulder. "I know it. I know it, they know it, Yanni knows it, it's what he does—he was psyching you. He was getting you on tape."

"He said I flunked, didn't he?"

"For God's sake, that's part of it, that's part of the psychout, don't you understand it? You know what he was doing. The test wasn't over yet. He wanted a reaction, and you gave it to him."

"I'm still pulling up what I said." He took a second, still shaking. "I can remember what I meant. I don't kː ː I can figure Yanni well enough to know what he heard."

"Yanni's good. Remember that. *Remember that.*"

He tried to. He wrote: *The question is, whose side is he on?*

Horse dipped his head and took grain from Florian's palm. "See," he said to Catlin, "see, he's friendly. He just worries when it's strangers. You want to touch him?"

Catlin did, very carefully. Horse shied back.

Catlin outright grinned as she jerked her hand back. "He's smart."

The pigs and chickens had not impressed Catlin at all. She had just looked at the chicks in disgust when they piled up against the wall, and retreated from the piglets in some alarm when they rushed up to get the food. Then she had said they were stupid, and when he explained how smart they were about what they ate, she said they wouldn't be bacon if they were smarter about where they got what they ate.

The cows she said looked strong, but she was not very interested.

But Horse got the first real grin Florian had ever seen from Catlin, and she climbed up on the rail and watched while Horse played games with them and snorted and threw his head.

"We aren't going to eat Horse's babies," Florian said, climbing up beside her. "He's a working animal. That means they're not for food."

Catlin took that in the way she took a lot of things, with no comment, but he saw the nod of her head, which was Catlin agreeing with something.

He liked Catlin. That took a lot of deciding, because Catlin was hard to get hold of, but they had been through the Room a lot of times, and only once had he been Got and that was because they had Got Catlin first, and there had just been a whole lot of the Enemy, all Olders. Catlin had been Got twice in all, but the second time she had yelled Go! and given him time to blow a door and get through, which was his fault: he had been slower than he ought; so she Got all the Enemy but the one that Got her, and he Got that one, because *he* had a grenade, and the Enemy didn't expect him to have because he was a tech with his hands full. Catlin had been real proud of him for that.

He was just glad it was a game, and he told the Instructor it was his fault, not Catlin's. But the Instructor said they were a team, and it didn't matter.

He gave them half their Rec time.

Which was enough time to come over here. And this time he talked Catlin into coming with him and meeting Andy and seeing all the animals.

He was not sure Andy and Catlin got along. But Catlin said Horse was special.

So he got Andy to show Catlin the baby.

"She's all right," Catlin said, when she saw the girl Horse, and it played dodge with them, her tail going in a circle and her hooves kicking up the dust of the barn. "Look at her! Look at her move!"

"Your partner's all right, too," Andy said, with a nod of his head toward Catlin.

Which was something, coming from Andy. Florian felt happy, really happy, because all things he liked fell into place that way, Catlin and Andy and everything.

He remembered then, though, that they had to get back before curfew, which meant they had to hurry.

"Time," he said, and to Andy: "I'll be back as soon as I can."

"Goodbye," Andy said. "Goodbye," Florian said with a little bow, and: "Goodbye," Catlin said, which was very unusual, Catlin usually letting him do the talking when they dealt with anybody but Security.

They had to walk fast. He had showed Catlin the shortcuts on the way and she knew all of them on the way back, which was the way with Catlin.

She was also longer-legged than he was, and she could pick him up. He had thought boys were supposed to be taller and stronger. The Instructor said not when you were seven.

So he felt a little better about it. And he walked fast keeping up with Catlin, breathing harder than she was when they got to Green Barracks.

But when they checked in there was a stop on both of them at the desk. The azi there looked at his machine and said:

"Report to the Super, White section."

That was clear across the Town. That was Hospital. That meant tape. Instead of going to their quarters. "Yes," Catlin said, taking her card back and clipping it to her shirt. He took his back.

"Same instruction," the azi said.

"I wonder why," he said when they went back out onto the walk, headed for White.

"No good wondering," Catlin said. But she was worried, and she walked fast. He kept up with little extra efforts now and again.

The sun had gone behind the Cliffs a long time ago. The sky was going pink now and the lights were going to be on before they could get back. The walks and the roads were mostly deserted because most everyone was at supper. It was a strange time to be going to take tape. He felt uneasy.

When they got to the Hospital the clerk took their cards and read them; and told them each where to go.

He looked at Catlin when she went off her own way. He felt afraid then, and didn't know what of, or why, except he felt like he was in danger and she was. If you took tape you went to Hospital in the daytime. Not when you were supposed to be having dinner. His stomach was empty and he had thought maybe it was going to be a surprise exercise: they did that to the Olders, hauled them out of bed and you could hear them heading down the hall in the middle of the night, fast as they could run.

But it was not a Room when they got there, it was truly Hospital. You couldn't do anything except what you were told, and you didn't *think* in Hospital, you just took your shirt off and hung it up, then you climbed up on the table and sat there trying not to shiver until the Super got there to answer your questions.

It was a Super he had never had before. It was a man, who turned on the tape equipment before he even looked at him; and then said:

"Hello, Florian. How are you?"

"I'm scared, ser. Why are we getting tape now?"

"The tape will tell you. Don't be scared." He picked up a hypo and took Florian's arm and shot him with it. Florian jerked. He had gotten nervous about noises like that. The Super patted his shoulder and laid the hypo down. And held on to him because that was a strong one: Florian could feel it working very fast.

"Good boy," the Super said, and his hands were gentle even if he didn't talk as nice as some Supers. He never let him go, and swung him around and helped him get his legs up on the table, and his hand was always there, under his shoulders, on his shoulder or his forehead. "This is going to be a deep one. You aren't afraid now."

"No," he said, feeling the fear go away, but not the sense of being open.

"Deeper still. Deep as you can go, Florian. Go to the center and wait for me there. . . ."

xiii

"I don't *want* a party," Ari said, slouching in the chair when uncle Denys was talking to her. "I don't want any nasty party, I don't like any of the kids, I don't want to have to be nice to them."

She was already in bad with uncle Denys for borrowing Nelly's keycard, because Nelly, being Nelly, had told uncle Denys and uncle Giraud the whole thing when uncle Denys asked her. Nelly didn't want to get her in trouble. They had caught her anyway. Nelly had been awfully upset. And uncle Denys had had a severe Talk with her and with Nelly about security and safety in the building and going where she was supposed to.

Most of all he had said he was mad at Justin and Grant for not calling him and telling him that she was where she wasn't supposed to be, and they were in trouble too. Uncle Denys had sent them an angry message; and now they were supposed to report her if she came by there instead of the halls she was supposed to be in.

Ari was real mad at uncle Denys.

"You don't want the other kids," uncle Denys said, like a question.

"They're stupid."

"Well, what about a grown-up party? You can have punch and cake. And all of that. And have your presents. I wasn't thinking of having the whole Family. What about Dr. Ivanov and Giraud—"

"I don't like Giraud."

"Ari, that's not nice. He's my brother. He's your uncle. And he's been very nice to you."

"I don't care. You won't let me invite who *I* want."

"Ari, —"

"It's not Justin's fault I took Nelly's keycard."

Uncle Denys sighed. "Ari, —"

"I don't want an old party."

"Look, Ari, I don't know if Justin *can* come."

"I want Justin and I want Grant and I want Mary."

"Who's Mary?"

"Mary's the tech down in the labs."

"Mary's azi, Ari, and she'd feel dreadfully uncomfortable.
But if you really want to, I'll see about Justin. I don't promise,
mind. He's awfully busy. I'll have to ask him. But you can
send him an invitation."

That was better. She sat up a little and leaned her elbows on
the chair arms. And gave uncle Denys a lot nicer look.

"Nelly isn't going to have to go to hospital, either," she
said.

"Ari, dear, Nelly *has* to go to hospital, because you made
Nelly awfully upset. It's not *my* fault. You put Nelly in a hard
place and if Nelly has to go to rest a while, I'm sure I don't
blame her."

"That's nasty, uncle Denys."

"Well, so is stealing Nelly's card. Nelly will be back tomorrow morning, Nelly will be just fine. I'll call Justin and I'll tell
Mary you thought about her. She'll be very pleased. But I
don't promise anything. You be good and we'll see. All
right?"

"All right," she said.

She was still mad about having to stay in the downstairs hall
on her way back and forth to tape; and she tried and tried to
think how she could get around that, but she hadn't figured it
out yet.

So they were not going to have a party in the big dining
room downstairs this year because uncle Denys said there was
so much work lately anyway that a lot of people couldn't
come. So they were going to have just a little one, in the apartment, but the kitchen was going to do the food and bring it up;
and there would be just a few grown-ups, and they would have
a nice dinner and have punch and cake and open her presents.
She would get to plan the dinner with Nelly and sit at the head

of the table and have anything she wanted. And Justin and Grant might be able to come, Denys said.

So they did.

Justin and Grant came to the door and Justin shook uncle Denys's hand.

Then the scared feeling shot clear across the room. Justin was scared when he came in. Grant too. And everyone in the room was stiff and nasty and trying not to be.

It was her party, dammit. Ari got up with the upset going straight to her stomach, and ran over and was as friendly as she could be. You didn't get anywhere by telling people to be nice. You just got their attention and shook them up until they fixed on you instead of what they had fixed on, and then you could do things with them. She didn't have time to work out who was doing what—she just went for Justin: he was the key to it and she knew that right away.

Uncle Giraud was there, and Giraud's azi Abban; and Dr. Ivanov and a very pretty azi named Ule, who was his. And Dr. Peterson and his azi Ramey; and her favorite instructor Dr. Edwards and his azi Gale, who was older than he was, but nice: Dr. Edwards was one of her invites. Dr. Edwards was a biochemist, but he knew about all sorts of things, and he worked a lot with her after her tape. And there was uncle Denys, of course, who was talking to Justin.

"Hello!" she said, getting in the way.

"Hello," Grant said, and gave her their present. She shook it. It wasn't heavy. It didn't rattle. "What is it?" she asked. She knew they wouldn't tell her. Mostly she wanted to get hold of them. And they were looking mostly at her.

"You have to wait to open it, don't you?" Justin said. "That's why it's wrapped."

She bounced over and gave it to Nelly to put with all the others that were stacked around the chair in the corner. It was like the whole room took a breath. She let it go a minute to see what the grown-ups were going to do now that they knew for sure that Justin and Grant were her invites.

The grown-ups had drinks and got to talking, and everyone was being nice. It was going to be nice. She would make it nice even if uncle Denys was getting over a mad with Justin. It was *her* party and *her* say-so, and she intended to have it, and to have a good time. No one was going to spoil it; or she would get them good.

Giraud was the nasty one. She was watching him real close, and she caught his eye when no one else was looking, and gave him a real straight look, so he knew that. Then she bounced back over and took Justin's hand and had him look at all her pile of presents, and introduced him and Grant to Nelly, which embarrassed Nelly, but at least you knew Nelly was going to be nice and not make things blow up.

She went into her suite and brought out some of her nicest and most curious things to show everyone. She got everyone fixed on her. Pretty soon everybody was being a lot nicer, and people started talking and having a good time, having a before-dinner drink. But she didn't. She didn't want to spoil dinner.

It was different than parties she had had before, with the kids. She had a blue blouse with sparkles. A hairdresser had come in the afternoon and done her hair up with braids. She was very careful of it, and careful of her clothes when she sat on the floor. She was very pretty and she felt very grown-up and important, and she smiled at everybody now that they were being nice. When Seely said it was time to eat and the kitchen staff was going to be bringing the food in, she had Justin sit by her on one side at the table and Dr. Ivanov sat down next to him on the other, with Dr. Edwards across from him, so he was safe from Giraud, especially since Dr. Peterson sat down next to Dr. Edwards. Which left uncle Denys and uncle Giraud farthest away. You weren't supposed to have an odd number at table. But they did. She had wanted Grant to be there, but uncle Denys said Grant would enjoy the party more with the other azi, and even Nelly said, while she was helping her get dressed, that Grant would be embarrassed if he had to be the only azi at the table where the CITs ate. So since Nelly said it too, she decided uncle Denys knew what he was talking about.

She got to sit at the head of the table; and she got to talk to adults, who talked about the labs and about things she didn't know, but she always learned something when she listened, and she didn't mind it at all when the adults quit asking her questions about her studies and her fish and began talking to each other.

It was a lot better, she was sure now, than kid-parties, where everybody was nasty and stupid.

When Justin and Grant had come in everyone had acted just exactly the way the other kids acted when *she* came near them. She hated that. She didn't know why they did it. She had thought grown-ups were more grown-up than that. It was depressing to learn they weren't.

At least adults covered it up better. And she figured it was easier to deal with if you weren't the target of it. So she started figuring out where the problems were.

Uncle Giraud was the worst. He always was. Uncle Giraud was minding his manners, but he was still sulking about something, and talking about business to uncle Denys, who didn't want him to.

Justin wasn't saying anything. He didn't want to. Dr. Peterson was just kind of dull, and he was talking to Dr. Ivanov, who was bored and mostly trying to listen to what Dr. Edwards was saying about the problems with the algae project. Uncle Denys was watching everybody and being nice, and trying to get Giraud, who was next to him, to stop talking.

She knew about the algae. Dr. Edwards had told her. He showed her all these sealed bottles with different kinds of algae and told her what Earth's oceans had in them and what the difference was on Cyteen.

So she was trying to listen to that and she answered Dr. Peterson sometimes when he tried to talk to her instead of Dr. Ivanov.

It was still better than playing with Amy Carnath. And nobody was being nasty.

So when they got past cake and punch, and it was time for the adults to drink their drinks, she grabbed Justin by the hand and sat him in the circle of chairs right on the end next to uncle Denys. And, oh! that made Justin really nervous.

That was all right. That was because Justin was smart and knew if uncle Denys got mad at him everything was going to blow up. But she was too smart for that to happen. She opened uncle Denys' present first. It was a watch that could do most everything. A real watch. She was delighted, but even if she hadn't been she would have said she was, because she wanted uncle Denys happy. She went and she kissed uncle Denys on the cheek and was just as nice as she could be.

She opened uncle Giraud's present next, just to make uncle Denys *real* happy, and it was an awfully nice holo of the whole planet of Cyteen. You moved it and the clouds went round. Everybody was real impressed with it, especially Dr. Edwards, and uncle Giraud explained it was a special kind of holo and brand new. So uncle Giraud was a surprise: he had really tried hard to find her a nice gift and he really liked it himself. She had never known uncle Giraud liked things like that, but of course, he was the one who had given her the bird in the cube, too. So she understood something about Giraud that was different than him being nasty all the time. She gave him a big kiss and skipped off to open Dr. Ivanov's present, which was a puzzle box. And Dr. Edwards', then, which was a piece of gold plastic until you put your fingers on it or laid something like a pencil on it, and then it made the shadow in different colors according to how warm it was, and you could make designs with it that stayed a while. It was real nice. She had known whatever he gave her would be. But she didn't make any more fuss over it than over Dr. Ivanov's puzzle and Dr. Peterson's book about computers, and certainly not more than over uncle Denys's watch or uncle Giraud's holo.

It was working, too. They were having a good time. She opened Nelly's present, which was underwear—oh, that was like Nelly—and then she opened Justin's; which was a ball in a ball in a ball, all carved. It was beautiful. It was the kind of thing maman would have had and said: *Ari, don't touch that!* And it was hers. But she mustn't fuss over it. No matter how much she liked it. She said thank you and got right into the huge pile of other things from people who hadn't come to her party.

There were things from the kids. Even nasty Amy sent her a scarf. And Sam gave her a robot bug that would really crawl and find its way around the apartment. It was expensive, she knew, she had seen it in the store; and it was awfully nice of Sam.

There were a lot of books and tapes and some paints and a lot of clothes: she thought uncle Denys probably told people the sizes because everybody knew. And there was clay to work and a lot of games and several bracelets and a couple of cars and even a roll-the-ball maze puzzle from Mary the azi, down in the labs. That was awfully nice. She made a note to send Mary a thank-you.

And Sam too.

Presents were good for making everybody feel happy. The grown-ups drank wine and uncle Denys even let her have a quarter of a glass. It was suspicious-tasting, like it was spoiled or something. All the adults laughed when she said that; even Justin smiled; but uncle Denys said it certainly wasn't, it was *supposed* to taste like that, and she couldn't have any more or she would feel funny and get sleepy.

So she didn't. She worked her puzzle-box and got it open while the grown-ups drank a lot and laughed with each other and while uncle Denys finally got her watch set with the right date. It was not a bad party at all.

She yawned and everybody said it was time to go. And they called the azi and wished her happy birthday while she stood at the door with uncle Denys the way maman would have and said goodbye and thank you for coming.

Everybody was noisy and happy like a long time ago. Denys was really smiling at Dr. Edwards and shook his hand and told Dr. Edwards he was really happy he came. Which made Dr. Edwards happy, because uncle Denys was the Administrator, and she wanted to get uncle Denys to like Dr. Edwards. And uncle Denys even was nice to Justin, and was really smiling at him and Grant when they left.

So *all* of her invites worked.

Everyone left, even uncle Giraud; and it was time to clean up the presents and all. But Ari figured it was not too late to get another point with uncle Denys, so she went and hugged him.

"Thank you," she said. "That was a nice party. I love the watch. Thank you."

"Thank *you*, Ari. That was nice."

And he smiled at her in a funny way. Like he was really happy for a lot of reasons.

He kissed her on the forehead and told her go to bed.

But she was feeling so good she decided to help Nelly and Seely pick up the presents, and she gave Nelly special instructions to be careful with her favorites.

She turned on Sam's bug and let it run around real fast. "What's that?" Nelly cried, and uncle Denys came out again to see what the commotion was.

So she clapped her hands and stopped it, and snatched it up and took it to her room.

Real fast. Because she was really trying to be good.

—————————————— xiv ——————————————

Ari waked in the morning with the Minder dinging away and told it shut up, she had heard it. She rubbed her eyes and really wished she could stay there, but she was supposed to go to tape, it was that day. And there was no more going by Justin's office either.

She had a lot of new toys in her bedroom, and a lot of new clothes; but mostly she would like to just lie here and go back to sleep, except pretty soon Nelly would be in telling her she had to move.

So she beat Nelly. She rolled over and slid over the side of the bed. And went to the bath and slid out of her pajamas and took her shower and brushed her teeth.

Usually Nelly was in the room by now.

So she put on the clothes Nelly had laid out for her last night and said: "Minder, call Nelly."

"Nelly isn't here," the Minder said. "Nelly's gone to the hospital."

She was scared then. But that could have been the old message. She said: "Minder, where's uncle Denys?"

"Ari," the Minder said, in uncle Denys's voice, "come to the dining room."

"Where's Nelly?" she asked again.

"Nelly's in the hospital. She's fine. Come to the dining room."

She brushed her hair fast. She opened the door and walked down the hall of her suite past Nelly's room. She opened the door to the main apartment and walked on into the sitting room.

Uncle Denys was at the table beyond the arch. She walked in, clipping her keycard on, and uncle Denys said she should sit down and have breakfast.

"I don't want to. What's the matter with Nelly?"

"Sit down," uncle Denys said.

So she sat. She wasn't going to learn anything till she did. She knew uncle Denys. She reached for a muffin and ate a nibble dry. And Seely came and poured her orange juice. Her stomach felt upset.

"There," uncle Denys said. "Nelly's in hospital because she's getting some more tape. Nelly's not really able to keep up with you, Ari, and you're really going to have to be careful with her from now on. You're getting bigger, you're getting very clever, and poor Nelly thinks it's her duty to keep up with you. The doctors are going to tell her it's not her fault. There's a lot Nelly has to adjust to. But you do have to remember not to hurt Nelly.''

"I don't. I didn't know the bug was going to scare her.''

"If you'd thought, you would have.''

"I guess so,'' she said. It was a lonely morning without Nelly. But at least Nelly was all right. She put a little butter on her muffin. It tasted better.

"One of the things Nelly has to adjust to,'' uncle Denys said, ''is two more azi in the household, because there will be.''

She looked at uncle Denys, not real happy. Seely was bad enough.

"They'll be yours,'' uncle Denys said. ''They're part of your birthday. But you mustn't tell them that: people aren't birthday presents. It's not nice.''

She swallowed a big gulp of muffin. She wasn't at all happy, she didn't want any azi but Nelly to be following her around, and if it was like a present, she didn't want to hurt uncle Denys's feelings, either, for a whole lot of reasons. She thought fast and tried to think of a way to say no.

"So you don't have to go to tapestudy today,'' uncle Denys said. ''You go over to hospital and pick them up. And you can spend your day showing them what to do. They're not like Nelly. They're both Alphas. Experimentals.''

A large gulp of orange juice. She didn't know what to think about that. Alphas were rare. They were also awfully hard to deal with. She was sure they were supposed to be watching her. That sounded an awful lot like uncle Denys was going to make it really hard for her to do *anything* she wasn't supposed to. She wasn't sure whether this present came from uncle Denys, or uncle *Giraud*.

"You go to the desk,'' uncle Denys said, ''and you give your card to Security, and they'll register them to you. Effectively, you're going to be their Supervisor, and that's quite a lot different than Nelly. *I'm* Nelly's Supervisor. You're only her responsibility. This is quite different. You know what a Supervisor does? You know how responsible that is?''

"I'm a *kid*," she protested.

Uncle Denys chuckled and buttered another muffin. "That's all right. So are they." He looked up, serious. "But they're not toys, Ari. You understand how serious it is if you get mad at them, or if you hit them the way you hit Amy Carnath."

"I wouldn't do that!" You didn't hit azi. You didn't talk nasty to them. Except Ollie. And Phaedra. For different reasons. But they were both special, even Phaedra.

"I don't think you would, dear. But I just want you to think about it before you hurt them. And you can. You could hurt them very, very badly, a lot more than you can Nelly—the way only I could hurt Nelly. You understand?"

"I'm not sure I want them, uncle Denys."

"You need other children, Ari. You need somebody your own age."

That was true. But there wasn't anybody who didn't drive her crazy. And it was going to be awful if they did, because they were going to live-in.

"The boy is Florian, the girl is Catlin, and it's their birthday too, well, just about. They'll live in the room next to yours and Nelly's, that's what it was always for. But they'll have to go back to the Town for some of their lessons, and they'll do tapestudy in the House, just like you do. They're kids just like you, and they have Instructors they have to pay attention to. They're very quick. In a lot of things they're ahead of you. That's the way with azi, especially the bright ones. So you're going to have to work to keep up with them."

She was listening now. No one had ever said she wasn't the best at anything. She didn't believe they could be. They wouldn't be. There was nothing she couldn't do if she wanted to. Maman always said so.

"Are you finished?"

"Yes, ser."

"Then you can go. You pick them up and you show them around, and you stay out of trouble, all right?"

She got down from table and she left, out into the halls, past Security and the big front doors and across the driveway and along the walk to the hospital. She ran part of the way, because it was boring otherwise.

But she was dignified and grown-up when she passed the

hospital doors and gave her card to hospital Security at the desk.

"Yes, sera," they said. "Come this way."

So they brought her to a room.

And they left and the other door opened. A nurse let in two azi her own age. The girl was pale, pale blonde, with a braid; the boy was shorter, with hair blacker than their uniforms.

And uncle Denys was right. Nobody ever looked at her that way when she had just met them. It was like friends right off. It was more than that. It was like they were in a scary place and she was the only one who could get them out of it.

"Hello," she said. "I'm Ari Emory."

"Yes, sera." Very softly, from both, almost together.

"You're supposed to come with me."

"Yes, sera."

It felt really, really strange. Not like Nelly. Not like Nelly at all. She held the door button for them and she took them out by the desk and said that she was taking them.

"Here are their keycards, sera," the man at the desk said. And she took them and looked at them.

There were their names. Florian AF-9979 and Catlin AC-7892. And the Alpha symbol in the class blank. And the wide black border of House Security across the bottom.

She saw that and a cold feeling went through her stomach, a terrible feeling, like finding the Security guard in maman's apartment. She never forgot that. She had nightmares about that.

But she didn't let them see her face right then. She got herself straight before she turned around and gave them their cards, and they put them on.

And they had different expressions too, out here, very serious, very azi: they were listening to her, they were watching her, but they were watching everything.

You had to remember how they had been in the room, she thought. You had to think how they had looked in there, to know that that was real too, and that they were two things.

They were Security and they were hers, and it was other people they were watching like that, every little move that went on around her.

I wanted an Ollie, she remembered, but that was not what uncle Denys had given her. He gave her Security.

Why? she wondered, a little mad, a little scared. *What do I need them for?*

But they were her responsibility. So she took them out and down the walk to the House and checked them in with House Security. They were very correct with the officer on duty. "Yes, *sera*," they said very sharply to the officer, and the officer talked fast and ran through the rules for them in words and codes she had never heard. But the azi knew. They were very confident.

Uncle Denys hadn't said they had to come straight home, but she thought they should. Except she went by uncle Denys's office and uncle Denys was there. So she took them in and introduced them.

Then she took them home and showed them where they would live, and their own rooms; and explained to them about Nelly.

"You have to do what Nelly says," she said. "So do I, most of the time. Nelly's all right."

They were not quite nervous; it was something else. Especially Catlin, who had this way of looking at everything real fast. Both of them were very tense and very stiff and formal.

That was all right, they were respectful and they were being nice.

So she got out her Starchase game, set it up on the dining table and explained what the rules were.

None of the other kids ever listened the way they listened. They didn't tease or joke. She passed out the money and dealt out the cards and gave them their pieces. And when they started playing it got real tense.

She wasn't sure whether it was a fight or a game, but it was different than Amy Carnath, a lot different, because nobody was mad, they just went at it; and pretty soon she was leaning over the board and thinking so hard she was chewing her lip without knowing it for a while.

They *liked* it when she did something sneaky. They were sneaky right back, and the minute you got your pieces where you could get Florian in trouble, Catlin was moving up on the other side.

Starchase was usually real fast to play. And they were at it a long time, till she could get enough money to get enough ships built to keep Catlin off till she could get Florian cornered.

But then he asked if the rules let him join Catlin.

No one had ever thought of that. She thought it was smart. She got the rulebook out and looked.

"They don't say you can't," she said. And her shoulders were tired and she was stiff from sitting still so long. "Let's go put the board in my room so Seely won't mess it up and we'll have lunch, all right?"

"Yes, sera," they said.

They had a way of doing that to remind her they weren't just kids, every time she tried to make them relax.

But Florian carried the board in and he didn't spill it. And she thought she had rather go have lunch in North wing: uncle Denys let her go to the restaurant there, the little one, where the azi and the manager all knew her.

So that was where she took them, to *Changes*, down next to the shops, at the corner, where mostly Staff had lunch. She introduced them, she sat down and told them to sit down, and she had to order for them: "Sera," Florian whispered, looking awfully embarrassed after a moment of looking at the menu, "what are we supposed to do with this?"

"Pick out what you want to eat."

"I don't know these words. I don't think Catlin does."

Catlin shook her head, very sober and very worried-looking.

So she asked them what they liked, and they said they usually had sandwiches at lunch. She ordered that for them and for herself.

And thought that they were awfully nervous, and kept looking at everything and everyone that moved. Somebody banged a tray and their eyes went that way like something had exploded.

"You don't have to be worried," she said. They made *her* nervous. Like something was going to happen. "Calm down. It's just the waiters."

They looked at her, very sober. But they didn't stop watching things.

Just as serious and just as sober as they were in the game.

The waiter brought their drinks and they looked at him, all over, real fast, so fast it was hard to see them do it, but she knew they were doing it because she was watching.

Nothing like Nelly.

Uncle Denys talked about being safe in the halls. And got

her two azi who thought the waiter was going to jump them.
"Listen," she said, and two serious faces turned toward her
and *listened*, azi-like. "Sometimes we can just have fun, all
right? Nobody's going to get us here. I know all these people."

They calmed right down. Like it was magic. Like she had
psyched them exactly right. She let go a little breath and felt
proud of herself. They sipped their soft drinks and when the
sandwiches came with all the extra stuff that came with them
they were real impressed.

They liked it. She could tell. But: "I can't eat this much,"
Florian said, worried-like. "I'm sorry."

"That's all right. Quit worrying about things. Hear?"

"Yes, sera."

She looked at Florian, and looked at Catlin, and all that seriousness; and thought of ways to un-serious them; and then remembered that they were azi, and it was their psychset to be
like that, which meant you couldn't *do* a lot of things with
them.

But they weren't stupid. Not at all. Alphas were like Ollie.
And that meant they could take a lot that Nelly never could.
Like in the game: she pushed them with everything she had,
and they didn't get mad and they didn't get upset.

They were a big job. But not *too* big for her.

Then she thought, not for the first time that morning, that
they were a Responsibility. And you didn't take on azi and
then just dump them, ever. Uncle Denys was right. You didn't
get people for presents. You got somebody who wanted to love
you, and you couldn't ever just move away and leave them.

(Maman did, she thought, and it hurt, the way it always hurt
when that thought popped up. Maman did. But maman didn't
want to. Maman had been worried and upset for a long time
before she went away.)

She would have to write and tell maman about them, fast, so
maman would know she had to tell uncle Denys to send them
with her. Because she couldn't just leave them. She knew what
that felt like.

She wished she had gotten to pick them out, because her
household was getting complicated; she would much rather
have an Ollie for hers, and one and not two. She could have
said no. Maybe she should have said no, and not let uncle

Denys give them to her. She had thought she could sort of go along with it. Like everything else.

Till they looked at her that way over at the hospital, and they just sort of psyched her, not meaning to, except they wanted to go with her so much; and she had wanted somebody to be with her, just as bad.

So now they were stuck with each other. And she couldn't leave them by themselves.

Not ever.